"A master of smart, snappy repartee."

—*Kirkus Reviews*

PRAISE FOR THE NOVELS OF AYELET WALDMAN

BYE-BYE, BLACK SHEEP

"Satisfyingly vivid . . . Excellent characterization and swift action make for an involving leisure choice." —*Midwest Book Review*

"As always, Waldman manages to depict the life of L.A.'s yuppie parents with humor while showing genuine compassion for the less-fortunate inhabitants of the city." —*Booklist*

"Whether scrambling for child care or bribing pimps, Juliet is resourceful, and her humor shines through in this brisk, thoroughly readable tale." —*Publishers Weekly*

THE CRADLE ROBBERS

"Witty . . . smart sleuthing." —Marilyn Stasio, *The New York Times Book Review*

"Human and credible characters—in particular, a smart, sensitive sleuth . . . should delight committed fans and attract new ones." —*Publishers Weekly*

"Fabulous." —*Midwest Book Review*

"Waldman always provides full-bodied characters, humor, and a socially conscious plot that entertains as it enlightens." —*Booklist*

continued . . .

Murder Plays House

"Well-plotted . . . Juliet is a wonderful invention, warm, loving, and sympathetic to those in need, but unintimidated by the L.A. entertainment industry she must enter to search for clues . . . What a motive, what a resolution, and how clever of Juliet to figure everything out."

—*Publishers Weekly*

"As always, Waldman uses humor to portray the Los Angeles scene while making some serious points about what is really important in life. This thoroughly modern cozy will be popular."   —*Booklist*

"Witty Waldman is so endearingly pro-kid that you may run right out and get pregnant."   —*Kirkus Reviews*

Death Gets a Time-Out

"Juliet and her patient husband make an appealing couple—funny, clever, and loving (but never mawkish). Waldman has an excellent ear for the snappy comeback, especially when delivered by a five-year-old."

—*Publishers Weekly*

"Waldman is at her witty best when dealing with children, carpooling, and first-trimester woes, but is no slouch at explaining the pitfalls of False Memory Syndrome either."   —*Kirkus Reviews*

"Arguably the best of Waldman's mysteries . . . Think *Chinatown*, but with strollers and morning sickness."   —*Long Island Press*

A Playdate with Death

"Smoothly paced and smartly told."   —*The New York Times Book Review*

"Sparkling . . . Witty and well-constructed . . . Those with a taste for lighter mystery fare are sure to relish the adventures of this contemporary, married, mother-of-two Nancy Drew."   —*Publishers Weekly*

"[A] deft portrayal of Los Angeles's upper crust and of the dilemma facing women who want it all."   —*Booklist*

The Big Nap

"Juliet Applebaum is smart, fearless, and completely candid about life as a full-time mom with a penchant for part-time detective work. Kinsey Millhone would approve."

    —Sue Grafton, *New York Times* bestselling author *W Is for Wasted*

"Waldman treats the Los Angeles scene with humor, offers a revealing glimpse of Hasidic life, and provides a surprise ending . . . An entertaining mystery with a satirical tone."   —*Booklist*

Nursery Crimes

"[Juliet is] a lot like Elizabeth Peters's warm and humorous Amelia Peabody—a brassy, funny, quick-witted protagonist."   —*Houston Chronicle*

"Funny, clever, touching, original, wacky, and wildly successful."
    —Carolyn Hart, *New York Times* bestselling author of
    Death at the Door

continued . . .

"A delightful debut filled with quirky, engaging characters, sharp wit, and vivid prose."

"[Waldman] derives humorous mileage from Juliet's 'epicurean' cravings, wardrobe dilemmas, night-owl husband, and obvious delight in adventure."

AND MURDER MAKES THREE

AYELET WALDMAN

BERKLEY PRIME CRIME, NEW YORK

An imprint of Penguin Random House LLC
375 Hudson Street, New York, New York 10014

AND MURDER MAKES THREE

BERKLEY® PRIME CRIME and the PRIME CRIME design are registered trademarks of
Penguin Random House LLC.
For more information about the Penguin Group, visit penguin.com.

ISBN: 978-0-425-28088-1

PUBLISHING HISTORY
Berkley Prime Crime trade paperback omnibus edition / August 2015

Penguin
Random
House

CONTENTS

NURSERY CRIMES

For Michael

1

'M NOT SURE whose fault it was, Ruby's or mine, that we didn't get in. Let's just say neither of us aced the admissions interview. I knew we were in trouble as soon as Ruby woke me up, at 6:00 A.M., with a scowl as black as the cowboy boots she had insisted on wearing to bed the night before. She refused to let me comb the left half of her hair, so I ended up walking out of the house holding the hand of a tiny little carny sideshow attraction: a half adorable, beribboned angel, half street urchin from hell. The effect was dramatized further by her chosen attire: Superman T-shirt, magenta miniskirt, and bright yellow clogs. She was impervious to my pleas, and seemed uninterested in my explanation of how not going to the right preschool would preclude Harvard, Swarthmore, or any other decent college. She'd end up at Slippery Rock State, like her dad. Even if she hadn't been two and a half years old, this would likely have made little impression on her. Her un-Ivied father made about ten times as much money as her thickly Ivied mother, and had an infinitely more satisfying career as a screenwriter than mine had been as a public defender.

By the time we got into the car, we were all three, Mama, Daddy, and Baby, in matching moods. Bad. Really, really bad. Peter was irritated because he'd had to get up before eleven. Ruby was irritated because I had turned off *The Big Comfy Couch* and forced her to eat some Cheerios and get out of the house. I was irritated at Ruby for being such a stubborn little brat, at Peter for failing to help me get her ready for the interview, and at myself for having gained fifty-five pounds in the first thirty-two weeks of my second pregnancy. I'd already outgrown most of my maternity clothes, and the only thing I could fit into was an old, dusty-black smock that I had worn to shreds when I was pregnant with the tiny Hell's Angel herself.

As we drove up Santa Monica Boulevard I desperately tried to give Ruby some last-minute admissions hints.

"Listen, Peach Fuzz, it's really important that you try to be sweet today, okay?"

"No."

"Yes. Yes. It is. You have to try to share with other kids. Don't grab toys or fight. Okay?"

"No."

"Yes. Hey, I have an idea! You can tell some of your funny stories. How about that story about the crazy kitty? Want to practice that now? That's such a great story."

"No."

I sighed. Peter looked over at me and raised his eyebrows.

"She'll be fine," I said. "As soon as she's around the other kids, she'll be her sweet, agreeable self."

I glanced into the backseat. Ruby was grimly picking her nose and wiping it on the armrest of her car seat. When she saw me looking at her, she covered her eyes with her hands.

THE HEART'S SONG School was widely considered the best preschool in the city of Los Angeles. The competition for the seventeen spots that opened each fall in the Billy Goat room was cutthroat. It was probably easier to qualify for the Olympic gymnastics team. It was certainly easier to get into medical school. Everyone who was anyone in Hollywood had a little Billy Goat. The school's spring fund-raiser, a talent show, had boasted original songs by Alan Menken, dance numbers by Bette Midler, and one legendary reenactment of Romeo and Juliet's balcony scene starring Arnold Schwarzenegger and Whoopi Goldberg.

Our interview at the preschool took place with two other families. We perched on miniature chairs, covertly sizing each other up while waiting for the school principal. One family seemed pleasant enough. The parents were exhibiting the same slightly manic good cheer as Peter and I. The father had a kind of artistic look, with longish, tousled hair. I decided he was probably a cinematographer or a moderately successful film director. He wore the same dress-up uniform as Peter, chinos and a slightly wrinkled oxford shirt. The mother was an attractive, dark-haired woman about my age, thirty-two or -three, wearing a long sweater over leggings and pretty brown boots. When she caught me looking at her, I smiled ruefully and rolled my eyes. She smiled back. Their son sat quietly in his father's lap and buried his head in his father's shirt whenever anyone looked at him.

The other couple was a whole different kettle of fish. First of all, he was wearing a suit, a double-breasted sharkskin. Definitely Italian. He was substantially older than the rest of us, at least forty-five or fifty, but trying real hard to look thirty-five. He sported an expression that managed to look tense and bored at the same time. Skinny wasn't the word to describe his trophy wife. Emaciated more like. Her very young, twiglike body was wrapped in an elaborate slinky skirt with a Lycra top that revealed a strip of bare midriff. She sported a diamond the size of a small puppy on one finger. She had a gash of bloodred lipstick in an otherwise alabaster-white face, and her petulant pout precisely matched that of her daughter. I discreetly snuck a tongue out over my lips to see if I had remembered to put makeup on. Of course not. I rummaged in my purse for a lipstick, but had to satisfy myself with a tube of Little Mermaid Junior Lip Gloss.

The hyperelegant couple's daughter wore black velvet leggings and a red tunic with shiny black cuffs and pockets. Ruby was transfixed by her red patent-leather boots. She pointed at them and said, "Mama, buy me that"—*dat*—"I want *that*!"

Normally that kind of demand would be greeted with a minilecture on why we can't have everything we see. It is a mark of how desperately I wanted Ruby to get into that school that I leaned over and whispered in her ear, "I'll tell you what, kiddo. If you are really, really good I'll try to find you a pair of those boots."

The principal walked in just in time to hear Ruby say to the proud owner of the boots, "I'm getting those boots if I'm weawy good!"

I blushed to the brown roots of my red hair, and Peter snorted with laughter. The nice couple smiled and the not-so-nice couple looked superior. Trophy wife hissed "Morgan, come here," and hustled her daughter away from Ruby as if she imagined that my baby would try to wrench the boots clean off her little treasure's feet. As if Ruby would ever have tried that. At least not with me right there.

Abigail Hathaway, the founder and principal of the Heart's Song School, was a woman in her mid- to late fifties, tall, thin, and striking.

She had black hair, shot lightly with gray, that she wore rolled in a chignon at the nape of her neck. Her clothes were gorgeous, conservatively elegant, and obviously expensive. She wore a fawn-colored wool jacket buttoned loosely over a thick, creamy, silk blouse. Her skirt was in a matching herringbone. It occurred to me to wonder how she kept herself looking so splendid when she was surrounded every day by forty or so frenetic and filthy preschoolers. Ruby and I had already managed to acquire matching milk stains on our shirts, and my shoulder was festooned with a pink splash of toothpaste where she had wiped her mouth after brushing her teeth. I looked like the "before" picture in a Calgon bubble bath ad. Abigail Hathaway looked like she was heading out to lunch at the hunt club.

She perched herself on the edge of a minichair, introduced herself, and told us how she had come to start this most elite and special preschool fifteen years before. I put on my alert and interested expression, the one I had perfected in law school to impress professors with my zeal and engagement with the material. Actually, I was listening with only about fifteen percent of my brain. The other eighty-five was concentrating on Ruby as she wandered around the room, picking up toys and books.

"Heart's Song is designed to be a place where children learn the most important of lessons, how to cooperate and communicate," Ms. Hathaway said. "To that end we try to inculcate values such as empathy and concern for others."

At that moment Ruby plucked a toy from the nice couple's son's hand. He began to cry.

"Look, Mama, I'm gwabbing!" she announced proudly.

"Ruby!" I snapped. "Don't grab."

"But Mama, I *love* to gwab." She smiled hugely. I shot a quick glance at Ms. Hathaway to see if she'd heard. She had and was looking at me expectantly.

"Ruby, these toys belong to all the children and we have to share." I was using my best Miss Sally, Romper Room voice.

"It's virtually impossible for children of this age to share, Ms. Wyeth," the principal said.

"Actually, it's Applebaum, Ruby and Peter are Wyeth, I'm Applebaum," I said automatically, then winced. Like I really had to make that particular point at that particular moment. I looked over at my daughter. "Never mind, Ruby."

At that point Peter decided to take over for me, since I was obviously not wowing the room with my parenting skills.

"Hey, Rubes, come over to Daddy." She ran over and jumped up into his lap.

The school principal continued on for a while, describing how at the end of the afternoon those of us who had been selected to move on to the next stage of the application process would be given forms to fill out and send in, along with the $125-dollar, nonrefundable application fee. After about five minutes of sitting quietly, Ruby had had it. She wriggled out of Peter's arms and leaped off his lap. She was making a beeline for the sand table and had mischief on her mind. As she blew by me, I reached out an arm, stopping her in midrun. I hauled her onto my lap.

"If we're all ready to settle down," said Ms. Hathaway with a disapproving glance in my direction, "I'd like to tell you about the pedagogical goals of the Billy Goat program."

RUBY, IT TURNED out, was on her best behavior after all. She played nicely and managed not to break anything. But none of that mattered. My parenting skills had not impressed Ms. Hathaway. As we gathered our belongings at the end of the morning, I watched as she handed a thick manila envelope to the pleasant couple, who, laughing delightedly, scooped up their shy little boy and rushed out the door. No packet came our way. I had a moment of sadness thinking that we probably would never get to know that nice family, who had seemed like people we could be friends with. Those thoughts were interrupted by a scene unfolding at the other end of the room.

"Excuse me. We haven't received our application packet." Morgan's father had reached his arm out to stop Ms. Hathaway as she walked toward the door.

"I'm sorry, Mr. LeCrone," she said.

"Sorry? What do you mean, you're sorry? Where is my application packet?" He leaned over her, threateningly.

"We are only able to extend an invitation to apply to a small number of those who visit. I am sorry."

"Look, what the hell are you talking about? Do you realize that I employ the parents of half your students? I suggest that you get me an application."

His wife put her hand on his arm. "C'mon, Bruce. Let's just go. Who gives a shit."

Ruby, who had been staring at the drama unfolding in the doorway, gasped. "She said 'shit,' Mama!"

I leaned down and picked her up. "Shh, honey-pie," I murmured. I wanted out of that room right away, but they were blocking the only exit. Peter and I looked at each other. Neither of us could figure out what to do.

"I give a shit, goddamn it. Who the hell do you think you are, lady?" LeCrone's grip tightened on Ms. Hathaway's arm. Two spots of color appeared high on her cheeks. She looked genuinely frightened.

"Bruce, I'm leaving right now," LeCrone's wife said, grabbing their daughter by the hand. She pushed by him, out the door. He opened his mouth to speak, but before he could say anything more, Peter walked over.

"Hey, let's just chill out here a minute. We're all a little tense. Nobody means any harm," my husband said as he put an arm around LeCrone's shoulder. "I don't know about you, man, but my back's killing me from those little chairs, and I'm seriously coffee-deprived."

LeCrone looked, for a moment, like he was going to snarl. But suddenly he seemed to change his mind. Angrily shrugging off Peter's arm, he spun on his heel and marched out the door. Ms. Hathaway sighed with relief. She hugged her waist with her arms and shivered.

"Mr. Wyeth, if you'll wait a moment, I'll go get you an application."

"That's okay. You don't have to reward me. We understand you have your selection process. It's no big deal," Peter said, motioning to me. I scooped Ruby up in my arms and accompanied him out the door.

"Thanks for everything and have a nice day," I said, smiling over my shoulder at the principal. I'm not sure what prompted that, maybe I just wanted to show her that we were fine and unscathed by her rejection. At any rate, it turned out to be a singularly inappropriate comment, given what happened later that evening.

2

RUBY FELL ASLEEP in the car on the way home and Peter and I sat quietly, each immersed in private thought. I figured he was probably thinking about his latest script, the third in a lurid series about a marauding group of urban cannibals. It was definitely Peter's biggest movie so far, and he was under a lot of pressure to make the script satisfy all the various parties, including a director who spoke virtually no English and a studio executive with artistic pretensions.

When Peter and I had met in New York City, seven years before, he was working at Movie Madness, a cult video store in the East Village, and writing horror screenplays in his spare time. Actually, he'd been writing screenplays at work instead of waiting on customers. Our first conversation involved my threatening to report him to his boss and his asking me out for a beer instead. I still have no idea why I went out with him. It probably had a lot to do with his soft, sexy, gray eyes.

At the time Peter and I met, I had been earning big bucks at a prestigious New York law firm. I married him six months after that first beer, fully expecting to support him for the rest of our lives together. Three weeks after we came home from our honeymoon (beach-hopping and rain-forest-trekking in Costa Rica), he got a call from his agent. Slasher movies were suddenly in vogue, and one of that year's hottest producers had gotten his hands on Peter's script for *Flesh-Eaters I*. He optioned it for more money than I made in a year.

Much to my joy, Peter's success allowed me to quit my job. The short and only answer to the question of why I had ever become a corporate lawyer in the first place was money. I graduated from Harvard Law School owing seventy-five thousand dollars. Delacroix, Swanson, & Gerard offered me a starting salary of just under ninety thousand dollars a year.

After two years at the firm I had lowered my debt to a mere fifty thousand dollars, higher than my parents' mortgage but a slightly more manageable monthly payment than when I had started out.

During those two years I had billed six thousand hours, represented an asbestos manufacturer and a toxic-waste dumper, and helped to bust a union. My garment-workers'-union-organizing grandfather must have been spinning in his grave. I'd spent three weeks trapped in a warehouse in Jersey City, sifting through documents, and a month in a conference room in the Detroit Airport Hilton, listening to lying corporate executives. I'd done so many all-nighters that for a while Peter was certain I was cheating on him. The lunches at Lutèce and the Lincoln Town cars that drove me home each night were no compensation for the misery I felt during every one of my fourteen-hour days. By the time Peter got his big break, I was way past ready to quit.

We used Peter's advance to pay off my law school loans, packed the contents of our apartment into a U-Haul, hooked it to the back of my aunt Irene's 1977 Buick, and took off for the promised land, Los Angeles. We ended up in a 1930s apartment chock-full of period details and period appliances in Hancock Park, near Melrose Avenue, and I got the job I'd always wanted, as a federal public defender. For the next couple of years Peter wrote script after script, some of which were actually made into movies. We met a lot of interesting and creative people: writers, directors, and even an occasional actor. I represented gangbangers and drug dealers and became familiar with a side of L.A. that most of our new Hollywood friends tried to pretend didn't exist. I was the only one of our set not either writing a script, producing a movie, or trying to do one or the other. Nonetheless, I managed to hold my own at industry cocktail parties, regaling studio executives with stories about my cross-dressing bank-robber clients and how I was "protected" by the Thirty-seventh Avenue Crips.

I loved my job, and I was really good at it. Everything was going wonderfully, and we were really happy. And then something happened that destroyed it all: We had a baby.

Anyone who tells you that having a child doesn't completely and irrevocably ruin your life is lying. As soon as that damp little bundle of poop and neediness lands in your life, it's all over. Everything changes. Your relationship is destroyed. Your looks are shot. Your productivity is devastated. And you get stupid. Dense. Thick. Pregnancy and lactation make you dumb. That's a proven, scientific fact.

I went back to work when Ruby was four months old, and I quit ten months later. I just couldn't stand being apart from her and Peter. I'd call in the afternoon, snatching a few minutes to pump breast milk between court appearances and visiting clients at the detention center. Peter would tell me the latest cute Ruby story. I missed her first word ("boom") and the day she started to walk. Peter wrote at night, slept in, and took over for the nanny at eleven each morning. He and Ruby spent the day together, going to the park, playing blocks, lunching with pals from Mommy and Me. I was jealous. Completely, insanely jealous.

I was also doing a lousy job at work. I didn't want to be there any longer than I absolutely had to. I was relieved when clients pled guilty because that meant I wouldn't have to put in the late nights a trial demands. I finally realized that I was giving everything short shrift—my work, my husband, and most of all, Ruby.

So I quit. I dumped three years of Harvard Law School into the toilet and became a full-time mom. That decision blew everyone away, including me. My boss, the kind of working mother who came back to work when her kids were three months old and never looked back, thought I'd lost my mind. My mother kept me on the phone one night for two hours, crying. I was supposed to have the career she'd never been able to achieve. She felt like I had betrayed her feminist dream. My friends who hadn't yet had kids looked at me with a kind of puzzled condescension, obviously wondering what had become of the ambition that used to consume me.

As for myself, I couldn't really believe what I had done. For months, when people asked me what I did, I continued to reply, "public defender." If pressed, I would clarify by saying that I was on leave to be with my daughter. I never really came to grips with my status as a "stay-at-home mom." I'd always had just a little bit of disdain for women who devoted themselves completely to their families. I'd always assumed that they were home because they couldn't cut it, out in the real world. It had never occurred to me that a person would voluntarily leave a career in which she excelled in order to spend her days changing diapers and playing "This Little Piggy."

But that's what I had done. The worst part of it was that I wasn't especially proud of my skills as a mother. Ruby was turning out fine, if willful, stubborn, brilliant, and funny qualify as fine, but I wasn't any June Cleaver. I did all the things mothers aren't supposed to do. I yelled. I was sarcastic. I let her watch TV. I fed her candy and almost always forgot to wash the pesticides off the fruit. I never kept up with the laundry. My shortcomings as a mother bothered me enough to make me consider going back to work, but then I found myself pregnant again. That settled it. Awash in ambivalence, alternately bored and entranced, full of both joy and despair, I joined the ranks of stay-at-home moms. At least for the time being.

By the time we arrived back home from our debacle at the preschool, we were all sufficiently recovered from our ordeal to joke about it. Peter treated us to a dead-on imitation of Bruce LeCrone. Ruby and I invented a new game that consisted of pinching each other, shrieking "I love to gwab!" and then collapsing on the floor in giggles. By that evening our family's failure to enter the social register of the preschool set was forgotten.

After we had bundled Ruby into bed, and Peter had read that night's installment of *Ozma of Oz,* we settled down for the night. Peter went to work in his office, a converted maid's room at the back of our apartment, and I got into bed with my evening snack of ice cream and salted almonds. The calcium needs of my pregnant body provided sufficient rationalization for my astronomical ice cream intake. A few almonds made my decadent snack a protein-rich necessity. Or at least that's what I liked to tell myself. The increasing spread of my thighs I attributed to my body's stockpiling fat in order to breast-feed.

I flicked on the TV and spent the next couple of hours watching a movie about a woman with lymphoma whose anorexic daughter is sexually abused by a cross-dressing drug addict while a mudslide threatens their home (or something like that; I don't really remember). I was in hysterical tears from start to finish. I love watching disease-of-the-week films when I'm pregnant. That extra burst of hormones makes for a delightful two-hour sobfest. After the movie was over, I was about to turn off the set when the lead-in for the eleven-o'clock local news caught my attention.

"A prominent nursery school principal died tonight in an apparent hit-and-run. Angie Fong is live at the scene of the crash."

No way. It wasn't Abigail Hathaway. It couldn't be. After all, there were umpteen preschools and nursery schools in the Greater Los Angeles area. I stayed glued to the set through the commercial break.

The perky, helmet-haired news reporter stood in front of a cordoned-off street corner. Behind her I could see a mailbox tipped over on its side and crushed. I could swear I saw a woman's shoe lying next to it on the sidewalk. As soon as I heard Abigail Hathaway's name, I yelled for Peter. He came rushing in to the bedroom, looking panicked.

"What? Are you okay? Is it the baby?"

I pointed wordlessly at the television.

"Abigail Hathaway, the founder and director of the exclusive Heart's Song School, was killed in an apparent hit-and-run outside of the school entrance this evening. Witnesses say a late-model European sedan, either gray or black, swerved onto the sidewalk, crushed the victim against a mailbox, and then took off at a high rate of speed. No suspect has been apprehended."

The news reporter turned to a man in a baseball jacket with long, stringy hair. He was standing next to a shopping cart piled high with empty cans and bottles.

"Sir, you saw the accident?"

"It was no accident, man," he said. "This car comes speeding 'round the corner, goes up on the curb, bashes into her, and then takes off. I swear it was aiming right for her."

"And did you see the driver, sir?"

"Nah, but I saw the car. Silver Mercedes or maybe a black Beemer. Something like that. It was aiming for her, swear to God."

The screen switched back to the news anchor in the newsroom.

"Police are asking that anyone with any information about this incident please call the number on the bottom of your screen."

A commercial began, and I switched off the set. I had this strange, nauseated feeling in the pit of my stomach.

"Oh my God. I just can't believe it. We saw her today. *Today*." I felt tears rising up in my eyes. Peter sat down on the bed and pulled me to his chest. I started to cry.

"I know, honey, I know," he murmured, stroking my hair with his hand.

"I don't know why I'm crying," I said, sobbing. "I didn't even like her."

"I know, honey."

I stopped my tears. I had the hiccups. "I'm okay. Really. You can go back to work."

"You sure?"

"Yeah, it's okay. I'm going to call Stacy." Stacy was an old friend from college, whose six-year-old son was a graduate of Heart's Song. Peter went back to his office and I dialed the phone.

"Hello?" Stacy's voice sounded groggy.

"It's me. Sorry to wake you, but have you heard?"

"What?"

"Somebody killed Abigail Hathaway."

"What?" She perked up. "Are you serious? What happened?"

"I was just lying here watching the news. We didn't get in, by the way. And they come on with this story about how somebody mowed her down with their car. I couldn't believe it. I started crying."

"What do you mean, you didn't get in? She didn't give you an application?"

"No. Anyway, are you listening to me? The woman is *dead*!"

"Jeez. Wow. It was a car accident?"

"Yes. I mean, no. She was on the street outside of the school and some car hit her and then took off."

"Outside of the *school*?" Stacy sounded horrified. "Outside of Heart's Song?"

"Right on the corner. A car hit her and knocked her into a mailbox. At least I think that's what happened. Anyway, she's dead."

We talked for a while longer, speculating that the driver must have been drunk. I told Stacy about the interview and described the scene between the angry father and Ms. Hathaway.

Suddenly something occurred to me. "Oh my God, Stace. Maybe he killed her! Maybe he freaked after not getting into the school! Maybe he snapped!"

"Oh, for Pete's sake, Juliet. He did not kill her. Bruce LeCrone is a studio executive. He's the president of Parnassus Studios. And he used to work at ICA. He's not a murderer."

Stacy is an agent at International Creative Artists, one of the most prestigious talent agencies in town. She knows everybody in Hollywood.

"How do you know what he's capable of?" I said. "You didn't see this guy. He was furious. Insanely furious."

"Juliet, Bruce LeCrone's temper is legendary. That was just par for the course with him. You should hear how he treats his assistants."

"I still think there was something bizarre about how angry he got. I think I'm going to call the cops and let them know what happened."

"I really don't think that's such a hot idea. If you make trouble for LeCrone, and he finds out it was you, Peter will never sell a script to Parnassus. You don't want to go throwing wrenches into your husband's career just because you have some wacked-out theory."

That stopped me in my tracks. I certainly didn't want to ruin Peter's chances of doing a movie with one of the biggest studios in town.

"I'll talk to Peter about it before I do anything."

"You do that."

"So, what were you up to tonight?" I asked.

"Nothing! What do you mean? What are you suggesting?"

"Jeez, Stacy. Get a grip. I wasn't suggesting anything. I just wanted to know what you were up to."

"Oh. Nothing. I worked late."

"Poor you."

"Yeah, poor me."

We said good night and I turned off the light. Shivering, I snuggled down into my bed, tucked my body pillow under my heavy belly, and pulled the down comforter up to my chin. I couldn't seem to get warm. It was a long while before I fell asleep.

ABIGAIL HATHAWAY'S HOMICIDE happened too late at night to make that morning's *Los Angeles Times,* but the morning news shows each aired the story. I watched all three networks and got three very different stories. One referred to the death as a traffic accident. Another said the police had suspects under investigation. The third reported that the police were treating the death as a hit-and-run and were looking for the driver, whom they believed might have been under the influence of drugs or alcohol. Much to my embarrassment, I found myself vaguely disappointed that it appeared to have been a random accident. Over the course of my long, sleepless night I had worked up a head of steam about Bruce LeCrone. He seemed decidedly murderous to me.

The problem with having experience as a criminal defense lawyer is that you tend to see criminal violence everywhere, in everyone. One of Peter's and my biggest sources of conflict is that despite the fact that he spends his days thinking up new and exciting ways for people to be killed, preferably with as much blood and pain as possible, he is an eternal optimist who always believes every human being to be basically good at heart. I've spent too much time with apparently normal guys (and some women, too) who've done heinous things and am always willing to believe someone capable of extreme violence.

Not surprisingly, we got into an argument when I told Peter that I was suspicious of LeCrone. I had just woken him and was standing in the doorway of my closet, desperately searching for something to wear. Ruby was happily ensconced in the living room, glued to *The Lion King*.

"Oh, right, Juliet," Peter said, obviously irritated. "That's what most studio heads worth nine bazillion dollars go around doing. Murdering preschool teachers."

"He's not most studio heads! Tell me you didn't think he was psychotic."

"I didn't. Aggressive, yes. Used to getting his own way? Yes. But psychotic? No. If he's psychotic then so are two-thirds of the executives in Hollywood."

I thought about that for a moment while I rummaged through a pile of trousers, looking for some maternity leggings. Stacy had said the same thing, and it did have a ring of truth to it. Peter was always regaling me with stories of his dealings with various producers. One guy, in particular, was legendary. He had a phone with buttons on it marked "rice cakes"; "diet Coke"; "sushi." If he punched a button and his assistant didn't show up immediately with the requisite item, heads rolled. This same producer was famous for having been arrested on a flight from New York to Los Angeles for refusing to give up the in-flight phone and screaming obscenities at the flight attendant who tried to pry it away from him. He was probably single-handedly responsible for the appearance of phones on the backs of airplane seats. Bruce LeCrone was certainly no more horrifying a character than he.

On the other hand, as far as I knew, neither the flight attendant nor any of the assistants of the ranting and raving producer had ended up dead. It was one of LeCrone's enemies who had gotten herself mashed against a mailbox by a luxury car.

However, giving my already stressed-out husband grounds for an anxiety attack was not on my list of appropriate activities for the day. I decided to drop it—or at least to let Peter think I had.

"You're right. I know you're right. Listen, you remember I'm supposed to be having lunch with Marla?" Marla Goldfarb was the Federal Public Defender, and my old boss.

"Was that today?"

"Yeah. I told you yesterday. Is that a problem? Do you have a meeting this afternoon? Can you watch Ruby?"

"Sure, no problem. I was going to take her on a comic-book-store crawl, anyway." Peter's idea of a good time is hitting every comic-book store in Hollywood in a single afternoon. If he doesn't get the latest *Hellboy* or *Eightball* on the very day it's issued, he's completely inconsolable.

"Thanks, sweetie." I finally found a pair of leggings with relatively intact seams, threw one of Peter's freshly laundered dress shirts over it, and accented the ensemble with a jauntily tied scarf. I looked at myself critically in the full-length mirror. At least my hair looked good. I'd dyed it to match Ruby's red curls. I'd even kept dyeing it while pregnant, figuring that the damage to the baby from an ugly and depressed mother would be worse than whatever the hair dye might do to him.

"Not bad for a fat girl," I said.

"You are NOT fat. You're pregnant. You look great." Peter walked over to me and slid his arms around my waist, his hands gently cupping my protruding belly. I leaned back against his chest and smiled. My husband always knows how to make me feel sexy. The night before I gave birth to Ruby, he gave me a black, lace maternity negligee and told me that nothing turned him on like the sight of my huge, pregnant body. What a guy. I have no idea if he was telling the truth, but I decided to believe him. We're both convinced that the subsequent events were what put me into labor. Who needs labor-inducing medication when you've got a willing and able man around?

3

THE OFFICE OF the Federal Public Defender is in downtown L.A., in the U.S. Courthouse. I had always loved appearing in those courtrooms; the large, wood-paneled rooms have a solemn ambience that well matches the seriousness of the proceedings that take place there. The defender offices are, on the contrary, fairly typical, hideous, government offices with dingy carpeting and glaring, fluorescent lights. The low-rent atmosphere never helped convince my clients that their lawyer was competent and capable. Criminal defendants, like the rest of the world, tend to believe the old adage "You get what you pay for." Since the indigent don't have to pay their appointed counsel, they usually feel like they are getting their money's worth. The constant battle to convince drug dealers and bank robbers that I was good enough for them had contributed to the malaise that eventually precipitated my departure from the office.

Walking into the office that day, I felt an almost overwhelming pang of nostalgia and longing. I missed the place. I missed going to court. I missed my clients. I even missed the lunatics I used to work with. Criminal defense lawyers are a strange lot, arrogant and usually somewhat nuts, but genuinely and fiercely committed both to their clients and their ideals. You need a special personality to take on the forces of the government day after day, particularly when most people despise what you do and generally feel quite comfortable telling you that. I can't count how many times people have asked me, usually in tones bordering on disgust, what I would have done if I ever found out that a client of mine was guilty. I always reply that the real question is what I would have done if I had ever found out that a client of mine was innocent. The truth is that I probably would have collapsed with horror. If you do your best, lose, and a guilty person goes to jail, at least you can sleep at night knowing you've done your job. If you do your best, lose, and an innocent person goes to jail, that could pretty much ruin your life. Since, no matter how good a lawyer she is, most of a public defender's clients end up in jail, defending a truly innocent person would be a nightmare.

I tamped down my emotions enough to have a nice lunch with Marla. I even managed to limit my discussion of Abigail Hathaway's death to my feelings of shock and my ambivalence over whether to tell Ruby. I refrained from accusing prominent local businessmen of murder. When we got back from our Chinese chicken salads, I said good-bye and went out to the elevator bank, punched the down button, and tried to resist the little voice in my head. If the elevator that showed up hadn't been bulging with blue-suited prosecutors, I might have gone home that day, and avoided all the stress and fear of the next few weeks. But, as luck would have it, there was no room for a pregnant woman and no suit feeling chivalrous enough to give me his spot. The door closed and instead of hitting the down button again, I walked back into the federal defender's office and headed to the lair of the investigators. I've never been very good either at resisting temptation or minding my own business. That's what made me such a good lawyer.

No criminal defense lawyer could function without the assistance of an able investigator. These are often retired cops who see nothing strange in their decision to spend their golden years keeping people out of prison after having spent their youth putting people in. My favorite investigator was a man named Al Hockey, an ex-LAPD detective who took a bullet to the gut in his twenty-fifth year on the force. Al had tried to play golf for a year or so after leaving his job, but at a mere fifty was too young to spend his days chasing a little white ball around a green lawn. He'd been with the federal defender's office going on ten years, and during my time as an attorney there we were a terrific team. The first time we'd worked together, he'd managed to drum up fifteen bikers, each of whom claimed to have slept in my client's camper and most of whom surprised the heck out of the prosecutor, judge, and jury by acknowledging more than a passing acquaintance with methamphetamine. It didn't take the jury long to decide that any one of them could have left the packet of crank in my client's glove compartment. That was my first not-guilty verdict.

I walked into Al's office, plopped myself into a beat-up vinyl armchair, and put my feet up on the desk.

"Hey, old man. Miss me?"

Al knocked my feet to the floor and flashed me a huge grin.

"I was wondering if you were going to grace me with your presence. I heard you were around today."

"Wow, you must be using your keen detective skills again, Al."

"You know it, fat girl."

"I am not fat," I sputtered. "I'm pregnant."

"Whatever. All I know is that it's been a mighty long time since I've seen you in your leathers."

I'd earned the eternal devotion of the sexists in the investigator's office by showing up on my third day of work in a black leather miniskirt coupled with a conservative black blazer. I liked to pretend that I was making a statement, but the truth was I had spilled coffee that morning on the skirt that matched the blazer and, since I had eaten French fries and pie at every truck stop between New York and California, my mother's old leather mini (circa 1960) was the only thing in my closet that fit. I've never regretted my fashion *faux pas*. It can be next to impossible for an aggressive woman to earn the respect and cooperation of her colleagues, particularly if those colleagues are a bunch of beer-bellied, bellicose ex-cops. For some reason, my willingness to seem decidedly female, even sexy, made the guys feel better about accepting me as an equal. I wasn't someone they had to watch themselves around for fear of being reported for sexual harassment. Perversely, wearing a leather miniskirt made me one of the guys.

"Peter's keeping you barefoot and pregnant, Juliet." Al laughed.

I lifted a sneaker-shod foot. "Well, pregnant anyway," I said.

"What exactly is it that you do all day?"

"Oh, you know, bake cookies. Drive car pool. Run the PTA."

He looked at me seriously. "And that's enough for you?"

I had no ready answer. No, it wasn't enough.

"It's enough for now." I said and then changed the subject. "So Al, I have a favor to ask."

"A favor?" Al asked, his eyebrows raised.

"Yeah. Nothing big. Well, not too big. Well, maybe kind of big. Will you run someone through NCIC for me?"

NCIC stands for National Crime Information Center. It's the computer system listing everyone with a criminal record in the United States. The investigators have access to it so they can get the skinny on the informants, witnesses, and other nefarious characters the defender's office deals with. They are specifically not allowed to use it to, for example, check if someone's daughter's fiancé has a record. Al's daughter was, by the way, still single despite a couple of offers.

Al got up, poked his head out of his office door, looked up and down the hall, and sat back in his chair.

"Got a name and Social for me?"

"No Social Security number, but I do have the name. Bruce LeCrone."

"Capital 'C'?"

"Yeah."

"What about a birth date?"

"No, but he's probably about forty-five or fifty years old."

"Okay, give me a minute." Al scribbled the name on a Post-it and headed off down the hall to the computer terminal with the NCIC link. While he was gone I nosed around the files on his desk. Nothing seemed very interesting, just the usual bank robberies, mortgage frauds, and drug deals. Ten minutes passed before Al came back.

"Well, your boyfriend's got a record."

"No kidding! Great. Fabulous. He's not my boyfriend. Gimme that." I grabbed the printout.

In 1994 Bruce LeCrone had pled guilty to chapter 9, section 273.5.

"Do you know what section 273.5 is?" I asked Al.

He looked over my shoulder. "No idea. Here, look it up." He handed me the blue paperback *California Penal Code*.

I leafed through the book, found the appropriate section, and read aloud, "Willful infliction of corporal injury. Any person who willfully inflicts upon his or her spouse—"

"Domestic violence," Al interrupted.

"A batterer." I said.

I was flabbergasted. I knew how prevalent domestic violence is, even in educated, wealthy families. Nonetheless, it still shocked me to hear that someone in my world was a wife-beater. Recent events notwithstanding, most of us probably still believe that that kind of thing happens only in trailer parks, not in Brentwood.

"Any jail sentence?" Al asked.

I looked back at the printout. "Nope. Probation."

Al leaned back in his chair and looked at me speculatively. "Juliet, what gives? What are you up to?"

"What do you mean?" I asked disingenuously.

"You know what I mean. Are you working on something?"

I considered whether to take him into my confidence. I trusted Al, I always had.

"I'm checking into the background of a man I think might be responsible for a murder. Have you been paying attention to the case of the nursery school director who was hit by a car?"

"I think I saw something about it on the local news. What's your connection to the case?"

"I knew the woman."

"So you're playing detective?"

"I'm just looking into a few things."

"That sounds like so much nonsense to me."

"What?" I was genuinely shocked.

"Look, Juliet, the cops can do their job. They don't need you investigating this murder, if that's even what it is. They'll figure out who done it without any help from you."

I sputtered.

"This is about *you*," he continued. "You are doing this for yourself."

I shrugged, angry at him but knowing, deep down, that he was right.

"You've always been a ball of fire, Juliet. It was obvious from that first day I saw you come in here looking like Tina Turner. You just like mixing it up."

"That's probably true," I admitted.

"Not much opportunity for that, driving around in that big blue Volvo of yours, is there?"

"Nope. There isn't. What do you want me to say, Al? That I'm playing private eye because I'm bored with the daily grind of motherhood?"

"Well, are you?" He asked.

I considered for a minute. "Probably. Is there anything wrong with that?"

Al looked at me and shrugged. "How should I know? Who do I look like, Dr. Laura?"

I had to spend a few minutes promising Al that I wasn't involved in anything dangerous before I could gather my things and leave.

I drove home, strangely excited and energized by my discovery. I walked in the door to find Ruby and Peter immersed in an art project that involved sprinkling purple glitter all over the kitchen floor. I was about to berate the two of them for their sloppiness when Ruby held up a piece of paper covered in glitter and crayon.

"Look, Mama. This says 'I love you, Mama, because you are so beautiful.'" My eyes filled with tears as Peter and I smiled hugely at each other over Ruby's head. Sometimes it just takes you by surprise. Who was this fabulous little person careening around our house, and exactly what had we done to deserve her? How could I possibly consider leaving this delightful creature and going back to work?

4

THAT EVENING PETER, Ruby, and I went to dinner at one of our regular restaurants, Giovanni's Trattoria. Giovanni himself greeted us, as usual, and scooped Ruby up in his arms, taking her back to the kitchen to be petted and spoiled by his brother, the chef, and his mother, a sweet old woman in a long, black dress whose sole job seemed to be criticizing her sons and feeding bits of cannoli to my daughter. Peter and I sat down at our usual table in the corner near the kitchen, and ordered a bottle of mineral water. Giovanni had known I was pregnant before my own mother did. He figured it out the night we declined our usual bottle of pinot noir and asked for one of fancy, Italian sparkling water instead.

"I'm getting the pasta with clam sauce," Peter said.

"That's what I want. Get something else."

"You know, Juliet, we can both order the same thing. It won't kill us."

"God forbid. That's the difference between you WASPs and the rest of us. Two people dining together cannot order the same thing. What's the point of sharing if we both order the same thing?"

"What if I don't *want* to share?"

"Then you should have married Muffy Fitzpatrick from the tennis club instead of Juliet Applebaum from the delicatessen." I smiled sweetly at my husband and reached out to take the piece of bread he had put on his plate, just to illustrate my point. "You get the clams. I'll get the Arabbiata. And we share."

Peter smiled and grabbed his bread back.

"So, Juliet, what are we going to do about preschool?"

In my investigative zeal I had completely forgotten about what had involved me with the whole Hathaway affair to begin with.

"Oh, God. I don't know. We didn't even get an interview at Circle of Children or First Presbyterian. Maybe we could just forget about it. Do kids *have* to go to preschool? Wait, I have a terrific idea! We'll home-school her!"

"Right. I can definitely see you doing that. I can see you preparing elaborate lesson plans with multicolored charts and stickers while you're cooking up a batch of homemade papier-mâché and creating dioramas of early Colonial life. And all this with a baby attached to your breast. That is just so *you*, Juliet."

I shot my husband a glare. "Okay, maybe I'm not the most patient parent in the world, and maybe I've never done finger painting or played with Play-Doh or made a model of the Eiffel Tower out of Popsicle sticks, but don't you think I could handle it for a year?"

He looked at me balefully.

"How was your lunch with Marla?" he asked, changing the subject.

"It was fine. The office is hiring again."

Peter raised his eyebrows.

"No, no. I'm not thinking of going back. I'm seven months pregnant. How could I go back?"

"But you want to." Peter was trying to look as if he didn't care whether I went to work or not. Yet I knew how much he liked having me home. It wasn't a sexist impulse, but rather a selfish one. He liked the companionship. He liked the idea of being able to rush off spontaneously to Paris or Hawaii or Uttar Pradesh even though, in reality, we never rushed off anywhere more exciting than Home Depot.

"No," I answered quickly. "Not really. I mean, I wouldn't mind having something to do for a few hours a week, but I'm definitely not interested in full-time work!"

"Oh, good. I was afraid you were getting bored."

"Just because I'm bored sometimes and just because I'm not some kind of arts and crafts supermom doesn't mean I want to leave you guys. I love staying home. Really. I love it." Maybe I could convince myself if I said it often enough.

Peter looked relieved. I decided to take advantage of the goodwill I had engendered.

"I found out something interesting about our friend Bruce LeCrone."

"Juliet." His mood was not as receptive as I had thought. "I thought we decided you were going to give that a rest."

"*We* didn't decide anything. You did. And, anyway, I'm not doing anything. I just checked to see if he has a record."

"That seems like doing something to me." Peter looked irritated.

I said nothing. I could see his curiosity slowly getting the better of him. "Does he?"

"Excuse me?" I asked mock-innocently.

"LeCrone. Does he have a record?"

"Oh, so you *are* interested."

"Fine, don't tell me." He frowned and began earnestly studying the menu.

"He was convicted of domestic battery."

"Domestic battery?"

"You know, wife-beating."

"Holy cow!" Peter exclaimed.

"Exactly what I said. I was on the right track after all."

Peter looked doubtful. "Just because he beats his wife doesn't mean he killed Abigail Hathaway."

"Maybe not, but it sure does mean he's capable of violence. Anyway, I think it must have been his ex-wife. The charge is seven years old, and unless he married the present Mrs. LeCrone when she was in junior high, I don't think she's the one he beat up. Although, I suppose he could be beating her, too. Did you notice any bruises on her?"

"Don't get carried away, Juliet. Granted, this doesn't make him look good, but it's hardly evidence of murder." Peter poured some olive oil onto his bread plate, dipped his bread, and took a bite. "Still, I guess we should tell the police about his fight with Hathaway."

"You read my mind, my love." I reached out with my napkin and wiped away the trail of oil dripping down his chin.

At that moment Ruby came running out of the kitchen, chocolate smeared all over her chin.

"Giuseppe made me fed-up-cino alfwedo. Is that okay?"

"Sure, Peanut," Peter said. "But only if I get a bite."

"No, Daddy. Alfwedo is only for me an' Mama today. Right, Mama?"

"Right, kiddo," I said, somewhat amazed that Ruby was sharing with me rather than her dad. When faced with a choice between the two of us she never picked me.

Peter turned back to me. "Do you want me to call the cops for you?"

"Of course not. I'm the one who figured this out; I'm the one who should call. And I'd like to ask them one or two questions about the investigation."

Peter smiled. "Be sure to tell them you were a public defender. That'll put them right in your corner."

THE NEXT DAY I called the Santa Monica Police Department and asked to speak to the detective in charge of the Hathaway investigation. I was connected to the homicide unit and spoke to a woman who informed me that Detective Mitch Carswell was out of the office but would return later in the day. I told her that I had information regarding the death of Abigail Hathaway, and she said she would pass my message along to Detective Carswell. He called back later that afternoon while Ruby and I were making Play-Doh pasta.

"Juliet Applebaum?"

"This is she. Ruby, not in your mouth!"

"Detective Carswell, Santa Monica Police Department. I understand you called regarding the Hathaway case?"

"Yes, I did. Ruby! Can you hold on for a second, Detective?"

Without waiting for his answer I quickly put the receiver down on the table, leaned across, and hooked my finger into Ruby's mouth. Over her screams of protest I scooped out clumps of turquoise blue Play-Doh.

"But it's *pasta*!!" she shrieked indignantly.

"For heaven's sake, Ruby. It's pretend. It's pretend pasta. You can't eat it!"

PlaySkool puts huge quantities of salt into its Play-Doh with the idea that that will make it unpalatable and prevent tiny sculptors from consuming their medium. This precaution is wasted on a child whose idea of a snack is sucking the salt off of an entire bag of pretzels.

I picked up the receiver again.

"Sorry. I have a two-year-old and I'm trying to keep her from killing herself."

Detective Carswell didn't laugh.

"I'm kidding," I said, just to make sure he didn't actually show up at my door with an arrest warrant and a couple of social workers from the Department of Youth and Family Services.

The silence on the line was deafening.

"Are you still there?"

"Yes, Mrs. Applebaum. Can you talk now, or shall I call back at another time?"

"Ms. And now's fine."

"You have some information for me regarding the Hathaway hit-and-run?"

"Yes. That is, I think so. I mean, I have the information, but it may or may not be relevant to the Hathaway case."

"Why don't you let me be the judge of that," Detective Carswell said.

"Right. Sure. Um, where do I begin? My husband, daughter, and I were at Heart's Song, that's the school Ms. Hathaway ran."

"I'm familiar with it."

"Of course you are." Did I detect a note of sarcasm? "We were there for an admissions interview with two other couples. At the end of the morning, one of the people there got into a fight with Ms. Hathaway."

"A fight?" Carswell interrupted. "What kind of fight?"

"It was actually pretty ugly. Ruby! Stop that! Put that Play-Doh down, *now*!" I pried the purple gunk out of my daughter's hands and did my best to scrape it off the underside of the kitchen table.

"Detective, hold on a sec, okay?" I put the receiver down again.

"C'mon, honey, let's watch a video."

I loaded up *The Lion King*, a film that by a conservative estimate Ruby has seen 237 times, hit the play button, and picked up the receiver again.

"Sorry. Where was I?"

"There was an ugly fight at the preschool."

"Right. This one guy, Bruce LeCrone, grabbed Ms. Hathaway and started yelling at her because she didn't accept his daughter to the school."

"She told him that at the interview itself?"

"I know. Pretty obnoxious. They have this procedure where they give out applications to the families who move on to the next step of the application process. She gave one to this other couple but not to LeCrone or us."

"Wait a minute." Carswell sounded genuinely astonished. "You people were applying to *preschool*, right?"

"Well, yes, but this isn't just any preschool. It's a really good school and it's very competitive." As I explained this to the detective I became decidedly embarrassed at being involved in the whole preschool rat race. What were we thinking? If we ended up in this kind of frenzy over preschool, imagine the horrors of college applications!

"Let me get this straight. You all come for an interview, and at the end she only gives an application to the people she likes?"

"Right."

"And she didn't like you?"

"Right. I think she thought I was beating my kid."

"Excuse me?" He sounded confused and a bit suspicious. "You were beating your child?"

"No, no!" I nearly shouted. "It's just that Ruby was about to destroy the sand table and I grabbed her and . . . oh, never mind. It's not relevant. I don't know why I even mentioned it."

Detective Carswell sighed. "What exactly is the *relevant* information you have for me?"

I really needed to get to the point. I could almost hear his thought: "Who is this crazy broad who's wasting my time?"

"Bruce LeCrone's daughter didn't get in either. He began yelling at Ms. Hathaway and grabbed her arm. He left without doing anything more, but I think he's worth investigating. He has a criminal record for domestic violence!" I ended, dramatically.

Detective Carswell didn't respond.

"He beat his wife!" I continued just in case he hadn't understood.

"Mrs., er, Ms. Applebaum, how is it that you are familiar with his criminal record?"

Now it was my turn to be quiet.

"Are you a friend of his wife?" he asked.

"No. Nothing like that. Anyway, I think it was his ex-wife."

"How do you know about his record?" he repeated.

I paused. "I'd prefer not to answer that question. But, if you don't believe me, feel free to check it out on your own. It's capital L, E, capital C, R-O-N-E."

"I'll do that," Detective Carswell said. "I have a few more questions for you, if you don't mind. For starters, why is it that you prefer not to answer my questions?"

"I have no problem answering your questions, just not that particular one." I knew I sounded defensive, but I couldn't help it. No way was I going to get Al into trouble.

I peeked into the family room, where Ruby was singing about how she couldn't wait to be king.

"Go ahead. Ask away," I said.

"Abigail Hathaway rejected your daughter from the Heart's Song School?"

"Right."

"And that upset you?"

"Of course. Wait a minute. Are you actually suggesting that I killed her?"

"I'm not suggesting anything. I'm just trying to get my facts straight."

"Fine. We were rejected at the school. We spent the rest of the day at home and I was in bed when I found out that Ms. Hathaway was killed. The phone rang any number of times during the evening, in case you want to verify my alibi."

"There's no need for that."

The detective paused. "Ms. Applebaum, now, I want to make sure you understand that the Santa Monica Police Department is doing everything we can to find the driver of the car that hit Abigail Hathaway. Leaving the scene of an accident is a very serious offense and, rest assured, we intend to find the person who did this."

"I'm glad to hear that."

"Ma'am, we deal with cases like this all the time. Drivers operating under the influence, uninsured drivers, they drive off after an accident all the time. But we'll find him. We usually do."

"So you're certain that this was a hit-and-run?" I asked. "Aren't you even considering the possibility of murder?"

"We haven't ruled out anything, ma'am."

"Good." I could hear myself starting to get a little snippy. That invariably happened when I was confronted with the hyperpolite condescension of your average police officer. I changed my tone. "Thank you for calling me back."

"That's quite all right, ma'am. Good-bye."

And he hung up.

I stared moodily at the receiver. I considered the idea that Detective Carswell might view me as a suspect in Abigail's murder, but pretty quickly dismissed that. Peter and I had each other as alibis and, if the detective was crazy enough to investigate a hugely pregnant woman, I could always pass a lie detector test. They might not be admissible in court, but they usually convince a prosecutor of a suspect's innocence or guilt.

What really worried me was that it sounded like the detective wasn't looking that hard for anyone to suspect of murder. In a city replete with drive-by shootings, gangland-style hits, and domestic murders, a simple hit-and-run car accident, even one that cost the life of a prominent citizen, wasn't going to get much police investigation. I'd seen it before. The cops would put a few signs up in the neighborhood, friends and family would raise funds for a reward, and in a year or two people would ask, "Hey, did they ever find out who ran over poor Abigail Hathaway?"

I sat down on the couch and pulled Ruby into my lap. Idly twirling her curls in my fingers and humming "Hakuna Matata," I puzzled over my next step. Detective Carswell wasn't going to change his approach to this case just because some housewife told him to. The truth was, he was probably right. It probably wasn't a murder, but rather at worst a vehicular homicide—drunk or reckless driving. But Bruce LeCrone's past made him worth investigating. And if the cops weren't willing to do it, I could. After all, this was something I'd been trained to do, and something I was actually very good at.

Only a very small fraction of a criminal defense attorney's job involves dancing around a courtroom turning prosecution witnesses into quivering lumps of jelly. The vast majority of the job is investigation. The lawyer has to figure out what happened—not what the police say happened, and sometimes not what actually happened, but what, if any, scenario exists to make her client's claim of not guilty at least plausible. That involves long hours at crime scenes, interviewing witnesses, talking to family members, and more. If a client is convicted, there's even more investigation to be done. The lawyer has to find enough information to convince the judge that a lighter sentence is warranted. It's all about fieldwork, and I had always loved that part of the job. There was no reason I shouldn't exercise that atrophied muscle in the service of Abigail Hathaway. At worst, I'd find out nothing. And, maybe, just maybe, I'd discover something that would give the police a reason to consider the possibility of murder.

I WAS STILL puzzling out my next step an hour later, when Ruby danced over to the VCR and pressed the rewind button.

"Wanna play trains, Mama?" she asked.

I sighed, already bored at the prospect of toddler games. I looked at my watch. I had a whole hour to kill before I could expect to see Peter walk through the door and relieve me of my Romper Room duties.

"Why don't you play by yourself, Ruby."

I looked up in time to see a fat tear rolling down my baby's face.

"You never wanna play with me," she whispered.

"Sure I do. I play with you all the time. Don't I?"

"No."

I thought for a moment. She was right.

"Okay, honey, let's play trains," I said, pushing thoughts of Bruce LeCrone and untimely deaths out of my mind and lowering my substantial bulk onto the floor.

Ruby hauled out her plastic bin full of Brio trains and tracks. Peter had brought the little magnetic train set home with great fanfare as part of our campaign to ply Ruby with gender-neutral and boy's toys. She loved it from the moment she set eyes on it. Much to Peter's horror, however, she was not at all interested in setting up the tracks and making the little train run around them. Instead, she liked to play "train family." Lately, the train babies all had bad colds and were in bed, being cared for by the train mommies. The engine, in its role as train doctor, gave them frequent shots and pills. These games drove her normally patient father to distraction, and I'd once heard Peter wail, "Can't they just pull *a heavy load*?"

Balancing a little caboose on my round belly I said, "Hey look, Rubes, the train baby is stuck on top of a mountain! Can the train mama rescue her?"

By the time Peter got home we'd been playing for close to an hour and my eyes had long since glazed over. What was it about me that made it so hard for me to enjoy these games? Peter loved playing with Ruby. I often saw other mothers playing with their kids. Was I the only one who found it cataclysmically boring?

At the sound of the garage door opening, Ruby and I rushed to the front door like a couple of golden retrievers who'd been left alone all day. Peter walked in wearing his gym clothes and carrying a brown paper bag that gave off the most tantalizing aroma.

"Guess what?" he said.

"What?" Ruby shouted.

"I went to the gym and guess what?"

"What?" she shrieked again.

"What's next door to the gym?" He matched her yell.

"What?" This time I thought the windows would shatter.

He lowered his voice to a stage whisper. "Barbecue!"

Peter and I had celebrated the pink line in the pregnancy test by ordering a pizza—stuffed, no less—and had been going strong ever since. While he didn't quite match me inch for inch, Peter's belly was slowly creeping outward. I found this to be a considerable comfort. The last thing a rotund, pregnant woman needs is a guy with a washboard stomach lying next to her in bed.

We feasted on our ribs, dipping the pieces of spongy white bread that Ruby liked to call "cottony bread" into the barbecue sauce. Finally, chins and fingers sticky and stomachs content, Peter hustled Ruby off to her bath and bed. I picked up the receiver. Stacy was where I knew she'd be at seven thirty at night. At work.

"Hey."

"Hey to you, too. Did Bruce LeCrone confess yet?" she asked.

"Ha, ha, ha. You'll all be sorry you gave me such a rough time when the guy's trying to run the studio from San Quentin."

"Oh, please, Juliet. You are really being ridiculous. Seriously, have you found out anything new?"

I brought her up to date on my phone conversation with the police detective and what I had found out about LeCrone. When I told her about the domestic violence charge she gasped.

"Oh, for crying out loud, Juliet, you are so full of it," she said.

"What are you talking about?" Sometimes Stacy really made me angry. "I am not full of it. I put his name through the computer. The guy was convicted of beating up his wife."

Stacy was silent.

"Stacy? Are you still there?"

No reply.

"Stacy, come on. Would I lie to you?"

She sighed. "No, I suppose not."

"Look, I need some information from you," I continued.

"What?" She sounded suspicious.

"Nothing too big. I just need to know LeCrone's address."

"Oh, for God's sake, Juliet. I'm not going to give you his address."

"Why not?"

"Because he used to be a colleague. He worked here before he left to run Parnassus. I can't just give you a colleague's address."

"Well, can you tell me approximately where he lives?"

"No!"

"Just look it up on your database. Don't give me the address, just the neighborhood. C'mon, I'd do it for you," I wheedled.

She fell silent for a moment and then said, "Are you sure about this domestic violence thing?"

"Absolutely. I couldn't be more sure. I saw the printout of his record myself."

"All right. Give me a second, I'll check in the computer." She sounded grim. I heard her tapping a few keys.

"He lives in Beverly Hills a little east of the Century City Mall."

"Near Roxbury Park?"

"I think so," Stacy said.

"That's a nice park," I said. "Ruby would like it. Maybe we'd better go check it out."

"I'm not even going to bother telling you to be careful, Juliet. It doesn't do any good."

"I'm careful. I'm just taking my daughter to the park. What could possibly be wrong with that?"

5

THE NEXT MORNING dawned warm and beautiful. It was one of those days that remind you that Los Angeles is just a desert covered in freeways and parking lots. The light was so bright it hurt my eyes, but it seemed as likely to be emanating from the white lines in the road as from the sky above. I usually greeted this kind of day with a scowl and a muttered, "Great, another beautiful day. Who needs it?"

Not so today. Today we had plans. Ruby and I donned matching purple sunglasses and, careful not to wake Peter, gathered up her pails and shovels and headed out to Roxbury Park, a lovely expanse of green grass, play structures, and *bocci* and basketball courts on the southern end of Beverly Hills. The children playing there generally reflected the demographics of the neighborhood, primarily wealthy white kids with a smattering of Iranians and Israelis who'd made good in the jewelry, film, or air-conditioning business.

When Ruby and I arrived we found the play area packed with toddlers. I dumped Ruby's sand toys out in the pit and set her up next to a dark-haired little boy with a bulldozer, and a little girl with blond pigtails who was making sand pies. Ruby and the tiny chef immediately struck up a conversation and I headed out to the benches, satisfied that she was busy for a while at least.

As in all Los Angeles area parks (and maybe those in all affluent cities), the benches were strictly segregated. About half were populated by a rainbow coalition of women—Asians, Latinas, black women with lilting Caribbean accents. Those women chatted animatedly, sharing bags of chips and exotic-looking treats, stopping only to scoop up fallen children or take turns pushing swings. The children they watched over were, without exception, white.

The tenants of the other benches were the Los Angeles equivalent of the suburban matron, of whom there are two distinct types. One group, with impeccably manicured nails and carefully blow-dried hair, called out warnings to their little Jordans, Madisons, and Alexandras. The other group, the ones I liked to think of as "grunge mamas," were just as carefully turned out, in contrived rags artfully torn at knee and elbow. They wore Doc Martens and flannel shirts, and their shouts of "Watch out for the swing!" were directed at little boys named Dallas and Skye and little girls named Arabella Moon. I belonged somewhere between the two. My overalls disqualified me from membership in the Junior League, but, since I'm a lawyer and not a performance artist or jewelry designer I wasn't quite cool enough for the alternative music set.

It took me only a moment to spot Morgan LeCrone. She sat on the top of a high slide, looking imperiously down at the children playing below her. Behind her, a towheaded boy whined for his turn down the slide. At the bottom, a middle-aged Asian woman waved both hands wildly, beseeching the child to go.

"Morgan, time come down. Come down, Morgan. Other children want play, too."

Morgan ignored the woman.

I walked over and stood next to the Asian woman, who obviously had the unpleasant job of nanny to the LeCrones' spoiled princess.

"Mine does that. Drives me nuts," I said, smiling.

"She never come down. She go up and sit. I always gotta go up and get her."

"Maybe if you just leave her she'll have no choice but to slide down on her own," I suggested.

"You think that okay?" the woman asked.

"Sure. I think that would be fine. Let's just walk over to that bench and have a seat. She'll come down."

I led the woman over to a nearby bench under a shady tree and she sat down, clearly happy to get out of the glaring sun.

"My name is Juliet," I said, holding out my hand.

She took it. "I'm Miriam, but everyone call me Lola."

"That means grandmother," I said.

"You know Tagalog?" she said, surprised.

"Not really. My daughter, Ruby, has a friend who's Filipina, and she calls her grandmother Lola."

"Yeah. Lola mean grandmother. All my kids calls me Lola."

"Do you baby-sit for other kids or just Morgan?"

"She my only one now but she number thirteen for me. I got six of my own, too." Lola looked proud.

Reminded of her charge, we both looked up in time to see Morgan fly down the slide, hair blowing out behind her, a huge smile on her face.

"Hmph. That something I don't see alla' time," Lola said. "She don't like to smile."

"No?" I asked. "That must be pretty hard to deal with."

"I tell you something: I take care lotta kids in my life. I got six my own kids, I been nanny plenty times. But this kid the hardest. I call her Amazona, she always hittin' and beatin' other kids. She even hit me!" Lola shook her head, obviously scandalized at Morgan's misbehavior.

I murmured sympathetically, shaking my head.

"It's okay. I love her anyway. I love alla' my kids." Lola leaned back against the bench. "Which one yours?"

I pointed to Ruby, who was still busy in the sand pit.

"Nice red hair. She get it from you," Lola said.

I smiled. "I hope not! I get it from a bottle."

"You lucky! Everybody think yours real because of her."

I pulled a pack of gum out of my pocket and handed her a piece. We sat, companionably chewing, for a moment.

"So, do you like being a nanny?" I asked.

"I love my kids," Lola repeated.

"And the job?"

"That depend. Some jobs I like more than others."

"I guess it must depend on the family."

"Yeah, mostly it the family. If the kids happy. If the mom and dad happy. One time I work for couple in the middle of divorce. That was terrible. Poor kids."

"Are Morgan's parents good to work for?" I asked nonchalantly.

Lola paused. "They okay. Not so bad. They not there so much, so it's okay.

"Her parents both work?" I asked.

"He workin' alla' time. She, I dunno, maybe she shoppin' alla' time."

"They don't spend much time with Morgan?"

"No. The father sometimes go work inna morning before she awake, come back after she asleep. Don' see her all week. They go out every night. Never even eat dinner with that kid!"

"That's terrible! You wonder why some people have children. What's the point if they're not going to spend any time with them?"

Lola and I nodded, agreeing with each other. I glanced over at Ruby, who had come upon Morgan playing on the slide.

"I know you!" I heard my daughter shout. "Mommy! I remember her!"

Hurriedly, I tried to distract Lola. The last thing I wanted was for her to discover that I had ever seen Morgan before. "So, do you live in?" I asked.

"Yeah. First Monday to Friday, but now they pay me extra and I stay all weekend, too."

"You work seven days a week?"

"Sure. They pay me fourteen dollars a hour. My daughter in medical school in Manila. It's very expensive."

"I'll bet. When's the last time you had a day off?"

"Not so long ago. Monday night she tell me go home. She gonna stay in."

My ears pricked up. This was just the information I was looking for!

"Wow. They both actually stayed home with their daughter for once," I said, with just the slightest hint of a query in my tone.

"Her, but not him. I put Morgan to bed, I clean up, I go to my sister's house. I left maybe eight thirty. He not home yet."

Pay dirt. Abigail Hathaway was run down on Monday at about nine in the evening. Bruce LeCrone may have had another alibi, but he wasn't home immediately before the murder.

I decided to try to find out if LeCrone's violent tendencies had reared their ugly head.

"You know, Lola, I just read this article that said that men who work all the time are more likely to be violent. You know, like hit their wives or their kids." Embarrassingly unsubtle, but what the heck.

Lola got very quiet.

"I wonder if he's like that. Like what the article said." I pressed.

She said nothing.

I pushed harder. "Do you think he might be like that?"

"He don' hit that baby, I know that. I would never let him hit that girl," Lola blurted out. She was clearly hiding something but just as clearly worried about how much she had already said.

"I gotta go. It late now," she said, gathering her bag.

"Wait!" I said. I hadn't gotten nearly enough information from her. I decided to bargain that Lola's antipathy toward her employers would keep her from giving me away. Reaching into Ruby's diaper bag, I rustled around until I found an old business card. Crossing out the federal public defender's phone number, I scrawled in my home number. "Please give me a call if anything happens, or if you want to talk, or anything," I said, pressing my card into her hand.

Lola nodded quickly, crammed my card into her pocket, jumped up, and rushed off to the slide, where Morgan had once again begun her slow, deliberate assent. She scooped the little girl off the ladder and, despite Morgan's howls of protest, hustled her off the playground.

"See you again!" I called after her retreating back.

"Okay. Bye," Lola said, without stopping or even turning back to look at me.

I'd obviously touched a raw nerve. I believed the nanny when she said that LeCrone didn't hurt Morgan. Not because I didn't think him capable of beating his child, but rather because I didn't think Lola would stand for it. That little Filipina grandmother seemed perfectly capable of protecting her charge. Her reaction, however, made me think that LeCrone's capacity for violence was not unfamiliar to the members of his household. It seemed pretty likely that he was beating up on someone, and I was willing to bet that it was his wife.

While all this was certainly disturbing, it didn't get me any closer to proving that the man had killed Abigail Hathaway. All I'd succeeded in doing was ruling out one possible alibi.

I decided to put the LeCrones out of my mind for the time being and went over to Ruby, who was wistfully watching the children on the swings.

"Hey, big girl! You want me to push you?"

"Yes! As high as the sky, Mama! As high as the sun, moon, and stars!"

"Hey, what a coincidence! That's how much I love my girl! As much as the sun, moon, and stars," I said, kissing the top of her head. I picked her up and deposited her on the swing.

"I got a coincident, too, Mama. Mines is that I love you as much as there are elephants in the zoo!" Ruby squealed, her legs kicking in the air as the swing rose higher and higher.

"That's a lot of elephants, Sweetpea." I pushed her again. For one of the few times in my life I was distracted completely from everything except my daughter, rushing toward the glare of the sunless sky, her copper curls shining and her mouth open in a yowl of glee. My breath caught as I tried to freeze that moment in my memory. I wanted to be sure I never forgot her that way, full of joy and absolutely certain that the world is a wonderful place, a place where Mama is always there to push, it's possible to reach the moon on a swing, and the zoos are bursting with elephants.

6

THAT NIGHT PETER and I had planned one of our infrequent, much-anticipated date nights. I fed Ruby her favorite dinner, macaroni and cheese. I tossed in a couple of microwaved broccoli florets (which would, of course, never actually pass Ruby's lips), and I had a well-rounded meal sure to satisfy even the most scrupulous of nutrition advocates. Okay, not the *most* scrupulous, but good enough for me.

Once Ruby had finished her macaroni and cheese and pushed her broccoli into a pile at the side of her plate, I rousted Peter from his office, where he was pretending to work but really busily clicking his mouse and slaying Ganon and other cybervillains.

Once I'd convinced him that it was really time to go, I yet again found myself standing naked in my room, idly scratching my itchy belly and studying the contents of my closets, like I expected to find lurking therein a Sasquatch, a paving stone from the lost city of Atlantis, or the propeller of Amelia Earhart's airplane. Or, at the very least, something to wear. Early in my first pregnancy I had excitedly gone to a maternity store, happily imagining myself in all sorts of elegant ensembles that artfully disguised my girth while showing off my glow. Yeah, right. Elegant is not what the designers of maternity wear have decided is the appropriate look for their corpulent clientele. "Cute" is the adjective of choice. Bows, ribbons, little arrows pointing down at the belly. Prints of smiley faces and happy flowers. Lots of pink.

I don't know who decided that pregnancy requires the infantilization of a woman's wardrobe, but I'd like whoever it was to spend a few moments with me while I model those outfits. It's hard enough for me to look like a grown-up, since I'm only five feet tall. With my width fast approaching the same dimensions as my height and my face assuming the proportions of the moon, the last thing I needed was a frill on the collar of a pastel blue ruffled smock.

I'd stocked my closet with black leggings and oversized shirts in neutral colors. Each day I resolutely tried to find a new and interesting combination. Raiding Peter's wardrobe helped alleviate the monotony, but that was becoming less of an option as I slowly but surely inched up toward and, horrifyingly, past his weight. I was outgrowing his clothes as fast as I had outgrown my own.

Tonight I was determined to look decent. Peter and I were going to a movie premiere. We didn't often get invited to these Hollywood events. We're not exactly A-list material. However, the producer who'd optioned Peter's latest script had just released a new film, a typical shoot-'em-up action movie starring a taciturn, kickboxing Swede who made Steven Seagal look like a candidate for the Royal Shakespeare Company. While the movie was bound to be both jarringly loud and earth-shakingly dull, I was looking forward to the premiere hoopla. It had been quite some time since I'd hobnobbed with Hollywood's elite.

I dragged on a pair of my ubiquitous black leggings, hauled them up over my belly, and confronted my closet yet again. A flash of sequins caught my eye. There, in the back of my closet, lurked a seemingly ill-advised purchase, a sequined shirt of clingy spandex in a deep, shining green. I'd bought it years ago when I went through a brief club-hopping phase. I used to wear it tucked into that leather skirt. I pulled the shirt over my head and snapped it down over my bulging belly.

There are, I believe, two ways to dress when pregnant. One possible avenue hides the belly under loose, smocklike tunics. It is the more obvious choice. The second celebrates the size of the belly, calling attention to its contents. Green sequins drawn tight enough to see the outlines of my navel fall squarely into the latter category. It was a risk, but I have to say it worked.

I made up my eyes elaborately and chose a dark red lipstick. I jammed my puffy feet into open-toed platform sandals and waddled into the bathroom.

"So? Whaddya think?" I asked in my best Jewish-princess-from-Long Island voice.

Ruby was sitting in the tub, her hair full of shampoo and pulled into triceratops horns at the top of her head. Peter sat on the floor next to her, attacking her with a three-inch blue *T. Rex* figurine. They turned to look at me.

"Wow, Mama, you look so fancy!" Ruby said, smiling.

"Wow, Mama, you look so sexy!" Peter said, leering.

My two loves, each with trashier taste than the other.

"Do I look good enough for Hollywood?"

"You look good enough to eat," Peter said, grabbing a fistful of my rear end and squeezing.

ANDREA, RUBY'S ANOREXIC baby-sitter, showed up on time for once. As usual she had brought a Tupperware container full of carrot sticks and celery stalks. I'd long ago gotten over asking her to help herself to the food in our kitchen. For a while I'd even provided her with her favorite veggies, but to no avail. She always brought and ate her own. It was as if she thought our carrots had soaked up extra calories by virtue of their presence in our fat-polluted fridge. Like the bacon was secretly rubbing itself on them when the door was closed.

Eating disorders aside, Andrea was a great sitter, responsible and creative. Ruby loved her. They were playing a round of Candyland as we left, and Ruby didn't even look up to say good-bye.

Peter parked the car as close as he could to the movie theater, but it was almost a ten-minute walk before we arrived at the edges of the bleachers that had been set up for the Swede's adoring fans. By that time I was limping in my platform shoes and holding my stomach with both hands, hoisting the load off my bladder. Peter gripped me by the elbow, propelling me through the throngs of hysterical kickboxing fanatics, many of whom actually seemed to be practicing their favorite moves while they waited for their idol to appear.

"Hey, watch it, pregnant woman here!" he said, deflecting a Nike that grazed my belly.

We finally made it to the police barricades set up to keep the crowds off the red carpet leading into the theater. Peter thrust his engraved invitation into the face of one of the security guys manning the entrance. The guard motioned us through a gap between two barricades, and we stepped up on the red carpet. The area in front of the theater was lit by a huge phalanx of hot, white Klieg lights. The carpet was crowded with reporters fawning over stars and thrusting microphones in their faces. As we stepped up, the crowd of hoi polloi behind the barricades turned in one motion to look at us. An audible sigh of disappointment escaped them as they realized we were nobody. A camera operater who had turned his oversized video camera in our direction snapped off the light and turned away, leaving us in a little, dark island of anonymity in the midst of the bright, star-filled field of red. Peter and I looked at each other and smiled ruefully. There's nothing like a Hollywood opening to make you feel like you don't exist.

We walked quickly up the carpet toward the door of the theater. Suddenly, a hand reached out and grabbed my arm, jerking me roughly. I staggered, my balance thrown off. Peter threw his arm around my waist to keep me from falling, and I turned around to see where the hand had come from. I found myself staring up at the beet-red face of none other than Bruce LeCrone. He was already screaming by the time I turned my head.

"Who do you think you are, you bitch! I'm going to have you arrested for stalking! What the hell do you think you're doing? Do you know who I am, you disgusting cow?"

My mouth dropped open and I stared at him blankly, utterly taken aback by his invective. Not even my creepiest clients had ever abused me that way.

Before I could gather myself together to blast him back, Peter took hold of LeCrone's hand, wrenching it off my shoulder and pushing it away.

"Back off. Back off, now," Peter said quietly.

LeCrone leaned into Peter's face. "Your wife has been following my nanny around, accusing me of beating up my kid. I'll kill her *and* you!"

Peter, his white face and set chin the only outward evidence of how truly angry he was, put his hand on LeCrone's chest and pushed him gently but firmly away.

"No one has accused you of anything. Now we're going to turn around and go into the theater and I suggest you do the same."

By now everyone was staring at us. The reporters had stopped in midinterview. The videographer who had previously considered us too boring to merit his attention had his camera trained firmly in our direction. From the corner of my eye I could see two security officers rushing our way.

"Look, I happened to bump into your nanny at the park and we got to talking, that's all," I said, hoping to calm the furious man down. What had possessed Lola suddenly to turn loyal? Peter turned to look at me in surprise.

"You just happened to ask her if I beat up my kid? Bullshit!" LeCrone said, his voice only slightly quieter than a shriek.

"Can we just cut out the screaming?" Peter said. "There's obviously been some kind of misunderstanding here."

"Exactly," I interjected. I decided to go for broke. After all, I couldn't get the guy any *more* furious than he already was. "I was actually trying to find out if you had an alibi for the night Abigail Hathaway was killed."

LeCrone exploded. With a bellow, he reached his arm back and shot out a fist, aiming it directly at my face. Peter jumped in to deflect the blow, managing to put his shoulder between LeCrone's balled hand and my nose. Peter took the punch and staggered back with the force. LeCrone was getting ready to deliver another strike when the two security officers finally arrived at our sides. They grabbed LeCrone, one on each arm, and hauled him back a few feet. One raised a warning hand at Peter.

"That's it, buddy," the officer said.

As they hustled LeCrone off, he turned back and shouted over his shoulder, "I was at a reception at ICA, you dumb broad. That's my *alibi*." The last word was delivered in a snide snarl.

I turned to Peter, who was staring at me, shaking his head.

"I guess he has an alibi," I said sheepishly.

At that moment a long white limo pulled up at the curb and the Swede leaped out the door, arms outstretched to greet his public. A roar rose up from the crowd, and all attention was diverted from us and toward the evening's kickboxing prince.

"Juliet, what in God's name were you thinking? Are you trying to get yourself killed?" Peter said as he grabbed my hand and dragged me into the theater.

"Hardly," I responded. "I just asked his nanny a question. How was I supposed to know that the guy would lose his mind?"

We walked down the aisle and found ourselves two seats toward the back.

"Might I remind you that you yourself called him psychotic and capable of murder?" Peter said.

I settled myself into the chair. "Yeah, well, I guess I didn't realize exactly how psychotic. Anyway, he has an alibi." I reached across Peter's body and gingerly touched his hurt shoulder. "I'm so sorry, honey. Are you okay? Does it hurt?"

"Yes, it hurts. And don't touch me," Peter said, wincing and shrugging my hand off his shoulder.

"My knight in shining armor. My hero," I said, smiling sweetly.

Peter snorted and turned his face to the screen. I could tell that under his irritation was a wellspring of macho pride happily bubbling to the surface. He'd protected his woman!

"Thank God you were there. I swear he would have knocked me out if you hadn't deflected that punch," I said, leaning my head against his good shoulder and staring up at him admiringly.

Peter grudgingly reached his arm around me and gave me a squeeze.

"I love you," I said.

"I love you, too. Even if you are an idiot." He smiled despite himself. "I was about to really let him have it when those security guards showed up."

"It's lucky you didn't. You're in much better shape than he is and you probably really would have hurt him," I said, exaggerating more than a little but not more than necessary. A man's ego is a fragile thing. It never hurts to give it a few pats every once in a while.

We settled in to watch the movie.

News travels fast in Hollywood. Bad news faster than good, and misinformation at the speed of light. By the time we got home that night our answering machine was blinking like a hopped-up cokehead with a twitch. Peter's agent had called to ask if he had given any thought to his career before punching out the head of Parnassus Studios. My prenatal Yoga teacher had called because she'd heard I'd been beaten up and gone into early labor. Stacy left a hysterical shriek on the machine, shouting, "Juliet, my God, are you okay? I heard that you got into a fistfight with Bruce LeCrone at the premiere of *Rumble in Rangoon*! Did he hurt you? My assistant just told me that LeCrone knocked Peter out and had to be dragged off by four cops! What did you say to him? Are you nuts, Juliet? Are you totally insane? Call me as soon as you get this message. Call me right now!"

I called.

"Hi, Stace. It's me. I'm fine. Nothing happened."

"What do you mean 'nothing happened'? Everyone is talking about this. The only people not talking about this are lying under slabs at Forest Lawn. What in God's name happened?"

"Nothing happened. Nothing serious. LeCrone started screaming at me at the theater in front of every camera in Los Angeles, and that's about it. Except that he also tried to punch me but Peter got between us. Peter's fine. LeCrone hit him on the shoulder."

"And no one's in the hospital?"

"No, unless they locked LeCrone up in the booby hatch, which I hope they did because that is clearly where he belongs."

"But what did you *do*? Why did he try to kill you?"

"Oh, for crying out loud, he did *not* try to kill me. Jeez, Stace, you're beginning to exaggerate worse than I do! He took one tiny punch."

"But what did you *do*, Juliet? People don't just hit other people for no reason, not even studio executives."

"Nothing, really. I just met his nanny in the park. I might have asked her if she thought he might have any violent tendencies. Nothing more than that." I sounded defensive, but I knew she would flip out. And she did.

"Are you kidding me? What are you *doing*? What did you *expect* to happen? My God!"

"Well, it's all moot now, and anyway, I'd like to point out that you could have prevented this whole incident if you'd told me that LeCrone was at one of *your* parties on Monday night."

"What? One of *my* parties?"

"He said he has an alibi. He said he was at an ICA cocktail party."

"Monday night? Monday night. What was Monday night?" She seemed to be flipping through a mental calendar. "Oh, right! Monday night was the unveiling. We had a cocktail party to celebrate the new Noguchi piece in the office lobby. I think I even remember seeing him there, now that you mention it."

"Gotta say, Stace, I wish you'd remembered this a couple of days ago," I said, trying not to sound irritated. After all, it wasn't Stacy's fault that I was playing Hercule Poirot.

"Gotta say, Jule, it never occurred to me that you would be accosting LeCrone's household employees in the park. Otherwise, I might had worked harder to provide him with an alibi."

Stacy wouldn't let me hang up until I'd promised to leave the sleuthing to the professionals with the badges and the guns. I crossed my fingers and vowed to concern myself with more appropriate things, like whether I'd have another C-section or manage to deliver the new baby in the old-fashioned way or where we would send Ruby to preschool now that Heart's Song was no longer an option.

As I returned the handset to its cradle it suddenly occurred to me that perhaps Abigail Hathaway had been killed before putting her official rejection in Ruby's file. Maybe we should apply again! I wouldn't want to present too obvious a motive to Detective Carswell, but, on the other hand, I had Ruby's future academic career to think about.

Peter came in from walking Andrea to her car and locked the front door behind him.

"Sorry your agent is so mad at you," I said.

"Don't worry about it. You know, I think that's the first time *she's* called *me* in about two years!" He kissed me on the forehead and headed off to the bathroom to get ready for bed.

I followed him and we brushed our teeth side by side, alternating spitting in the sink. I pulled off my sequin shirt and leggings and climbed into bed. I dragged the full-length body pillow up alongside me and tucked one end up under my belly. As I was plumping the other pillows into position, Peter lay down on his side of the bed.

"Construction complete yet?" he asked.

"Almost," I said, giving the pillow behind my back a last punch and settling down with a groan.

"You're going to have to redo the whole thing in ten minutes when you get up to pee."

"I know. Isn't being pregnant fun?"

He put his head down on the lone pillow I'd grudgingly left for his use. Looking up at the ceiling, he said, "Well, at least this whole thing is over. We know LeCrone didn't murder Abigail Hathaway, and you can stop obsessing over this."

"I suppose," I said.

Peter sat up. "Juliet!"

"What?"

"Your own best friend gave him an alibi. What more do you need?"

"I suppose," I said again.

Peter rolled his eyes.

"Look," I said, "doesn't it just seem a little pat to you? I mean, why would Stacy suddenly remember that she'd seen him? I talked to her the night of the murder. I even told her that I suspected him. So why didn't she tell me then? Why didn't she give him that foolproof alibi then?"

That seemed to bring Peter up short. He paused for a moment and then shook his head. "You know what, Juliet? I don't care. All I care about is that next time, you might just get one of us killed. Promise me that you're not going to do any more investigating."

"You're right. Of course you're right. I'm sorry I even mentioned it." I didn't promise anything.

"Are you working tonight?" I asked.

"Yeah," Peter said, and hoisted himself up off the bed. "See you in the morning."

"I love you."

"Me, too. Good night."

7

THE NEXT MORNING I woke Peter up at eleven o'clock, as usual.
"I have a midwife's appointment today," I said as I handed him
his coffee.

"Thanks." He took a sip. "Do you want me to come?" When I was
pregnant with Ruby, Peter had come to every single prenatal appointment.
This time around he missed them more often then not.

"No, that's okay. It's just a standard eight-month checkup. And I might
go to prenatal Yoga afterward."

"Okay. Ruby and I'll go to the Santa Monica pier, maybe ride the
carousel."

I gave him a kiss. "See you later," I said. I had the afternoon to myself.

Dorothy, my midwife, shared offices with an acupuncturist and a mas-
sage therapist. The place had seemed a little kooky to me at first, but I had
gotten used to it. Stacy had convinced me to use Dorothy instead of an
obstetrician and, just as she'd promised, my prenatal care definitely had
a more personal touch this time around. I'd gotten pretty sick of my old
doctor asking me if I had any questions with her hand on the doorknob
and her body half out in the hall, heading to the next patient.

When I got to the office, I took off my shoes and stepped onto the scale.
Gasping in horror, I stripped off my socks. No substantial difference. I
took off my glasses, headband, and earrings. The scale began to wiggle a
bit, like it was considering whether to cut me some slack. It decided not
to. I'd gained seven pounds in the previous four weeks. I was tipping the
scales at a cool 170. If the NFL was in the market for any short, female
linebackers, I was ready to answer the call.

I was tempted to take off my shirt, leggings, bra, and even my panties
to try to bring the numbers down out of the leviathan and into the human

range, but the scale was in the hall, and there were a couple of expectant fathers milling about. Modesty prevailed.

Once inside the exam room, I listened patiently to Dorothy's lecture about the dangers of excessive weight gain, and lay on my back as she palpated my belly.

"Little guy been kicking much?" she asked.

"Less than before," I said. "That's normal, right?"

"Sure. There's less room for him to move around in there. He's getting big!"

I smiled, imagining a big, fat boy curled up inside of me.

"How are you doing, Juliet? You seem much happier to me. Last month you were a little blue." Sometimes Dorothy seemed almost psychic. She immediately sized up my state of mind, and even seemed to know better than I how I was doing. She considered the emotional health of her patients to be as important to a successful pregnancy and birth as their physical condition. My emotions had been on something of a roller-coaster ride over the past eight months.

I considered what she had just said. "You know, I *am* happier." I hadn't even noticed. "I've actually been feeling pretty good for the past few days!"

"Terrific. Is something going on? Are you involved in a new project?" she asked.

"No, there's nothing going on. Not really. Maybe I'm just getting used to the idea of having another baby. It's about time."

"True, true," she said. "I've been hoping this would happen for a while now. Let's listen to the baby's heart."

I lay back as she moved the portable Doppler over my belly. After a few false starts we heard the rapid thump-thump of my baby's heartbeat. My eyes welled up for a moment as I imagined him, this mysterious new creature, so completely familiar to me and so totally unknown.

"He sounds great. And he's perfectly in position, with his head down," Dorothy said.

"Hi, baby Isaac," I murmured.

"So it's Isaac?" Dorothy asked.

"Yup. We let Ruby choose between Isaac and Sam. She actually wanted to name him Odysseus but we nixed that."

"Odysseus! My goodness."

"She knows her Romans," I said, smiling proudly.

"Greeks."

"Right. I knew that."

Dorothy bustled around the room, putting away her instruments. She reached an arm out for me to hoist myself up off the table. I got myself dressed, scheduled my next appointment for two weeks hence, and went out to my car. I squeezed myself behind the wheel and turned on the radio to my favorite talk-radio station. Unfortunately, the Fates were conspiring to keep me involved with Abigail Hathaway. I tuned in just in time for the hour's news wrap-up, including an announcement that crowds of Hollywood luminary-parents were expected at the preschool director's memorial service, to be held at two o'clock that afternoon. I looked at my dashboard clock. It was one forty-five.

For a split second I actually considered going to my prenatal Yoga class and forgetting about Abigail, LeCrone, and the whole Heart's Song debacle. For a split second, only. I made a U-turn on Santa Monica Boulevard.

Naturally, there was valet parking. I gave the keys to my Volvo station wagon to a perky young blonde in a blue jacket with "Valet Girls" embroidered on the pocket. She could barely contain her disgust at the state of my car, which really irritated me because I had thoughtfully swept the used Kleenex, dried-out baby wipes, partly eaten apples, ancient Ritz crackers, chewed-up plastic dinosaur, and slightly rancid sippy cup of milk off the passenger seat and onto the floor. Maybe she was just disappointed because she had to park a beat-up old station wagon instead of a brand-new Porsche. As Ruby would say, tough noogies.

I walked by the ubiquitous television cameras and into the chapel. The pews were crowded, and I saw a surprising number of children's faces. My impression of her skill with children to the contrary, Abigail Hathaway must have been popular with her students. I was scanning the rows, looking for a spot large enough for my considerable bulk, when I heard a voice.

"Juliet! Juliet!"

I looked over my shoulder and spotted Stacy seated near the back of the chapel. She was wearing a severe black suit that showed off her creamy white skin. Her thick, blunt-cut blond hair was hidden under a hat that was, perhaps, a bit too elegant for a funeral. She leaned down her row, and with a flash of red nails motioned to her pewmates to move over. Miraculously, a space was made. I squeezed in, apologizing to those I mashed on the way. I've never figured out what is the appropriate way for a pregnant woman to move down a row of seats. Do you stand with your belly toward the people you are passing, impaling their noses on your jutting navel? Or do you go rear end first, forcing them to contort away from that particular body part? Obviously both options are an exercise in tackiness, but which is worse? I opted for the butt-in-the-face on purely selfish grounds—I wouldn't have to look at them while I squeezed by—and sat down next to Stacy.

"How come you didn't tell me you were coming?" I whispered.

"It never occurred to me that you'd be here. I mean, you didn't get in, right?" Stacy didn't whisper. Up and down the row, heads swiveled in my direction. I blushed.

"Nice, Stace."

"Sorry."

"Forget it. What a turnout!" I said, changing the subject.

"I know! Unbelievable. Look over there. There are Nicole and Tom sitting next to Michelle. She's a client of ours. Michelle! Hi, Michelle." Stacy waved at the movie star, who stared back, nonplussed.

"For God's sake, Stacy, this is a funeral, not a cocktail party! Keep your voice down!" I said.

Chastened, Stacy assumed a stage whisper. "So, what are you going to do about preschool?"

"I don't know. We missed the deadline for most places."

"What were you thinking?" Stacy seemed genuinely disgusted. "How many schools did you apply to?"

"Three. And we got rejected everywhere."

"Three? That's it? Are you nuts?"

A woman in the row ahead of us turned around to get a good look at the mother of the preschool reject. I smiled at her and waved. She blushed and turned back around.

"Stacy, can we just drop this? I'll figure something out."

"No, we cannot drop this. This is terrible. You don't seem to understand. If Ruby doesn't go to the right preschool, there is no way she'll get into a decent elementary. Then you can kiss high school good-bye. And let's not discuss college. This is a crisis. An absolute crisis."

"You mean a crisis as in the AIDS crisis? The dissolution of the Soviet Empire? The massacres in Rwanda? Would you please get some goddamn perspective?" I was hissing like an angry rattler.

Stacy looked at me and rolled her eyes. "We'll talk about this later. Maybe there's someone I can call."

"Oh my God, really? Is there? I'm sorry for losing my temper. Do you really think there's something you can do?" My own indignantly expressed sense of perspective lasted about fifteen seconds. Stacy patted my hand and turned back to scanning the crowd.

"You see down front? That's Abigail's husband, Daniel Mooney. He's a real estate developer or something." She pointed out a tall man in his mid- to late fifties, with salt-and-pepper hair done up in long, Byronesque curls falling to his shoulders.

"*That's* her husband?" I was astonished. "That hippie dude is married to her?"

"Was. And he's not a hippie. He's more of a Boho, Euro-trash type. Except I think he's from Iowa or something. Her daughter is sitting next to him."

Abigail Hathaway's daughter looked to be about fifteen. My heart went out to her as she sat there, a chubby adolescent with a pale face trying unsuccessfully not to cry. Her hair was dyed a sickly purple and shaved on one side. She had obviously tried to tone it down for her mother's memorial service, combing the long side over the top and clipping it with a plain tortoiseshell barrette. There was a foot of space between her and Daniel Mooney. Neither so much as glanced at the other. He looked straight ahead, and she stared into her lap.

"Poor thing," I said. "Why doesn't her father put his arm around her or something?"

"Oh, that's not her father," Stacy replied. "He's Abigail's third or fourth husband. They'd only been married for a few years. Audrey's father was her first husband, I think. Maybe her second."

"Abigail Hathaway had four husbands? Are you serious?"

"Three or four. I don't remember."

Just then the hall filled with the sound of an organ, and we all hushed. A small man in a cleric's collar walked solemnly onto the altar, raised his hands to the gathered mourners, and led us in a hymn. Stacy pointed out the words in the hymnal, but I didn't need to look. I'd memorized Judy Collins's rendition of "Amazing Grace" long ago. I even knew the harmony.

I found most of the service remarkably moving, but then I've been known to cry at Lysol commercials. One of Abigail Hathaway's oldest friends gave the eulogy, recalling her as a wonderful wife, mother, and a resource to the entire community on child-rearing. A moderately famous movie star, the father of a student at Heart's Song, wiped away tears as he told us how Abigail Hathaway had helped his daughter through the difficult period of her parents' moderately notorious divorce.

After the movie star sat down, the pulpit remained empty for a few moments. Suddenly, with a toss of salt-and-pepper curls, Daniel Mooney rose from his seat. He stepped up to the pulpit with a long, loose stride and lifted his arms to the assembly.

"I embrace you. I embrace you and thank you for your love, for your support, for your memories of our dearest Abigail.

"I see that some of you are crying. Don't cry for her. Life is simply an illusion. The tears you shed are for yourselves, for us all. For we are here in the time-space of earthly life and she has gone forward, gone upward to the realm of complete being. She has gone home.

"If you grieve for Abigail you will hold her back from that place. You will hold her back from the light. Celebrate for her. Be joyful for her. Let your joy propel her ethereal body to the home we all crave."

Daniel Mooney blathered on in this manner for a good half hour and actually succeeded in drying up all the tears that might have been shed for his wife. Periodically during his oration, he would pause dramatically and sweep his hair off his forehead with a flourish of thumb and ring finger. And, he never, not once, looked down at his stepdaughter, sitting alone in the front pew, isolated and abandoned in her misery. By the time he finally sat down, I had found another suspect in Abigail Hathaway's death.

The minister led us in a final hymn, then stepped down off his pulpit and led the dead woman's husband and daughter out of the chapel. Once they had walked down the aisle, the rest of us stood up to leave. Stacy turned to me and said, "Do you want to grab something to eat? I don't have to be back at the office for an hour or so."

"Who, me? Eat? Never," I replied.

As we made our way through the crowd, Stacy stopped every few feet to greet another one of her acquaintances.

"Hello! Tragic, isn't it?" she said. And again.

"How *are* you? Isn't this just awful?" And yet again.

"Hi. So sad. Isn't it just so sad?"

I was impressed at her capacity to sound both genuinely grief-stricken and happy to see someone at the same time. We finally reached the door and walked out into the bright, dry sunlight. Making our way to the curb, we waved our claim checks in the direction of the parking attendants and waited for our cars. Just then, a young woman with a long brown braid down her back and red-rimmed eyes touched Stacy's shoulder.

"Oh, Stacy. I'm so glad you came. Is Zachary okay? Does he know?" she asked.

"Maggie! Dear, sweet Maggie! Zack's fine, he's doing great. I told him about Abigail, but he doesn't really understand. How are *you* holding up?"

"Um, I don't know. I'm like, totally in shock. You know, we were together until just before it happened," the young woman said, her eyes welling up with tears.

That caught my attention. I immediately butted in on the conversation.

"You poor thing," I said. "You saw her right before she died?"

Stacy shot me a warning glance.

"*Juliet*. This is Maggie Franks. She's one of the teachers in the Billy Goat room. Maggie, this is my friend Juliet Applebaum."

I reached out my hand and shook Maggie's limp one.

"Did you know Abigail?" she asked.

"No, not really," I replied. "I just came to keep Stacy company."

Stacy snorted derisively. I hurriedly continued, "We were heading out for some lunch. Would you care to join us?"

Maggie looked at me gratefully. "You know, I think I would. Mr. Mooney isn't having any kind of reception today, and I really don't feel like being alone right now."

Stacy, who had been glaring at me incredulously, politely seconded my invitation and we arranged to meet at Babaloo, a little restaurant nearby. We retrieved our cars and set off in a convoy. It didn't occur to us to go in one car, but then why would it? This was L.A., after all. Stacy and I each found parking right away and waited in the restaurant while Maggie circled the block, looking for a space.

"What's this all about, Juliet? Why did you ask her to join us?" Stacy asked me.

"Well, she's Zack's old teacher."

"And?"

"And she may have been the last person to see Abigail alive. I just want to find out if she knows anything that might be useful."

"I thought you had decided to give this up after your brawl with LeCrone. I thought we'd agreed that you were going to leave the detective work to the professionals."

"First of all, *we* didn't decide anything, you did." I paused for a moment, distracted by the thought that I'd used precisely the same line on Peter. Giving my lack of originality an inward shrug, I continued, "And second of all, it seems to me that the police have pretty much decided that this is a random hit-and-run. If that's the case, then they're not going to be doing much investigating. And if they aren't, why shouldn't I? I'm trained for it. I know what I'm doing. There's no harm in me looking into things a bit."

"LeCrone might take issue with that point of view." Sometimes Stacy can be downright snide.

At that moment we spotted Maggie's car pulling into a space that had opened up in front of the restaurant.

"Just do me a favor, Juliet. Don't be too pushy with Maggie. She's a real sweetheart, and I'm not sure she can hold her own with you."

"I'm not going to be pushy. When am I ever pushy?"

Stacy raised her eyebrows.

"Trust me," I said hurriedly as Maggie walked into the restaurant. "I'll be gentle and restrained."

"You'd better be," she whispered to me, waving her hand at Maggie. "Honey! We're over here!"

STACY ORDERED HER usual—diet fare. This time it was plain grilled fish and a salad with no dressing. Someday I'm going to tattoo "No butter, no oil" onto her skinny butt. Come to think of it, there's probably not enough room. Maggie got something multigrained and sprout-filled. I got a steak sandwich and fries. I didn't really want the fries, but someone had to fulfill our table's daily caloric requirement.

As we sipped our iced teas, I gently directed the conversation back to Abigail Hathaway.

"Maggie, you mentioned that you saw Abigail right before she died?"

So, maybe I wasn't so gentle.

"Yes. No. I mean, not right before. But that evening. After school," Maggie said.

"What time?" I asked.

She looked at me curiously, but answered my question. "About 6:10 or so. After the last late pickup."

Stacy interrupted. "Maggie runs the afternoon day-care program. School ends at one, but some of the kids stay until six."

"Nine to six?" I was surprised. "That's a really long day for a three-year-old."

Maggie nodded. "I think so, too. But we only have a few who stay that late. Most of them go home at three. That's why we have two teachers in the early afternoon, and only I stay late."

"Abigail always stayed with you?" I asked.

"Usually," Maggie said. "She didn't like to have just one teacher there, in case something happened, so she'd do administrative work until the last pickup at six. I don't know who's going to stay late with me from now on." She sniffed loudly as her eyes filled with tears.

Stacy patted her on the hand. "Don't worry, sweetie. I'm sure the new director will stay with you."

I hadn't even thought of that. "Who is going to be taking over the school now?" I asked. "Does anybody know?"

Maggie shook her head. "The board of directors will have to decide. It seems so weird. It's Abigail's school! It's not like they could just hire someone new to take her place."

I turned to Stacy and asked, "Is Heart's Song a nonprofit? Is it run by a foundation or something, or did she just own it outright?"

Stacy thought for a moment. "I'm pretty sure it's like any other private school. It's officially run by a board of directors, although they're just figureheads, really. Abigail made all the decisions. I know it's a nonprofit because I used to deduct all the donations I made every year."

"Unless you were just committing tax fraud," I said.

"Well, if I was, then my accountant was, too. His kids are Heart's Song alumnae."

"Okay, so we're pretty sure the school is going to continue, even without Abigail. The question is, who's going to run it? Who's going to get her job?" I mused.

Maggie gave a little sob. "Oh, no, I hope they don't make Susan Pike the new director. If they do, I'm quitting, I swear."

"Susan Pike? Who's that?" I asked.

Stacy answered, "She was one of the first teachers Abigail hired. She's been there as long as the school's been open. She's kind of an old dragon, but really good with the kids."

"She may be good with the kids, but we all hate her," Maggie said vehemently. "I don't feel bad about telling you that now, Stacy, because Zachary's graduated. The only person who can stand to be around her is Abigail."

"Then I'm sure they won't make her the new director," I tried to reassure Maggie.

"Did anything unusual happen the night Abigail was killed?" I asked, changing the subject. "Did you notice anything out of the ordinary?"

"The police already asked me that. I told them everything was just the same as always."

"So it was just your basic Monday night?"

"I guess so."

"Like every other day of the week?"

"Yeah. Well, no."

"No?" I asked.

"Fridays are different," Maggie said. "On Fridays Abigail leaves at a quarter to six because she's got therapy at six. But on every other day she stays late with me. Just as she did that night." Maggie started to sniffle.

"She was seeing a psychologist?" I asked. It was hard for me to imagine supremely confident Abigail Hathaway in therapy. I'm not sure why, since it seems like everyone in Hollywood is seeing a shrink, but I wouldn't have expected Abigail Hathaway, the frost queen, to regularly unburden her soul. It just didn't seem her style.

"There's nothing wrong with seeing a therapist," Maggie said defensively. "Anyway, she'd only been going for a few months. It's not like she was crazy or anything."

"Do you know who she was seeing?" I asked, not really imagining that Maggie would, or would say so.

"Well, let me think. A couple of months ago the doctor called and canceled the appointment because she was sick. I took the message because Abigail and Susan were having a f— discussion. Let me see if I can remember the doctor's name."

"Try. Try hard," I pressed.

"I remember thinking it was Chinese. Tang? Wong? Wang, that's it, Wang!"

"The doctor's name was Wang?" I asked. "Was it a woman? Do you remember the first name?" It couldn't be the same one, could it?

Back when Ruby was first born, and Peter and I were going through our difficult period of adjustment, we had, on the advice of a friend, visited a couples counselor. Peter had had a movie in production just then and he had gotten friendly with the lead actress, Lilly Green, a budding starlet who soon thereafter surprised everyone by winning a supporting-actress Oscar for her first serious film performance. At the time she was shooting Peter's movie, she had been in the process of dissolving her own rocky marriage and gave Peter the name of her therapist, one Dr. Herma Wang.

We'd made an appointment with Dr. Wang, who turned out not to be the tiny, slim, Asian woman I had been expecting, but rather a somewhat overweight Jewish matron with a thick Long Island accent, who used her married name.

Peter and I had lasted exactly one session with the good Dr. Wang. In the first three of our fifty minutes she'd managed to drop the names of three or four hundred of her most famous patients. Not their last names, mind you. She'd say things like, "As I said to one of my patients, 'Warren, every marriage is a partnership,'" or "As I often tell a patient, 'Julia, you can't expect him to understand you if you don't utilize your three-part communications technique.'"

Technically, I suppose, she wasn't violating anyone's confidences, but really, how many of us *don't* know who those folks are? Peter and I decided that whatever problems we had weren't worth spending a hundred bucks an hour to hear Dr. Wang wax poetic about the trials and tribulations of Mel, Matt, Bruce, and Susan. We never went back.

"Yes, it was a lady doctor, but I don't really remember her first name," Maggie said.

"*Could it* have been Herma?" I asked.

"Maybe. I don't know. Why are you asking me all these questions?"

"Juliet's just a busybody," Stacy said, pinching my leg under the table.

Realizing I wasn't likely to get any more out of Maggie, I stopped the interrogation and kept my mouth shut for the remainder of the lunch. While Stacy and Maggie spent the next half hour or so sharing fond memories of Zachary's years at Heart's Song, I sat and pondered what I had discovered. If Abigail Hathaway was really seeing Dr. Wang, marriage counselor to the stars, then she was most likely going to couples counseling. If she was going to couples counseling, that meant her marriage to Daniel Mooney might be in trouble. And if that were the case, maybe he plowed her into a mailbox! It might be a huge jump from getting a little marital counseling to murder, but as I said before, Daniel Mooney had really rubbed me the wrong way. It wouldn't make any sense *not* to investigate this lead, even if it was a little far-fetched.

The waitress stopped by to clear our plates, and asked us if we were interested in coffee.

"I'll have a double, half-caf, nonfat latte," Stacy ordered.

I thought for a moment. Had I exceeded my caffeine allotment for the day? I decided that I probably had. "I'll have the same. But not a double. And not nonfat. And decaf," I said.

The waitress looked at me, confused.

"A single, decaf latte," I said. "Full-fat."

"Oh. Okay," she replied.

"I don't think I'll have anything," Maggie said. "Actually, I think I'd better get going. I should do prep for tomorrow. It's music day and I want to teach the kids a new song."

Neither Stacy nor I objected. Maggie gathered herself together, kissed Stacy warmly on the cheek, shook my hand coldly, and left.

I watched her walk out the door and, once she had gone, turned to Stacy.

"So, what's the deal, Stacy? What's going on with you and Bruce LeCrone?"

She jerked her head up at me and blanched. "Nothing."

"Baloney."

"Seriously, nothing. Ooh, look, our coffee is here." She busily engaged herself in pouring copious amounts of artificial sweetener into her tall mug.

"Stacy."

My friend looked up at me. "How did you know?" She whispered.

"I talked to you on Monday night. I even said something like, 'Maybe LeCrone killed her,' and you never mentioned that you saw him that night. You never mentioned the party."

"Didn't I?" She looked pale and almost frightened. "Juliet, promise me you won't say anything. Please. It's over. I swear it's over. It was over as soon as you told me about what he did to his wife."

"What's over, Stacy?"

"Me and Bruce. It was nothing, really. Just a fling. I mean, for Christ's sake, I'm entitled. Do you know how many times I've had to deal with Andy's little adventures? It's about time it was my turn."

Stacy's husband, Andy, has always been a notorious womanizer. Stacy knows it. Her friends know it. Everyone knows it. Every couple of years they separate, only to get back together again a few weeks or months later after therapy and lots of promises of eternal fidelity. I'd thought Stacy had reached some kind of peace with it—that she'd gotten used to it in a way. Maybe she had. Maybe betraying him back was her way of dealing with Andy's treachery.

"How long were you seeing LeCrone?"

Stacy laughed mirthlessly. "I'd hardly call it that. We had sex a few times. The first time was in his bathroom in the middle of a party."

I grimaced. She looked at me, almost defiantly. "We got carried away."

"I guess you did," I said. Then I felt bad about sounding so judgmental. "It sounds pretty exciting."

"It was. I met him a couple more times. And then, that Monday night we got a room at the Beverly Wilshire. That was the last time." She was looking straight into her coffee cup, and it took a moment for me to realize that she was crying.

"Oh, Stacy, honey, don't cry," I said. "You're right, you do deserve it. Andy's been doing this kind of thing to you for years. You are entitled. Really you are."

"But you wouldn't have done it," she said.

That brought me up short. No, I couldn't imagine cheating on Peter. But then, I couldn't imagine him cheating on me, either.

"I don't know, Stacy. I have no idea what I would do under similar circumstances. But that doesn't matter. All that matters is how you feel."

"Well, I feel like I'm the one who was hit by a car."

I reached my hand out across the table, and she took it. We sat there silently for a few more minutes and then paid the bill, gathered our things together, and left. We stood awkwardly in front of my car. I reached out my arms and hugged my friend.

"Call me, okay?" I said when I released her.

"Okay. I love you, Juliet."

"I love you, too. You're my best friend. You know that, don't you?"

"Yeah. I know. You're mine, too."

I waved good-bye, opened my car door, and squeezed myself behind the wheel. I headed for home, thinking about all those terrible marriages around me. LeCrone and his wives. Andy and Stacy. Abigail Hathaway and Daniel Mooney. It often felt like Peter and I were the only happily married couple we knew. Sometimes that made me feel complacent, better than anyone else. Sometimes it just scared me. Maybe we weren't any different. Maybe it was just that our misery simply hadn't started yet.

8

$\mathcal{I}$ WALKED IN THE house and, not hearing Ruby's voice, peeked my head into Peter's office. He was lying on his stomach on the floor, surrounded by *Star Wars* action figures, carefully putting the mask on Darth Vader.

"*Luke*, it is your destiny," I said.

"Hi." He didn't look up.

"Where's Ruby?" I asked.

"Nap."

"Whatcha doing?"

"Playing."

"Hmm."

Peter's "office" looks like an eight-year-old boy's clubhouse. The book-shelves are crammed full of action figures. He's got every comic book hero placed carefully next to the appropriate villains. I'm convinced Peter collects all these toys not, as he insists, because they are valuable (although his collection of vintage '70s Mego Superheroes was once appraised at $4,750), or even as inspiration for his writing, but because as a kid he was deprived of them. His mother did her best, but she just barely managed to support her three children after his father walked out on her. Whatever money she had went to cover the basics, such as food and shelter and, of course, television.

Peter spent his childhood craving the toys he saw on TV. He tells one story that always makes me cry, although he tells it as a joke. One year at Christmas he desperately wanted a G.I. Joe Frogman. His mother couldn't afford the doll, but she did get him the doll's diving suit. He used a tiny, plastic G.I. Joe coat hanger for a head and shoulders, and tugged the empty wet suit around a bucket of water. I like to tease him that his next feature will star the archvillain "Hangerman." Every time Peter shows up with another two-hundred-dollar Major Matt Mason figurine in the original 1969 packaging and I want to wring his neck, I try to remember that boy with no dolls.

I walked into the room, straddled his prone figure, and lowered myself onto his rear end.

"Ooph." He grunted. "You weigh a ton, babe. It's like having Juggernaut sitting on my butt."

"Gee, thanks. Come to think of it, I do feel sort of like a fat mutant."

"You're not fat, you're pregnant."

"That's turning into your mantra."

"Yeah? Well, I'll stop saying it as soon as you get over your lunatic obsession with your weight."

"First of all, I'm *never* going to get over that particular lunatic obsession, and second of all, you're no stringbean yourself."

"Oh, yeah?" he said, flipping over under me so that I was straddling his crotch. He started tickling me in the ribs.

"Stop! Oh, please stop. Please please please." By then I was laughing so hard I was crying. I rolled off of him and onto my side on the floor, curling up into as small a ball as I could—that is to say, not very small. He kept tickling me.

"Peter! Stop it right now or I'm going to pee in my pants! I'm serious!"

That made him quit. He leaned down and kissed me on the mouth, lingeringly.

I won't describe what happened next. Suffice it to say we did what most couples do when they find themselves at home on a lazy afternoon with the kid down for her nap and no laundry to be done.

Afterward, as we lay on the floor of his office, tucked together like spoons—well, like a spoon and a ladle—I reached under me and grabbed a little figurine. "Boba Fett is poking a hole in my back," I said, handing Peter the toy.

Holding the doll puppet-fashion, Peter deepened his voice and said, "May the force be with you!"

"It already was, baby," I said. "Hey, guess where I went this afternoon?"

"Yoga?"

"Nope. Abigail Hathaway's memorial service." I winced, waiting for the bomb to drop. Surprisingly, it didn't.

"Hmm," he said.

"That's it? Hmm? Aren't you angry? Aren't you going to tell me to mind my own business?"

"Nope."

"Why not?"

"Well, Juliet, I've been thinking about it a lot. For the past year or so you've been sort of at loose ends. It's like you know you should be staying home with Ruby, but something in you doesn't really like it. You're used to being useful. You're used to helping people. And for some reason, being useful to us, helping your family, isn't as satisfying to you as doing for other people. Ever since you've started looking into this Hathaway thing, you've been different. It's like you've got your old sense of purpose back."

"You know, Dorothy noticed that, too," I said. "I definitely feel like I can contribute something here. But I'm surprised that you're not worried about me."

"Well, I'm not," he replied. "I'm not worried because I know that you know what you're doing. I wasn't worried when you were out canvassing witnesses in Crip or Blood territory. Why should I worry now? I assume that you aren't going to do anything that will put yourself in any danger. I assume that you will nose around and give whatever information you uncover to that detective you spoke to. I assume you'll be sensible."

"I will be sensible. I *am* being sensible, really."

"Good."

"Do you want to hear what I found out at the service?"

"Sure."

"First of all, I saw her husband, who is a total creep. He looks like some Yanni-wannabe."

"Really? That doesn't seem like the kind of person she would be with."

"Exactly what I thought. You should have seen this creep. His stepdaughter was sitting there, weeping, and he barely noticed her. It was awful. I felt like scooping the poor thing up and taking her home."

"I'm glad you didn't. I don't think I could be so understanding about kidnapping."

"Teenagernapping, actually. She's about fifteen or so. Anyway, it turns out that Abigail was seeing a shrink, and you'll never believe who."

"Who?"

"Herma Wang!"

"Herma Wang, celebotherapist?"

"Wouldn't it be celebratherapist?"

"Celebo is better."

"Whatever. Yes, her! I was thinking I would call Lilly and see if she's still seeing Wang. If she is, maybe she can find out for me whether Abigail was seeing her, too, and if she was, whether it was for couples counseling."

"Lilly's in town," Peter said. "She left a message on the machine this morning. By the way, do we want to stay with her and the twins at the Telluride Film Festival this year?"

"Um, Peter, I don't know if you've noticed, but I'm about to have a baby. I don't thing we're going to make it to Telluride this year."

"Oh, right." He laughed. "I keep forgetting."

"Maybe I'll give her a call and ask her about Wang."

"You do that. I'm going to get back to work," Peter said.

"*Back* to work?"

He blushed. "To work."

"Um, Peter, I found out something else."

"Hmm?" He was already thinking about his script.

"Stacy was with Bruce LeCrone the night of the murder."

"At the ICA party. You knew that."

"No, Peter. She was *with* him."

He looked at me. "With as in *with*?"

I nodded.

"Wow. Does Andy know?"

"I don't think so. At least not yet."

"Wow."

We looked at each other and recognized the emotion we were both feeling. Relief. Profound relief to be married to one another. To be married to someone we not only loved, but also trusted.

I kissed Peter and, leaving him to his toys, went to call Lilly from our bedroom. Lilly Green is definitely our most famous friend. She's the only one who's really achieved movie-star status. Despite this, she's managed to stay unpretentious and almost normal. She has the usual Hollywood retinue of personal assistants, business managers, and household staff, but she still drives her twin daughters to school every morning that she's not working.

One of her assistants answered the phone and put me on hold while she checked if Lilly was "available."

"Juliet! Great to hear from you. So, do you guys want to join us at Telluride?" Lilly shouted in the receiver.

"I wish we could, but I don't think we'll be able to manage it with the new baby."

"Oh, that's right, I totally forgot! When are you due?"

"In about a month."

"How fabulous! Boy or girl?"

"A little boy. His name is Isaac."

"That's so sweet! What a terrific name. I can't believe you've picked out a name already. The girls were almost a month old before we'd settled on Amber and Jade. And even then I wanted to change it two weeks later!"

"Well, you know me, decisive to a fault. Listen, I was wondering if you could help me out with something?"

"Sure."

"Remember that therapist you recommended to Peter a couple of years ago? Herma Wang?"

"Of course." Lilly's voice lowered in sympathy. "Do you need her number? Is something going on with you two? Are you okay?"

"No, no, we're fine, it's not that. It's just . . . where do I begin here?" I launched into the long, tangled story of why I wanted to track down the good Dr. Wang. When I'd finished, Lilly whistled.

"Juliet, you are so cool! The crime-solving soccer mom!"

I snorted. "Ruby hasn't started soccer yet. And I haven't solved any crimes."

"I haven't seen Wang as a patient in about a year, but ever since I got my Oscar she's called every couple of months inviting me to lunch."

"How starstruck *is* she?"

"She's pretty bad. It was kind of icky by the end of therapy. She *always* took my side, not that I minded, but it did get a little ridiculous."

"Starstruck enough to breach confidentiality? Could you try to find out if she was seeing Abigail alone, or if she was treating her and her husband, together? And it would be really good to know *why* she was seeing her, okay?"

"I bet I could find out *something* from her. She's so completely indiscreet. I'll take her to the Ivy. That'll knock her onto her butt-kissing butt. This is kind of fun; I feel like Miss Marple!"

"Only much better-looking," I said.

"You flatter me, dahling," Lilly replied, doing her best Zsa Zsa Gabor. "I'll call you as soon as I talk to the doc."

"Great! Talk to you soon."

I hung up the phone just in time to hear Ruby yelling from her bed.

"Mama! Nap all done! Come get me! Mama come *now*!!"

"I'm coming!" I yelled back. "And stop yelling at me!"

I walked into Ruby's room and found her standing in her crib, one leg hoisted over the side.

"What are you doing, Houdini-baby?" I said, grabbing her just in time to break her fall.

"Nap all done," she said. "I want out."

"I see that," I said. "If you're big enough to climb out of your crib, maybe you're big enough to get a big-girl bed. Do you want a big-girl bed?"

"No."

"You could pick one out by yourself."

"No."

"It could be a really pretty bed," I wheedled. I needed to get her out of that crib before her brother made his appearance. No way was I buying a second crib.

"No." *Jeez*, this kid was stubborn. Wherever did she get that?

"It could be pink," I said in a singsong voice.

That sparked her interest. "Pink?"

"Sure. Wouldn't that be great? Let's go buy you a pink big-girl bed!"

"No."

Time to quit while I was behind. "Okay. Never mind. Let's go find Daddy."

It took all of three seconds to pry Peter away from his work. The bait was a trip to the grocery store to buy the fixings for chicken tacos. The man is easily distracted.

Peter wheeled our big cart down the aisles, Ruby trundled along behind wheeling her minicart, and I brought up the rear, wishing that one of them was wheeling me. In the produce aisle I caught up to Peter and asked, "Do you *goyim* have any ritual where friends and family pay visits on the bereaved after a death?"

"You mean like a wake?" he asked.

"No. Not like a party or anything. More like . . . well, like a *shiva* call."

"What's a *shiva* call?"

"You know, we paid a *shiva* call on my aunt Gracie when Uncle Irving died."

"Oh, right. Of course. When they sat around on stools for seven days and everybody came by with food."

"Exactly."

"Nope. I don't think there's a WASP equivalent."

"Really? That's so cold! You just let the family mope in their house all alone?"

"No, Juliet. We all meet up at the country club and play a round of golf. And then we have a big meeting and discuss how to keep the Jews and blacks out of the neighborhood."

I laughed. "Seriously, there's no time where you just drop by and visit the family?"

"Not really. Although my mom is always dropping off casseroles for eligible widowers. Does that count?"

"No, I don't think . . . Wait a minute, maybe that *could* work."

"What could work?"

"Maybe I could make a casserole for Abigail Hathaway's husband!"

"That's a terrible idea."

"Why? I think it's a great idea."

"First of all, didn't you say she had a daughter?"

"Yes. So what?"

"It's hardly fair to leave her an orphan. I can't imagine a surer way to kill the poor girl's stepfather than feeding him a casserole that you made."

"Ha, ha. You're a laugh a minute."

"Seriously, Juliet. You don't even know these people. You can't just show up with food."

"Why not? I'm just showing support. Helping them out. And I did *so* know her."

"You did not. She probably wouldn't even have recognized you."

"Yes, she would have. She would have remembered that you saved her from Bruce LeCrone. And anyway, *they* don't know how well I knew her."

"Juliet, be careful around that family. This isn't a game. They're grieving."

"I will be careful. I just want to get a sense of them, on a more personal level. I'm not even going to ask any questions."

"I'm just giving you my two cents."

"Duly noted. And I will be discreet. I promise." I gave his arm a reassuring squeeze. "Okay?"

"Okay."

"Peter?"

"Yes?"

"How would you feel about cooking up a little casserole?"

"Oh my God. No. Definitely not."

"Please. Oh, please." I kissed him on the cheek.

"I can't believe you."

I reached out to a grocery bin and tossed a few bags of spinach into our cart.

"What's that for?" Peter asked.

"Spinach lasagna. Only make it with fewer onions this time. Most people don't like as many onions as you do."

9

THE PRESCHOOL GIG sure paid well, I thought as I pulled up in front of Abigail Hathaway's oversized Tudor house in the Santa Monica Canyon, one of the most prestigious neighborhoods on the Westside. A manicured lawn stretched from the brass-riveted front door down to the curb. A brick path meandered down the lawn between carefully tended beds of winter flowers. In the driveway were parked two cars—a bright-blue Jeep, and one of those BMW two-seaters that a certain kind of middle-aged man feels compelled to purchase immediately upon seeing James Bond tooling around in one on the silver screen.

Gee, I wonder which car belongs to Daniel Mooney? I thought.

I got out of my suburban-matron heap, careful not to wrinkle the baby-blue maternity smock I had found crumpled at the back of my closet and had actually managed to iron in preparation for my incursion into Mooney territory. I looked innocuous and very, very sweet.

Reaching into the backseat, I grabbed the handles of a shopping bag containing a spinach-and-feta-cheese lasagna that Peter had obligingly whipped up. I walked up to the front door, stretched my face into a sickly sweet smile, and knocked briskly. While I waited for an answer, I reached into the shopping bag and took out the foil pan of lasagna. Without warning and with a sudden jerk, the door opened. Startled, I gave a little jump. Not much, but just enough to tilt the lasagna pan and send a stream of tomato sauce out from under the foil wrapper and all over the front of my smock.

"Oh!" I said with a gasp.

Abigail Hathaway's daughter stood in the doorway. "Oh, no!" she said, reaching out and steadying the pan. "You got it all over yourself!"

I looked down at the splash of red festooning my chest and belly.

"Lovely. Just lovely," I said, ruefully.

"I'm so sorry," the girl said.

"No, no! It's not your fault! Don't be sorry. It's me. I'm just a complete klutz. I'm the one who's sorry." I motioned toward the sauce-covered pan. "This is for you and your . . . your dad."

"Thanks," she said, although she clearly didn't mean it.

"It's lasagna."

"Great." Looking vaguely nauseated, she gingerly took the pan from my outstretched arms.

"Would you like to come in and get cleaned up?"

"That would be terrific. My name is Juliet Applebaum. I knew your mom."

Standing in the doorway, holding a pan of lasagna, Abigail Hathaway's daughter started to cry. She cried not like the grown woman she looked like, but like the child she was. Huge, gasping sobs shook her narrow chest and tears poured down her face. Her nose streamed and, arms filled with lasagna, she turned her head to the side, trying ineffectually to wipe her nose on her shoulder. As she lifted her shoulder to meet her nose, the pan slipped from her hands, falling to the floor with a wet *splat* and spilling tomato sauce over her shoes.

"Oh, no! Oh, no!" the girl wailed, dropping to her knees and trying to stem the tide of sauce making its way across the floor in the direction of a pink and white Oriental floor runner.

I looked around me for a cloth, anything to catch the spill before it ruined what was surely an expensive carpet. Unsurprisingly, there was nothing to be found. I looked down at my shirt, and, with a helpless shrug, whipped it off over my shoulders and, joining Audrey Hathaway on the floor, used it to mop the spilled sauce. She sat back and stared at me, her surprise completely stopping her tears. I finished cleaning up the spill, tossed my filthy shirt on top of the lasagna pan, and hoisted myself to my feet, holding the by now quite disgusting offering in my arms.

"Where's the garbage pail?" I asked.

"In the kitchen. Through there." The girl pointed down the hall. I first checked my shoes to be sure they were clean of sauce, and then headed down the hall toward the perfectly appointed kitchen. I glanced at a gilt-framed mirror that I passed and was horrified to see myself in my black-and-white-spotted maternity bra, the one Ruby likes to call my cow bra. My stomach bulged over the top of my leggings, and my belly button made a little tent in the black fabric. Shuddering, I rushed into the kitchen. I crammed the pan, shirt and all, into the stainless steel trash bucket under the sink, found some paper towels on the counter, unrolled a few dozen sheets, and soaked them with warm water. Carefully squeezing out the towels, I made my way back to Audrey, who was still kneeling in the middle of the entryway. She hadn't moved, but neither had she resumed her sobbing. I took each of her hands and gently cleaned them. Then, I wiped the sauce off her shoes and scrubbed up the last traces from the floor. I went back to the kitchen, threw out the mess of paper towels, and returned to the hall. Audrey hadn't budged.

Groaning, I lowered myself next to her and stretched my arms out to her. Silently, she inched over to me and awkwardly leaned into my arms, resting her head on my chest. She started to cry again, but without the violence of the first episode. This time her tears fell quickly and silently, dampening my bra. I rocked her gently, smoothing her hair with my hand.

We sat like that for a few minutes. Finally, Audrey Hathaway sat up.

"I'm sorry," she said. It sounded like she'd been saying that a lot.

"Don't be sorry, honey. You have nothing to be sorry about."

"I miss my mom."

"I know, sweetie. I know."

"You're a friend of hers? I've never met you before."

"Well, no. Not a friend. I met your mother right before . . . right before she died. My daughter applied to her school."

She looked at me, still obviously not understanding what I was doing there.

What *was* I doing there? What had I been thinking? "I didn't really know your mom at all. She didn't even accept my little girl to Heart's Song. After I heard what happened I just thought you and your dad might not be that interested in cooking," I finished lamely. I looked around at the devastation I had wrought on her house and on myself.

I couldn't help it. I laughed. Audrey looked startled.

"Look at me!" I said with a gasp through my guffaws.

She seemed to see me for the first time and suddenly burst out laughing, too.

Wiping tears from our eyes, we got up from the floor.

"Can you just see me driving down Santa Monica Boulevard in this?" I asked her.

"You'd probably get arrested!"

"For solicitation! Of cows!" That set us off again.

Once we finally managed to catch our breaths, Audrey stuck her hand out.

"I'm Audrey."

"I know. My name is Juliet." I shook her hand.

We stood looking at each other for a moment and then I remembered something.

"Oh my God, your father. I can't let him see me like this."

"Stepfather. And don't worry. He's not here."

"You're here alone?" I was astonished. What kind of a man leaves a child alone just days after her mother is killed?

"Yeah. He had to go out. He'll be back soon. Maybe I can find you something to wear."

"That would be great, although I hate to bother you."

We both looked down at my stomach at the same time.

"I guess it would kind of have to be, like, a big shirt or something," she said.

"Like, a really big shirt."

"Wait just a sec, okay?" She ran up the stairs. A moment later she was back, holding a man's Oxford-cloth, button-down shirt, frayed at the collar and cuffs. I looked at it doubtfully.

"Is this your stepfather's? Do you think he'll mind?"

"It's mine. It used to be my dad's. My real dad. Not Daniel." She spat her stepfather's name out of her mouth as if it tasted bad.

"Do *you* mind if I borrow it?" I asked. "It looks kind of special."

"I don't mind."

"I promise I'll wash it and bring it back tomorrow."

"Okay."

We looked at each other, awkwardly, for another minute. It didn't feel right for me to be there, but I didn't want to leave the girl all alone. Someone had to take care of her, and it was clear that her stepfather wasn't interested in the job.

Audrey reached up and brushed a lock of purple hair out of her eyes. I smiled and said, "I like your hair."

She blushed. "My mom hates . . . hated it."

"I'll bet."

"It's not permanent or anything. It washes out after a while."

"Did you do it yourself?"

"Yeah. I mean, I did the purple part myself. I got the haircut on Melrose." She fingered the shorn side of her head. By now a fine fuzz covered the half that had looked shaved when I saw her at the memorial service.

"Can I feel it? I love the way a buzz cut feels."

She leaned her head over to me and I rubbed my palm across the soft fuzz. "Mmm," I said. "Soft."

She smiled. "Hey, want something to drink? Like tea or something?"

"Sure."

While Audrey bustled around the kitchen putting on the kettle and putting tea bags into pretty ceramic mugs, I perched on a stool at the counter.

"Is there anything you need, honey?" I asked. "Are you doing okay?"

It was a stupid question. She was pretty clearly not doing okay.

"No. I mean, yes. I'm doing fine, I guess. I don't need anything."

For the next fifteen minutes or so I sat sipping tea at Abigail Hathaway's kitchen counter, next to her grieving daughter. Neither of us spoke much, except to comment on the flavor of the tea (peach ginseng) or the weather (chilly, for Los Angeles). There was, however, an odd companionable feeling between us, not like friends and nothing like mother-daughter, but some kind of link nonetheless. Audrey seemed comforted by my presence. Maybe it had nothing to do with me. Maybe the girl was so lonely and so sad that any living, breathing presence would have been enough for her. Whatever it was, by the time I got up to leave, I felt like I had formed a bond with the awkward, sad child.

After my cup had long been empty, I kissed Audrey good-bye, gave her my phone number, and left. As I drove away I turned back to see her standing in the doorway, staring after me. I waved and she lifted her hand for an instant before disappearing into the house.

I drove down the Pacific Coast Highway, onto the Santa Monica Freeway, and into an impenetrable wall of traffic. As my twenty-minute ride stretched to an hour and then some, I had plenty of time to reflect on my actions of the past few days. Investigating Abigail's death had seemed like something I could do. More importantly, maybe, was that it was something *to* do. Meeting Audrey Hathaway had changed all that. Suddenly I was confronted with what I should have understood from the very beginning.

This was not a chapter out of a Nancy Drew story. It was a real, live tragedy. Abigail's death was not an excuse for activity for a bored house-wife, but the worst thing that would ever happen to a teenage girl. How dare I even attempt to "investigate"? How arrogant of me to think I was competent to solve this crime! Who did I think I was, running all over town, questioning nannies, brawling with studio executives, crashing funerals? I was deeply embarrassed by my gall in showing up at that poor girl's house with a Trojan horse in the shape of a spinach-and-feta lasagna.

By the time I made my way home, I had firmly resolved to give up my investigative efforts. I decided to leave it to the people who really knew what they were doing: the police. I walked in the door, scooped up my own little girl, and squeezed her as hard as I could. As Ruby wriggled and howled in protest, I breathed in the puppy-dog smell of her hair and wordlessly promised her that I would never leave her like Abigail Hatha-way had left her own little girl. My baby would never ache so for a moth-er's touch that she needed to cry in the arms of a stranger.

I kissed Peter on the cheek and was just about to tell him about my decision to give up investigating the murder when he handed me a scrap of paper on which he'd written the following message:

"Lilly called. Says 'PAY DIRT!' Call her ASAP."

"When did she call?" I asked.

"Just a couple of minutes ago," he replied.

I had to at least find out what she'd discovered. I called her. The answer-ing machine picked up the phone.

"Lilly? Are you there? It's Juliet. Pick up. I know you're screening, because Peter says you just called. Pick up pick up pick up pick up pick up."

By now Ruby had joined in and was shrieking "Pick up" and dancing around the room.

"All right, already. For goodness sake!" Lilly's exasperated voice inter-rupted our song-and-dance number.

"Hi."

"Hi, yourself. Boy, do you owe me. That was the worst lunch of my life. The woman brought a camera and kept asking the waiters to take our picture. By the time dessert showed up she'd taken enough for an entire album."

"I'm so sorry I put you through that," I said with a laugh.

"Doesn't matter. Anyway, do I have some gossip for you!"

"Great!" I said. Then I remembered my decision. "Except I'd sort of decided not to look into this anymore."

"What?!" She sounded genuinely angry. "Do you mean to tell me I withstood two hours of fawning by Herma Wang for nothing? I don't think so, girlfriend."

"I'm so sorry. It's just that I met Abigail Hathaway's daughter, who is in a really bad way, by the way, and I started feeling guilty about playing this Agatha Christie game. I should leave it to the cops, don't you think?"

"Listen, what *I* think is that you are doing this girl a favor. You could find out who killed her mother! You have a civic duty to do whatever you can to help solve this murder. And, moreover, you started this ball rolling, and you should follow it up. At least listen to what I have to say. You can always just call the police and pass the information on to them!"

"I guess you're right. Anyway, I'm dying to find out what Wang told you. I can't believe she really said *anything*. Didn't she take some kind of oath of confidentiality? Does that woman have no ethics?"

"Apparently not. Although it's not like she told me intimate details or even really admitted to treating Abigail Hathaway."

"What *did* she tell you?"

"She said she did have a patient named Abigail, no last name, wink, wink. Wang had been treating her primarily, but she saw the whole family at various points. You were right: Daniel-no-last-name-either and Abigail were having problems—serious ones, according to Wang. She wouldn't tell me what, but she did say that divorce was possible, even likely."

"I knew it. I just *knew* it."

"That's not all. Apparently she also saw the daughter a few times. There were some serious problems there, too."

"I called that, too. I stopped by Abigail's house today and found Audrey, the daughter, all by herself. Her mother *just died*, and her stepfather can't be bothered to keep her company."

"Nasty."

"Yup. Did Wang give you any ideas about what was going on with Audrey and her stepfather? Any abuse or anything like that?"

"She didn't say. All she would say was that the problems they were all having seemed more serious than normal marital difficulties or adolescent angst."

"Lilly, you've outdone yourself. This is all *really* interesting. I'm not sure that it's a motive for murder, but it sure does paint our grieving widower in a different light. I knew the guy was rotten the first time I saw him. And my first impressions are *always* right."

"You know what I like best about you, Sherlock?"

"What, Watson?"

"Your self-effacing nature."

"I *am* modest, aren't I?"

I thanked Lilly for her time and, promising to see her soon, hung up the phone.

"What's this I hear?" Peter said. "Giving up the private-eye biz?"

"Oh, I don't know," I said with a sigh. "I guess so. I started feeling really guilty once I met Audrey, Abigail's daughter. The poor thing cried in my arms today."

"Jeez. I heard what you told Lilly about the stepfather. He sounds like a real creep."

"Totally," I agreed.

Peter, Ruby, and I got up a game of Chutes and Ladders, which I played absentmindedly, all the while trying to decide whether to act on the information Lilly had given me. Every time I landed on the boy stealing cookies or the girl coloring on the wall and had to slide my piece down a chute into a losing position, I felt like someone was trying to tell me something. Finally I decided that the only responsible thing to do was let the police know what I had discovered and leave it at that. Let Detective Carswell do his job.

After losing to Ruby as usual (Peter placed a distant third), I called the detective. I managed, miraculously, to find him at his desk.

"Detective Carswell? This is Juliet Applebaum. We spoke about the Hathaway affair, if you recall."

"Yes, Mrs. . . . er, Ms. Applebaum. I do recall our conversation."

"I have some more information for you."

"Relevant information?"

Was it just to me, or was this guy this sarcastic to everyone he dealt with?

"Yes, *relevant* information. At least I think it's relevant," I answered, trying to keep my own voice as neutral as possible. The detective obviously thought I was a hysterical ninny, and I didn't want to give him any more fuel to add to his snide little fire.

"Why don't you let me be the judge of the information's relevance," the detective said.

I gritted my teeth with irritation. Why is it that a certain kind of man thinks that just because you happen to be a mother you also are necessarily an idiot? In my prior incarnation as a criminal defense attorney, I had grown used to being taken seriously. Very seriously. Prosecutors might not like what I had to say, and they might not be willing to give my clients the deals I wanted, but they never condescended to me. Now, suddenly, just because I had doffed my barrister's wig and donned a housewife's kerchief, people like Detective Carswell thought they could pat me on the head and send me on my way.

"Well, Detective Carswell, how do you judge the relevance of the fact that Abigail Hathaway and her husband were going through serious marital difficulties and, in fact, were considering divorce?"

That got his attention.

"How do you know this? Who told you about this? How reliable is your source?" His sentences tumbled out in a rush.

Well, well, well. Now I was suddenly someone with sources.

"The information is very reliable. Ms. Hathaway and her husband were seeing a marital counselor named Herma Wang. According to Dr. Wang, they were in serious trouble, perhaps enough to lead them to divorce."

"And you spoke to Dr. Wang?"

"No, *I* didn't speak to her. A mutual friend and onetime patient of hers spoke to her and was told about this."

"The psychiatrist discussed the case with your friend?"

"Yes and no."

"Yes and no?"

"Yes, they discussed the case, but Dr. Wang, who's a psychologist, by the way, kept the conversation hypothetical. It was clear who she was talking about, however."

"Clear to whom?"

"To my friend."

"And who is this friend?"

"I'm afraid I can't divulge that information. I promised my 'source' confidentiality."

"Ms. Applebaum, this is a murder investigation. You are hindering the investigation of a murder. Do you understand that?"

That really ticked me off. "Hindering? Hindering? How, exactly, is telling you something that you obviously don't know and can clearly help you, hindering? Precisely the opposite, I would think."

Realizing that the detective was more interested in finding out who my link to Wang was than finding out whether the information I had could provide a clue to what had happened to Abigail Hathaway, I decided to end the call.

"Listen, Detective, I'm not going to tell you who told me about the shrink. You'll have to subpoena me for the information. I'm hanging up now." And I did. So much for passing my information along to the police and letting them figure out what to do with it.

10

THE NEXT MORNING I woke up early and spent the first twenty minutes of my day hunched over the toilet seat, vomiting up not only last night's dinner but also everything I'd eaten in the previous six weeks or so. Why do they call it morning sickness? It's pretty much an all-day affair, and what's worse, it can disappear for months and then suddenly rear its truly ugly head. During my pregnancy with Ruby, I had once been overcome by it on my way to work. There I was, walking up the front steps of the courthouse in my navy suit, holding my Coach briefcase and matching purse. I nodded a grave but courteous good morning to the jurors who were milling about, smoking their last cigarettes before heading inside to decide the fate of my cross-dressing bank robber. A few of them returned my greeting, then recoiled as I proceeded to lean over the balustrade and puke my guts out over the side. I then had the humiliating task of asking the judge to instruct the jurors that defense counsel's tossing of cookies should not be construed as an indication of her confidence in the strength of her client's case.

This time around I threw up with Ruby standing behind me, her chubby arms wrapped around my legs and her head resting on my ample behind. It would have been the greatest luxury to be able to deal with my bathroom business unaccompanied. I couldn't remember the last time I was allowed the extravagance of a closed door.

Cooking Ruby's scrambled eggs almost sent me back to the bathroom, but I managed to restrain myself, cram her into her booster seat, and put her breakfast in front of her. I then tiptoed into my bedroom and retrieved Audrey Hathaway's father's Oxford shirt. I washed it in cold water on the most gentle cycle of my washing machine. I was terrified that I would somehow damage it. I imagined myself standing at Audrey's front door, a shredded piece of stained cloth in hand, explaining to the poor orphan how my spin cycle had eaten her prized possession.

By the time the shirt was dried, fluffed, and folded, Ruby and I were dressed and ready to face the day. I didn't particularly want to take a toddler with me on this errand, but Peter was still sound asleep, and I didn't have much choice. We set off for the Hathaway house.

I pulled up in front of the Tudor palace and looked in the driveway. Both cars were there. Suddenly something occurred to me. Yesterday, when I'd visited Audrey Hathaway, the cars had been in the driveway. Yet, her stepfather hadn't been home. The BMW, however, had to be his. So why hadn't he been driving it? Los Angelenos like Daniel Mooney do not take public transportation or taxicabs. They drive. Moreover, they drive themselves. People don't generally drive one another around. It's not at all uncommon to see convoys of cars following one another as their occupants go to dinner and a movie "together." Maybe Daniel Mooney had *two* cars. Or, maybe, I thought, he had a friend. A very *close* friend.

I unsnapped Ruby's car-seat straps and lifted her out of the car. Together, we walked up the path.

"Are we having a play date, Mommy?"

"No, peachy. We're just dropping something off at this house. Then we'll head over to the park."

"Let's go to the Santa Monica Pier!"

"Not today, Ruby. That's a big outing. We'll do that with Daddy soon."

I glanced down and saw her fat lower lip begin to tremble ominously.

"Ruby," I said, perhaps a bit too sharply, "no tantrums. I'm not kidding. If you throw a tantrum about the pier we're not even going to go to the park."

She mustered up every ounce of willpower in her three-foot body and calmed herself down.

"Maybe we'll go to the pier tomorrow!" she said.

"Maybe. We'll talk about it tonight. Good job holding it together, kiddo."

By then we'd reached the front door. I let Ruby press the doorbell, grabbing her hand after she'd rung it six or seven times. Daniel Mooney opened the door. He was taller than I'd remembered, maybe six-foot-two or so. His long hair was gathered in a ponytail, a style I've never been that fond of, especially when sported by aging men with an outsized sense of "cool." He was wearing a luxurious black shirt in a thick, soft-looking, sueded silk, and I had an almost irresistible urge to stroke it. Ruby had the same idea, and I had to jerk her arm back to keep her from fondling Abigail's widower.

"Yes?" he said. "Didn't you see the sign?" He pointed at the "No Soliciting" sign posted prominently on the door.

"Oh, no, I'm not selling anything. I'm just returning this to Audrey," I said, holding out his stepdaughter's folded shirt.

"Are you a friend of Audrey's?" he asked suspiciously.

"Not really. I borrowed this shirt from her yesterday. I came over to drop off a lasagna and spilled most of it on myself. She lent me this since I had nothing else to wear. I knew your wife." Babbling again. Terrific.

"Oh. You're a friend of Abigail's. Come in." He opened the door and stepped back, making room for me to enter.

"I wasn't really a friend," I said as Ruby and I walked through the doorway. "I knew her from the school. I just wanted to bring something by for you two. You and Audrey, I mean."

Mooney seemed to suddenly notice Ruby. "She's a student," he said.

"No, not yet." I blushed. I decided that now wasn't the time to tell him that his wife had rejected us.

"Please sit down." He motioned toward an archway that led into the formal living room. "I'll get Audrey." He walked up the stairs. I noticed then that he was barefoot and that his toenails sported a decidedly glossy sheen. What kind of a man gets a pedicure?

Ruby and I walked into the elegant living room. The furniture was country French, and the chairs and couches were upholstered in a pale, pink silk. There were end tables everywhere, all of them covered with highly decorative and very breakable knickknacks. I grabbed Ruby just before she could send a collection of tiny music boxes crashing to the floor and sat gingerly in a spindly chair, holding her firmly in my lap.

"Honey, it's too dangerous in here," I said, wrapping her wiggling legs in my own. "I can't let you touch anything. You might break something."

"I won't," she whined. "I'll be careful. Please. Please. Please."

"I'm sorry, sweetie."

We were distracted from our wrestling match by Audrey, who came down the stairs wearing blue-and-green plaid flannel pajamas, and rubbing sleep from her eyes.

"We woke you up! I'm so sorry, Audrey."

"That's okay, I've been sleeping a lot lately," she said in a small voice. I inwardly cursed her stepfather for letting her sleep all morning instead of getting her up and distracting her from the depression into which she had clearly sunk.

"I brought back your dad's shirt, honey," I said. "Thanks so much for lending it to me."

"That's okay. Is this your daughter?"

"I'm Ruby. Who are you?" Ruby piped up.

"Hi, Ruby. I'm Audrey." She had crouched down so that she was eye level with the little girl. Audrey clearly had a way with small children. Maybe that was something she inherited from her mother.

"Hey, Ruby, will you thank Audrey for lending Mommy her shirt?"

"Thanks, Audrey."

"You're welcome, Ruby."

"Hey, Audrey, are you okay?" I asked.

"No. I mean, I guess so. I dunno." Her face began to turn a blotchy red, and her eyes filled with tears. Once again, I found myself sitting on the floor holding Abigail Hathaway's daughter while she sobbed. Within moments, Ruby, who hadn't seen that many grown-ups, or almost grown-ups, in tears before, also began quietly crying. I stretched out an arm to my own daughter and rocked them both for a while. I kept looking over Audrey's head in the direction of the stairs, hoping that her stepfather would hear her and come offer his comfort. Nothing. Maybe I'm being ungenerous—maybe he didn't hear her. But why wasn't he there? Why wasn't he with her? Why had he disappeared up the stairs to begin with?

Audrey soon gathered herself together.

"Sorry. I keep doing that to you," she mumbled, extricating herself from my embrace.

"That's okay. At least I didn't spill anything on you this time," I replied. She smiled politely.

"I think I'm going to go back to bed."

"Honey, do you really want to do that? Isn't there someone you can call to spend some time with you? A relative? One of your friends?" By then I knew enough not to even bother mentioning her stepfather.

"I'm going over to my friend Alice's house this afternoon. Her mom's gonna come get me later."

"Oh, okay," I said, relieved. "Why don't I leave you my number and you can call me if you need anything." I handed her one of my old cards with my home phone number scrawled on it.

I gathered up a still distraught Ruby and headed to the door. Audrey walked me out. She surprised me by giving me a quick, almost embarrassed hug in the doorway. I hugged her back and carried Ruby to the car.

"She's a sad girl," Ruby said as I buckled her into her seat.

"Yes, she is."

"Why is she a sad girl?"

"Well, Peachy, she's sad because something terrible happened to her."

"What happened?"

I dreaded having to say this, but I had no choice. "Her mommy died."

"Did she get trampled by wild-a-beasts?"

"What?" I answered, shocked. "Wild beasts? No. Are you afraid of wild beasts?"

"No, not wild beasts. Wild-a-beasts. Like Mufasa."

The Lion King. Right. Life lessons brought to you by Disney.

"No, Ruby. Her mommy did not get trampled by wildebeests. She died in a car accident."

"Oh." Ruby seemed satisfied by that answer, and I closed her door and walked around to the driver's seat.

I started the ignition and pulled out into the street. I had just stopped at the stop sign at the end of the block when Ruby announced, "We don't have any wild-a-beasts, but we *do* have a car."

I pulled over to the side of the road, stopped the car, and turned to her. "Ruby, I promise you Mommy is not going to die in a car accident." I'm sure there are hundreds of child-development experts who would be horrified that I said that. After all, it is possible that I could die in a car accident. But, the way I figure it, the chances are pretty slim. And, if I do die, Ruby is going to have a lot more serious traumas to deal with than the fact that her mother promised she wouldn't die. Sometimes you just have to tell your kids what you think they want and need to hear and hope for the best.

"Promise?" she asked in a tiny little voice.

"Promise."

"Okay."

"I love you, Ruby. You are my most precious girl in the whole wide world."

I turned around and glanced in my rearview mirror before pulling into the street. I was just in time to see a car come to a stop in front of Abigail Hathaway's house. I couldn't make out the driver of the cherry-red, vintage Mustang convertible. Curious, I idled at the side of the road.

The door to Abigail's house flew open, and Daniel Mooney bounded out. He loped down the path and fairly leaped into the passenger seat, and the car pulled away from the curb with a screech. I didn't have time to think about what I was doing—I just acted. As the Mustang blew by me I waited a moment and then gave chase.

Ruby and I followed the car all the way down the Pacific Coast Highway to Venice. I did my best to be discreet, keeping one and even two cars between us. Lucky for me, a bright red Mustang is maybe the easiest car in the universe to tail. It wasn't hard to keep my eye on it. Luckily, also, Ruby fell asleep. I'd like to see Jim Rockford engaging in a car chase while handing juice boxes and Barbie dolls back to a demanding toddler. I certainly couldn't have managed it.

Finally, the Mustang pulled up in front of a fourplex on Rose Street. It was one of the *faux* Mediterranean structures that had sprung up all over Los Angeles in the 1930s, all arches, plastered domes, and Mexican tiles. This one looked like it had seen better days, but it retained a kind of blowsy, overdone elegance.

I drove by the Mustang and pulled into a bus-boarding lane at the end of the block. Slouching down in my seat, I angled my rearview mirror so I could see the car. As I watched, the driver's door opened and a woman got out. She was a tall, striking redhead, no more than twenty-five or twenty-six years old. Her hair hung in thick waves down her back, and she wore jeans and cowboy boots. She carried a large leather bag that looked artfully beat up.

Daniel Mooney got out of the passenger side, and the two of them walked into the building. Just as they reached her front door, I saw him grab her hand and press it to his lips. I gasped, although I'm not sure why, because by then I was sure I'd found his paramour and the motive for his murder of the woman I'd by then decided was a martyr in a miserable marriage to a selfish, heartless beast.

I circled the block and made sure I had the number of the apartment building correct. Then I drove quickly back home. I made it in record time.

Peter was sitting at the kitchen table, hunched over a cup of coffee, when I rushed in.

"You just get up?"

He grunted.

"Ruby's asleep in the car. Will you go get her and put her in her crib?"

Grunting again, he got up and went out to get his sleeping child. I poured myself a glass of juice and drained it. Detective work made me thirsty.

Peter settled Ruby down for her nap and came back to his coffee.

"Listen," I said, "do you mind if I run out? I'll be back in about an hour." I waited for him to ask me where I was going.

"Yeah, fine, whatever," he mumbled. A morning person my husband is not.

I paused at the front door, giving him another moment to ask where I was off to. Nothing. I jumped back into my car and sped down the freeway in the direction of Venice.

The parking gods were not on my side. I circled the block twice before I finally gave up and parked in the tow-away zone directly in front of the apartment building. I flicked on my hazard lights, jumped out of the car, and walked quickly to the front door.

There were four buzzers next to the door behind which Mooney and his redhead had disappeared. Below each one was a narrow mailbox. One mailbox had no name tag, one read "Jefferson Goldblatt," and one was marked "Best & Co." Taped above the fourth bell was a small slip of cardstock elaborately decorated with scrolls and flowers in an Art Deco design. The name "N. Tiger" was hand-calligraphed in a luscious purple ink. The red-haired woman had to be N. Naomi. Nancy. Nanette. Nicole. Noreen. Nesbit. Nefertiti. Noodleroni.

I casually looked around to make sure I wasn't being watched. Satisfied that there was no one in sight, I pulled on the little metal door to N. Tiger's mailbox. It was locked. Thinking it hopeless, but somehow not able to help myself, I yanked a little harder. With a tiny shriek of metal the door popped open, only slightly bent. I gulped but, the damage having been done, looked inside the narrow box. At first sight it appeared to be empty, but then I saw a piece of crumpled white paper flattened against the back of the box. I slid my hand inside, and with the tips of my fingers I could just reach the paper. I grabbed it between my index and middle fingers and eased it out. It was a piece of junk mail, one of those cards with the picture of a missing child on the front and an ad on the back. This one was for a dry cleaner. The card was addressed to "Miss Nina Tiger or Current Resident." I had her.

I shoved the card back into the mailbox and closed the little door as best I could. I had bent the latch just enough to make it impossible to shut. I tried jamming the door shut, and when that wouldn't work I opened it up again and did my best to bend the latch in the other direction. I was engaged in this futile and highly illegal activity when the door to the building opened. I jumped, in part because I was startled and in part because the door smacked me on the hip.

"Sorry," I heard a woman's voice say.

Cringing, I looked up into the face of Nina Tiger. She had brown eyes and a splash of freckles. She glanced at me and started to look away when she noticed what I was doing.

"That's my mailbox. What are you doing?" she demanded.

"Um. Um. Nothing." Quick with the retort as ever.

"Are you going through my mail?" She pushed me aside and reached into her mailbox. She grabbed the door and noticed the latch.

"You *broke* it? Who the hell are you? What's happening here?"

"I did not break anything," I replied indignantly. "I'm just leaving a note for my friend Jeff Goldblatt. I noticed that your mailbox door was open and that . . . that . . . a letter had fallen out of it. I picked it up and put it back for you. I was trying to close the door so that nothing else would fall out when you opened the door on my stomach." I reached for my belly and gave a little grimace of imaginary pain.

She wasn't sure whether to believe me. We looked at each other for a long moment. "You're a friend of Goldblatt's?" she finally asked.

"Of course," I said. "I was dropping off a check, if you must know."

That extra detail seemed to convince her.

"Well, sorry," she said, and brushed by me.

"Apology accepted," I called to her back and followed her down the path. She stopped at her car, opened the trunk, and took out a shopping bag. I walked quickly back to my car and jumped inside. Breathing heavily and more nervous than I'd ever been in my life, I drove off as fast as I could without speeding. I was home within ten minutes.

Peter was in the same position he'd been when I left, although he seemed to have finished the pot of coffee.

"Hi," I said.

"Hi."

"Awake yet?"

"Getting there."

"Ruby still asleep?"

"Isn't she with you?" He looked confused.

"Peter! You put her in bed forty minutes ago."

"I did? Oh, right. Yeah. She's asleep."

"Will you wake up, already, for crying out loud?"

"I got E-mail from your mother last night," he said, changing the subject.

"What? Why is she writing to you?"

"She's been writing to you, apparently, but you haven't answered. She asked me if there's anything wrong."

"I haven't checked my E-mail in ages," I said. "I'll go log on right now."

It took more than ten minutes for all my E-mail messages to download. I hadn't checked my E-mail since the day before Abigail Hathaway died, and I had a huge backlog of messages. E-mail is a big part of my social life. I write regularly to friends from college and law school as well as to my old colleagues at the federal defender's office. I don't think I've spoken to my mother since she got her first laptop with a modem. She spends all her free time surfing the Web, so her phone line is permanently engaged and she communicates exclusively by E-mail.

After I'd finished answering my mail, I logged on to the Web. I was checking out a few of my favorite sites when an idea suddenly occurred to me. I clicked over to Yahoo, input the name "Nina Tiger," and requested a search. It was only moments before I got my results. One hit. I clicked on the icon and found myself looking at a review of a children's book called *Nina Tiger and the Mango Tree*. Probably not who I was looking for, unless the red-haired woman doubled as an exuberant tiger cub.

I leaned back in my chair, rubbed my belly, and considered the situation. If this woman had a computer and spent time on line, I should be able to find her. It was worth a try. I've never been a big one for newsgroups, those message boards of strangers who share a common interest, although at one point, when I was feeling particularly exasperated with my mother, I posted for a while to a group called alt.reddiaperbaby. While it was entertaining for a while to compare stories about socialist summer camp with twenty or thirty strangers, most of whom were named Ethel or Julius, ultimately I got bored. But I remembered how to use Dejanews, the site that digests all the hundreds of thousands of posts to the thousands of newsgroups on topics ranging from alt.misc.parents to alt.dalmatians to alt.gunlovers. I clicked over to it, typed in the red-haired woman's name, and ordered a search. Success. I found an E-mail address registered to a Nina Tiger: tigress@earthweb.net. Cute. Crossing my fingers, I asked for tigress's author profile. If she posted to a newsgroup, I would find out.

Tigress, it turned out, was a big-time cyber-geek. Dejanews provided me with listings of her participation in a whole variety of newsgroups. I checked out her postings to alt.postmodern—tigress was not a fan of Jeff Koons. She did, however, enjoy *Star Trek: The Next Generation* and French cooking. I scrolled down past postings to those groups and others, including one dedicated to the Rajneesh and another whose topic I couldn't figure out—it had something to do with witchcraft, or rugby. One of the two. Then I found something interesting: Tigress spent a lot of time chatting with folks on the topic of alt.polyamory. That sounded like sex to me.

I clicked on tigress's most recent posting to the newsgroup. The protocol of newsgroup participation is to include a portion of the person to whom you are responding's message at the top of your own so that readers will know what the topic of conversation is. Otherwise it would be almost impossible to follow the train of various comments and responses. Tigress had excerpted a prior message from someone named "monkey65" and responded to it.

<<Given tigress's frequent lambasting of this poor woman, I'm not sure why we are all expressing sympathy for her loss. IMHO, she didn't lose jack other than an impediment to her relationship with Coyote. He deserves our support, but she certainly doesn't.>>

My loss is immeasurable because my love's loss is immeasurable. I feel his misery in my own soul. His wife's refusal to embrace our love and make it part of her own doesn't ease the pain of her being violently thrust from this life into the next passage. I ache with Coyote

as I love with Coyote. Our intertwined souls feel this wrenching
together as we feel all else together. We will celebrate her voyage
into the next life with a tantric love dance.
    tigress

It was difficult to keep myself from gagging. I wasn't sure what made
me more sick to my stomach: Nina Tiger's pretentious, New-Age pseudo-
mourning, or the idea of Daniel Mooney—it had to be he—performing a
"tantric love dance," whatever the heck that might be.

I snipped the message and copied it into a file on my computer. In the
interests of security, however paranoid, I labeled the file "Animal Musings." No way a hacker, police detective, or nosy husband would figure
that out.

I then went back to Dejanews and searched for more information on
my pair of tantric murderers. After about an hour I could stand no more.
My back ached, my eyes were blurry, and I was thoroughly disgusted. I
logged off, put my computer to sleep, and staggered out to the kitchen. I
found Peter just where I'd left him. He was still hunched over his empty
cup of coffee but seemed to have progressed through all the various sections of the *Los Angeles Times*. The Trades were spread out in front of
him, and he was busily circling items with an angry red marker.

"Hey. Whatchya doing?" I asked.

"Figuring out who's getting paid more than I am."

"Oh, for Pete's sake, Pete, tell me you're not serious."

"Totally," he said, miserably. "The *Hollywood Reporter* has this long
article on some twenty-eight-year-old hack writer who just turned down
one point seven million dollars to write the script for *Revenge of the Killing Crows*. Turned it down. Meaning, it wasn't enough money. Meaning,
he's planning on making *more* money doing something else."

"You don't know that. Maybe the guy has some artistic integrity and
doesn't *want* to write the *Killing Crows* thing," I said.

"Give me a break, Juliet. First of all, this is Hollywood. No one has
artistic integrity. And even if they did, they wouldn't for one point seven
million dollars. And second of all, I would *kill* to write the movie that you
seem to think is so artistically bankrupt." He positively snarled at me. My
sweet, unflappable spouse had turned into a character from one of his
own scripts.

"What has gotten into you this morning?" I asked, trying to keep my own temper. For some reason, my moods always seem to adjust to match Peter's. When he's depressed, I'm depressed. When he's angry, I'm angry. Unfortunately, his positive emotions don't seem anywhere near as contagious.

Peter moaned, reached over, and hugged me. "I'm sorry, sweetie. I'm being a bear. I was up until four in the morning trying to finish that scene I'm working on. I am never going to finish this script. Which means I'll never get another movie."

Suddenly he dropped his arms from around my neck and looked at me, horrified. "Oh my God, do you think *I'm* the reason we've been rejected at all the preschools? They know I'm going nowhere, and they don't want their precious kids to associate with the spawn of failure."

I rolled my eyes. Before I could express a reassuring word, Peter started scrambling around the table.

"Where's a pencil? I have to write that down. *Spawn of Failure*. Great title."

Laughing, I kissed the top of his head. "I love you," I said.

"Love you, too. What have you been up to all morning? How's the baby doing?" He scribbled on a corner of the newspaper and then leaned over and gave my belly a kiss.

"Isaac and I are fine. We were just . . . um . . . driving around."

"What?" he asked. "Driving around?"

"I mean, Ruby and I went to Abigail Hathaway's house to return the shirt to her daughter, and after I dropped her off at home I . . . I . . . I just drove around." I paused. "I'm lying," I said.

"What?"

"I didn't want to tell you what I really did, so I lied. But I can't lie to you. I did go to Ms. Hathaway's house. But, then, I sort of followed Daniel Mooney."

"You *what*?"

"I followed him. But listen, here's why—"

"I don't care why!" By now he was yelling. "You took our two-and-a-half-year-old daughter on a car chase?"

I yelled back, "It wasn't a car chase! We very slowly and carefully followed Daniel Mooney and his *girlfriend* to her house, and then I immediately brought her back here before I went back to figure out the girlfriend's name. Do you honestly think I would ever risk Ruby's safety?"

Peter paused. "Girlfriend?"

"Yes, girlfriend. And you'll never believe the stuff I found out about the two of them on the Web."

Peter was interested despite himself. "Go on."

"Turns out this creep is sleeping with this woman, Nina Tiger, or "tigress," as she likes to call herself. They met about a year ago on a newsgroup for people interested in polyamory."

"Poly what?"

"Love relationships among more than two people."

"Ick."

"My feelings exactly. Anyway, they met on the Web, and pretty soon were having very public and very raunchy Internet sex. Finally, it wasn't enough for them. They decided they needed to consummate their cybersex. The whole time, mind you, they kept the entire population of their newsgroup apprised of every single sordid detail of their relationship. They started sleeping together, sneaking around behind Abigail's back.

"Within a couple of months, the newsgroup freaks started hounding them. Remember, the whole point of this movement or whatever it is is that they are supposed to by polyamorous, not just adulterous. Tigress and Coyote—yes, that is indeed his *nom de guerre*—finally succumbed to the pressure and decided to include Abigail in their little love nest or cesspool, whatever you want to call it. And, get this, they decided, with the help of their comrades in arms—and legs, for that matter—that the best way to get Abigail to go along with this multiple-partner thing is to have her walk into her bedroom one fine day and find ol' tigress and Coyote waiting there, buck naked."

"Are you kidding?"

"Nope. They planned their moment, and one fine evening there they were, waiting for Abigail when she walked in from work. Surprise, surprise, Abigail was less than thrilled with the little *Wild Kingdom* tableau awaiting her. In fact, she freaked out—which, by the way, totally confused everyone in the newsgroup, all of whom apparently were under the impression that she would rip off her clothes and jump into the sack with the fabulous twosome.

"Not one to be trifled with, Abigail threw Coyote out on his butt, and he, bizarrely, to my mind, began this desperate siege to try to get her back. Finally, after about a week or so of flowers, phone calls, etc., she relented, on the condition that he stop seeing tigress and get some marital counseling, which he did. Go to therapy, that is. He did *not* stop sleeping with the hungry jungle cat. They just went back to doing the nasty in secret. They seem to have been under the impression that Abigail didn't know about it, or at least that's what they told the newsgroup."

"Holy cow."

"Cows say 'Moo!'" a high-pitched voice squealed.

Peter and I spun around to find Ruby standing in the doorway. How long she'd been there and how much she'd heard we never did figure out. I didn't have time to mention to Peter that Nina Tiger had caught me going through her mail.

11

S O DANIEL MOONEY had killed his wife for the second-oldest reason in the book: love. Something still bothered me, however: This was a full thirty years after the "me decade" and the divorce revolution. By conservative estimates, one in every two marriages doesn't make it. Why didn't Daniel Mooney just divorce his wife and marry his trophy, like most other philandering husbands? Why did he kill her, exposing himself to the possibility of taking up residence on San Quentin's death row?

There were two possible explanations that occurred to me. The first had the benefit of a little drama and just a hint of Jacqueline Susann. Mooney, acting in the heat of his overwhelming passion, overcome with lust and despair, struck out in a blind rage. Since Mooney seemed about as capable of passion as your average android, I could pretty much rule that possibility out. That left me with the single biggest motivator of all, the reason most crimes are committed to begin with. Filthy lucre. Money.

That night, after I put Ruby to bed and after Peter had gone to work, I went back to my computer. I logged on to a legal search engine that I'd been subscribed to while at the Federal Defender's office. Surprisingly, my password still worked. Promising myself that I would notify Marla Goldfarb that she should adjust the office's subscription to exclude me and any other ex-employees just as soon as I was done, I began a search of the real property files.

Real property means just that—land, houses, apartments, and the like. The search engine listed appraised values and title histories of all pieces of real property in most if not all areas of the country. In the California real estate market, average, and even not so average, wage earners have the vast majority of their assets tied up in their homes. One of the best ways to figure out what someone is worth—one of the only ways, unless you're the FBI or the IRS and can subpoena bank records—is to figure out what kind of money she has invested in her house.

It took me no time at all to find Abigail Hathaway's property interests. In addition to her house in Santa Monica, she owned eight rental units in East Los Angeles and three small apartment buildings in South-Central L.A. and Watts. Lovely, elegant Ms. Hathaway was a slumlord. Slumlady? Anyway, she collected rent on a number of buildings in decidedly dicey parts of Los Angeles. She also owned a commercial building on Wilshire Boulevard and a couple of empty lots downtown. A real estate magnate in preschool teacher's clothing.

Scrolling down through the document that my entry of her name had generated, I found another listing—a large holding on the central California coast. A ranch, most likely, since it listed agricultural uses under its property description. Old California families often used to own vast ranches all over the state. William Randolph Hearst's San Simeon is the most famous of these, but families such as the Hewletts, Packards, Browns, and others still keep their "rustic" family retreats. It appeared that the Hathaways were part of that select group.

Now the question became how Abigail Hathaway had come into these various properties and what kind of stake, if any, Daniel Mooney had in them.

Before I continued my search I got up and tiptoed into the hall. I paused outside of Peter's office and listened to the rapid-fire click-clack of his computer keys. His work was obviously going better. I continued down the hall and stopped outside of Ruby's door. Opening it a crack, I peered into the semidarkness. She lay on her bed, arms and legs spread wide. That child sure knew how to take up space. Smiling at the sound of her snores, I softly closed the door and headed to the bathroom. The minute dimensions of my pregnant bladder were having a detrimental effect on my stamina.

Business accomplished, I headed back to my desk. Thankfully, I had not been logged off in my absence. Going back to my search, I began with the Santa Monica house. According to the record, it had been purchased in 1983 by Abigail Hathaway and Philip Esseks. 1983. I did some quick math. (Okay, not so quick, but I'm a product of the new math of the early 1970s, and it is simply not my fault that I need to add and subtract using my fingers and toes. And let's not even talk about my times tables.) Sixteen years ago. Abigail's daughter, Audrey, looked to be about fifteen years old or so. That made it likely that Philip Esseks was Audrey's dad and one of Abigail's first few husbands.

Married couples generally purchase residential property as joint tenants. That means each has a right of survivorship. If one dies, the other owns the whole thing. The house was Abigail's. Even more interesting, there was no bank lien on the property, meaning that it had either been fully paid for when bought or the mortgage had been paid off.

Since Abigail owned the house before her marriage to Mooney, the house was hers and hers alone. Under California's community property laws, each person retains ownership of whatever assets he or she brings into the marriage. It's only what they earn or acquire during the time they are together that gets split down the middle. The house belonged to Abigail, and unless she had expressly made it part of their community property (something I couldn't see a woman who'd been through a divorce or two doing), if Mooney divorced her, he wouldn't get any of it.

I then checked the house's appraised value. Scrolling down, I let out a long, low whistle. Wow. Here was the reason Peter and I would never be able to buy a house in a place like Santa Monica. Abigail's admittedly lovely but certainly not palatial home was appraised at 2.1 million dollars. Yes, you read that right: 2.1 million. And that was only the appraised value. Who knows what she could have sold it for on the open market?

So much for the house. I clicked over to the central coast property. The line of title on that was even simpler. The property had been purchased in 1914 by Alexander Hall Hathaway. It was now owned by the Hall Hathaway Family Trust, with Abigail Hathaway listed as trustee. The ranch's appraised value was a cool twenty-six million dollars. Good news for Abigail, but meaningless to Mooney. Inherited property is not subject to the community property laws. He would have gotten none of it had they divorced. Presumably, however, he wouldn't get any part of it at her death, either. I was pretty confident that the ranch would go to the Hathaway heir—Audrey.

The only thing left to figure out was the ownership status of the commercial holdings—the various apartment buildings and lots sprinkled throughout town. It took me a while, but I finally managed to figure out who owned what. It appeared, curiously, that Abigail was the sole owner of each of the rental units and of the vacant lots. The commercial building on Wilshire Boulevard was owned by an entity called "Abigail Hathaway Ltd.," a limited partnership. Clicking over to the business listings, I entered the name "Abigail Hathaway Ltd." and, after a short wait, came up with a description of the partnership. Its sole member was Abigail Hathaway herself.

I returned to the property screens and spent some time trying to figure out the chain of title of the various buildings. They were all sold to Abigail Hathaway between 1989 and 1995. Interestingly, all the properties except the Wilshire office building and one of the empty lots had been sold to Abigail by the same entity, Moonraker, Inc. Moonraker—it had to be Daniel Mooney.

I tried to figure out who, exactly, constituted Moonraker, Inc., but found myself lost in a tangled web of owners, partners, lienholders, and the like. Finally I gave up. I needed someone with real experience in the field to help make sense of what I'd found. I carefully downloaded all the relevant documents and put them into my Animal Musings file.

It was only once I'd logged off, and put my computer to sleep, that I realized how sore my neck was and how my back ached. I stretched my head from side to side and cracked my neck. Detective work was exhausting. And it made me hungry. I waddled to the kitchen and made myself a bowl of ice cream. I added a dollop of butterscotch sauce and a squirt of whipped cream. I was about to return the whipped cream canister to the fridge when I had a sudden, irresistible urge: I leaned my head back, opened my mouth, and sprayed it full of whipped cream. Coughing and swallowing, I took my light snack to bed.

12

THE NEXT MORNING, after I'd fed Ruby and settled her in front of *Sesame Street*, I sat at the kitchen table and tried to think of someone who could help me figure out the meaning of what I'd discovered the night before. I needed a real estate lawyer. Fortunately, one of the benefits of going to Harvard Law School is that my old friends and classmates are successfully employed all over the country in good law firms, and, generally, when I need some legal advice, it's easy to find. Unfortunately, in this particular instance, I could come up with only one name: Jerome Coley. Jerome had come to Harvard Law School via the governor's office in Sacramento, where he'd been one of the youngest press secretaries ever to hold the position. Before that he'd been a linebacker for Stanford's football team and had been named All-American two years in a row. He was a complete hotshot. After graduation, Jerome had taken a job in Los Angeles at a prominent local firm and, as I recalled, specialized in real estate law.

There was, however, a slight complication: Jerome had been my boyfriend throughout my second and third years of law school, although our relationship never got as serious as it might have. We just weren't meant to be. He was one of those guys whose ambition is palpable. He knew exactly what he was going to do with his life. He told most people that his goal was to be a senator from the state of California. He confided in me his real dream: to be president. I didn't have much doubt that he'd succeed.

Jerome had his whole life planned out. After establishing himself in the legal community, he intended to run for Congress, serve a few terms, and then make a play for the Senate seat. A white wife didn't figure into his plans. Jerome believed that Californians would have a hard enough time electing a 6-foot-6, 280-pound black man to office without the added benefit of a 5-foot-tall Jewish wife standing proudly at his side. He was probably right.

Anyway, after we'd broken up he'd met and married a sweet young woman of the correct race, the daughter of friends of his parents. We hadn't spoken since our final blowout in the middle of commencement ceremonies (I'd accused him of being a calculating son of a bitch, and he'd responded by accusing me of using our relationship as a sop to my white, liberal guilt), and I wasn't sure how he'd react to a phone call from me. But no matter how hard I racked my brain, I could not come up with a single other real estate lawyer. I had no choice but to give Jerome a call.

I telephoned information, got the name of his firm, and dialed the number before I had time to change my mind. The receptionist put me through to him.

"Jerome Coley." He answered his own phone.

"Hi, Jerry. You'll never guess who this is."

"Juliet Applebaum." There wasn't even a pause!

"Wow. You recognized my voice after all this time!"

"I'd never forget your voice. How you doing, baby?" Baby?

"Um, okay, pregnant. Again."

"Really? I'd heard you had a kid. Girl, right?"

"Right. Her name is Ruby. This one's a boy."

"Ruby. Pretty name. Is she as beautiful as her mama?"

"Well, since her mama weighs about three hundred pounds right now and has ankles the size of soccer balls, I'd say she's definitely more beautiful."

"I can't believe that. You always look good. Even fat, you'd look good."

This conversation was unbelievable. With a little shiver I remembered how Jerome had always made me feel. Kind of like a melted ice-cream cone. Pulling myself together, I quickly redirected the conversation.

"So you're not mad at me anymore?" I asked.

"Of course not. Are you still mad at me?"

"Of course not. Bygones and all that."

"Right. So you calling to ask forgiveness, or is there some ulterior motive up your adorable little sleeve?"

I laughed. "You still know me a little, don'tcha, Jer."

"Yes, I surely do."

"Well, I do have an ulterior motive, but first tell me how you're doing. How's Jeanette? Do you guys have any kids yet?"

"She's fine. She's been home for the past year and a half with our twin boys, Jerome, Jr., and Jackson."

"Twins? Wow! You must be exhausted!"

He laughed the deep, rolling chuckle that I remembered so well.

"Indeed. Indeed we are."

"And your job, Jer? How's that going?"

"Just fine. I made partner last year."

"I'm not surprised." I wasn't. He was a smart guy, and more importantly, he had always been a team player.

"Congratulations. That's terrific."

"And, Juliet, you probably won't be surprised to hear that I'm running for Congress next fall. Richard Baker is stepping down, and I'm going to be running for his seat."

"Now, that's what I expected to hear!" I said. "I figured it was about time for you to be heading to Washington."

"You know the plan, girl. You know the plan."

We both paused, considering for a moment that, but for "the plan," there was a good chance we would be living together right now, making little *café au lait* babies of our own. Ah, well, such is life. We were both happily married, at least I was, and the better off for our breakup.

I decided to get down to business. "Jerome, I have a couple of questions about a series of real estate transactions that I've been looking into, and I wonder if you might be able to give me some help."

"Of course, baby."

Baby again. He used to call me that in that same deep, sweet voice while we made love. Over and over again. Steeling myself, I got my mind out of the gutter and into the present and concentrated on my questions.

"Okay. First of all, do you have any idea what Moonraker, Inc., is? Have you ever heard of them?"

"Moonraker. Moonraker. That rings a bell. Hmm." He paused for a moment. "I think I remember something about that company. Hold on a second, let me check a file."

He put me on hold long enough for me to get a little too involved in a fond recollection of the past.

"I'm back. I just checked with a colleague. I thought I'd remembered that name. Moonraker played a small role in a series of deals the firm did in the mid-eighties or so. Things got a little ugly when the market went bust in 1989, and we haven't done any work with them since. They might have gone under. A lot of smaller companies did back then."

Pay dirt.

"Do you happen to remember the name of the principal owner of Moonraker?"

"I didn't, but my partner did. He told me that it was owned by a guy named Mooney. Hence the name. Cute."

"Daniel Mooney?"

"He didn't say. Maybe. Are you doing some kind of deal with Moonraker? Is he back in business?"

"No, nothing like that. Tell me, can you think of a reason why Moonraker would sell off its properties?"

"Well, that's a no-brainer. Real estate transactions are highly leveraged. That means everyone borrows heavily to make each deal. If enough of its deals fell through to force Moonraker to go under, it would have to sell off its assets to pay off its debt."

"That makes sense. Now, can you think of a reason why Moonraker would sell its assets to Mooney's wife?"

"Interesting. Well, maybe Mooney wanted to protect his properties from creditors and was under the impression that if he made them the personal property of his wife they would be exempt from dissolution and distribution. That would have been a mistake on his part, however. You can't protect property just like that."

"Why not?" I asked. I didn't do that well in property law.

"Well, think about it, baby. If you could just sell off your assets to your family, no creditor would ever get anything when a business went bankrupt."

"Oh, right. Then why did he do it?"

"Maybe his wife bailed him out. That's the only thing I can think of. Maybe his wife bought his properties to give him the cash to pay off his creditors. Does she have that kind of money?"

"I think she must have." Abigail Hathaway had the money to pay off her husband's debt, but instead of giving it to him, she bought his properties. So she ended up owning everything and he ended up owing her for the rest of his life.

"Juliet, what's your interest here? Who are you representing?"

"Nobody. I'm not representing anybody. I'm just, well, I'm just sort of investigating a murder."

"You're *what*?"

"Abigail Hathaway, Daniel Mooney's wife, was killed last week. I knew her and I'm sort of trying to figure out who killed her."

"You know, I always thought you'd make a good cop. So you think this guy Mooney killed her and you're going to cuff him and bring him in."

"Ha, ha. Very funny, Jer. I'm not cuffing anybody. It's just that the cops have decided that this is a hit-and-run, which it may well be. Nonetheless, I think it's worth an extra look. I've been spending a little time nosing around. I think you've helped me discover something pretty important."

He laughed again. "Juliet Applebaum, private eye. Hey, girl, don't go getting yourself into any trouble."

"You know what, I kind of like the sound of that: Applebaum, P.I. Anyway, don't worry, I'm not getting into any trouble. And, Jerome?"

"What?"

"Thanks. You've been a great help."

"You're welcome, baby. Anytime."

"Watch out or I'll take you up on that. Regards to your wife and sons."

"Good luck with your new baby, baby."

Now it was my turn to laugh. I said good-bye, thanking him again for his advice, and hung up the phone.

I sat for a moment, staring into space, indulging a brief but nonetheless highly disconcerting fantasy about Jerome and the lazy afternoons we used to spend in his studio apartment in Cambridge. I had fond, very fond, memories of the god-awful, green shag carpeting. It was made out of some horrible acrylic and once gave me such a bad rug burn on my rear end that I could barely sit for a week. With a shiver, I realized that there was only one way I was going to exorcise the demon of Jerome Coley. After checking to make sure that Ruby was still busy with the number 16 and the letter R, I snuck into my bedroom and woke up my husband. Substituting reality for fantasy turned out to be just what I needed.

AFTER I HAD successfully reminded myself that I was happily married, Peter and I took a quick shower together. I grabbed a pink razor that was sitting in the soap dish and tried to shave my legs. I leaned over and, about halfway down toward my knees, I got stuck. I couldn't bend over far enough. I looked up at my husband, who was rinsing the shampoo out of his hair.

"Um, honey?" I said beseechingly, holding the razor up to him. "It's that time again."

"Really? Already? Last time you could shave your own legs up until the last couple of weeks," he said with a laugh.

"Well, I'm just fatter now, if you don't mind."

"All right, prop your leg up here."

Groaning with the effort, I balanced my leg on the side of the tub. Peter bent down under the spray of the shower and delicately and carefully shaved my leg clean. I reached over and wiped the streaming water out of his eyes. What I really wanted to do was kiss the top of his head, but I couldn't reach it. What a lovely man. How many guys do you know who would shave their pregnant wife's legs? I know exactly one. And I married him.

Suddenly, with a crash, the bathroom door burst open. Peter and I both jumped, and I felt a sting as the razor sliced into my shin.

"Ow! Dammit!" I hollered. "Ruby! What in heaven's name are you doing?"

"Nothing!" she wailed. "I'm lonely!" I ended up crouched on the bathmat, soaking wet and dripping blood and water, trying at the same time both to dry off and to comfort a righteously indignant toddler.

13

PETER DID ME a favor and took Ruby out for the rest of the morning so I could do a little more research. I noodled around on the Internet for a while, trying to see if I could come up with some more dirt on either Daniel Mooney or his feline friend. After an unsuccessful hour or so, I was getting very frustrated. Looking at my watch, I realized that if I rushed, I could make my prenatal Yoga class. I definitely needed to clear my head, and moving my body probably wasn't a bad idea. I hoisted myself out of my chair, waddled into my bedroom, and began the arduous process of cramming my body into my maternity Yoga cat suit. Getting my thighs into that Lycra outfit was an awful lot like stuffing a sausage casing.

I was stuck somewhere between my knees and my butt when the phone rang. I lunged over to the nightstand, and fumbling for the phone, knocked the receiver onto the floor. I spent a couple of frantic seconds on my hands and knees, tangled in my leggings, trying to reach under the bed where the receiver had rolled. Finally, I managed to herd the dust bunnies into a corner and answer the phone.

"Yeah? Hello?" I was panting from exertion.

"Um, hello? Juliet? Are you okay?"

"Yeah, fine. I'm fine. Who is this?"

"It's Audrey. Audrey Hathaway. Abigail's daughter. I'm sorry. I hope it's okay to call you. I mean, you said I could call but you were probably, like, just being nice or something. I shouldn't have called. Forget it. I'm—"

"Audrey! I'm so glad to hear from you," I interrupted her. "Of course you can call. I wanted you to call. Are you okay? Why are you calling? I mean, it's fine, but is there something wrong?"

"No. Yes. I dunno." And she started to cry. I sure had a calming effect on that girl.

"Honey, shh. It's okay, sweetie. Are you just sad? Is that it?"

"No." She hiccuped. "I mean, yes, I'm sad, but that's not why I'm calling. I'm totally freaking out here and I have no one to talk to and then I found your number and you're so sweet and I thought you maybe might be there because you're, like, pregnant and can't go anywhere anyway." With that, she began to wail.

I looked down at my legs, still trapped in Lycra. She wasn't far wrong—I certainly didn't give the appearance of anyone who should be leaving the house.

"Should I come over? Do you want me to come over?" I asked.

"No!" she shouted. "No! Not here!"

"Can I meet you somewhere? Do you want to come over to my house?"

She was sitting in my kitchen, drinking hot chocolate, within twenty minutes.

I LET AUDREY sit quietly for a little while, slurping cocoa and eating cookies. Her multicolored hair was shoved into a baseball cap, and she was wearing an oversized sweatshirt and a pair of pants so big they looked like I could climb into them with her. I wasn't sure if she was pathologically ashamed of her body, or just expressing the height of a teenage fashion I was too clueless to even know about. Finally Audrey squared her shoulders and seemed to make some kind of decision.

"If I tell you something, like absolutely, totally insane, will you swear that you won't think I'm crazy?"

"You're not crazy, Audrey."

"I know I'm not crazy. I just don't want *you* to think I am."

"I won't. I don't. What is it?"

"The cops are, like, all over my house and they won't tell me why, but I think I know."

"You do?" Did she? Could she know about her stepfather?

"Yeah. It's Daniel. I know it is. He killed my mom. I'm so completely sure he did it." She wasn't crying anymore. She seemed grim, and certain, and scared.

"Your stepfather? Are you just guessing, or do you have proof?"

"Well, it's not like he's confessed or anything. It's just that he hates me and my mom. He left once, you know. He was having an affair, and my mom threw him out."

I decided that it was better to play dumb. "An affair? Really? With whom, do you know?"

"I don't know her name or anything. But I know that he met her online, how lame is *that*? He's like some pathetic old man having *cybersex*. It's so totally gross." Audrey no longer sounded upset. Just really angry.

"How did you find out about this?" I asked.

"My mom made him go to therapy and the two of them dragged me with them a couple of times. So we could 'deal with our family issues.'" Her voice dripped sarcasm. "They were supposed to be talking about me, but my mom ended up screaming about his computer slut. The shrink made her shut up, but I heard enough to figure out what the creep was up to."

"Creep is right," I agreed. "Audrey, I think you should be telling this to the police. Don't you?"

"No! No way. He'll kill me if he finds out I told on him." She started to cry again.

It occurred to me that she might be right. Kill her, as in really kill her, not just be angry enough to ground her for the weekend.

"Okay. Okay. Do you want me to tell the police, and leave you out of it?"

"Would you? Would you do that?"

"Of course, honey. Of course I will. But what are you going to do? You can't go home, can you?" I reached my arm around her and hugged her. I tried to imagine Peter's face when I told him that I'd invited Abigail Hatha-way's daughter to stay with us until I could prove that her stepfather was a murderer. I opened my mouth to invite her to stay, but she spoke first.

"I can stay at my friend Alice's. I was going to do that anyway, at least until my aunt comes back. My aunt was here for a couple of days, but then she had to go home. She's coming back soon, that's what she said. She wants me to go live with her in New Jersey, but I don't know if I want to. I mean, who the hell wants to live in New Jersey?"

"I'm from New Jersey," I said, smiling and trying to cut the tension a bit.

"Oh. Sorry."

"Don't worry about it. It's not so bad, New Jersey. But what about school? Don't you want to stay in your school?"

"To hell with school. I'm flunking out anyway. Who cares?"

I didn't want to touch that. The weeks following her mother's death were not the time to lecture Audrey on the importance of an education.

"Okay, you go to your friend Alice's and I'll call the police and tell them what you told me."

"But don't mention my name, okay? Tell them you heard about it from, like, anonymous sources or something."

"I'll tell them something."

I packed a Baggie with some cookies for Audrey. She swore to me that she was going right over to Alice's house, and left the number for me. Then I called Detective Carswell's office and left an urgent message for him to call me.

Checking my watch, I realized that I had a few more minutes before Ruby and Peter were likely to get home. I contemplated getting back onto the computer, but decided that I needed help if I was going to get any more information on Mooney. I decided to call in yet another favor. I dialed the federal defender's office and asked to speak to Al Hockey.

"Hey, it's the Old Woman Who Lived in a Shoe! Have you figured out what to do with all your children?"

"Ha. Funny, Al. Two. Exactly two children. One and a half, really. Less than you, I might add."

"Is it just two? All those months spent barefoot and pregnant for two kids?"

"Al, this line of discussion is getting old. Really old."

"I'll tell you what, Juliet. I'll stop when you get yourself out of the kitchen and back here, where you belong."

"Thanks. And I miss you, too."

I could almost hear him blushing on the other end of the line. "Enough of this mushy stuff. Why are you calling? Who do you need me to run through NCIC now?"

"I'm trying to get some information about someone who does a lot of messing around on the Internet. I found out a bunch of stuff, but I'm no hacker, and I've kind of hit a brick wall. I was hoping you'd have some ideas for me."

Al paused, and it seemed to me that there was an uncomfortable silence.

"Al? You there? Got any ideas?"

"Yeah, I'm here. Okay, Juliet, can I trust you?"

"Sure. Of course you can trust me. You know that."

"I do have someone I've gone to a number of times for—let's call it specialized information. But if the boss lady found out I was using this guy, she'd hang me by my nuts."

"Nice image, Al. You've piqued my interest. Who's your expert?"

"I'm swearing you to secrecy, Juliet."

"I'm sworn, Al."

"Okay, remember Julio Rodriguez?"

A year or so before I'd quit, the office had represented Julio Rodriguez, a skinny kid from East L.A. who happened to be a computer genius. Using his cousin's ten-year-old Mac and an old acoustic modem, Julio managed to hack into the Immigration and Naturalization Service's files. It was months before anybody noticed that the number of green cards being issued to immigrants in Boyle Heights had shot through the roof. The papers had dubbed Julio the "Robin Hood of the Bario," and by the time the feds had tracked him down, he'd become a local folk hero. Marla Goldfarb herself had represented him and lost. Last I heard, Julio was serving a four-year sentence at FCI Lompoc.

"No kidding! Julio is out of jail? Is he some kind of expert witness or something?"

"No and yes," Al said.

"No and yes? What's that supposed to mean?"

"Yes, he's doing some, er, consulting, and no, he's not out of jail."

"Let me get this straight. Julio is still in jail?"

"At the Farm at Lompoc." The Farm is the minimum-security facility at Lompoc Federal Correction Institution. It's where white-collar criminals such as Michael Milkin and, apparently, Julio Rodriguez, serve their time.

"And you're using him as a consultant?"

"It's really not a big deal, Juliet. Sometimes, if I happen to have a question or two about a specific computer issue, and if I happen to be heading up to Lompoc anyway, I stop in to have a little conversation with Julio. And sometimes I give his mother a few bucks."

"How few?"

"A hundred dollars for every hour I spend with Julio."

I whistled. "Wow. Where the heck do you get that kind of money? You work for the federal defender, not for Johnny Cochran."

"I expense it. Over a couple of weeks. You see why Marla would lose her mind if she found out? I can't exactly submit this on a reimbursement form to the court, can I?"

All expert fees paid out by the federal defender's office have to be filed for approval with the federal district court. Marla, as a court officer, has the right to approve them herself, but ultimately the chief judge gets the paperwork. Al was right. There was no way Marla would ever approve payments to Julio Rodriguez, a former client, even if he was the smartest cybergeek in all of California.

"So, Al, if I needed to have a chat with Julio, what would I do?"

"Are you still a member of the bar?"

"Of course I am."

"Then you would head up to Lompoc for a legal visit. If you tell Julio you used to work for us, he might not make you pay his mother in advance."

I considered for a moment whether I really wanted to be stuck behind the wheel of my car for the three hours it takes to get to Lompoc. Then I thought of Audrey.

"Thanks, Al. I'm going tomorrow."

"Tomorrow? Want some company?"

"What? You can go with me to Lompoc tomorrow? Are you serious?"

"I'm investigating a habeas case and I haven't been up to interview the client. He's at Lompoc."

"Al, I love you. I really do."

"We've got to get an early start. I'll pick you up at six."

"Jesus. That *is* early."

"You want to go or not?"

"Yes, yes. I want to go. Do you have my address?"

"Orange Drive, in Hancock Park, right?"

"Indeed."

"See you tomorrow."

"Okay. Thanks, Al."

"Thanks for what? We're just carpooling to Lompoc, right?"

"Right."

PETER WASN'T THRILLED when I told him he'd have to take the night off so I could wake up at the crack of dawn and head up to Lompoc, but he didn't freak out, either. He seemed sort of resigned to my investigation by that point.

The next morning I hauled myself out of bed before it was light and allowed myself a rare extra-large cup of coffee. One caffeine drink wouldn't kill the baby. Neither would two. Three was pushing it, but it was five thirty in the morning, for crying out loud. I was waiting out on my front steps when Al pulled up in his monstrous Suburban.

"Nice to see you're taking that dependence on foreign oil thing to heart," I said as I scrambled up into the passenger seat, which seemed, to me at least, to be about eight feet off the ground.

"The United States has plenty of oil. We aren't dependent on anybody. That's all just lies spread by the government so we wouldn't figure out their real agenda in the Gulf War."

"And that was?"

"Illegally testing biological weapons on U.S. troops."

There was no way I was going to spend the next eight hours exploring the depths of Al's paranoid conspiracy theories.

"You're right, Al. Absolutely right. How could I have been so stupid? Can we change the subject now?"

"Fine. Live in ignorance. I don't care. Coffee?" He leaned over and picked up a thermos that was tucked under his seat.

"Mmm. Real coffee. I shouldn't. I had a cup or two this morning."

"Why shouldn't you?"

"Oh, you know, the baby and all."

"Oh, for Pete's sake. Elaine drank two pots of coffee a day when she was pregnant with our kids. And let's not even talk about the drinking and smoking."

"I know, I know. And you never put them in car seats, either, right?" I noticed, then, that Al had devised an intricate system of tucking his seat belt over his body and through his arm so that it appeared that he was wearing it while, in actuality, it hung, unbuckled and useless, at his side.

"Right," he said.

"Give me the thermos." I grabbed it, opened the top, and poured a few steaming inches into the little orange cup. Sipping the coffee, I grimaced at the weak, sour flavor. Obviously not a gourmet blend. But caffeine is caffeine, in whatever form it comes. I guzzled the last few mouthfuls in the cup and handed the thermos back to Al.

"Thanks," I said, and meant it.

We passed the rest of the drive in silence, listening to Al's favorite talk-radio host denounce the United Nations as a tool of the New World Order and claim to have personally witnessed black helicopters in formation over Roswell, New Mexico.

We pulled into Lompoc and headed over to the visiting building. We stopped at the reception desk, handed over our identification, and each filled out the form indicating that we were there for a legal visit. I glanced over at Al's form and noticed that he'd only written Julio's name.

"What about your habeas case, Al?" I asked.

"That? I decided not to bother with it today. I've got plenty of time before the petition is due."

"So you're just here for me?"

"Yup."

I smiled at him. What a guy.

We passed through the metal detectors, surrendering our cell phones to the guards, to be held until we left. I had a brief moment of panic, imagining something terrible happening to Ruby, and Peter unsuccessfully trying to reach me on my phone, but I pushed it out of my mind. Parents had survived thousands of years without cell phones. I could live without mine for a couple of hours.

Al and I walked up to the first door to the visiting room and stood, holding our passes up to the window and waiting, more or less patiently, for the guard manning the door to notice us. Despite the fact that I caught her eye through the reinforced window more than once, it took at least five minutes for the guard to buzz us in. By the time she had deigned to move her hand the two inches it took to reach the buzzer, I had begun, as always, to fume.

Prison guards can sometimes be the worst of the worst: petty, bureaucratic, wannabe cops who get off on asserting whatever power they can muster. Who in their right mind would want to spend his or her entire working day lording it over a bunch of pathetic, sometimes violent, losers whose fondest wish is usually to see you, if not dead, then beaten to a pulp? You have to really like the power dynamic to be willing to put up with the misery.

I can count on the fingers of one hand the number of times I've been treated with any kind of respect by a prison guard. They tend to view defense lawyers as one rung *below* their clients on the social scale. There's not a lot you can do about it, however. You just have to grit your teeth and do your best to ignore their games. So Al and I stood and waited for the rotund little guard in the too-tight uniform to buzz us through the steel-and-glass door. Then we walked through the hall and waited at the next locked door to get into the visiting room. It took us almost fifteen minutes to walk about twenty feet.

We made ourselves comfortable at one of the tables reserved for legal visits and waited some more, this time for Julio to be brought down to the visiting room. Visiting a client involves a whole lot of waiting. Just when I feared I was going to have to go out, visit the bathroom, and repeat the whole entrance rigamarole again, Julio was brought through a barred door into the room. One of the guards pointed him in our direction and he ambled over.

Julio was a good-looking kid, small and dark with decidedly Indian features. He wore his hair long and parted at the side like a curtain falling over his right eye. His face was broad and angled, with sharp cheekbones and a nose that was almost hooked. He looked like a Mayan statue—regal and just a little scary. He wore a pair of pressed jeans with a knife edge of a crease running precisely down the middle of his legs, a blue button-down shirt, and perfectly white Nikes—his prison uniform, but with a touch of class. He sat down gracefully and reached a small, strong hand with well-kept nails across the table.

"Al," he said, shaking his hand.

"Julio. Good to see you," Al replied.

"Ma'am." He extended a hand to me.

"Juliet Applebaum," I said, surprised at the softness of his palm, especially when contrasted with the firmness of his grasp.

"What can I do for you today?" Julio asked. In his voice I could hear the faintest trace of a Mexican accent.

"I was hoping you might be able to help me with a case I've been investigating," I said.

Al looked at me, eyebrows raised. I guess I'd never put it so bluntly before. The truth was unavoidable, however. I was investigating the murder of Abigail Hathaway, albeit unofficially.

"Has Al explained my terms to you?" Julio asked softly.

"One hundred dollars per hour, to be paid to your mother."

"Yes. I usually require some proof of prepayment, but if Al can vouch for you, I will allow you to pay after we speak."

"I can vouch for her," Al said.

"Fine," Julio replied.

"Okay, so here's the situation," I began.

It took about fifteen minutes for me to explain the entire history of Abigail Hathaway's death, her husband's affair, and the polyamorous computer club to Julio. He listened intently, never taking his eyes off mine. Initially it was disconcerting to have him staring at me so tenaciously, but I got used to it. I had never met anyone who sat as still and as quietly as Julio. Every once in a while he would nod at something I had said, or raise a quizzical eyebrow, asking, without words, for more information. Other than that, he was made of stone. Finally, when I had finished, he spoke.

"You should not have come here."

"What?" I was confused and not a little irritated. I mean, I'd driven three hours when I could barely manage to sit in one place for more than five minutes without my back seizing up, and this little creep was telling me I shouldn't have come? Wasn't my money good enough for him?

"You have wasted your time and money."

"And why would that be?" My voice came out stiffer and a little more prim than I would have liked.

"Because a computer-literate eight-year-old could have solved this problem for you."

"Well, Julio, here's the thing: I don't happen to know any computer-literate eight-year-olds, and my two-and-a-half-year-old can barely manage to surf the Barbie website. So you're what I've got. Are you going to help me or not?"

"Yes. I will. But it is important for you to understand that this problem of yours is very easily solved."

"I understand."

"I am capable of much more demanding tasks."

"I understand."

"Despite that, you understand, my fee must apply."

"I understand."

"This is what you must do." Julio then described to me how I could access Daniel Mooney's account and trace his virtual steps. I have no idea if what he taught me was legal, but I decided not to worry about it. I took careful notes on Julio's instructions, not trusting my pregnancy-addled brain to remember anything. After he had finished, he asked for a sheet of paper and carefully wrote out a bill for one hour's work.

"Please deliver this to my mother with payment."

I took the bill and put it in my briefcase with the legal pad on which I'd made my copious notes. I reached out my hand to Julio who shook it once again.

"Good afternoon, Mrs. Applebaum," he said.

"Ms. But you can call me Juliet."

"Of course, Ms. Applebaum. It was a pleasure to assist you."

"Thank you, Julio. Is there anything we can help *you* with? Do you need anything?"

Julio smiled faintly. "Unless you have in your pocket a presidential pardon, I think that no, there is nothing you can do for me."

I smiled back at him. "Nope, fresh out of those. Sorry."

"Ah, well. Until next time, then."

"*Hasta luego,*" Al interrupted, making no attempt at a Mexican accent whatsoever.

"*Hasta proxima vez,* Al," Julio said.

He rose and with a fluid, almost elegant stride, walked over to the guard, indicating that he was ready to go back up into the prison.

Al and I gathered our things and executed the elaborate door ballet in reverse, once again waiting much too long to be buzzed through.

"So, private eye Applebaum, did you get what you needed?" Al asked once we had settled ourselves into his car and driven through the gates of the prison.

"Yup. I think so. Now we'll just have to see if I can actually do this stuff on my computer."

"Julio's directions are usually pretty clear. Call me if you have any problems. Maybe my nine-year-old nephew can help you out."

"Ha, ha. Very funny, Al. Hey, listen, if I give you the hundred bucks, will you deliver it to Julio's mother?"

"Sure."

I wrote Al out a check, balancing my checkbook on my stomach.

"Hey, Juliet, interested in some barbecued oysters?"

Of course I was. We stopped at a little roadside shack and prepared to feast. I wasn't technically supposed to be eating oysters, but these were cooked, so I figured it was okay. Besides, there was no way I was going to sit and watch Al slurp up the contents of the oyster shells and lick sauce off his fingertips without having a plate of my own. I waited impatiently for my paper plate full of steaming shells drenched in spicy red sauce, and dove in headfirst when it arrived. As we gobbled our food, I brought Al up to date on my investigation. When I finished, he took a long draft of the one beer I had allowed him to order, swallowed loudly, belched, and pointed a thick finger at me.

"You, girl, have found your calling."

"What do you mean?"

"Investigation. Detection. Forget the courtroom crap. Figuring out who done it. That's the fun part."

"You know, I always enjoyed that part of it. You're right."

"You should hang out a shingle: "Juliet Applebaum, Private Eye.""

"You're not the first person who's said that. Anyway, stop worrying about my career and finish your food, man! Let's get on the road."

We ate quickly, racing to see who could consume more oysters. Al won. With a final belch, he pushed back his chair and got up.

"Lunch is on you, Detective," he said.

I GOT HOME in plenty of time to hang out with Ruby and Peter before dinner. We played a vigorous and cutthroat game of Hungry, Hungry, Hippos, in the midst of which I noticed that I was actually having a good time. While Ruby accumulated every marble in the game, as she always did through some innate power of control over plastic marble-devouring hippopotamuses, I brought Peter up to speed on what I had discovered. He seemed pretty impressed at my detective skills, and even promised to help me surf the Net for dirt on Daniel Mooney and Nina Tiger after Ruby went to bed.

That night, Ruby seemed to sense that we wanted her to get to bed so we could get to work on the computer. First she needed an extra story. Then she needed another drink of water. Then she peed in her overnight diaper and couldn't stand the idea of sleeping in it. And so on. After the third trip to the bathroom, I threatened her with no candy the next day if she didn't go to sleep once and for all. That got her. It's amazing how quickly kids discover that candy is, in fact, the reason and purpose for human existence.

Peter and I settled ourselves in front of the computer and did our best to carry out Julio's instructions. Honestly, I have no idea what we did. While I love using my computer, the technical details never remain in my brain for very long. I always have the same experience as when I took the bar exam. Walking in, the Rule Against Perpetuities was as clear to me as the nose on the proctor's face. As soon as I'd filled in my last circle and lay down my number-two pencil, my brain flew open and promptly flushed away that and every other arcane law that remains on the books just to torment law students. They were gone, as if they'd never even been there.

Somehow Peter and I managed to follow Julio's directions, and it didn't take long to accumulate a list of aliases for both Daniel Mooney and Nina Tiger. We started with Nina and spent a couple of hours tracing her cyber-footsteps. I wasn't surprised to discover that Nina, using different aliases, was an active member of a number of sex-based newsgroups. As "muffdvr" she explored her lesbian sadomasochistic side. As "kittyhowl" she was an expert on clitoral piercing. Most bizarrely, as "judyspal" she had a couple of hundred gay men convinced that she was one of them. All pretty weird stuff, but nothing particularly incriminating.

Finally, worried that spending too much time associating with the likes of Nina Tiger would kill our sex drives once and for all, Peter and I decided to explore Daniel Mooney's seamy side. Like Nina Tiger, he had his own bunch of aliases—"mchoman," "boytoy2000," and even his own transvestite alias, "GRrrrL." The same kinky stuff as Nina, with the added twist that "GRrrrL" liked to pretend to be a pubescent girl and flirt with older men.

It didn't take long to find the piece of evidence that would put Daniel Mooney behind bars for the murder of his wife.

14

ANIEL MOONEY'S FAILING as a murderer was that he had the sophistication of a twelve-year-old. Using the alias "doll-parts," and going no farther to cover his tracks, Abigail Hathaway's husband had posted the following advertisement on a website called "Soldiers of Fortune":

> *Wanted: Experienced soldier for special project. $5,000. Interested? Go to dollparts's private chat room on this site Monday nights, 2:00 A.M.*

That was all, but it was everything. I immediately understood that Daniel Mooney had tried to hire someone to kill his wife. I hoped that Detective Carswell would understand the same. I'd been leaving him messages every couple of hours since two days before, when Audrey had come over to tell me about her suspicions about her stepfather, but Carswell still hadn't called me back. I called him again anyway. He wasn't at work. I spoke to the desk sergeant, asking him to find Carswell and let him know that it was a matter of great urgency that he call me, at any time, day or night. I could tell I wasn't being taken seriously and was pretty sure I wouldn't hear from Carswell that night.

Peter didn't go to work that night. Instead we crawled into bed together, both overcome with the enormity of what we had discovered. We lay side by side for a while, silently. Then, suddenly, I jumped.

"Oh my God, Peter. Audrey. I don't know if she's still at her friend Alice's. What if she's home? What if she's all alone with him?"

"Abigail's daughter?"

"She could be in the house with him! What's to stop him from killing her, too?"

"She's probably at her friend's. That's where she told you she was going, right?"

"Yeah, but that was yesterday!"

"I'm sure she's still there. And, anyway, there's nothing we can do right now, Juliet. You called the detective."

"Maybe we should call nine-one-one. Or Social Services. Or something!" I was panicking.

"And tell them what? That we think her dad's a murderer because he was looking to chat with an experienced soldier on the web? No one would believe us. We need to talk to Detective Carswell."

"You're right. I know you're right. But what if something happens to her tonight and we could have prevented it? I couldn't live with myself. You didn't see her, Peter. She's so vulnerable."

"Look, he has no reason to suspect that she knows anything. And anyway, he'd have to be a total moron to hurt her now, so soon after her mother's death. That would immediately draw attention to him. He won't do it. It wouldn't make any sense."

"No, it wouldn't. We'll just have to hope that he acts sensibly."

Peter and I slept little that night. Finally, at about 6:00 A.M., I couldn't wait any longer. I picked up the phone and dialed the Santa Monica P.D. Miraculously, Detective Carswell was in.

To my surprise, he didn't dismiss me right away. On the contrary, he took me much more seriously than I had expected and every bit as seriously as I hoped. Within half an hour he was on my doorstep, accompanied by another detective, a younger man who sported the same military haircut but wore, instead of a suit, a pair of khakis and a blue blazer. Kind of like an oversized Catholic schoolboy.

I showed the two into my kitchen and offered them coffee. They accepted.

"Ms. Applebaum, please tell us what you've discovered," Carswell said, not patronizing me in the slightest. Finally.

I described my computer investigation. Carswell seemed impressed at my savvy.

"You figured out how to track his steps through all his various aliases?" he asked.

I certainly wasn't going to tell him about Julio.

"It's really very easy," I replied. "Any computer-literate eight-year-old could do it."

"Still, I'm impressed," he said, not quite grudgingly.

I smiled, feeling like I'd earned a gold star from my kindergarten teacher.

"We'd like to see the files you've downloaded," the other officer said.

I showed them into my office and to my computer. The ad, which I had not only copied into my hard drive but also bookmarked, was on the screen. The young detective sat down at my chair, pulled a couple of floppy disks out of his coat pocket, and proceeded to make copies not only of the ad but also of the many conversations of the polyamorous newsgroup. Then the two sat with me for another hour, taking notes, while I described in detail all my investigations of the past week. I left out Audrey's visit to me, because I'd promised her that I wouldn't tell them about her, and my meeting with Julio, because I didn't want Al to get into trouble.

I actually intended to tell Carswell about how Nina Tiger had found me going through her mailbox, but I couldn't bring myself to do it. It was, after all, a crime, and I hope I can be forgiven for failing to confess it to a police officer. Detective Carswell didn't *need* to know that I'd broken into her mailbox or that I'd had a confrontation with her. It wouldn't help or hurt his case any. I was rationalizing and I knew it, but I couldn't help myself.

Detective Carswell and his partner made me go over everything a second time and then rose to leave.

"Wait!" I said. "What are you going to do now?"

The two cops glanced at each other. "We'll review this information and have our computer experts track Mooney's Internet activities," Carswell said.

"And then?"

"Well, if it all checks out, if we're convinced from the evidence that this was murder and not a hit-and-run accident, and if we can convince the judge that the evidence against him amounts to probable cause, then we'll get a warrant and arrest Daniel Mooney."

I couldn't resist. "Pretty relevant information, after all, don't you think?"

Carswell looked at me for a moment. Then, miraculously, his stony face cracked into a smile. "Pretty relevant after all," he agreed.

"Ms. Applebaum, it's very important that you tell no one of the things you have discovered. We don't want to take the chance that word will get to the suspect before we're absolutely ready to act on this information," he continued.

"Right. Of course. I was a public defender. I know how it works."

At that piece of information Carswell's partner looked really worried.

"Ms. Applebaum, your defense prejudice isn't going to influence you, is it?" the young officer asked.

This steamed me. "Look, I just spent who knows how much time and energy trying to prove that this guy killed his wife! Why would I blow it now?"

Somewhat mollified, the two detectives left our house.

15

THE NEXT MORNING, Ruby woke me up earlier than normal. I plopped her in front of *Sesame Street* and headed out to the curb to get the newspaper. Cursing the delivery boy who had once again tossed the paper directly onto one of our sprinkler heads, I threaded my way, barefoot, over the grass. I picked up the soggy paper by one corner and went back inside. I tossed the paper into the oven and turned it on to about 200 degrees. I figured that as long as I stayed well below the famous Fahrenheit 451, nothing would burst into flames. I made myself a cup of tea, microwaved a few pancakes for Ruby, and settled down at the kitchen counter. Hoping that the paper was dry, I reached in with an oven mitt, grabbed it by a corner, and pulled it out. And then I started shouting.

"Peter! Peter!"

My husband came tearing out of the bedroom, stark naked.

"The baby? Is it the baby?"

I shoved the paper into his hands. He screamed and dropped it.

"Ouch! That's hot!" he howled.

"Oh. Sorry. Look! Look at the front page!"

He leaned over the floor and read aloud, "Nursery School Teacher's Husband Arrested for Murder!"

"They arrested him!"

"I can see that."

Carswell wouldn't give me any more information when I called him, so whatever I know I learned from that front-page article in the *Los Angeles Times*. Abigail Hathaway's own car matched the description of the one that had run her down; she drove a two-year-old Mercedes sedan, black. Her car wasn't at home, and when asked about it, Daniel Mooney apparently claimed to have assumed it was at the school. He said he hadn't bothered to look for it after she'd been killed. But it wasn't in the nursery school parking lot. The police searched the city, but unsurprisingly, it was nowhere to be found. The newspaper speculated that if the car had been abandoned after the murder, particularly if the keys had been left in the ignition, one or another of Los Angeles's hyperefficient car theft rings would have had it lifted, painted, and on its way to Mexico or China within a couple of hours.

So there it was: Abigail was murdered by her own husband, driving her own car.

Peter and I read the newspaper article together, sitting side by side at the kitchen table. Reading about the crime, I felt this weird combination of sadness for Abigail and her poor daughter, and satisfaction at a job well done. It was sort of like what I'd felt after winning a trial. I'd be feeling on top of the world, proud of my success, and flying high on my ego. Then I'd look over to the family of the victim, or the victim himself, and feel a little deflated. Sure, my client had gotten off because I'd done such a good job of convincing the jury of his lack of guilt or of the victim's complicity. But criminal law isn't a computer game. It isn't just a question of winning or losing and racking up points. My victory meant that someone else lost. When that someone was just the government—if, for example it was a drug case and nobody except the DEA cared if my client was convicted— then it was easy to revel in my success. But often enough, my clients had actually hurt someone. It was a heck of a lot harder to find myself happy about winning their freedom under those circumstances.

I felt a similar bittersweetness that morning. Yes, I succeeded. I'd found Abigail's murderer. But while Audrey was surely a lot safer with her step-father behind bars, she was still an orphan, now more than ever.

"Maybe I should give Audrey a call," I said. "She's probably at her friend Alice's house."

"That's not a bad idea," Peter answered.

I reached for the phone, but before I even dialed, it rang.

"Hello?"

"Juliet! This is Audrey! Isn't this awesome! Isn't this just totally bitchin' what happened to Danny? That nimrod's in jail! He is *in jail*!" Audrey was positively giddy.

"Yes, I guess it's awesome. But how are you doing? You must be pretty freaked out by this all." I looked over at Peter and mouthed silently, "Audrey." He nodded.

"Freaked out? No way! I'm happier than I've ever been in my whole life! He is G-O-N-E gone! Out of my life forever!" she shouted.

"So what are you going to do now?" I asked her.

"My aunt's flying in tonight, so I guess I'll just stay at home with her. I've gotta decide about New Jersey. What do you think I should do?"

I thought for a moment. "I guess I think you should go. New Jersey's not so bad. It's close to New York!"

"Hey! I didn't think of that. New York. Now, *that* would be bitchin'."

I laughed. "I guess it would. It sure can be. Promise me you'll keep in touch, okay?"

"Definitely! What's your E-mail address? I'll E-mail you!"

What would the world be like without the Internet? I wonder. How did we ever survive, a mere five years ago, before everyone had her very own E-mail account?

I gave Audrey my E-mail address, and she promised to write. I hung up the phone.

"She's staying with her friend until her aunt comes," I said.

"How did she sound?"

"Relieved. Happy really," I said. "I'm just glad she's safe."

The phone rang again. It was Stacy.

"Can you believe this?" she positively shrieked.

"Yes, actually because—"

"And you thought it was Bruce LeCrone! Ha. Please!"

"Well, actually, I was the one who—"

"Like Bruce would do that. Really. But her husband! I always knew that there was something fishy about—"

"Stacy! If you'd just shut up for a moment, I'll tell you how I solved this murder!"

That shut her up. I described the events of the past week or so to Stacy, lingering over details of my derring-do. Once again I kept Julio out of it, as I'd promised Al, but no other element of the story was spared my dramatization. By the end of my tale I'd actually managed to leave Stacy speechless. I think that's the first time that anyone has ever accomplished that. My story complete, I said good-bye, hung up the phone, and looked complacently over at Peter.

"Uh, Juliet, didn't Detective Carswell ask you not to reveal any details of the investigation?" he said.

I blanched. "I totally forgot. Do you think it's okay? Do you think Stacy will tell anyone?"

He looked at me.

I answered my own question. "Of course she will. Oh, no no no no."

I immediately dialed her number, but got voice mail. She had already begun to broadcast. I left a frantic message, begging her not to tell a soul. She was definitely going to ignore it, but it was the best I could do. I put my head down on the kitchen counter and moaned. "I had to tell the single biggest gossip in Los Angeles. I hope this doesn't get back to Carswell."

"Don't worry, sweetie," Peter said, patting my head. "Stacy and the detective don't exactly travel in the same circles. It'll probably be fine."

I didn't make the same mistake again. Both Al and Jerome called me that morning, and I remained discreet, expressing only my happiness that Daniel Mooney had been apprehended and nothing else. I didn't let my guard down until I heard from Lilly Green.

Lilly called me from her car phone.

"Juliet! I just got my nails done and I'm right around the corner from you. Meet me for a cup of coffee at the Living Room and tell me everything about your murder!"

I threw a baseball cap on over my hair, quickly dragged on a pair of leggings and one of Peter's flannel shirts, and, promising Ruby and Peter that I would not be gone long, rushed out the door. As I was tearing up the block on my way to meet Lilly at the homey little café she favored, it occurred to me to wonder if I would have dropped everything so quickly for a friend who wasn't a famous, Oscar-winning movie star. Just how starstruck was I? I couldn't answer the question and decided not to bother trying. I liked Lilly, and if I also liked being seen with her, well, that didn't make me any worse or any better than the rest of Los Angeles. In L.A., being starstruck is one's civic duty.

By the time I got to the café, huffing and puffing and beet-red with the exertion of my block-and-a-half walk, Lilly was already there, lounging on an overstuffed sofa, sipping a latté out of a cup the size of a basketball. She wore a pair of jeans and an old, ratty turtleneck sweater. Her hair was casually wound around her head and held in place with a chopstick. She looked gorgeous. I sighed for a moment, imagining just how beautiful I looked right then, exploding out of Peter's old shirt, my leggings fraying at the seams with the effort of containing the bulk of my thighs. Silently repeating my mantra "I'm not fat, I'm pregnant," I gave Lilly a hug and sank down next to her on the couch.

"Nonfat latte," I said to the rail-thin young thing who had instantly appeared to take my order. I got service like that only when I was with Lilly. Alone, I'd have been waiting for hours.

"Decaf?" she asked, except it sounded like "detaf" because she was having difficulty talking through the large silver stud embedded in her tongue.

"No. Caf-caf," I said.

The waitress looked disapprovingly at my belly and turned away.

"Lilly, can I bum a cigarette? Or a line of cocaine?" I asked, loud enough for the waitress to hear. Her back stiffened and she hustled off. "Why is it everyone thinks they can tell a pregnant woman what to drink, eat, whatever? I mean, for crying out loud, it's only coffee. Women in France drink coffee and swill red wine the whole time they're pregnant. No one bugs *them*."

"Yes, but then they give birth to little Frenchmen."

"Good point."

"So, you were right about Abigail Hathaway's husband!" Lilly said, getting to the point.

Once again conveniently forgetting my promise not to discuss the case with anyone, I filled Lilly in on my role in the arrest of Daniel Mooney.

"Herma Wang should have her license revoked," Lilly said once I'd finished.

"Why?"

"For not figuring out that he was so violent, that's why. She was perfectly willing to tell me that the family is in crisis and go on and on about all the suppressed rage, but did she put two and two together and realize someone was actually in danger? God forbid."

"She told you that? What is she, the Liz Smith of shrinks? Confidentiality be damned—I know a movie star!"

"I know. Ridiculous, isn't it? I can only imagine what she's told people about *us*." Lilly grimaced. "I'm doing my best just not to think about it."

"She wouldn't talk *about* you. She just likes talking *to* you. She's telling you stuff so you'll keep having lunch with her and she can tell people she's friends with a movie star. It's hardly unusual. I mean, look at me, running out of my house at a moment's notice to meet you for coffee."

Lilly laughed uncomfortably, not sure if I was kidding.

At that moment my coffee showed up. I slurped at it loudly, for the pierced waitress's benefit.

"Anyway, what else did Wang tell you?" I asked.

"Oh, not much more than that. The family was having terrible problems. They were considering divorce. The daughter was acting out, having problems in school, hanging with a fast crowd. That kind of thing."

"Audrey, she's the daughter, is kind of a lost soul," I said. "She has this horrible shaved and dyed hairdo that I'm sure she got just to torture her mother."

"They did a lot of torturing of each other, according to Herma," Lilly said. "Not a very easy relationship. Abigail had high expectations, and Audrey had a hard time fulfilling them, or something like that. Apparently Mooney and the girl didn't like each other, and that was a source of real tension in the marriage."

"High expectations? Sounds like every mother-daughter relationship I've ever heard of," I said.

"Not mine." Lilly sounded bitter. "My mother expected me to get pregnant at fifteen and spend my life living in a trailer park with six kids by six different men. She's sorely disappointed that I've exceeded her expectations."

"God, are our kids going to be sitting here in thirty years having this discussion about us?" I asked, imagining Ruby and the twins bemoaning our various flaws over latte or proton shakes or whatever they'll be drinking then.

"God forbid." Lilly shuddered. "Why didn't he just leave her? Why *kill* her?" she asked.

"Money. It must have been about money. She owned everything they had as her separate property. It's likely that he would have had to walk away from the marriage empty-handed."

"But I imagine that he must have hated her, too. Don't you think he would have had to, to murder her?"

"I wonder."

"It's always someone in the family, isn't it?"

"What do you mean?"

"It's always a family member who's the murderer."

"Usually. Or, if not family, then certainly someone the victim knew. Stranger-on-stranger crimes are much rarer."

"But that's what we're all afraid of. Isn't that ironic? We're so afraid of being killed by some serial killer but it's our loved ones we really should be afraid of."

I looked at Lilly for a minute, wondering what was inspiring these morbid thoughts. "Lilly, are you trying to tell me something? Have you murdered someone?"

She laughed. "Actually, you know what? There are only two people I can even imagining killing. Guess who?"

"Your agent?"

"No. Although that's an idea."

"The director of your last picture."

"Ouch. That stings."

"Sorry. So who?"

"Well, one is my ex-husband, obviously. The other is my mother." Lilly laughed grimly. "And instead of killing either of them I bought them each a house."

"You bought Archer a house?" I almost shouted.

"Community property bought Archer a house. And a boat. And two cars. And a share in Planet Hollywood and so on and so on and so on."

"Wow. You know what, Lilly? Maybe we should get married. I could use some extra cash."

"Very funny. Ha, ha, ha."

Suddenly I had a thought. "Hey, Lilly, are the twins still in preschool?"

"Yes. Next year they'll start kindergarten at Crossroads," she said proudly.

It occurred to me that I didn't even know where Amber and Jade went to school. "Where do they go now?"

"Temple Beth El," she said.

That stopped me in my tracks. Lilly Green, the personification of blond, Aryan womanhood, sent her kids to a Jewish school? She noticed my bemused expression.

"Archer's mother is Jewish," she explained. "And the girls didn't get in anywhere else. We applied pre-Oscar."

"Oh. Do you like it?"

"I love it. I love that the girls walk around the house singing "*Shabet shalom,* hey!" she warbled.

"*Sha*-bat."

"Right, right. *Shabat shalom,* hey! I have a terrific idea! Why don't I ask the principal if they still have slots available for next year?"

"No. No. That's okay." It probably sounds crazy, but Peter and I had never discussed the religion thing. We celebrated whatever holiday came around and just sort of assumed that things would work themselves out. I couldn't see asking him to send Ruby to a Jewish preschool. That would be like taking sides.

"Really, I don't mind. I'll ask her when I pick up the girls tomorrow."

"You'd better not. You know, the whole Jewish thing."

"Oh, don't be ridiculous. There are plenty of *goys* like me at the school. I'm going to ask her. It can't hurt."

We talked for a while longer about Daniel Mooney and about whether he'd plead guilty or go to trial. After we'd finished our coffees, Lilly offered me a ride home.

"No, I think I'll walk. I need the exercise."

It was only after she'd gone that I realized she'd left me with the check. Again.

16

OVER THE NEXT few weeks the newspapers were full of the tragedy of Abigail Hathaway and Daniel Mooney. The case was taken away from the Santa Monica D.A. and moved to downtown Los Angeles. Mooney was charged with first-degree murder, which carries the death penalty, and thus no possibility of bail. Audrey called a few more times, but we never got together. She told me that she had decided to finish out the school year before moving to New Jersey and was living in her house with her aunt. She seemed to have gotten over her first blush of giddiness at her stepfather's arrest, and expressed her eagerness to put the whole ugly business behind her. I agreed that that was probably a good idea, but secretly wondered if she ever would be able to put the loss of her mother behind her. Could anyone?

My pregnancy proceeded and I closed in on the final month, looking forward with mounting impatience to Isaac's arrival. I tried to spend as much time as possible with Ruby, preparing her as best I could for the upheaval the new baby would cause in all our lives.

One night, after putting Ruby to sleep and sending Peter off to work, I lay in bed, trying to fall asleep. I tossed and turned, or rather, I tried to toss but couldn't quite manage to heft my belly from one side of the bed to another. Finally, frustrated and hungry, I got up and made myself a peanut-butter-and-jelly sandwich. Recalling Peter's recent irritation at me for getting crumbs in the bed, I decided to eat in my office, and play on the computer for a while. I logged on, licked my fingers clean, and checked out what was happening on *Moms Online*. I lurked for a while in a chat room, but couldn't manage to work up any interest in the sore-nipple discussion.

I decided to check out how Nina Tiger was dealing with the arrest of her lover. I clicked over to Dejanews and plugged in her name. I soon tired of reading her vitriolic defenses of Mooney's innocence but, unfortunately, I wasn't tired enough to go to sleep. Bored, I typed in Daniel Mooney's screen names. As I had already read in tigress's correspondence, Coyote was the topic of much conversation among the polyamorous. Nobody had seemed to notice mchoman's absence from the newsgroup in which Mooney had participated using that alias, but boytoy2000 had been sorely missed by the more raunchy of his cyberpals. Because none of his buddies had linked him to Daniel Mooney, there was much speculation about where boytoy2000 had gone.

I input the last of Mooney's aliases, GRrrrL. That's when I got the shock of my life. GRrrrL, Mooney's female alter ego, had posted as recently as last night. Shaken, I called out for Peter. He came tearing into my office.

"Is it happening? Are you in labor?" he asked, almost hysterically.

"No. Look." I held a trembling finger out to the screen.

"Juliet! You have *got* to stop doing that to me. Look at what?"

"Dejanews has postings from GRrrrL, Daniel Mooney's alias, from last night."

Peter quickly scrolled down the screen.

"This is what our tax dollars are going for? Web access in prisons?" he asked, outraged.

"There is no Web access in the county jail. GRrrrL is posting from outside."

"Then there's got to be a mistake. Mooney's in jail. Dejanews must be wrong."

"They're not wrong. GRrrrL is posting."

Peter and I sat staring at the screen for a moment.

"I'm going to find GRrrrL," I said.

"How?"

"Watch."

I scrolled up and found the address of the newsgroup on which GRrrrL's most recent post had appeared. I clicked the "new message" box and posted the following message under the subject heading "GRrrrL sought":

GRrrrL—I want to talk to you. E-mail me and set up private chat.

"Why not just E-mail GRrrrL directly?" Peter asked.

"Because I want whoever's using the account to know just where I tracked GRrrrL down."

"Oh. Now what?" Peter asked.

"Now we wait," I said grimly.

We waited. We waited for two hours and heard nothing. Finally, exhausted and drained, we set the computer to download E-mail every half hour and went to bed. The next morning I leaped out of bed and rushed to the computer. At 6:30 A.M. I had received a message from GRrrrL. Fingers shaking, I opened it.

Private chat at 4:00 P.M. See you there!

The rest of the day passed in something of a blur. Ruby, sensing that I was preoccupied and tense, matched me mood for mood. When she wasn't whining she was throwing a tantrum or stomping around the house in a huff. Peter and I spent the day frantically trying to entertain her, but she had the attention span of a flea. No game was good enough, no toy fun enough. Finally, in desperation, Peter took her to our old standby, the Santa Monica Pier. We figured he'd tire her out on the carousel and rides. While they were gone I mostly paced around the house. Oprah distracted me for a few minutes but not long. Finally, at ten minutes to four, I heard Peter's car pull in the driveway.

I rushed to the front door and opened it in time for him to tiptoe in, carrying a sleeping Ruby in his arms. Walking as quietly as possible, he took her into her room, put her in her crib, and closed the door.

"Let's go," he said.

We went into my office, closed the door, logged on, and entered the chat room.

GRrrrl? Are you here?
Here I am. I know who you are.

I looked up at Peter, scared. "How does he know me?"

"I don't know. Is your tag line somewhere on your message?"

"No, just my E-mail address."

How do you know who I am? I wrote back.
Never mind. What do you want?

I paused for a moment. What did I want? To know who he was, I suppose.

Who are YOU? I typed.
GRrrrL.
No, who are you IRL?

"IRL?" Peter asked, reading over my shoulder.
"In real life."

Who do you think I am? GRrrrL asked me back.
This screen name belongs to Daniel Mooney.
Then I'm Daniel Mooney.
Daniel Mooney is in the county jail. He can't log on.
Poor Daniel. Locked in jail.

I looked up at Peter again. "What's going on here?" I asked.

He shook his head. "Juliet, what if GRrrrL placed the ad for the hired killer? What if Daniel Mooney didn't do it?"

The thought had crossed my mind at the same time. After all, the only hard evidence against Mooney was the ad. The rest was purely circumstantial. I decided to give it a shot.

Do you know who killed Abigail? I typed.
Daniel Mooney killed Abigail.
Is that true? Do you know that for a fact?
Do YOU know that for a fact? GRrrrL asked back.

Now GRrrrL was messing with me.

"Peter, maybe I should just ask him straight out."

"Go for it." He squeezed my shoulder and kissed my cheek. I took a deep breath and then started typing.

Did YOU kill Abigail?

There was a pause. Finally GRrrrL replied,

Did YOU?
No, I did not. You didn't answer my question. DID YOU KILL ABIGAIL
HATHAWAY?
Bye-bye, Juliet.

And GRrrrL was gone. Peter and I sat, staring at the computer screen
for a moment. I copied the text of our conversation into a file on my computer and sent it to print. As I clicked the print button, I had an epiphany.

"I know who that was."

"You do?" Peter asked doubtfully.

"Nina Tiger."

"His lover?"

"It's got to be her. Think about it. They have the same access provider.
All she'd have to do would be to log on as a guest and input the password
he uses for that alias. Who else would know his password? It has to be her."

"You don't know my password. Why would she know his?" Peter said.

"Gee, I don't know. Could it be, perhaps, Cthulhu?"

"Hey!" he shouted. "How did you know that?"

"Oh, please, Mr. Owns a First Edition of Every Book H. P. Lovecraft
Ever Wrote."

"I can't believe you."

"Could we get back to the issue at hand?"

"I can't *believe* you."

"Peter!"

"Okay, okay. How would Nina Tiger have known who you are?"

"She must have compared notes with Mooney. I introduced myself to
him, and he probably told her about me. How many pregnant women with
red hair could have been following them around? She put two and two
together and came up with me."

"Juliet?"

"What?"

"What are you talking about?"

Then I remembered that I hadn't mentioned my run-in with tigress.
With a huge amount of trepidation, I told him about it. To Peter's credit,
he managed to suppress whatever anger I knew he must have felt. He looked
at me horrified and then seemed to make a decision not to discuss it.

"Okay, so it's Nina Tiger. So what?" he said.

I thought. True, so what? So what if she was logging on as her imprisoned lover? It was weird, but it didn't mean anything. Then I realized something.

"She never answered my question."

"What?"

"She never said she didn't kill Abigail."

17

CALLED DETECTIVE CARSWELL and left another of my famous messages for him. This time I asked for and received his fax number and faxed over a copy of my chat with GRrrrL. That would make him call back.

"Peter?" I said.

"What?"

"If tigress killed Abigail, that means that Daniel Mooney didn't."

"Unless they were in it together."

"Either way, the murderer is still out there, and so is Audrey." I began to pace nervously. "I wish that detective would call me back."

"Juliet, there's no reason to think that Audrey is in any danger. Tigress hasn't done anything to her yet. Why would she start now?"

"I suppose. God, I wish Carswell would call me."

I called the station house again, telling the woman who took my call that it was an emergency. Something about the tone of my voice must have convinced her how serious I was. She put me on hold. Within a couple of minutes I was talking to Detective Carswell.

I apprised the detective of my online conversation with GRrrrL and explained why I thought that Nina Tiger was the only person who could have had access to Daniel Mooney's alias and password. Sounding somewhat dubious, he asked me to explain how I'd tracked GRrrrL down. After a couple of frustrating minutes trying to explain Dejanews to a man who just barely understood the concept of E-mail, I asked him to please come over so I could show him what I was talking about. He agreed. He and his young sidekick showed up at our door half an hour later.

I led the police officers directly to my computer, and I logged on and showed them what I'd found.

The young cop looked at Carswell. "Maybe we should talk to Ms. Tiger," he said.

"We'd planned on interviewing her anyway. She's on the witness list," Carswell said, nodding his head.

The younger officer borrowed my phone and called the station house. Eavesdropping, I heard him ask for a DMV address on Nina Tiger.

"Is that all you have?" he said into the receiver.

He covered the receiver with his hand and spoke to Carswell. "Last known address is in Santa Barbara."

"She lives here, in Venice," I interrupted. "Remember, I told you that I followed her?"

He turned back to the phone. "Check for a Venice address." He waited a moment and then replied, "Okay, we'll get it from the witness."

"What's going on?" Carswell asked.

"No Venice address listed."

"Ms. Applebaum," Carswell asked me, "do you remember the address of her apartment in Venice?"

"It was on Rose Street," I said. "A fourplex."

"The house number?" he asked.

I racked my brain. "I'm sorry. I don't remember. It was in the middle of the block. Mediterranean. Kind of like all the others on that block."

"Would you know it if you saw it?"

"I think so. And I'd definitely recognize her car."

I DROVE WITH the detectives in their unmarked car, an anonymous blue, late-model American sedan, to Venice. Peter had been loath to let me go, but I had insisted. We drove onto the block, and I directed Carswell and the young detective to Nina Tiger's apartment building. I pointed out the Mustang convertible parked at the curb.

"That's her car," I said.

"Now, you wait right here, Ms. Applebaum," the young detective said.

"Don't move," Carswell reiterated.

I promised not to, and settled more comfortably in the backseat of the car, propping my feet up. I watched them head off up the path and imagined tigress's face when she opened the door to them.

I hadn't gotten very far in my fantasy when I noticed the door to the building open. With a flash of red hair and long legs, Nina Tiger strode down the path toward her car. They must have missed her!

For a moment I puzzled over what to do. I was under strict orders not to move. On the other hand, no way was I going to let her get away. She might have been on her way to Audrey's house! I wrenched the car door open, leaned my head out, and shouted.

"YO! Tigress!"

She stopped dead in her tracks and looked around her, finally spotting me. Meanwhile, I was having problems getting myself out of the car. I gave a final heave and staggered out onto the sidewalk. She looked at me blankly for a minute, and then I could see a flash of recognition cross her face.

"My mailbox!" she said, and ran over to me, hands on her hips. "Who are you? Why are you calling me 'tigress'? Are you on one of my lists? What's your name?"

With the final question she reached me and, sticking a finger out, poked me in the chest. Hard.

"Hey! Watch it!" I said, batting away her hand.

"No! *You* watch it." She pushed me. I staggered back and swayed, scrambling with my feet to keep from falling. At that moment I heard a voice shout, "Police, put your hands up!"

"What the hell?" tigress said, turning around and spotting the detectives running from the house. "Are you out of your goddamn minds?" she screeched. "This bitch is assaulting me!"

"I am not!" I said indignantly. "She pushed me!"

"She broke into my mailbox!"

"Well, yeah, but not today!"

By then the detectives had reached us. Carswell grabbed tigress by the arm and dragged her away from me. The young guy helped me steady myself.

"Are you okay, Ms. Applebaum?" he asked.

"You know her? What's going on here? Is she a cop?" Nina yelled.

Carswell led her a few feet away and asked calmly, "Are you Nina Tiger?"

"Yeah. So what? Am I under arrest?"

"I have some questions for you, Miss Tiger. Shall we continue this inside?"

"No way you are coming into my apartment!" she said with a snarl.

"Shall we continue this at the station house?"

She shrugged off his hand, angrily. "Look, if this is about Abigail Hathaway, I had nothing to do with that. I was in Santa Barbara, at my mother's house. Three of her bridge partners saw me there. You can call them all!"

Detective Carswell paused for a minute and then said, "We simply have a number of questions for you. Nothing serious. Why don't we go upstairs and discuss it."

"Fine." She stormed up the path to her front door.

Carswell looked at the younger detective and said, "Take Ms. Applebaum home and then come get me. ASAP." He followed tigress into the house.

THE DETECTIVE DROPPED me off at home, and I walked in, shouting out, "I'm home!"

"How'd it go?" asked Peter.

"She has an alibi."

"Oh. Sorry."

"She could have hired someone to kill Abigail," I said, grasping at straws.

"I guess so. The police will figure it out," Peter said.

"Yeah, I suppose they will. Is Ruby still asleep?"

"I guess so."

"You guess so? It's late. We'd better wake her up."

I walked into Ruby's room and gently shook her awake. She responded by squawking in outrage and promptly bursting into tears. I tried pulling out her Tickle-Me-Elmo. The screaming continued. I grabbed her Madeline doll. No effect. Finally, desperate, I said, "Hey, Peanut, want to go visit the Barbie website?"

"No. I hate Barbie."

"You do not, Ruby. You have twenty Barbies. You *love* Barbie. Let's go visit the website. It'll be fun, I promise."

I plopped Ruby on the chair at my desk and logged on. I quickly found the Barbie website, and set Ruby up selecting the accessory set for her personalized "Friend of Barbie" doll.

I leaned against my desk, too tired to stand but too lazy to get another chair. Ruby looked so sweet, her curls tumbling into her eyes, her face screwed up with concentration. I wondered, for the thousandth time, how she was going to tolerate another baby in the house. This child was so used to being the center of attention, the queen of the castle. The birth of a prince was going to be quite a shock.

Ruby interrupted my reverie. "Mommy, the computer said 'You've got mail.'"

"Oh, that means an E-mail came in. Want to help me get it?"

"Yeah!"

"Move the mouse over to the little mailbox symbol."

She followed my instructions.

"Now click twice."

She did.

It was a piece of junk E-mail—spam. I showed Ruby how to delete it and then helped her click back over to Barbie. And then, watching her dress Barbie in a fuchsia boa and purple pedal pushers, I figured it out. I figured out who GRrrrL was.

18

I'M NOT SURE why I did what I did next. In hindsight, it was definitely an idiotic move. But, at the time, I really didn't think I was putting myself in harm's way. I felt pretty confident that I was right, but I knew that after the tigress fiasco the Santa Monica Police Department wasn't going to accompany me on any more detective expeditions. I certainly wasn't going to ask Peter to come with me, as that would have meant bringing Ruby along, too. So I told my husband that I had to go out, making up an excuse about going to the drugstore to buy pads for when I came home from the hospital. He was only too glad to watch the baby, relieved that I hadn't sent him off to buy feminine hygiene products.

I drove across town on the freeway and up the Pacific Coast Highway to Santa Monica Canyon. I was going very fast, and it's a miracle I wasn't pulled over for speeding. Still, it felt like hours before I finally pulled up in front of Abigail Hathaway's Tudor house. I rammed the car into park and, slamming the door behind me, ran up the path. I rang the bell and, too impatient to wait, pounded on the door.

After a moment or two, Audrey opened it. She looked the same as always, except she'd had half her hair shaved off again and the rest redyed a sapphire blue. She sported a new stud in her nose, a stone that matched her hair. She smiled nervously when she saw me. "Hi, Juliet! What's going on? You look . . ." She didn't finish the sentence.

I looked at my reflection in the long, narrow window next to the front door. I was wearing my usual uniform of leggings and shirt, but a length of thigh was peeping out a torn seam. I hadn't even noticed. My hair was dragged off my face with a rubber band, and I wore not the slightest trace of makeup.

"Are you okay?" Audrey asked me.

"We need to talk. Is your aunt home?"

"No, she just left for the grocery store. Talk about what?" She held the door halfway closed.

"Let me in, Audrey." I pushed against the door.

She held it against my hand.

"What's going on, Juliet? You looked freaked."

"Let me in *now*." I jerked the door open and pushed by her.

"Fine, come in. What's up with you?" she asked. She sounded angry but also a little nervous.

"I know about GRrrrL, Audrey," I said, standing in the hall.

"Who? What girl?"

"Don't lie to me, Audrey. I know that you're using your stepfather's computer and that your screen name is GRrrrL."

"It is *not* his computer. My mom bought it. It's a family computer. I'm perfectly entitled to use it. And anyway, I'm not even using that computer. I'm using my mom's laptop. One of the stupid teachers from her stupid school dropped it off a couple of days ago."

She stalked off into the living room and shut the door after herself. I hustled in behind her and opened it to find her bent over her mother's desk. She slammed shut a drawer as I walked in. Tossing her half-bald head, Audrey walked over to the couch and sat down. She held her chin high and crossed her legs primly. I could see the pulse beating in her throat.

"So you figured out my screen name. So what? What does that make you, some kind of genius? I, like, basically told you it was me."

I sat down next to her. She still looked so vulnerable to me, so young despite her pathetic attempts at "cool."

"Audrey, have you told the police about your screen name?" I asked her.

She looked at me incredulously. "No. Why should I? It's none of their business." She started picking at a cuticle on her right thumbnail. A bead of bright red blood appeared. She stuck her finger in her mouth and sucked on it, like a baby.

"Audrey, it is their business. You know that." Was she really as obtuse as she was pretending to be? "Listen to me. You have to tell the police, because you can be sure Daniel will."

"Oh, please, like they could care less about my screen name."

"Audrey, the police confiscated Daniel's computer, didn't they?"

"Yeah, that's why I had to wait like a week to get online. I couldn't do anything until Maggie suddenly remembered that she'd borrowed my mom's computer and brought it back to me. I'm surprised the bitch didn't just keep it."

I started to defend the nursery school teacher but then shook my head. I wasn't going to let Audrey distract me. I got back to the point. "Doesn't the fact that they took Daniel's computer make you think that they might be interested in whatever information you might have about his E-mail accounts?"

Audrey rolled her eyes at me. "GRrrrL isn't the one who tried to find someone to kill my mother. It was his faggot screen name 'boytoy2000' that did that."

She shouldn't have known about the ad Mooney had placed for the hired killer. I hadn't told her, it hadn't been in the papers, and there was no reason in the world for the police or the DA to give her that kind of information. There was only one way for her to know about the ad, only one possible reason for her to have that kind of information.

"And anyway, he didn't even hire someone to kill her. He did it himself, driving *her* car," she continued.

I sat there on the couch, next to Abigail Hathaway's teenage daughter, and felt sickened that what I had feared was actually true. She wasn't just GRrrrl; she was also the person who placed the ad on the bulletin board. And if she'd placed the ad, I could be sure that she was the person who killed Abigail.

I rested my hands on my belly and felt the little boy swimming in the warmth of my body. I wondered how it was possible to spend so much energy, love, and tenderness creating a creature who could one day hate you enough to kill you. I imagined Abigail Hathaway, stretched large with the shape of her daughter, dreaming a life for her just as I dreamed one for Isaac now and had for Ruby before him. Then I imagined Abigail's face as she was murdered. Did she see Audrey driving the car? At the moment of her death, did Abigail know that it was the baby she had borne and nurtured and, surely, loved who was bearing down on the accelerator pedal?

"Juliet?" Audrey said.

I couldn't answer.

"Juliet? Okay, fine, I'll tell the cops. Okay? Juliet?" Audrey's tone was now sweet and wheedling. I turned to her and felt strangely, absurdly unafraid of this violent child. I'd sat next to many violent criminals, people who'd done the same or even worse than Audrey, and never been afraid. My clients knew that they could trust me to have their interests at heart, and for that reason they never tried to hurt me. Never. So often I was the only one who saw the tough gang-banger put his head into his hands and cry for his mother. So often I was the shoulder the heroin-using bank robber leaned on while he confessed the horrors the white powder had wrought on his life. I was used to scared people who did scary things. I was used to them, and I wasn't afraid. I reached for the girl's hand.

"Honey, what happened? Tell me why you did it." Tears filled my eyes as I stared into hers. There had to be some reason, some hideous story of abuse and betrayal that would make sense of Audrey's horrifying deed.

The girl blanched and jerked her hand away from mine.

"What are you talking about?" She got up and walked quickly over to her mother's desk, turning away from me.

"Audrey, please, you can tell me about it. You can trust me," I begged to her back.

She spun around. "You think you know everything, don't you?" she screamed, suddenly and harshly.

"No, no, I don't. I know that something must have happened. You can tell me, Audrey. You can trust me. I care about you."

"You think it's so damn easy being Madame Perfect Mother's screwed-up daughter?" She was crying now, dry, hacking sobs that made her voice crack and break. Words poured from her in a torrent. "You all think that she was so great, but she wasn't. She was a nightmare! A nightmare! Nothing I ever did was good enough. Nothing! She loved every single one of those little brats in her school more than she ever loved me." She wiped at her nose, angrily, drawing a smear of tears and snot across her cheek. "I hated her!"

Whatever she had done, this child was in terrible pain. Whatever had made her do it, she really was nothing more than a poor, scared child.

I walked over to her, slowly, and reached my arms out for her. She fell against me, awkwardly because of the protrusion of my stomach, and rested her head on my shoulder. Sobbing heavily, she continued, "I hated her. So much. And she hated me. She did. I swear she did. They both did. They just hated me so much."

"Oh, honey." I stroked her hair.

"She married Daniel like fifteen minutes after my daddy died. She couldn't *wait* to marry him. And then they didn't want me. They never wanted me. Daniel used to hit me, you know that? He'd smack me and she'd stand right there and let him."

"It's going to be all right. I'll help you."

She stood up straight and looked at me in surprise.

"You will?"

"Of course I will. I'll call a really good lawyer right now. And I'll go with you to the police. There are a bunch of defenses we can use. We'll figure something out." I wasn't so sure that we could, but now wasn't the time to bring up my doubts about the abused-child defense.

Audrey looked at me, horror-struck. "What are you talking about? I'm not going to the police." She jerked away.

"You have to, Audrey. There's no other way. They'll figure it out somehow, and it'll be worse for you if they come to you instead of you going to them."

"I'm not going to the police!" She was screaming again, and her face had turned a deep, blotchy red.

"Honey, calm down. I know you're scared, but I'll be here. I promise I'll help you." I leaned over to her, reaching my arms out again.

Audrey looked at me, her face contorted with rage.

"No!" She screamed and ran around to the other side of the desk. Before I could follow, she wrenched open a drawer, the same one I had seen her close when I had first walked through the door. She reached in and took something out. For some reason, it took me a few seconds to realize what she was pointing at me. Maybe I couldn't figure out what it was because I just couldn't believe it. Her hand was shaking, and the little silver pistol jerked in her fist.

Before I even registered that she was holding a gun, I felt a thud in the side of my right thigh. I didn't hurt at first, but the force spun me around, and my leg collapsed under me. I fell to the ground. I did my best to break my fall, but I landed on my stomach, hard. Suddenly the pain in my thigh was unbearable, hot and sharp. My entire leg felt leaden and useless. I rolled onto my left side and, crying, tried to sit up. I felt like my leg was on fire and that, at the same time, it belonged to someone else—I couldn't make it move. I reached my hands down and covered what felt like the fiery center of the pain, and watched as blood seeped through my fingers.

It looked thick and viscous, and I felt faint. I lay back down again, closing my eyes. I thought of Isaac and began to whimper. I reached my arms around my stomach, almost as if I were reassuring myself that he was still there.

"Juliet." Audrey's voice wasn't angry anymore, it was small and quiet, or maybe that was because it sounded far away to me, like I was standing at one end of a long tunnel and she was at the other. I opened my eyes. She stood over me.

"I didn't want to hurt you," she said. I saw that she was crying again.

"Okay," I murmured, terrified that she was going to shoot again, but unable to get up or even move.

"It's just your leg. It's not such a big deal."

"Okay." That seemed to be all I could say.

"I'm going to go away. You wait ten minutes and then you can go."

"Okay," I said again, but she had already run from the room. I lay there, listening, as Audrey ran around the house for a few minutes. I heard her pound up the stairs and then down, a moment or two later. Finally, the front door slammed and an automobile engine started up.

I closed my eyes again, repeating her words to myself. "It's just my leg. The baby is fine. It's just my leg. Isaac is fine." Then I felt a familiar tightening across my belly. The contraction seemed to go on forever. The combination of that familiar but nonetheless awful pain and the new and terrible one in my leg were too much for me to bear. I tried to breathe through the contraction like I'd been taught, but every time I felt myself climbing on top of it, the agony in my leg sent me crashing back down. I lay on the floor of Abigail Hathaway's living room, crying with great, racking sobs. Finally, the contraction ebbed and stopped. I gave another small moan, this time of relief. My relief was short-lived, however, because the ache in my leg started to overwhelm me again. I realized that I might not have a lot of time before the next contraction came. I couldn't stand much more of these competing agonies. Using every ounce of strength I could summon, and keeping before me the vision of baby Isaac desperately trying to get out of his wounded mother's body, I bent my left leg and rolled over onto my left side. Keeping as much of my weight on my hands as I could, I slowly began pushing up off the floor. Every movement of my right leg brought another wave of pain crashing over me. I kept it as still as I could, and slowly, impossibly slowly, I dragged myself, using my hands and my left leg and pulling my useless limb behind me, over to the couch where my purse lay. I reached up for my purse, grabbed it, and collapsed onto the floor next to the sofa. I dug frantically for my cell phone. Then I dialed 911 and waited. Nothing happened. I began crying again, this time in frustration, and only a minute later realized that I'd forgotten to press "send." I jammed my finger onto the button and, wonderfully, heard the sound of the ringing. I was on hold for a while, how long I don't know, because I had a contraction during the wait. I surfaced from the haze of pain to hear a voice.

"What is your emergency? What is your emergency?"

"Help me. I've been shot and I'm in labor."

"Are you having a baby, ma'am?"

"Yes, but I'm also shot. My leg. It's bleeding."

I felt another contraction coming impossibly quickly behind the last and had time only to tell the operator Abigail Hathaway's address before I had to put my head down and fall into the pain.

The contractions seemed to be coming one right on top of another. After the next one, I held the phone in my shaking hand and dialed home. I began weeping with frustration when the answering machine picked up.

I have no idea what I said into the machine. I know I was hysterical with pain and fear, and I'm sure I absolutely terrified my husband. It was only after I'd hung up the phone that I realized that he would probably play the message in front of Ruby. I was crying too hard to call again. Hearing another hysterical message would only scare them more.

The wait for the ambulance was interminable. After a couple more contractions, during which I felt like I was drowning under waves of pain, I began dragging myself out of the living room and toward the front door. I turned once to look behind me at the beautiful Oriental runner in the hall and remembered how I'd been so afraid of ruining this same carpet that I'd cleaned up lasagna sauce with my shirt. Now I was leaving an indelible trail of blood.

I reached the front door just as the ambulance and police arrived. Reaching up to open it, I promptly collapsed into the arms of a man in a firefighter's black rubber coat. He had warm, brown eyes and sandy hair and looked exactly like the kind of person who could protect you from fires, earthquakes, and even homicidal teenagers. Holding me in his arms, he carefully eased me down onto the floor in the hall.

"Don't worry, ma'am. We're here. It's going to be all right."

I smiled at him and closed my eyes in relief. I felt another contraction begin, and barely noticed the police officers who were stepping over me and pounding into the house.

When I surfaced from the contraction, I found myself lying on a stretcher, the leg of my tights torn off above my thigh, and my rescuer leaning over me, his hands pressing a bandage onto my wound. He smiled reassuringly, and I closed my eyes again.

"Ma'am. Ma'am," a voice said urgently.

I opened my eyes to see a police officer bent over me.

"Do you know who shot you, ma'am?" he asked.

I just had time before the next contraction to tell the officer that Audrey Hathaway was responsible for my injury. I asked him to call Detective Carswell and tell him that Audrey had confessed to murdering Abigail Hathaway. Another contraction hit as I finished, and I don't remember anything about his response.

The next thing I knew, I was rolling through a white hallway. I saw faces leaning over me and heard a woman's voice asking me, over and over again,

"Mrs. Applebaum? Can you hear me? How far along are you, Mrs. Applebaum? Can you hear me?"

"Thirty-six weeks," I said. "It's too soon. The baby's coming too soon."

"It's all right, Mrs. Applebaum, you'll be just fine. Can you remember your home phone number? What's your home phone number, Mrs. Applebaum?"

I told her the number and then felt them hoist me onto a bed. I felt a sharp sting in my left arm and then, blessedly, nothing for a little while.

I awoke to hear the sound of voices.

"The bullet went clean through, and we've cleaned and sewed the wounds. The bleeding has stopped, and I don't think there's any collateral damage we need to worry about. The question is, do we allow labor to proceed, or do we do a crash C-section right now?"

"I'd like to get the baby out as soon as possible. The monitor is showing unfocused contractions two to four minutes apart. She's only two centimeters dilated. It could be hours before this baby shows up, and I don't like the idea of putting her through a long labor after the trauma of a GSW."

"No, no reason to do that. Anyway, there's evidence of a prior section, so we may as well go ahead with this one."

"*No!*" I shouted.

The two doctors looked down at me in surprise. One was an older woman and another a boy of about twelve. At least that's what it looked like.

"I'm having a vaginal birth," I said. "Call my midwife, Dorothy Horne. I'm having a VBAC."

They looked at me doubtfully. "Mrs. Applebaum, you've just been shot. Our primary concern is your health and that of your baby. You should not be going through labor right now."

"Look, I've been doing goddamn prenatal Yoga for six months so that I'd be in shape for a vaginal birth. I've read every goddamn book on vaginal birth after cesarean ever written. I'm not having a goddamn C-section. Anyway, I'm fine. I feel fine." And I did; I was in no pain.

"That's the lidocaine. We've given you a painkiller."

"It's working. So I can do this. Call my husband, call my midwife, and get me to labor and delivery." With that, I felt another contraction starting. The anesthetic had taken the edge off the pain, and this contraction was much more manageable. I breathed my way through it, making an ostentatious show of my Lamaze competence for the doctors who seemed so eager to cut me. They watched me, then looked at each other.

"Take her up to L&D. Let them decide," the woman said, snapping shut the medical chart she held and walking away.

Within minutes I found myself in an elevator and on my way to the maternity ward. I guess my gunshot precluded them from putting me in one of those lovely bedroomlike delivery rooms. I found myself in a decidedly medical setting, strapped to the fetal monitor, and watched over by two nurses and a doctor. The doctor was a man, about my age, who was going prematurely bald. He looked like a nice guy, like the kind of guy you'd want to be your doctor.

"We're going to prep you for a section, Mrs. Applebaum," he said in a soft but firm voice.

"I want a VBAC."

"I'm afraid a vaginal birth after cesarean isn't a good idea, given your injury."

"How long have I been here?"

He looked at my chart. "About two hours."

"Is the baby okay?" I asked.

"It's fine. The fetal monitor shows a nice, steady heartbeat."

"Is my leg okay?"

"Yes, it's fine. The bullet passed cleanly through, and both the entrance and exit wounds have been cleaned and stitched. You're on IV antibiotics now in case of infection."

"So if I'm fine, and the baby's fine, how come I can't at least wait until my husband and my midwife show up?"

The doctor looked down at me and finally smiled. "I'll tell you what. We'll put in an internal fetal monitor, and if the baby remains in good condition, we'll give you another hour before we do the surgery. That should give your husband time to get here." He patted me on the foot and turned to leave. At that moment, Peter rushed into the room. As soon as I saw him, I burst into hysterical tears.

Peter crossed the room in two huge steps, leaned over the bed, and scooped as much of me as he could reach into his arms. I couldn't seem to stop crying as I nestled my head into his chest. Suddenly I felt a hot flash as he inadvertently brushed against my right leg.

"Ow! My leg!" I hollered.

"Oh, no," he said, dropping me like a hot potato. "What hurts? What did I do? Oh, God, Juliet. What happened?" I could swear he was crying, too.

"It's just my leg. My thigh. She shot me. Audrey shot me." Then another contraction began and I couldn't speak anymore.

I surfaced to hear Peter slowly murmuring my name. I felt his fingers in my hair, gently rubbing my scalp.

"It's over," I said.

"I know," he whispered. "I can see it on the monitor."

"How did you find me?" I asked. "Where am I? This isn't Cedars Sinai." I'd planned on delivering my baby at the plush hospital to the stars.

"You're in Santa Monica Hospital," a voice interrupted. I turned to see a nurse dressed in pink surgical scrubs standing on the other side of the bed, fiddling with the monitor. "The anesthetist will be here in a moment to put in your epidural."

"I don't want an epidural," I said angrily. "I'm having natural childbirth."

Just then another contraction hit me. In the middle of it I turned to the nurse and said through gritted teeth, "Get that goddamn doctor in here right now. I want that goddamn epidural right now."

She smiled and left the room. Within twenty minutes I had a tube the size of a single hair dripping blessed pain relief directly into my spine. It put me into the most wonderful, magical pain-free mood.

I turned to look at Peter and smiled.

"It's working," I said.

"Good." He smiled back.

"So now tell me how you found me."

Peter told me how he and Ruby had come home about an hour after I'd called. Ruby had gone straight to her room to find her Barbies, and, thankfully, had not heard my phone message. Peter had immediately called 911. The emergency operator directed him to the Santa Monica police dispatcher and from there to the fire department. Within fifteen minutes he had tracked me to Santa Monica Hospital.

"Where's Ruby?" I asked, suddenly worried.

"At Stacy's. That reminds me: Stacy and Lilly both left messages on the machine. Lilly said that there's a space for Ruby at Beth El preschool. And Stacy said that a colleague of hers at the agency sits on the board of a nursery school called Robin's Nest . . . or was it Bluebird's Nest? . . . something's nest. Anyway, a kid is moving to Europe or New York or somewhere and there's a space for Ruby for next year."

"Wow. Two schools. An embarrassment of riches," I said.

"Should we go visit them?" Peter asked.

"You know what?" I said. "Let's just toss a coin. I don't think I have the energy for more than that."

Peter smiled. "How 'bout we just send her to the Jewish school?"

"Really?" I asked. "That won't make you uncomfortable?"

"Please. Of course not," he said. "It'll be nice. I'll learn all about Hanukkah and . . . what's that one where you eat in the hut?"

"Succot."

"Yeah, all those holidays. It'll be great. I'll call the school tomorrow."

"Thanks, sweetie," I said. Meaning thanks for calling. Thanks for letting Ruby go to a Jewish school. Thanks for finding me at the hospital. Thanks for marrying me.

"Let's call Stacy and let her know I'm okay. She's probably totally freaking out."

Peter picked up the phone. "What's her number?" he asked me. I told him and lay back on the bed, idly watching the fetal monitor.

"I'm having another contraction," I told him.

He put his hand over the receiver. "Can you feel it?"

"No. I can see it on the display."

"Hi. It's Peter," he said into the phone. "She's fine. Long story, but everything's fine now." He turned to me. "Do you have the energy to talk to Ruby?"

I grabbed the receiver out of his hand.

"Ruby? Rubes? Baby girl?"

"Hi, Mama." She sounded so tiny and sweet.

"Hi, honey."

"Are you in the hostible?"

"Yes. I'm in the hospital, having Isaac."

"Can I come, too?"

"Not right now, sweetie. But you can come tomorrow. How 'bout that?"

"Okay. Bye-bye."

"Wait! Ruby, wait!" But she was gone.

"She hung up on me," I said, handing the receiver to Peter.

The door swung open and Dorothy walked into the room, dressed in scrubs.

"Hello, folks," she said in her soft voice with its touch of East Texas twang.

"Hi." I said. "I've been shot."

She smiled at me and walked over to the fetal monitor. "So I hear." She picked up the strip and looked at it carefully.

"I've been talking to the doctor."

"And?" Peter asked, obviously worried.

"And I think this birth's not going to be exactly what you had in mind," she said.

"No kidding," I answered.

"You know, Juliet, Peter, they never go exactly as we plan. Every birth is a surprise to me. Some more than others." She sat down next to me on the bed and took my good hand in hers. "I know how much you wanted a VBAC, but I'm afraid that's not the best idea right now."

"Why not?" I asked, close to tears. "I'm fine. I don't feel anything. My leg is fine. The baby's fine. Isn't he?"

"You've lost some blood, Juliet. Not a lot, but enough to make you weaker. Isaac's doing okay, but he's not as strong as we would like. You know I wouldn't be saying this if I didn't think it was for the best, but I think it's time to get Isaac out of you and into this world."

Peter and I looked at each other.

"Your call, sweetie," he said, and kissed me softly on the forehead.

"Okay," I said. "Let's do the surgery."

19

ONCE I'D AGREED to the C-section, things went very quickly. I was shaved, swabbed with Betadine, and wheeled into the operating room in just a few minutes. Isaac Applebaum Wyeth made his entry into the world not long afterward. He was a little guy—only five pounds, four ounces—but considering that he was a full four weeks premature, the doctors were pretty happy about his size. They didn't even make him stay in the neonatal nursery that first night. They kept him for a few hours, but then let him come to my room. I don't remember much about the next couple of days. I was more tired than I'd ever been in my life, and when I wasn't nursing the baby, I was sound asleep. Luckily, Isaac was a quiet baby at first—he pretty much slept and ate for those first few days. He was probably stoned on all the various painkillers he was taking in through my breast milk, but I was just happy to be getting rest.

At some point, after the surgery, Detective Carswell came by, carrying, strangely enough, a blue, stuffed alligator. He stood awkwardly in the doorway and said, to Peter, "This is for you. I mean, for the baby. Is she strong enough to talk?"

"I'm fine," I said. "They pumped me full of morphine and I'm feeling absolutely splendid. Itchy, but splendid." I scratched my arm. One of morphine's more unpleasant side effects is that it makes you feel like you've been attacked by hordes of mosquitoes. The pain relief was worth it, however.

"Can you tell me what happened?" he asked.

I told him the story of how Audrey had shot me.

"You know, when police officers are in their last trimester of pregnancy, we pull them off the street. We don't send them out to get themselves shot," Carswell said.

"Lucky pregnant police officers," I said, gingerly shifting my thigh.

Carswell snapped his notebook shut. "You are one difficult lady," he said.

"No kidding," Peter interrupted.

"I may be difficult, but if it weren't for me you'd still be looking for the driver who left the scene of an accident," I said.

"I'm sure we would have ultimately come to the correct conclusions," Carswell said, not sounding sure at all.

He paused.

"Thank you," he said, and leaned over to pat me on the foot. He missed, and stroked the bed instead, but hey, it's the thought that counts.

After he left, Peter asked me, "I wonder if they'll find Audrey."

"They will. They almost always do," I said, and shut my eyes.

I was right. Audrey was arrested after using her mother's credit card to fill up her tank at a gas station in Oakland. I considered getting in touch with her after her arrest, but something held me back. I don't know, maybe it was that she had lied to me, manipulated me, and shot me. But I asked a friend, a very good criminal defense lawyer, to call her, and Audrey ended up hiring him. Luckily for her, she wasn't tried as an adult, and was instead allowed to plead guilty in juvenile court. She was sentenced to spend the years until her twenty-fifth birthday in the custody of the California Youth Authority.

Daniel Mooney was released from jail and promptly brought an unsuccessful malicious-prosecution suit against the city of Los Angeles. I wasn't surprised to hear that he also ended up in protracted litigation with the trustees of Abigail Hathaway's estate. Seems he felt that since Audrey was barred by California law from benefiting from murdering her mother by inheriting her millions, all the money should go to him.

Strangely enough, while I never spoke to or saw him again, I did end up hearing from Nina Tiger. She E-mailed me more or less to say no hard feelings and to ask to hear my "side of the drama." She was writing a memoir about the Hathaway murder titled, quite grotesquely, I thought, *From the Loins of a Closed Mind*. I politely declined to participate. I've never seen the book in bookstores and am grateful that the publishing gods were wise enough to keep that particular family saga out of print. So far.

Peter and I weren't so lucky with Bruce LeCrone. Not long after the events surrounding the Hathaway murder, the studio executive ended up losing his job at Parnassus in the most Hollywood of fashions. He was phased out of his executive position, set up in a luxurious office suite on the studio's lot, and given a multimillion-dollar production deal. I like to think that his calling a pregnant woman a disgusting cow in front of two-thirds of the Hollywood establishment and the television cameras of *Entertainment Tonight* had something to do with it, but I doubt it. More likely it was the box office routs of Parnassus' last few pictures that did him in. Before he left the studio he did manage, however, to tank a project of Peter's that came across his desk. It didn't end up being that big a deal, however. Paramount optioned *Ninja Zombies* and it sat around in development for a while, earning Peter a nice chunk of change and the revilement of every parent watchdog group that got hold of the script.

On my second day in the hospital, Peter brought Ruby to visit me. Her eyes grew wide as she walked in and saw me lying in bed. At first she seemed scared to come near me, but, Ruby being Ruby, she soon got over her shyness and within a few minutes was curled up next to me in bed, describing all the things she'd done with Stacy and her kids over the past few days.

I'd had the nurses take Isaac to the nursery so I could be with Ruby alone for a bit, but they soon brought him back for a feed. Ruby watched in uncharacteristic silence as the baby nursed. Finally, she turned to me and announced, derisively, "That baby is too little. He can't play anything."

Peter and I laughed. "That's true, Sweet Petunia," I said. "But you know what?"

"What?"

"He'll grow pretty soon, and I bet his most favorite thing to do will be to play games with his wonderful big sister."

"You mean me?"

"I mean you."

She looked at Isaac suspiciously.

"Okay, big sister," Peter interrupted. "Time to go home and let Mommy sleep."

"Okay," she said, and skipped over to plant a kiss on my cheek. "Bye-bye, Mommy."

"Bye, honey. I love you."

"I love you, too."

Peter bent down over the bed and softly kissed me on the lips.

"I'm proud of you, honey."

"For almost getting myself killed?" I asked.

"For figuring out that Audrey did it, for *not* getting yourself killed, and for giving birth to a wonderful baby boy."

My eyes welled up with postpartum tears, and I kissed him back.

After they left, I lay thinking about Ruby for a while. It seemed to me that my ambivalence about being home with her had so overwhelmed me that I couldn't simply relax and enjoy her. I had left work to be with my child and ended up resenting her for it. Surely she already sensed this; how long would it be before she ended up mirroring it? While I was pretty sure that Ruby would never do anything like the awful thing that Audrey had done, I realized that I had, like Ebenezer Scrooge, been given a glimpse of Christmas future, and an opportunity to change things before it was too late. Isaac gave a squawk and I leaned over his bassinet, thinking that I was going to have to figure out some way to be a good mother without losing myself in the process. But first I was going to have to figure out a way to talk one of the nurses into changing that stinky diaper.

THE BIG NAP

For Michael, Sophie, and Zeke

AUTHOR'S NOTE

For helping me to understand the Hasidic community I thank Karen Zivan, Alex Novack, and the incomparable Esther Strauss. All mistakes are most definitely my own. For medical information I thank Dr. Dean Schillinger. I am eternally grateful to Mary Evans and to my husband, Michael Chabon, without whom nothing is possible.

1

I PROBABLY WASN'T THE first woman who had ever opened the door to the FedEx man wearing nothing from the waist up except for a bra. Odds are I was not even the first to do it in a *nursing* bra. But I'm willing to bet that no woman in a nursing bra had ever before greeted our apple-cheeked FedEx man with her flaps unsnapped and gaping wide-open. You could see that in his face.

I thought about being embarrassed, but decided that since I'd been too tired to notice that I wasn't dressed, I was definitely too tired to care. "You have to air-dry them," I explained. "Or they can crack."

"That has to hurt," he said.

I signed for the package, which turned out to be yet another sterling silver rattle from Tiffany (that made seven), closed the door, and dragged myself up the stairs to the second-floor, duplex apartment where I lived with my husband, Peter, my three-year-old daughter, Ruby, and the mutant vampire to whom I'd given birth four months before.

"Yes, yes, yes. I know," I sang in a mock cheerful voice as I scooped my screaming baby out of his bassinet. "Finished your six-minute nap, have you? That's all the sleep you'll be needing this week, isn't it? Hmm?"

Isaac eyed my conveniently exposed nipple and increased the pitch of his wail. I settled my bulk into the aggressively ugly glider rocker that had taken pride of place in our living room and lifted him to my breast. He began suckling as though he'd just gotten home from vacation in Biafra. It had been all of half an hour since he'd eaten. I leaned back in the chair, ran my tongue over my unbrushed teeth, and looked up at the clock on the mantelpiece. Noon. And I'd been awake for eight hours. Actually, it's hardly fair to say that I woke up at 4:00 A.M. That was just when I'd finally abandoned the pretense that night was a time when we, like the rest of the world, slept. Isaac Applebaum Wyeth never slept. Never. Like really never. It was my firm belief that in the four months since his birth the kid hadn't closed his eyes for longer than twenty minutes at a stretch. Okay, that's not fair. There was that one time when he slept for three hours straight. But since I was at the doctor's office having a wound check (bullet and cesarean, but that's another story altogether) at the time of this miracle, I had only Isaac's father's word that it had actually occurred. And I had my doubts.

Sitting there, nursing Isaac, I entertained myself by imagining what I would be doing if I were still a federal public defender and not a bedraggled stay-at-home mom. First of all, by this hour of the day I'd have already finished three or four bail hearings. I might be on the way to the Metropolitan Detention Center, hoping my smack-addict clients were straight enough to have a conversation about their plea agreements. Or, I might be in trial, striding around the courtroom, tearing into a quivering FBI agent and exposing his testimony for the web of lies that it was. All right, all right. Maybe not. Maybe I'd be watching my client self-destruct on the stand while he explained that the reason he was covered in red paint and holding the sack of the bank's money complete with the exploding dye pack was because his friend borrowed his clothes and car and did the robbery and then mysteriously gave him the bag. And no, he doesn't remember his friend's name.

But I wasn't a public defender anymore. I wasn't even a lawyer. I was just an overtired, underdressed mother. I'd quit the job I'd loved so much when Ruby was a baby. This decision shocked the hell out of everyone who knew me. It certainly hadn't been part of the plan I'd set out for myself when I walked down the aisle at Harvard Law School with the big diploma emblazoned with the words "Juliet Applebaum, *Juris Doctorat*." I'd left Cambridge brimming over with ambition and student loans and began my career as a corporate lawyer, a job I hated but with a salary I really needed.

Then, one day, I got into an argument with the clerk in my local video store that changed my life. Never, when I started dating the slightly geeky, gray-eyed slacker who gave me such a hard time when I rented *Pretty Woman*, did I imagine that he'd pay off my student loans with the proceeds of a movie called *Flesh Eaters* and move me out to Los Angeles.

My husband, Peter's, success had given me the freedom I needed to have the career I really wanted, as a criminal defense lawyer. Our decision to start a family had derailed me completely. I know lots of women manage to be full-time mothers and productive members of the work force at the same time, but, much to my surprise, I wasn't one of them. When I tried to do both I succeeded only in being incompetent at work and short-tempered at home. At some point I realized that it would be better for my daughter to have me around, and if I was bored out of my skull, so be it.

Isaac must have gotten sick of listening to me yawn, because he popped off my breast, let loose a massive belch, and graced me with a huge smile. He was, like his sister before him, bald but for a fringe of hair around the sides of his lumpy skull. He had a little hooked nose and a perennially worried expression that made him look, for all the world, like a beleaguered Jewish accountant and inspired his father to christen him with the nickname Murray Kleinfeld, CPA.

I kissed him a few times under his chins and hoisted myself up out of the chair.

"Ready to face the day?" I wasn't sure who I was asking—my four-month-old son or myself.

Only a mother of an infant knows that it is in fact possible to take a shower, wash your hair, and shave your legs, all within a single verse of "Old MacDonald Had a Farm." The trick is finishing the E-I-E-I O's with your toothbrush in your mouth.

Balancing Isaac on my hip, I gazed at my reflection critically. Washed and artfully ruffled, my cropped red hair looked pretty good, as long as you weren't looking too intently at the roots. My face had lost some of that pregnancy bloat, although sometimes it did seem as though Isaac and I were competing to see who could accumulate the most chins. My eyes still shone bright green and I decided to do my best to emphasize the only feature not affected by my rather astonishing weight gain. I applied a little mascara. All in all, if I was careful not to glance below my neck, I wasn't too hideous.

"Isn't your mama gorgeous?" I asked the baby. He gave me a Bronx cheer.

I rubbed some lipstick off my teeth.

"Let's get dressed."

A mere half-hour later, a record for the newly enlarged Wyeth-Applebaum household, Isaac and I were in the car on our way to pick up Ruby at preschool. He was, as usual, screaming, and I was, as usual, singing hysterically along with the Raffi tape that played on a continuous loop in my Volvo station wagon.

One really has to wonder how children make it to the age of ten without being pitched headfirst out a car window.

2

ON THE WAY home, my children thoughtfully contrived to keep me from falling asleep at the wheel—not an easy task given that I'd been averaging more or less eleven minutes of sleep a night—by regaling me, at top volume with (in one ear) a long, involved story about Sneakers the rat and how he had escaped from his cage, and (in the other) the usual hysterical weeping.

As we pulled into our driveway, Ruby said, "Mama, can we go to the park? Please oh please oh please oh please."

It was only because I was momentarily distracted by thoughts of the proper diagnosis of sleep-deprivation psychosis that I forgot that I'd been looking forward to turning on *Sesame Street* and enjoying an hour or so of TV-induced stupor (mine rather than theirs).

"Okay, honey," I said. Oh well, there was always the possibility that Isaac would fall asleep on the way there. I bundled the two of them into their double stroller and set off for a walk to the playground.

Our neighborhood, Hancock Park, is one of the oldest in Los Angeles, dating all the way back to the 1920s. It's full of big old houses, most of them stuccoed Spanish-style numbers with the occasional elaborate English Tudor thrown in for variety. The broad tree-lined avenues arc in gentle, carefully planned curves. While the addresses might have hinted at a certain long-ago grandeur, the neighborhood's proximity to downtown L.A. and a number of less savory neighborhoods has, in the last couple of decades, made it a haunt of car thieves and even the odd mugger or two. That's kept the housing prices lower than in some tonier areas. It's also kept out the movie-industry riffraff for the most part. We lived in one of the many duplexes sprinkled throughout the neighborhood.

On our walk to the park, I was taking up quite a bit of sidewalk space—all of it to be exact. Without realizing it, I'd caused something of a traffic jam behind me, which I noticed only when a polite little voice said, "Excuse me, may we pass?"

I turned around to see a gaggle of boys, ranging in age from about six to ten, gliding on Rollerblades behind me. They looked like your basic boys, kneepads covered in mud, shirttails flying, except that their shirts were white button-downs and they wore black trousers. They also wore yarmulkes and sported long, curling sidelocks. Hasidic Jewish Rollerbladers.

Los Angeles, like New York, has a large and vibrant Hasidic community. These are the most observant Jews; they follow the rules of Judaism to the absolute letter. They wear traditional clothing, the men in dark suits with their heads covered at all times. The women dress modestly, in long dresses with sleeves past their elbows, and their hair concealed by wigs and hats. The Hasidim follow a *rebbe*, a spiritual leader. There are different sects that, if you are more familiar with them than I, can sometimes be told apart by their distinctiveness of dress; some groups of men wear knickers or fur hats, some women wear only dark tights and eschew light-colored stockings of any kind.

The Hasidic community is about as different from your basic, garden-variety assimilated Jew as the Amish are from the members of your local Episcopalian church.

Because my neighborhood is relatively inexpensive, and because the duplex apartments are large and comfortable, it has become home to much of Los Angeles's Hasidic community. The neighborhood boasts a number of yeshivas and synagogues, and it's always possible to find "a piece herring," as my grandfather would say—except on a Saturday. That's when the myriad little kosher grocery stores and markets close up tight until Sunday morning. Because this is Los Angeles, the land of weird contradictions, there's also a huge Honeybaked Ham store right in the middle of the Hasidic enclave. Go figure.

I didn't have a lot of contact with the Hasidim. They keep pretty much to themselves. The mothers rarely take their kids to the park, although the older children do seem to have free run of the streets—unlike the other neighborhood kids, most of whom are chauffeured by their ex-lawyer or stockbroker moms from carefully organized play dates to music lessons to ballet to soccer practice.

"Sorry, guys," I said, and pushed the stroller up a driveway so they could whiz past.

"Why do those boys dress so funny?" Ruby asked.

"They don't dress funny, sweetie. They're just wearing yarmulkes and *tzitzit*."

"They do so dress funny. What's a yummyka and tis tis?"

"Okay, maybe it is a little funny. A yarmulke is a little hat and *tzitzit* are those long strings hanging out of their pants. Those are special things Jews wear."

"We're Jews and we don't wear those."

"True." What to say? *That's because we're bad Jews?* I settled for something that one of the teachers at Ruby's Reform Jewish preschool would have said. "Everybody celebrates religion in a different way."

"Our way has Christmas."

"Well, that's not exactly how we celebrate being Jewish. That's more like how we celebrate being Christian. Sort of. Hey, look at that doggy!" It's nice that three-year-olds can't usually sense when their mothers are desperately trying to change the subject. Ruby and Isaac's status as children of a mixed marriage, while certainly run-of-the-mill, does bring up the occasional unanswerable question. My husband, Peter, is vaguely Protestant and decidedly nonpracticing. The closest he comes to religion is Santa Claus and the Easter Bunny. My approach to Judaism is similarly low-key, expressing itself primarily in a deep-seated identification with Woody Allen and a guilt-ridden love of bacon.

Up ahead of us the boys were gathered around a frisky golden retriever puppy on a leash. Its owner, a much-pierced, artfully bored, post-adolescent of indeterminate gender, was leaning against a tree.

One of the boys reached out his fingers and said, "Nice girl" as the dog sniffed his hand.

Another immediately piped up, "What for you tink she's a goil?" Here was this eight-year-old on Rollerblades with a thick Yiddish accent that made him sound like a pint-sized version of my great-uncle Moe.

I maneuvered the stroller around the Hasidic boys and continued up the street. On the corner of La Brea we passed a little kosher market.

"Hey, Ruby, want some gelt?" Ruby and I share a soft spot for the chocolate coins in gold foil that used to be available only around Hanukkah. You can get them year round in my neighborhood.

"Yes! Mmm!"

We walked up to the entrance of the store and I leaned forward over the stroller, trying to reach the door handle. No luck. I walked around to pull it open and then had to leap for the stroller, which was starting to roll down the sidewalk. The door slammed shut. This is the twenty-first century. By now weren't all doors supposed to glide soundlessly open, activated by heat-sensing devices? For that matter, weren't we all supposed to have personal antigravity packs that would make awkward double-strollers a fond memory?

For some reason, and totally out of the blue, this disappointment of the futuristic fantasies created in my generation by *The Jetsons* made me cry. I leaned against the handles of my stroller and sobbed, inelegantly and furiously. I just felt so overwhelmed and hopeless, and most of all, tired. Deeply and completely tired down to my very bones. I stood there weeping while my two children stared.

"Please, Mama. Don't cry," Ruby whispered. Isaac whimpered. The terrified looks on their faces sent a wave of guilt washing over me and made me cry even harder. Suddenly, the door swung open, propped by a small, sneakered foot. I wiped the back of my hand across my streaming eyes and nose and quickly wheeled the stroller through the door and into the small, dimly lit market. The store was packed with shelves overflowing with merchandise unknown to my usual grocery store: kosher canned vegetables, Israeli candies, products made by companies called Feingold and Essem and Schwartz's. I turned to thank the owner of the foot, a breathtakingly lovely teenage girl in a calf-length skirt, dark tights, a man's white Oxford shirt buttoned up to the neck and a pair of decidedly spiffy Air Jordans. She had long, dark hair plaited into a single braid down her back and the loveliest eyes I'd ever seen. They were a very dark blue, almost purple, and were fringed with thick dark lashes. A Jewish Elizabeth Taylor.

"Thanks so much," I said, gulping a little.

"You're welcome," the girl answered, in a soft voice. She looked away from my blotchy tear-streaked face and knelt in front of the stroller. "Hello there. What's your name?" she asked my three-year-old.

"Ruby," my daughter answered.

"Ruby! What a coincidence! I have a ruby ring." She showed Ruby the small gold band with a tiny sliver of a ruby she wore on her right hand.

"Bootiful," Ruby said, reaching out a finger to touch it. "My mama only has a stinky old plain ring." My daughter, Paloma Picasso Wyeth.

"That's my wedding ring, Rubes. It's supposed to be plain," I said.

"Her wedding ring has sparkling gems," Ruby answered derisively.

"Oh, that's not my wedding ring," the girl said with a smile. "I'm not married. My daddy gave me this for my sixteenth birthday."

"It's lovely," I said.

"Is this your little brother?" she asked Ruby.

"His name is Isaac," Ruby said. "He's a very bad baby. He cries all night long."

"Oh no. How can you sleep? Do you have to cover your ears?"

"No. He sleeps in Mama's room so he doesn't wake me up."

Suddenly, we were interrupted by a loud voice.

"Darling, what's wrong?"

I turned around to see the shop owner leaning over her counter. She was a middle-aged *baleboosteh* with round cheeks, deep-set eyes that were about half an inch too close together, and a bright blond wig perched on the top of her head. She motioned me over.

"Come here, darling. Wipe your eyes." She held out a box of tissues. I walked over to the counter, took one, and blew my nose loudly.

"I'm so sorry. This is so ridiculous. Bursting into tears like this."

"Don't be silly. Why do you think I keep a box of Kleenex on the counter? What's wrong, darling? Did something happen to you?"

"No, nothing happened. I have no idea why I'm so emotional. It's just that I'm so tired. Isaac, that's the baby, he never sleeps. He's up all night and all day. I haven't slept more than an hour straight in four months."

"Exactly like my brother Baruch! My brother Baruch didn't sleep until he was three years old," she said with a snort.

"Oh, my G—Oh no," I said. "Please tell me this won't last three years."

"Darling, it was awful, I can tell you. And my mother, *aleha ha-shalom*, wasn't like you, she didn't have just one other little one. She had four older. And then she had two more before Baruch shut his eyes."

"Did she survive?"

"I'm telling you, none of us thought she would. I remember she said to my father, *alav ha-shalom*, 'One more day of this and Baruch and I, we go over a bridge together. Over a bridge.' She wasn't kidding, I'm telling you."

I felt my voice begin to quaver again. "I don't think I can stand three years."

Things had been a lot easier at home when Ruby was a baby. There were two of us to deal with her back then. When I'd gone back to work, Peter had even been Ruby's primary caretaker. This time, it was different. When Ruby was a baby, Peter had been writing movie scripts and had at least some control over his schedule. A few weeks after Isaac was born, Peter sold an idea for a television series to one of the networks and was currently involved in shooting the pilot. As soon as that happened, it was as though he'd disappeared off the face of the earth. He showed up just in time to go to sleep and then slept like one of the corpses in his series (better, actually), until the next morning when he woke up and rushed off. I knew I should be supportive—after all, he was supporting *us*, financially at least—but it was hard not to be ticked off. I had, for all intents and purposes, become a single mother, and I resented every second of it. I'd been happier when he was working hand to mouth.

"Darling, it sounds to me like you need some help around the house," the shopkeeper said, handing me another tissue. "Does your mother live nearby?"

"No. In New Jersey."

"Ach. So far. What about your mother-in-law?"

"Up near San Francisco."

"Sisters? Sisters-in-law?"

"No. Nobody lives here. We're all alone." That set me off again and I buried my face in the tissue.

"Okay, okay, *mamaleh*. Enough with the crying. You need to hire a babysitter."

"I can't do that. I don't work. This is all I *do* all day. I shouldn't need any help." When I'd left work to be with Ruby, I'd fired the nanny who'd been coming in the morning to watch Ruby until Peter woke up. I was determined to do it all myself. After all, the world was full of women raising their children without professional help. Why should I be any different? But that was before I gave birth to the child who never slept.

The shopkeeper rolled her eyes at me. "Look, darling, you're clearly exhausted. All you need is a nice young girl to come spend a few hours with the baby every day so you can run some errands, maybe even take a nap. When's the last time you had a nap?"

I shook my head.

"*Nu?*"

I couldn't pretend the idea didn't appeal to me. I imagined myself handing Isaac to a babysitter, just for an hour or so. Just so that I could sleep. "You know, you're right. It's not like I'm hiring a nanny. I just need someone to come in for a couple of hours so I can take a nap."

"Listen, Fraydle." The shopkeeper turned to the teenager, who had, meanwhile, taken off Isaac's sock and was tickling his toes. "You help this nice lady out. It slows down here around ten in the morning. You go over to this lady's house and help her out a couple hours."

Fraydle looked up. "But Tante Nettie, my father said I could work for you here in the store. He didn't say I could babysit for . . . for . . ."

Tante Nettie put up a hand. "My brother won't mind if his girl helps out a neighbor." She turned to me. "You *are* Jewish?" she asked.

"Oh, yes," I said.

"You see?" she said to Fraydle. "You'll help out a nice Jewish neighbor lady and maybe you'll show her how to light the *Shabbos* candles while you're at it. Your father will love the idea. He'll *make* you do it, I'm telling you."

"And I'll pay you!" I said. "Just tell me how much."

"Of course you'll pay her," Tante Nettie said. "You'll pay her six—no, seven dollars an hour. For two hours. From ten to noon. Every day but Friday. Friday I need her here. For the *Shabbos* rush, I need her. By the way, I'm Nettie Tannenbaum, and this is my niece, Fraydle Finkelstein."

"I'm Juliet Applebaum and I am so incredibly pleased to meet you both." I turned to Fraydle. "You'll do it?" I asked.

"Yes," the girl almost whispered.

I scrawled my name and address on a piece of paper.

"Tomorrow?"

"Tomorrow," she replied, looking worried.

"Okay, enough," Nettie said. "Fraydle, run to your mama's garage and get us another case of Kleenex. This nice young lady used them all up." She cackled and poked me in the side. I laughed.

"You need anything else from the storage area, Tante Nettie?" Fraydle asked.

"Yeah, maybe another case of chocolate. I have a feeling some little girl might want some."

Ruby's eyes lit up. On our way home Isaac fell asleep, and Ruby and I felt happier than either of us had in weeks. She, because she had piles of chocolate coins in her lap, and I, because I had a nap in my future.

3

THAT NIGHT I informed Peter that I had hired a mother's helper for a couple of hours a day. He opened his mouth, probably to remind me that every time he'd suggested the same thing, I'd insisted that since I was staying at home full time we didn't need any help with child care. I shot him a look full of such murderous venom that he clamped his lips shut.

The next morning, at precisely 9:59 A.M., my doorbell rang. I'd showered and dressed early in the morning so that I wouldn't treat Fraydle to the terrifying sight of my unwashed, morning persona. On my way downstairs I checked my shirt front quickly, to avoid a repetition of the FedEx incident. I opened the door to find my babysitter standing awkwardly on the front step. She was wearing the same outfit as the day before. Isaac, who was perched on my hip, reached out a hand to her and cooed.

She smiled at him and held out her arms. "Come, *motek*."

"My grandmother used to call me that," I told her. "It means sweet, right?"

"Mmm." She was busy making googly eyes at the baby.

"Be careful; he can't sit up by himself yet, so you have to sort of prop him up on your hip."

"He's nice and big," she said. "I have a sister his age and she's much smaller."

"How many brothers and sisters do you have?" I asked.

"We're eight in all. Three girls and five boys. I'm the oldest."

"My God!" I exclaimed.

She looked up, shocked at the expletive.

"I mean, wow. Gosh. That's a lot of kids."

"Not so many. There are many families with more. Ten. Sometimes even twelve."

I shuddered. "I'm barely managing with two. I can't imagine dealing with eight. Your poor mother."

"She has me to help. And my younger sister Sarah."

"But still. It must be exhausting. Do you think she's finished having children?"

"Oh no. She's only thirty-five years old. I'm sure she'll have more."

My mouth hung open. Thirty-five? The mother of eight was only two years older than I? *Oy vey.*

I ushered Fraydle into the house and showed her around Isaac's bedroom. It, like the rest of our apartment, was full of huge piles of brightly colored molded plastic in various stages of disrepair. Our home had started to look like the "seconds" section of a toy store.

"Do you mind if I take him out in the stroller?" Fraydle asked. "That way you can maybe sleep a little."

"Oh, that would be wonderful. He loves the stroller. Usually. Did you see it parked at the bottom of the stairs?"

"I'll find it," she said.

"He shouldn't need to eat, but if he does, there's a little bottle of expressed breast milk in the fridge. You can heat that up."

Fraydle nodded.

"Don't forget to bring extra diapers."

She nodded again.

"So I guess I'll go take a nap now."

She nodded once more.

I walked slowly back to my bedroom. I perched on the edge of the bed, wondering exactly how I was ever going to fall asleep while I was so worried about my little boy off in the hands of a complete stranger. Two hours later I woke up with a start. I'd conked out, half-sitting, half-lying on the bed, and had rather elegantly drooled all over the quilt. Wiping my mouth, I got out of bed and staggered into the bathroom. I splashed some cold water in the general direction of my face and stared into the mirror. My right cheek was covered with angry red creases and my eye was puffy. My hair had flattened out on one side and was doing its best Eraserhead imitation on the other. I halfheartedly patted at it and, giving up, wandered out into the living room. It was silent. No baby. No babysitter. I opened the window overlooking the front of the house and leaned out. Below, I saw the stroller, carefully covered by a baby blanket. Presumably Isaac was inside. But could he really be sleeping?

I leaned out a little farther, looking for Fraydle. She wasn't on the stoop. Panicking a bit, I leaned out farther still. Suddenly, I caught a glimpse of her standing about thirty feet down the block. She was talking to a young man in a brown leather bomber jacket. Just then, she glanced back at the stroller and saw me leaning out the window. She gave a startled little jump and said something to the man, who hurried away. She ran back to the house and I started down the stairs to meet her.

I opened the door to find her blushing furiously and apologizing.

"I'm so sorry, Mrs. Applebaum. I only left Isaac for a minute. And he was sound asleep. I could hear him from where I was. I promise you I could."

"That's fine, Fraydle. I trust that you wouldn't leave him alone. You were close enough to hear him. It's really fine. You can call me Juliet, by the way."

She seemed to calm down. "I really am sorry."

"It's okay, Fraydle. I would do it, too, I'm sure. Except, I've never actually been in the position to. How the heck did you get him to go to sleep?"

"I just walked with the stroller. That's all."

"When did he go down?"

"Right after we left. As soon as we started walking."

"You mean he's been asleep for two hours?" I was utterly and completely shocked.

Fraydle looked at her watch. "A little less, maybe. I've got to go back. My aunt is expecting me."

"No problem. Just wait a sec and I'll get my purse."

"No, no. Pay me at the end of the week."

"All right, if that's really okay with you. Fraydle?"

"Yes?"

"Who's the boy?"

To her credit she didn't say "which boy" or "nobody" or anything else teenager-like and evasive. She just got very quiet.

"Please don't tell my aunt Nettie or my parents, Mrs. Applebaum."

"Juliet. Of course I won't tell your parents. Who is he?"

She paused and then breathed, "Yossi."

"He's not Hasidic."

"No."

"Why is his name Yossi? Is he Israeli?"

"Yes."

"Is he your boyfriend?"

"No!" She sounded almost terrified.

"Really?"

"We're Verbover Hasidim. Even stricter than Lubovitch. I can't have boyfriends. I'm not allowed to have boyfriends. The only thing I'm allowed to have is a husband. A husband my parents choose for me." Her voice was low, rushed, and even a little bitter.

"You're a little young to be married, aren't you?" I asked.

"My mother was seventeen when she married my father, and I'm eighteen. I've already turned down two matches. I'm going to have to accept one soon."

"Your parents have already tried to marry you off? Are you serious?"

"Twice. I said no to both, but there's only so many times a girl can do that before she starts to get a reputation as a snob. Or worse."

Eighteen years old and already being forced into marriage and a life like her mother's—baby after baby with menopause as the only end to it. I didn't know what to say.

"I'm sorry, Fraydle."

She looked up at me, paused a moment, and then seemed to close whatever window had been opened into her true feelings. She shrugged her shoulders and said, "My parents will make a good match for me."

"Okay."

"Aunt Nettie's waiting. I gotta go."

"Okay. See you tomorrow."

"Bye-bye." And with that, she ran down the path and up the block. I sat down on the stoop and enjoyed the quiet for a moment. But only for a moment. Sensing, no doubt, that he was in danger of ruining his reputation as the most obnoxious baby in Los Angeles, Isaac woke himself up and let out a howl.

4

THAT NIGHT ISAAC actually slept for three hours in a row, between the hours of 2:00 and 5:00 A.M. When I woke to the early-morning grunting that generally preceded his early-morning shrieking, I positively leapt out of bed. It's remarkable how fabulous three hours of uninterrupted sleep can feel when you're used to none at all. I scooped the baby out of his bassinet and hustled out of the bedroom so that he wouldn't wake Peter. I went into the living room, snapped on the radio, and settled in for our morning feeding and session of *Morning Edition* on National Public Radio. Isaac had gotten used to nursing to the comforting voice of Bob Edwards. Since I never got the opportunity to read the paper, my half-hour or so of listening to the radio in the early morning hours was all that stood between me and complete ignorance of world affairs.

After Isaac had sated his appetite I put him into the Johnny-Jump-Up clamped in the kitchen doorway. He began happily leaping up and down, and I, in a sudden and rather inexplicable bit of Martha Stewart–like ambition, decided to prepare a homemade breakfast. Soon I had a pile of lovely, golden, misshapen banana pancakes warming in the oven, the table was set for three with the juice poured and the syrup heated, and the coffee was hot in the French press. I went to wake up the other members of my family.

Ruby woke, groggy and grumpy, but cheered up when I told her that pancakes were in the offing. Her father needed a little more encouragement.

"Honey! Wake up!"

Grunt.

"Sweetie. Sweetie. SWEETIE." I grabbed the pillow off his head. "Wake up! I made coffee. And pancakes!"

"Five more minutes," he mumbled, burying his head under the covers.

"Oh, c'mon, Peter. The pancakes are getting soggy."

I leaned over him and started nuzzling his neck. "Please, wake up," I whispered. Then, I plunged my tongue into his ear.

"Eeew!" he screamed, leaping about six feet in the air. "For crying out loud, Juliet, what's your problem?" He sat on the edge of the bed, digging his finger into his ear. "That is just so disgusting."

I smiled sweetly. "I made breakfast."

He looked up at me, surprised. "What?"

"Pancakes. I made pancakes."

"Wow. Okay. I'm up." Peter scratched his little potbelly, pulled on a pair of pajama bottoms, and followed me into the kitchen. We stopped in the hall and watched Ruby and Isaac. They were holding hands, and Ruby was gently bouncing the baby in the Johnny-Jump-Up. Her red curls glinted in the morning sunlight that, unusually for L.A., a city where the fog and smog don't ordinarily burn off before midmorning, streamed in through the window. Isaac had a huge grin on his face. As we watched, Ruby leaned over and kissed him on the cheek.

"Jump, Izzy. Jump jump jump," she said.

"Hey, Peach," Peter called.

She ran across the floor and leapt into his arms. "Good morning, Daddy. Look at the bootiful day."

"It sure is beautiful, honey."

We had the most pleasant meal together that we'd had in months. Since Isaac's birth, Peter and I had been behaving less like lovers and more like fellow laborers in a baby factory. And he was definitely a part-time employee. We'd gone from spending virtually all day together—Peter had always worked at night while I was asleep—to seeing each other about as much as your average married, professional couple, that is, not very much. I didn't know if it was the lack of time, or my exhaustion, or just the added pressure of another baby, but something wasn't right between us. We hadn't gone out on a date or even had a good long talk in ages. And let's not even discuss our nonexistent sex life.

"Juliet," Peter said, "you seem like yourself for the first time in months."

I smiled at him. "I feel like myself for the first time in months. No wonder authoritarian regimes use sleep deprivation as a form of torture. It's amazingly effective."

He leaned over and kissed me on the cheek. "I've missed you."

I felt a twinge of irritation. It wasn't my fault I'd been out of sorts. How would he feel if he had to spend his nights comforting a fussy baby? And hey, I wasn't the one at the studio all day and half the night. However, I was determined not to let anything ruin the mood of my lovely day. I suppressed any and all negative feelings and smiled—a stiff little smile, but a smile nonetheless.

"Is your little Orthodox girl coming today?" he asked.

"Yup. At ten. I can't wait."

Peter dressed Ruby, made her lunch, and took her to school on his way to work. I waved good-bye from the front step and then took Isaac upstairs. By a quarter to ten we were both bathed, dressed, and waiting for Fraydle.

At ten we were sitting on the front step.

At a quarter past ten we were standing at the end of the walk.

At ten thirty we were halfway down the block.

At ten forty-five, I put the baby in his stroller and stormed off to Mrs. Tannenbaum's. When I got to the market, I saw that the door was locked and the CLOSED sign was up. I peered through the glass of the door, and spotted a young girl sitting in the back on a high stool, reading a book. I rapped a few times on the glass and she looked up. She shook her head and motioned toward the CLOSED sign. I rapped again, insistently. Finally, she got down off the stool and came to the door. Opening it a crack, she said, "She's closed today."

The girl looked like a less attractive version of Fraydle. Her hair was the same dark color and was worn in the same simple braid down her back, but it was thinner and less glossy. Her eyes were dark blue but without any of Fraydle's purplish vibrancy. Her mouth and nose were both just slightly larger than Fraydle's. But still, I was confident I knew who she was.

"Sarah?" I asked.

She looked puzzled. "How do you know my name?"

"My name is Juliet Applebaum. Your sister Fraydle works for me. She didn't show up this morning and I came to look for her." Sarah fidgeted uncomfortably with the button on her shirt. "Do you know where she is? Can you call her for me?" She didn't answer. "I'm not mad or anything. I just want to know if she's okay, and if she plans on coming to work today. Or ever, I guess."

Still nothing.

"Sarah," I said, sharply.

She looked up, startled. "You should talk to my father," she said.

"What? Did your father decide she couldn't work for me? Is that what happened?"

"Please, just talk to my father."

"Sarah, what's going on here?"

"Fraydle's gone."

Now it was my turn to be startled. "Gone? What do you mean, gone? Where is she?"

"She didn't come home yesterday. Everybody is looking for her right now. I'm supposed to stay in the store in case she calls or comes here."

I didn't know what to say. Suddenly, I remembered the young man in the bomber jacket. Could she have gone off with him? Could she have run away with Yossi? Should I tell her parents about seeing them together?

The shrill ring of the telephone interrupted my thoughts. Sarah snatched it up.

"Hello? No, *Abba*. She hasn't called. Okay, *Abba*. *Abba*, wait. That lady is here. The one that Fraydle babysat for yesterday. She came looking for her."

There was a pause.

"Yes, right now, *Abba*." She hung up the phone. "My father says come to our house right now."

I thought about it for a minute. Did I really want to get in the middle of this? What was I going to tell Fraydle's father? Fraydle had told me that her parents were planning an arranged marriage for her, a practice I thought had gone out with corsets and horse-drawn carriages. Maybe Fraydle had decided to run away rather than be forced into a marriage she hadn't chosen for herself. If that was the case, I certainly wasn't going to help her parents track her down.

Sarah had started out the back of the shop. Realizing that I wasn't following, she turned around and said, "You must come. Now. *Abba* is waiting."

"Sarah, give me your telephone number. I can't go to your house because . . . because I need to get the baby home. I'll call your father within half an hour or so." I wanted to talk to Peter before I did anything.

Sarah ran back to me and grabbed my hand. "No!" she said, almost yelling. "*Abba* said you have to come now!"

I extricated my hand from hers. "I'll call him as soon as I get home, Sarah. I've got to go now."

She shook her head frantically. "No! *Abba* said I had to bring you now. You have to come. Please. Please." She began to cry.

"Okay. Okay. I'm coming. I'm coming. Stop crying, for goodness' sake." It was clearly fear of her father and not concern for her sister that was causing this hysteria. I didn't have the heart to make her any more panicky than she was. Following the girl, I humped the stroller out the back door and down the few stairs leading to an alley.

"It's just down there." She pointed to the end of the alley. We reached the corner and turned into the fenced yard of a small stucco house. There was a small lawn and a few flowerpots with red geraniums on the long flight of steps that led up to the porch. The garage took up the first floor of the house, and the front door opened into the second floor.

I picked Isaac's stroller up in my arms and followed Sarah up the steps and through the front door of the house. Once inside, I put the stroller down and looked around. The living room was packed with bearded men in black suits and broad-brimmed hats. They were standing in little clumps, whispering to one another. I knew that shorn of their facial hair and side curls and wearing jeans and T-shirts, they could easily have been some of the many cousins and uncles with whom I'd attended bar mitzvahs and weddings, but it was almost impossible to imagine these men not garbed in their traditional attire. They looked as if they'd been wearing those coats and white stockings for two or three hundred years. As we entered, all conversation ceased as they looked silently and intently at us.

"Um, I'm Juliet Applebaum?" My voice cracked a bit. The men with their piercing eyes and unsmiling mouths made me nervous.

Suddenly, Mrs. Tannenbaum bustled out of what was most likely the kitchen and rushed over to me. She had obviously been crying; her eyes were rimmed with red.

"Come. Come," she said, grasping my hands and trying to drag me into the living room. At that moment, Isaac began to cry. I disentangled myself from her grasp and lifted him out of his stroller. Resting the baby on my shoulder, I patted his back and crooned softly to him.

"Come." Mrs. Tannenbaum pushed me farther into the room. The men backed away from us, leaving a little path for me. I knew that they were forbidden to touch me, a strange woman, who might even be in the middle of the unclean part of her menstrual cycle. A large man in shirt-sleeves with a thick, unruly black beard sat on the couch in the middle of the room. He looked to be in his early to mid-forties. He wore no hat, but an oversized black velvet yarmulke covered the entire top of his head. He rose as I approached.

"This is my brother, Fraydle's papa, Rav Finkelstein," Mrs. Tannenbaum said. "Baruch, this is the woman I told you about. The nice Jewish lady who Fraydle was helping with her baby." She stepped back.

The rabbi looked at me silently. I felt intensely self-conscious in a pair of Peter's jeans rolled up at the cuff and cinched as tightly as possible, that is to say, not particularly tightly, at the waist. Thank heavens I had on a long-sleeve shirt. Too bad it had a large picture of Madonna wearing a black leather bustier.

"Hello, Rabbi. My name is Juliet Applebaum." I instinctively extended my hand, but quickly withdrew it, remembering that he could not shake it.

"You know my Fraydle, my daughter," he stated.

"Yes."

"She worked for you yesterday."

"Yes."

"You know this was without my permission. You know that she did this without telling me."

"No. No, I didn't know that." I turned to glare at Mrs. Tannenbaum, who backed away still farther, her eyes boring a hole into the faded green carpeting.

"I most assuredly did not know that," I said firmly.

"But you did not ask her if she had her father's permission to work for you. To work for a . . ." He left the sentence hanging in midair.

I was beginning to get angry. "To work for a mother with a small child, Rabbi Finkelstein. A Jewish mother. With a Jewish child."

He gave my outfit an ostentatious and derisive look. "A Jewish mother," he spat.

Isaac began to cry.

"Excuse me," I said. "My baby is hungry. I need to go home and nurse him." I spun on my heel and walked toward the front door. Just then, a woman rushed out of the kitchen.

"No. No, please don't go." She took my arm. "Come, feed the baby in the kitchen. Come." Ignoring the men in the front room, she began dragging me into the kitchen. I couldn't shake her off without being violent, so I followed.

The kitchen was small, plain, and practical. The walls and cabinets were painted white and the only decoration consisted of dozens of children's paintings and drawings that covered every wall, every cabinet door, and the fridge. A large round table scarred by years of use was shoved into a corner. Sitting around the table and leaning against every counter were women. There were old women in stiff, discolored wigs, younger women wearing fashionable well-coiffed wigs or headscarves, and girls with long braids or hair cropped to chin-length. The room smelled warm and yeasty, like baking bread. The woman who had taken my arm was wearing a loose-fitting gray woolen dress. Her brown wig was slightly askew and her face was red and blotchy. Her large, violet, lavishly lashed eyes were bloodshot. Clearly she, too, had been crying.

"Please excuse my husband, Mrs. Applebaum. He is not used to dealing with . . . with other people. Not from our community, I mean. He is upset. We are all upset. Come through here to the back bedroom. Nurse your baby there. We'll talk in a minute, okay? Nurse your baby and then maybe you'll tell us what Fraydle did yesterday. Maybe you'll be able to help us figure out where she is, okay?" She led me into a back room and shouted over her shoulder, "Nettie! You come sit with Mrs. Applebaum." Mrs. Tannenbaum, who had followed us into the kitchen, quickly walked into the room. Fraydle's mother backed out the door and shut it quietly behind her.

I looked around me. Mrs. Tannenbaum and I were standing in a small bedroom with a twin bed tucked into a corner. There was a desk chair against one wall. The room was dim; the only window was covered by a dark shade pulled tightly closed.

Isaac was still crying, and I sat down on the bed and quickly undid my shirt. His tears had started my milk flowing and I had soaked right through the nursing pad and my bra. My shirt had a large wet spot right around Madonna's grimacing profile. I pulled out a breast and drew Isaac close to me. He began sucking desperately. I sighed and looked up at Mrs. Tannenbaum, the woman who'd gotten me into this mess in the first place.

"You told me that Fraydle's father wouldn't mind if she worked for me. That he'd *love* for her to work for me."

She didn't answer.

"But you didn't even ask him," I continued.

"I was going to tell him, I'm telling you." She sounded defensive. "I was going to talk to him today. I came over this morning to tell him. But by the time I got here, it was already a huge *balagan*. A mess. The girl was gone. My sister-in-law was hysterical. The men were here. My brother, he's out of his mind with worry. I told him right away about Fraydle's job." She sat down next to me and gently stroked Isaac's head. "*Oy vey*, what a catastrophe this is. A complete *imglik*."

"I'm sure she'll be back," I said. "Teenage girls run away all the time. Mostly they come home right away." I couldn't help thinking of all the girls I'd seen during the years I'd practiced as a public defender. Young girls who ran away from home and ended up on the street dealing drugs, turning tricks, doing robberies with their no-good boyfriends. I didn't mention them.

"Our girls don't run away, Mrs. Applebaum. They never run away, and certainly not when they are about to be married."

"Fraydle was getting married?"

"Of course, didn't she tell you? A wonderful *shiddach*, a match. A very important New York family, I'm telling you. The boy's father leads the biggest yeshiva in Borough Park. A wonderful family. Very important."

"Fraydle didn't tell me that."

"She's a shy girl. Quiet. Maybe she didn't feel like she knew you well enough. This is a very lucky match for our Fraydle. The boy is smart, destined to follow in his father's footsteps. And not bad-looking, either. *Oy*, Fraydle. If Rav Hirsch hears of this, he'll call off the wedding, for sure. He'll never let his son marry an uncontrollable girl. *Chas 'shalom* he should hear about this. I'm telling you, it'll kill my brother if Hirsch ends the match. Kill him."

I switched Isaac to the other breast. Mrs. Tannenbaum heaved a sigh and leaned back on her elbow. "*Gevalt*. Where is that girl?"

"Did Fraydle want to get married?" I asked.

"Of course she wanted to get married. What girl would turn down a match like that? A family like that? And the boy was even good-looking. Maybe a little skinny. Maybe a few pimples. They outgrow that. What twenty-four-year-old doesn't have pimples?"

"Had she spent much time with him?"

"Rav Hirsch brought his son here a little while ago. They met, the son said yes to the match. They met again, maybe twice more. They had some time alone. I'm telling you, when I was a girl, we didn't have such luxuries. We were lucky to see the boy's face once before the wedding. Now, these children, they meet again and again. *Oy*, Fraydle. Hirsch hears about this, it will be the end."

"Has it occurred to you, Mrs. Tannenbaum, that maybe that's exactly what Fraydle might want? Maybe she took off because she doesn't want to get married."

"Don't be ridiculous. This boy is special. This family is one of the Borough Park *machers*, the elite. The father, like I said, is an important rabbi. The mother is from money. Her brothers own half of Brooklyn. This match gives my brother ties to a powerful and important yeshiva and makes Fraydle a comfortable girl. We're not so rich that she can turn her nose up at such an arrangement." The woman once again patted Isaac on the head.

He rolled off my breast with a contented belch. She reached out her arms and took him. I waited for his shriek of protest, but he seemed perfectly content to lie against her shoulder. She burped him gently.

"Do you have children?" I asked.

"No. Mr. Tannenbaum and I were not so blessed. My brother's children are like my own." She sounded a little wistful as she rubbed my baby's back with the palm of her hand. He giggled with delight as she kissed him softly on the cheek.

"You're good with him. He's not usually so affectionate with strangers."

"What strangers? He knows me. He's been in my store. We're friends. Right, Izzaleh? We're old friends."

"Mrs. Tannenbaum, I don't really know how I can help you here. I just met Fraydle. I really have no idea where she is."

"I know. Just talk to my sister-in-law. Let her ask you a few questions. Let her reassure herself that she's followed every path."

"Okay. But I'm warning you, if your brother starts yelling at me again, I'm out that door like a bat out of hell."

She looked up and gave a snort. "I like that. Bat out of hell. I'm going to use that one. You, go talk to Sima. I'll stay here with the baby."

I left them sitting on the bed, cooing at each other, and walked back into the kitchen. Once again, all conversation stopped when the women

saw me. A young woman in a brown fake-Gucci headscarf patterned with
backward logos hurriedly rose from her chair at the table and motioned
for me to sit down. I did. A cup of tea and a plate of cookies materialized
in front of me and Fraydle's mother, Sima, sat down at my side.

"The baby's okay?" she asked.

"He's fine. He's in love with Mrs. Tannenbaum."

She smiled thinly. "Nettie is good with the babies."

"Mrs. Finkelstein, I can't give you much help. I don't know your daughter very well. I met her only once before she came to work for me, and she
only came to work once. I slept the whole time she was there. I didn't
really get a chance to talk to her."

"Did she tell you she had plans to go somewhere? Maybe ask your advice
about where to go?" She seemed embarrassed to be asking these kinds of
questions of a total stranger, but persisted. "Did you give her any money?"

"No. She didn't ask for my advice or tell me anything. She didn't even
let me pay her. I was expecting to pay her today."

I felt guilty for keeping Yossi's existence a secret, as though I were
lying. Before I had kids, when I'd only had the experience of being a
daughter. I would naturally identify with the children in any given situation. I'd only had the experience of being a daughter. As soon as Ruby
made her appearance in the world, I switched camps: Parents are always
right, and even if they're not, you should listen to them anyway. But these
particular circumstances were something altogether beyond the realm of
normal child-parent conflict. An arranged marriage seemed, to me at least,
to be almost barbaric. It was as though Fraydle's parents were offering
her to the highest bidder. Her theoretical right to turn down the match
certainly didn't seem to have much real effect. I could absolutely understand it if she had sought refuge in the arms of Yossi, the mysterious Israeli.
I would have done the same. I wasn't going to turn her over to the parents
she had run from.

"Did she maybe use the phone from your house? Did she call someone?
Or meet someone?" her mother asked.

"I'm sorry I can't help you," I said firmly. I couldn't bring myself to
tell an outright lie, but I felt fine about evading the question. Then I felt a
stab of guilt. The poor woman was obviously distraught, just as I would
be if Ruby had run off.

It occurred to me that if I could find Yossi, he might be able to either lead me to Fraydle or pass her a message. I could tell her to call her parents, to let them know that she was okay. "I'll tell you what," I said, "why don't you let me ask around the neighborhood, and if anyone has seen her, or has heard anything, I'll let you know."

She looked at me for a moment, perhaps sensing that there was something I wasn't telling her. Finally, she spoke. "Okay. You ask around." She took a piece of paper from a pad on the table and wrote down her number.

"Mrs. Finkelstein?"

She glanced up quickly. "Yes? You thought of something?"

"No, it's not that. But have you called the police? Do they know she's missing? You should file a missing persons report. They'll start looking for her."

"No! No police!" someone shouted. I jumped, startled, as did Fraydle's mother and all the other women in the room. I turned in the direction of the booming voice and saw Fraydle's father standing in the doorway.

"This is a family matter," he said, shaking a finger in my direction. "We don't need any help from your police."

"Fine. This is your business. But if you really want to find your daughter—"

"Our daughter is no longer any concern of yours. Thank you for your help. You may go now."

I looked at him, astonished by his rudeness. "I wasn't particularly eager to come here in the first place," I reminded him. "You ordered Sarah to bring me here." The women looked nervously at one another. They'd probably never heard a woman speak that way to their formidable rabbi. I rose from my chair and swept across the kitchen to the adjacent room. I held out my arms to Mrs. Tannenbaum, who gently handed a sleeping Isaac to me. I walked back across the kitchen to the doorway, where Rabbi Finkelstein stood, blocking my way out. "Excuse me, please," I said.

He moved out of the way and I walked quickly to the front door and strapped Isaac into his stroller. One of the congregation who'd been silently watching my exit, a tall, broad-shouldered boy of no more than eighteen, with smooth cheeks that had obviously never needed the ministrations of a razor, held the door open for me.

"Thank you," I said. He blushed a deep red in reply.

5

M Y TEMPER COOLED as I walked home, and by the time I'd dragged the stroller up the stairs to my front door I no longer wanted to knock the rabbi upside the head with a Honey Baked Ham. I did my best to put myself in his shoes. What if Ruby had run off? Wouldn't I be crazed with worry? Wouldn't I be ready to tear apart anyone who might have helped her? In my jeans and Madonna T-shirt I probably looked to Rabbi Finklestein like the personification of the evils of contemporary Los Angeles culture. If he only knew how unattractive my life must have seemed to Fraydle. Sure, I get to wear what I want and marry whomever I want, but when push comes to shove, I'm still an exhausted mother in unbecoming old clothes married to an invisible husband. Not entirely unlike her own mother. What was the difference, really? It occurred to me that one major difference between Fraydle's mother's life and my own was that she raised her kids with the help of scores of friends and relatives, all of whom piled into her kitchen to provide support in times of trouble. I was pretty much on my own.

I plopped Isaac into his Exersaucer and piled a bunch of teething rings and toys on the tray.

"Keep yourself amused for a minute, will you, kid? Mama's got to do a little detective work."

Just how was I going to go about finding an Israeli named Yossi? The only Israeli I knew was my father's cousin's son Amos, and he lived in Houston and drove an ice cream truck. I was actually contemplating calling him, when it occurred to me that my best friend, Stacy, styles herself as Los Angeles's expert on everything. It couldn't hurt to try her.

Stacy is one of those fabulous working mothers who manage to bring home the bacon and fry it up in a pan, all the while wearing a pair of

Manolo Blahniks. She's a high-powered agent at International Creative Artists, the most prestigious talent agency in Hollywood. She has a kid in elementary school who not only plays soccer like every other kid in the United States but is also a math whiz and creates elaborate trigonometry programs on his home computer, just for the fun of it. And Stacy is gorgeous. Her blond hair is always perfectly done in whatever is the style of the moment, and her nails are polished with what I swear is the same nonchip substance they use to paint the space shuttle. Sometimes it's hard to remember why she's my best friend. She's so put together that she makes me feel as though I just waddled in, unwashed and clad only in a black plastic garbage bag, after a year of living in the basement of a doughnut factory. But I love her.

"Stacy Holland's office." There was a new, chirpy little voice answering her phone.

"Hi. What happened to David?" Stacy went through assistants like pantyhose.

"Um, he moved on. Can I help you?"

"This is Juliet Applebaum. Is Her Highness around?"

"One moment, please." I heard a rustling sound. "Oh, yes, Mrs. Applebaum. I'll put you through."

The phone went silent for a minute.

"Juliet! How are you?" Stacy shouted.

"New assistant?"

"Excuse me?"

"You have another new assistant."

"Why? Was she rude? Hannah, get in here!" Stacy bellowed.

"No! She wasn't rude. God, Stacy. The poor kid. I just didn't recognize her voice, that's all. You're a goddamn tyrant!"

"Never mind, Hannah. Go back to your desk. So, darling, is there a reason for this call or are you just experiencing some free-floating hostility?"

I laughed. "No, there's no reason, really. I just was wondering if you have any bright ideas on how I might track down an Israeli named Yossi."

"Yossi who?"

"I dunno. I only have his first name."

"Juliet, that's like asking me if I know a guy named Juan from Mexico. Every other Israeli is named Yossi."

"Well, how many of them can there possibly be in Los Angeles?"

"I read somewhere that the INS estimates that there are three hundred thousand Israelis living in the Los Angeles basin alone."

"Jesus Christ! Who's back home fighting the Arabs?"

"I haven't any idea. Why are you looking for this guy? Did he sell you a bum stereo?"

"No, nothing like that. I think he's my babysitter's boyfriend and she's kind of disappeared. I'm trying to track her down."

"Oh, no. Oh, God no," Stacy moaned.

"What?"

"Need I remind you that last time you did something like this you ended up riddled with bullet holes?"

"Don't exaggerate. Anyway, I'm not investigating a murder. I'm just trying to track down a runaway girl."

"Whatever. I refuse to be a party to this masochistic nonsense. Find your Israeli yourself."

I blew a raspberry into the phone.

"Nice, Juliet. Pick that up from Isaac, did you? Try the air-conditioning companies."

"Excuse me?"

"For your Israeli. Try calling air-conditioning companies. Andy and I just had a new air-conditioning system installed. We had four companies come out to give estimates and Israelis ran all but one. Apparently they have a lock on the industry."

"Why does that happen?" I asked.

"Why does what happen? Israeli air-conditioning installers?"

"And Indian motel-owners, and Ethiopian parking lot attendants. Does one person go home and say, 'Ibrahim! Ganesh! Come quick to America, they have a Motel 6 shortage!'"

"Juliet, I'm going back to work. You might be able to while away the hours pondering that and other metaphysical questions, but I have to put my nose to the grindstone."

"Okay. Grind away. Thanks for the help. I knew you'd know where to start looking," I said.

"*Ciao*, kiss kiss," she said, and hung up the phone.

There were five pages of air-conditioning contractors. At least a third of them had names like Uzi's, Jerusalem Air, and Givati. Did it really make sense to call one hundred air-conditioning companies on the off chance that they might have someone named Yossi working for them, who might then turn out to be the same Yossi that knew Fraydle? I decided to try the first ten names and see what happened.

Just as I began to punch in the first number, Isaac started to fuss. Almost relieved at the interruption of what would surely prove to be a futile exercise, I scooped him up and settled down in the rocker. He nursed, voraciously as usual, and I pondered my dilemma. My search for this Yossi was beginning to feel like looking for a needle in a haystack—or, rather, a sesame seed in a bagel factory. I was contemplating my next move when I heard an explosion coming from the nether regions of my little baby boy. At almost the same moment I felt something wet spreading across my lap. I leapt out of the chair and, ignoring Isaac's angry shrieks, rushed into his bedroom. Laying him on the changing table, I looked down at myself. My jeans were soaked through across the thighs. And they didn't smell pretty.

"Oh, for God's sake, Isaac," I muttered as I peeled off his overalls. "Some leakproof lining." The child had managed to produce enough poop to drench not only his diaper, but the shirt that snapped over his bottom, his overalls, and me. Swearing under my breath, I stripped him naked and dropped the filthy clothes onto the floor. He wiggled energetically while I wiped him up. Finally, realizing that the world didn't hold enough baby wipes to clean that mess, I picked him up and marched to the bathroom. I pulled off my own disgusting clothes, turned on the shower, and stepped in, holding Isaac in my arms. He startled a bit as the water hit him, but I fixed the showerhead so that a gentle spray rained down on us. Within moments, Isaac was giggling delightedly and lifting his head to the spray, opening his mouth to catch drops of water. I grabbed the soap and scrubbed both of us down, holding his slippery body in a viselike grip.

"Hey, this is fun, isn't it?" I said.

He burped in reply and snuggled up against my chest. He suddenly seemed to notice that he was in close proximity to his favorite things in the world and he began rooting around for a nipple. I stood there for a while under the warm water, holding Isaac while he nursed. As I held his silken soft body close to mine, I felt genuinely happy. Happy to be a mother. Happy to be standing in the shower with such a delightfully sweet baby. So much of being a parent is about managing, or disciplining, or getting from point A to point B. Sometimes I wonder what the point of having children is if one spends all one's time as a parent trying to herd them in the direction you need them to go, or keep them quiet or, even better, asleep. It's even occurred to me that I'd be better off with a battery-operated infant that I could play with for an hour or so each day and then toss into the closet when I got bored with its company. And then one of those sweet but rare moments happens, and I remember why I did this in the first place.

Finally, and reluctantly, I turned the water off and bundled the two of us into warm towels. As I dressed him, I noticed that Isaac actually seemed to be nodding off. Gingerly, I picked him up and tiptoed over to his bassinet. I laid him down and backed out the door. Miraculously, he slept.

"All right!" I punched a fist into the air and cheered, soundlessly. And then I remembered Ruby. I ran into the kitchen and looked at the microwave. I was late. Five minutes late. And I hadn't even left the house yet. I rushed over to the phone and called the preschool, praying that there would be someone who would answer the phone.

"Hello, Beth El Nursery School."

"Hi. Hello. This is Juliet. Ruby's mother? I am so sorry, but I completely lost track of time. I'm still home."

"Hello, Juliet. Why don't I check if there's someone here who can drive Ruby home for you."

"Could you? That would be just wonderful. Thank you so much."

The teacher was back within a minute or two.

"Juliet, everything is fine. Jake's mommy lives over on Fairfax. She's says you're right on her way home. She'll take Ruby for you."

"Thank God. Thank *you*. Wait. Wait a minute. A car seat. Ruby needs a car seat!"

"Not to worry, dear. We have one here for just these occasions. Just make sure you return it tomorrow at drop-off."

"I am so sorry. Thanks so much."

"Not at all. Not at all. Good-bye, dear."

"Bye-bye." Bye-bye. I sounded like a flight attendant—a stewardess on Bad Mother Airlines.

6

I TOOK ADVANTAGE OF the half-hour before Ruby got home to do the laundry and call some of the air-conditioning companies. Three of the ten I tried had guys named Yossi working for them. Only one company receptionist would give me a physical description and it didn't match Fraydle's boyfriend. I couldn't remember much about how he looked, but I was fairly certain he wasn't six foot three and blond. The other two people I spoke to who acknowledged the presence of at least one Yossi agreed to pass a message on. I didn't have high hopes that if, by some miracle, the message actually got to the right man, he would call me. After all, if it was the right Yossi, and if he did know where Fraydle was, he was presumably helping her hide out. Why would he ever help a stranger locate her?

After exploring my ten dead ends, I decided to skim through the list and give it one final shot. My eyes stopped short on the *Y*'s. There, under air-conditioning contractors, was the name "Yossi Ya'ari, Lcd. Contractor. I quickly called the number. It rang twice.

"Allo?" The line was full of static and I could hear what sounded like cars driving by. A cell phone.

"Hello, can I speak to Yossi, please?"

"This is Yossi." The man spoke with a thick Israeli accent; it sounded sort of like a cross between Brooklyn and Kuwait.

"Hello. Hi. Um, are you by any chance the Yossi who is a friend of Fraydle Finkelstein?"

"Fraydle? Who?"

"Fraydle Finkelstein?" I was barking up the wrong Yossi tree, clearly.

"No. I don't know any Fraydle."

"Okay, thanks for your time." I was about to hang up when something occurred to me. "Listen, I wonder if you can help me."

"Yes?"

"I was just wondering if you might know of some place that's popular with Israelis. You know, like a restaurant or bar?"

"Why? You want maybe to find a handsome Israeli man? You don't need a bar; you need me!"

I laughed politely. "I'm trying to track down a young Israeli man named Yossi."

"I am not so old, only sixty-two! Is that good enough for you?"

My polite laugh was getting stiff. "No, I'm looking for a specific Yossi, around twenty-one or twenty-two years old."

"Not me. So sad. Listen, where does this Israeli live?"

"I'm not sure, but maybe around Hancock Park."

"Near Melrose?" he asked.

"Possibly."

"Try Nomi's on the corner of Melrose and La Brea. It's a restaurant. Every Monday and Wednesday they have there music from Israel. Very popular with the young people. Maybe you can find him there."

"Thanks! Thanks so much, Yossi."

"I hope you find your Yossi. Wait, one minute. You are not from the INS?"

"No. No. Nothing like that."

"Good. Try Nomi's. Maybe you'll find him."

I hung up the phone just in time to hear a horn beeping in front of my house. I ran down the stairs and out the door to find Ruby being extracted from a Mercedes four-by-four. The woman who was helping her out was obviously Jake's mom, but I couldn't for the life of me remember her name. She was wearing leggings, a matching sweatshirt, and a pair of cross-trainers. She'd clearly just finished a workout. I glanced down at my decidedly un-aerobicized body and sighed. Someday I would find the energy to exercise. Maybe.

"Thanks so much!" I said. "I've just had the most ridiculous morning. I can't believe I forgot to pick Ruby up!"

The woman began to speak, but I couldn't hear a word she was saying. Ruby's indignant howls drowned her out.

"You forgot me!" my daughter shrieked. "You forgot me! You are a very very bad mama!"

"I'm so sorry, honey." I picked her up and hugged her. "I'm so sorry, sweet girl."

I kissed her a few times. She glared at me, and then her lower lip began to tremble.

"Oh honey, don't cry. Mama is so sorry."

With that, the tears began.

"She wasn't crying at all on the way home," Jake's mom said. "The two of them were singing the whole way."

"I believe that," I said, over the top of Ruby's hysterical head. "Thanks again, it was really nice of you."

"No problem. I live just a little farther along towards the Beverly Center. You're right on our way home. My name is Barbara, by the way."

"Of course, Barbara. Was it that obvious? I'm terrible with names."

"Me too. Brenda told me yours, otherwise I'm sure I wouldn't have remembered it either." She was probably just being polite.

"The kids sure seem to have hit it off," she said.

"That's terrific." It was a relief to know that Ruby could make friends. I've never been the best at organizing play dates. I can't plan my *own* social engagements, let alone Ruby's.

"Juliet, I was wondering, my older son goes to Milken Community School. In a couple of weeks the seventh grade is doing a production of *The Boys From Syracuse.* Would you and Ruby like to come see it with us? I think the kids will really love it."

Yeah, right after I have my fingernails pulled out, one by one. "Sure, that sounds great. Just let me know the details."

Ruby and I waved good-bye and headed up the stairs. I set her up with some markers and paper and we spent the next hour or so drawing portraits of our family. In mine, Daddy was far off in the distance, in a land called Work. In Ruby's, he was the largest figure on the page. I think we were expressing the same emotion, each in our own particular way.

That evening, long after I'd started listening for his car in the driveway, Peter called to let me know he was going to be late. Again.

"I was really hoping to go out tonight," I said, not a little irritated.

"I'm sorry, doll. Did you have plans with Stacy? I didn't realize. Do you want me to see if I can juggle things around here?" Now that was as insincere an offer as I'd ever heard.

"No. No, it's okay," I said. "I have to go check out this Israeli restaurant. Today's Wednesday and if I don't go today, I'll have to wait until Monday."

"Come again?"

"It's a long story. I'll tell you all the details when you get home, but in a nutshell, Fraydle has disappeared and I'm hoping to bump into her boyfriend at this restaurant on Melrose. It's supposedly a big Israeli hangout on Wednesdays and Mondays."

"Disappeared? How disappeared?"

"I think she's probably run away with this guy. I'll tell you all about it when you get home. Maybe I'll just take the kids to the restaurant for dinner."

There was a moment of silence on the line. Then he said, "Juliet, you're not getting *involved* in anything are you?"

"Don't be ridiculous, Peter. I'm just trying to find my goddamn babysitter. The poor kid is probably on the run from a horrible arranged marriage. Like I said, I'll tell you all about it when you get home."

"You wouldn't take the kids any place dangerous, would you?"

"Of course not. But hey, if you're really worried, why don't you come watch them while I go out?" I knew that was a nasty thing to say as soon as I said it, but I was pretty fed up with playing the part of the brave little television widow.

"I'm not worried. And I can't leave. Things are insane right now, but you know it will mellow out as soon as the pilot is in the can."

"Yeah, maybe. Or maybe they'll buy twenty-two episodes and we'll never see you again."

There was more silence on the other end of the line. Suddenly, I regretted my snappishness. Here the guy was, trying to support us, with no help from me, and I was giving him grief.

"I'm sorry, Peter. I know you can't help it. I'm just tired. I'm always tired. Go back to work, honey. We're fine. I love you."

"You do? Because, lately, it doesn't really seem like it."

Did he really feel that way, or was he just trying to make me feel guilty?

"Oh, give me a break, Peter. I told you, I'm just tired. Of course I love you. You try waking up every fifteen minutes for four months and see how pleasant you sound."

Two could play at the guilt game.

"I know. I know," he said. "I'm sorry, too. This is just a really lousy time for both of us."

"No kidding."

"Listen, I've got to run. They're calling me. I love you."

"Me too."

"Me too, too."

Trying not to feel too miserable about the conversation, I went into the bedroom to change my clothes for dinner. My Madonna T-shirt hadn't served me very well with Fraydle's father and I needed a change of luck. I grabbed a long black skirt with an elastic waist and pulled that on over a pair of black leggings. I topped that with a freshly laundered, white button-down shirt of Peter's. I picked up the baby and was on my way out to the living room to get his sister when I glanced in the mirror above my dresser. Ugh. My hair. Somehow, during the course of the day, I'd managed to mash down the front while, at the same time, doing something to the back that made it look decidedly like a third-grader's diorama of the Rocky Mountains. Peaks and valleys. I grabbed an old black beret out of my closet and put that on my head in what I hoped approximated a jaunty angle.

Nomi's was unprepossessing, to put it generously. The sole decorations were a number of ancient posters of Israel taped crookedly to the walls. There was one of Jerusalem from the air, with the Dome of the Rock prominently featured. Another showed a laughing female soldier, securely buckled into what looked like a parachute. The third appeared to be a view of a nondescript Los Angeles neighborhood, but the caption informed me, in bold neon, that it was "Cosmopolitan Tel Aviv." There were about twenty scruffy-looking Formica tables crammed closely together facing the far right corner, where a small stage was set up with music stands and an amplifier.

I stood hesitantly in the doorway, wondering if I should seat myself at one of the few remaining empty tables. I looked toward the back, where a waitress was bustling out of the kitchen with a tray of food. She smiled and called out something incomprehensible, pointing in the direction of one of the tables. Within seconds a handsome young busboy showed up holding a booster seat and a wooden high chair. He set the booster on one of the chairs and lifted a charmed Ruby into the seat. He then flipped the high chair over, took Isaac's car seat from me, and settled it snugly between the bars of the overturned high chair.

"Cool!" I said. "Where'd you learn that?"

"Babies babies, everywhere babies!" he said with an accent, pointing around the room. There were, indeed, quite a number of infants and small children in the place.

"You need menu?" he asked.

"Sure, that would be great."

He hustled off, returning after a moment with a menu and a glass of water for me, and some crayons for Ruby.

"Mama?" Ruby piped up.

"Yeah, honey?"

"I love this restaurant. This is the goodest restaurant I've ever seen."

"Even better than Giovanni's?" Peter and I have been regulars at our neighborhood Italian restaurant since before Ruby was born. Giovanni and his brother Frederico taught Ruby to say *ciao* before she even learned how to say "hello."

She paused for a moment. "No. Giovanni's is the goodest. This is the gooder."

"I'm glad you like it. Let's see what you think of the food. How about I order you a felafel sandwich and some french fries?"

"Fel fel like Daddy gets me at Eata-Pita?"

"The very same."

"Yummy."

The waitress, a petite brunette with a nice smile and two of the deepest dimples I'd ever seen, bustled over to our table. Quickly realizing that Hebrew wasn't going to go very far with us, she asked for our order in almost unaccented English. I ordered Ruby's felafel and a platter of various Middle Eastern salads for myself.

"Excuse me, miss," I said to the waitress as she finished writing down our order. "I'm looking for a guy named Yossi, darkish hair, about twenty or twenty-two years old?"

She looked at me curiously. "What do you need him for?"

"I'm actually trying to track down a friend of his, a young Hasidic girl named Fraydle. She works for me."

The waitress paused for a moment, as if she were about to tell me something. Then she said, "There aren't many Hasidim who come here. Nomi's is kosher, but not kosher enough, if you know what I mean."

I didn't, but I decided it wasn't important.

"There's music tonight, isn't there?" I asked.

"Every Wednesday and Monday. Look for your friend tonight. They all come in to hear the music."

I thanked her and scanned the room. There were lots of young men with Yossi's short haircut. There were even a few wearing similar brown leather jackets. None of them looked familiar, though.

The truth was, I didn't have a lot of faith in my ability to recognize Fraydle's Israeli, even if he should walk into the room. Eyewitness identification is notoriously unreliable. When I'd been a federal public defender I'd represented people in cases where every single eyewitness had provided a detailed description of the perpetrator—each one completely different from the others. One person would insist that the bank robber had blond hair and was six foot two. Another would swear that a Filipino dwarf had committed the crime. More than one witness usually meant that my client had a fighting chance. The real problem was when there was only one. It was virtually impossible to convince a judge to let me present expert testimony on the problems with eyewitness identification. Even if the judge did let me put a couple of scientists on the stand, juries never could get beyond their reaction to the bank teller who'd pointed a trembling finger at my client, whispering, "His face is burned into my mind."

I knew firsthand just how often eyewitnesses made mistakes. In law school my evidence professor had started class one day with a whispered discussion with a strange man who then left the room. An hour later she stopped, mid-lecture, and asked us to provide a physical description of the man. I thought he was about six feet tall or so, and I was absolutely positive that he was a young Latino man in his early twenties. I knew that he was wearing a blue windbreaker and khaki pants. I raised my hand and described the individual, absolutely certain that I was correct. A good half of the class agreed with me. My professor then walked to the door and opened it. In walked the man. He was a light-skinned black man who looked about thirty years old. He was a good deal shorter than six feet, but looked taller standing next to my petite professor. He was wearing a denim jacket and a pair of stonewashed jeans. I'd been absolutely wrong.

And worse, the sheer force of my conviction had swept many of the other eyewitnesses along with me.

For all I knew, Yossi would turn out not to be the medium-height, brown-haired Israeli I remembered, but rather an eighty-year-old Inuit in a wheelchair.

While I pondered this and other challenges of detection, Ruby grew bored with her crayons and Isaac lost patience with his car seat. The next few minutes were taken up with bouncing him on my lap and trying to entertain her with a story. Finally, the food arrived. Ruby tucked into her felafel with vigor and I popped Isaac on my breast, covered his back with a napkin, and stared at the vast plate covered with multicolored salads that the waitress set before me. There was easily enough food for three hungry men or one nursing woman. I almost groaned with delight as I scooped up garlicky hummus with warm pita.

I was so engrossed in cramming as much food into my mouth as I could before Isaac finished nursing that I almost forgot the object of my search. Luckily, I had stopped for a breather when a group of young men walked into the restaurant. From across the room I heard a voice call out, *"Shalom Yossi, Yiftach! Ma ha-inyanim?* What's up?" Any one of the four or five guys could have been my particular Yossi. They were all of short to medium height with close-cropped, brown hair. Two were wearing bomber jackets. "Yossi!" I said loudly.

One of the young men turned to look at me. He pointed to his chest and frowned as if to ask, Who, me?

Of all the felafel joints in all the towns in all the world.

"Yossi?" I said again.

He walked over to me. "Do I know you?" he asked. His voice was soft with just the slightest trace of accent.

"I think you know a friend of mine, Fraydle Finkelstein?"

He stiffened for a moment and looked at me more intently. "Do I know you?" he asked again.

"My name is Juliet Applebaum. Fraydle was watching my baby the other day? On Orange Drive?"

"We did not meet."

"No. No, we didn't. But Fraydle told me all about you."

He looked doubtful.

"Well, maybe not all about you. She told me that you guys are friends."

He smiled ruefully. "Friends. Yes, we are friends, I suppose."

"Yossi, would you sit down a minute so that we can talk?"

"I'm sorry. I cannot help you. I know her only a little. Just from the neighborhood." He turned his back to me and began to walk across the floor.

"Yossi!" I was almost shouting.

He turned back to me. "Please. I don't know what you want from me. I barely know this girl. We talk once, maybe twice. I did nothing wrong."

I looked at him. What made him assume that I was accusing him of anything?

"Do you know where Fraydle is?"

"What do you mean? She is where she always is. She is with her father. The rabbi." He fairly spat the words out.

"Actually, that's just where she's not. She hasn't been home since yesterday." It suddenly occurred to me that I hadn't spoken to Fraydle's family all afternoon. For all I knew, she was back home safe and sound.

"At least, she hadn't come home as of this morning," I continued.

Either Yossi was an accomplished actor or he was genuinely surprised at what I'd said. He pulled a chair over from another table and sat down between Ruby and me.

"Hey!" my daughter cried. "This is our table!"

"Ruby, this is Yossi. Mama just has to talk to him for a minute. Eat your felafel."

Ruby listened to me for once and turned back to her dinner. At that moment, Isaac gave a belch and I switched him to the other side. Yossi studiously avoided looking at my exposed breast.

"You said Fraydle is not home?" he asked.

I recounted to him how she'd failed to show up for work and my subsequent experiences with her father. "Not the most easygoing of men," I said.

"I have not met him. Your name is Juliet?"

"Yes."

"Juliet, this is not good. This is not like Fraydle to go away. She is not, how do you say, sophisticate?"

"Sophisticated."

"Yes, sophisticated. She is not. She has not spent a night away from her parents in her life. She would not just go away."

"And you have no idea where she is?" I was suspicious. After all, the first thing this guy had done was proclaim his innocence. And that was before I'd told him there might be something for him to be guilty of.

"I? Is that what you think? That she is maybe with me? That is crazy. I know this girl only a little bit."

"So you said. But you do know her enough to know she isn't sophisticated. Right?" He didn't answer. "Yossi," I said, "is Fraydle your girlfriend?"

"No! No! Nothing like that. I know her from the neighborhood. I told you this!" He shook his head angrily. "None of this is important. Where is she, that is what is important. You said you did not speak to them, to her family, this evening?"

"No. I haven't."

"So maybe she is at home." With that, he got up to leave.

"Wait. Yossi. Please wait. Let me just call her mother and see if she's home. If she is, fine. I won't bother you anymore. If not, then don't you think we should try to figure out where she might be?"

He looked at me for a moment, and then, shrugging his shoulders, sat back down at the table.

Ruby mumbled something incomprehensible from around a mouthful of fries.

"Just a minute, peach. Mama's got to make a phone call," I told her.

Reaching around Isaac's head, I dug in my purse for my cell phone and the scrap of paper with the Finkelsteins' phone number. I punched in the numbers. The phone rang only once.

"Hello? Fraydle?" a voice shouted into the phone. She wasn't home yet.

"No, this is Juliet Applebaum. Is this Rabbi Finkelstein?"

"Mrs. Applebaum. Yes. You have news of my daughter?" I could tell that I was not high on the rabbi's list of desirable conversation partners. I could also tell that he was desperate for news of his child.

"No, no, I'm terribly sorry, Rabbi. I was just calling to find out if she'd come home."

"No." And he hung up.

I stared dumbly into the phone receiver. "He hung up on me!" I announced.

Yossi didn't look surprised. "She is not home," he said, rather than asked.

"No."

He shrugged his shoulders. "Well, I don't know where she is."

"Exactly what are you and Fraydle to each other?" He didn't answer. "I know that you don't think this is any of my business, but maybe we can work together to figure out where Fraydle has gone." He remained silent. "Is it that you're afraid I'll tell her parents about you two? Is that it?" Silence.

"Hey, mister! My mama asked you something!"

"Shh! Ruby!"

Yossi looked at me for a moment and then, his face pale, he stood up again. "I cannot help you. I know her only a little bit. From the neighborhood," he repeated and made as if to walk away.

"Wait, Yossi. Let me give you my phone number, in case you think of anything. He shrugged his shoulders and stuffed the card I handed him into his pocket without looking at it.

"What's your last name?" I asked.

"Zinger," he said, turning on his heel and walking across the restaurant to the table where his friends were sitting.

"I want to go home, Mama. I want to see Daddy," Ruby whined.

"Okay, honey," I said. I hustled the kids out of the restaurant and into the car and, within an hour, had them both bathed and ready for bed. Ruby was out like a light as soon as her head hit the pillow. Isaac, as usual, was ready to rock and roll until the wee hours.

I took him into my bed and faked sleep, hoping to trick him into following suit. He was unimpressed. He lay in the crook of my arm, grunting and waving his arms about, his fingers gracefully outstretched like a miniature Thai dancer. After a futile ten minutes or so of playing possum, I gave up.

"So, what do you want to do?" I asked.

"I don't know, what do you want to do?" I answered in a squeaky baby voice.

"I don't know, what do you want to do?" *Et cetera*.

This scintillating exercise was interrupted by Peter's arrival.

"Hey," he called as he thumped up the back stairs.

"Hey," I called back.

"Are you still up?"

"No. I'm asleep. Can't you tell?"

Peter walked into the bedroom, stripping off his clothes as he crossed the worn wooden floorboards. In seconds he was next to us in bed, clad only in his boxer shorts.

"Hi, Isaac," Peter said, scooping the baby up and buzzing him on his belly. Isaac giggled.

"Hi, Daddy," I said in my squeaky voice.

"Did you guys have a good day?"

"Not really."

Peter pushed a long curl out of his eye. "Me neither."

"You go first," I said, rather generously, if I do say so myself.

"Oh, you know, just the usual garbage. The studio guys are insisting that the special effects are too expensive for TV and the director is threatening to quit unless they're left in. Blah blah blah. I swear to God, if it weren't for Mindy, I'd be going out of my mind."

I felt a flash of jealousy. The producing partner Peter's agency had set him up with was a woman of about my age with the unlikely name of Mindy Maxx. She was blond and brilliant and weighed seventeen pounds.

"And what did Maximum Mindy do today?"

Peter laughed perfunctorily. "She's really adept at handling those network drones. She keeps them in check but somehow convinces them that they're in charge. She's amazing."

"So you've said before."

He was oblivious to my sarcasm. "You do remember that we're going to her house for dinner tomorrow night, don't you?" he asked.

I hadn't remembered. "Oh God, is that tomorrow? Peter, I totally forgot. I didn't set up a babysitter. And Fraydle, the girl who was supposed to sit today, has disappeared. I don't know where I'd begin to find someone to watch the kids."

"I figured. That's why I found someone."

"*You* found a babysitter? What are you talking about? How did you find a babysitter?"

"Well, actually, it was Mindy's idea. Her assistant, Angelika, is going to do it."

"Angel-eeeka? Who's Angelika? We can't just let some total stranger take care of the kids." What was he thinking? Did he really believe I'd leave my kids with someone I'd never met?

"She's not a total stranger. I've known her for months—since we started developing the series. She's a nice young kid, a year or two out of college. She went to Yale, like Mindy."

"Oh, well, if she went to Yale, by all means." I was being snide. I'm a Harvard girl, after all.

"Juliet, do I need to remind you that you left Isaac with some girl you met once in a grocery store?"

That shut me up, for a moment.

"It'll be fine," Peter continued. "Angelika is a sweet kid and she's very responsible. Ruby will love her; she's got a stud in her tongue."

"Oh, well, why didn't you tell me that to begin with? Sure, no problem, as long as she's heavy into self-mutilation. I mean, who would ever want a babysitter who couldn't set off a metal detector or two?"

Peter sat up and lifted Isaac up over his head, zooming him around like an airplane.

"She's a nice kid," he said.

I gave up. "I'm sure she is. Ruby will love her." I sighed. "Don't get the baby all revved up. I'm trying to convince him that it's bedtime."

"Okay." Peter brought Isaac in for a landing and handed him to me.

"Why was your day so bad?" he asked, finally.

I launched into the tale of Fraydle's disappearance. I had just started telling him about my conversation with Yossi when I noticed that he'd fallen asleep.

"I love you, too," I whispered. I looked over at Isaac, who smiled at me. At least *he* cared what I had to say. "C'mon, buddy. Let's let Daddy get some rest."

7

PETER WAS GONE by the time Isaac and I got home from driving Ruby to school the next morning. My darling husband had left a note on the kitchen table.

Sorry I crashed last night. I'll be home early to get dressed for Mindy's. Why don't you go buy something fabulous to wear? It'll make you feel better.

"Better? Why do I need to feel better? I feel just fine, thank you." I muttered to myself as I crumpled the note. I had already decided to go by Mrs. Tannenbaum's store. I wasn't up to facing Fraydle's father, but I wanted to find out if Fraydle had come home. Afterwards, if we had time, Isaac and I could hit the Beverly Center and try to find something to wear to Marvelous Mindy's dinner party.

I drove the block and a half to the kosher grocery and parked in front of the store. It was open. Measuring the distance between my car and the shop at about ten feet, I decided it was safe to leave the baby in the car. I opened his window a crack, hopped out, and went to the door of the shop. Poking my head inside, I called out to Fraydle's aunt. "Nettie? It's Juliet Applebaum."

She stood behind the register, ringing up the purchases of an elderly woman wearing a wig that appeared to be made out of molded plastic.

"Hello, darling. No word yet," Nettie said, looking up at me and shaking her head.

"Nothing?" I asked.

"Nothing."

I glanced out at Isaac, who sat, undisturbed, just as I'd left him. "I can't stay," I said. "Isaac is in the car. I was just hoping . . ." I let the sentence trail off.

"We're all hoping."

The customer looked up curiously. "What hoping?" she asked, in a thick Yiddish accent.

"Nothing, dear," Nettie reassured her. She gave me a warning glance over the top of the woman's head. I nodded and waited in the doorway, where I could watch Isaac. He was busy trying to fit both fists into his mouth.

In slow motion, the old woman packed her purchases into a net bag and crammed that into an incongruous, pink suitcase on wheels emblazoned with the words "Going to Grandma's." Finally, after about twelve hours, she trundled past me and out the door. Nettie came out from behind the counter.

"Come, we'll go stand next to your baby. *Chas v'shalom* someone should steal him out of the car."

Suitably rebuked, I followed Nettie to the car. I leaned against the front passenger door, watching her as she made goo-goo eyes at Isaac. She tickled him on his belly and spoke to him in Yiddish. The woman clearly had been born to be a grandmother. It seemed a cruel twist of fate that she'd been robbed of her chance to have children, let alone grandchildren.

"Nettie, has your brother called the police yet?"

She shook her head. "No. Baruch says we'll find her ourselves."

I shook my head, frustrated at the man's obstinacy. "And Fraydle's mother agrees with this? She's willing to let days and days pass without going to the police? For crying out loud, Nettie. What if she *hasn't* run away? What if something has *happened* to her? You could be making a terrible mistake by waiting."

Nettie whirled around to face me, her eyes flashing. "You think I don't know this? You think I don't imagine that girl dead somewhere? Or kidnapped? What do you think? I don't care? Her mother doesn't care? We don't love her? Is that what you think?"

"Of course that's not what I think. I know you love her. That's why this refusal to call the police doesn't make sense to me. It's almost as if her father doesn't want her to be found."

"Pah!" She flung her hand at me in a dismissive gesture. "What do you know? The poor man does nothing but look for her. He drives all over this city looking for her. I'm telling you, he hasn't slept since she left. The only thing he wants in the world is for her to come home."

I was silent for a moment. Nettie obviously believed what she was saying. And maybe she was right. Maybe Rabbi Finkelstein was doing everything he could to get his daughter back. And maybe he wasn't.

"I have to go," I said finally. "You'll call me if you hear anything?"

"Yes. I'll call you," Nettie said. She leaned into the car and gave Isaac a wet kiss on the cheek. He grabbed her wig and tugged it askew.

"*Motek*," she said, and patted it straight again. "A lovely boy you have, Mrs. Applebaum. Take care of him."

"I will," I said softly. I reached out and hugged the sweet older woman. She held me close for a moment and then, sniffing back tears, walked back into her store. I watched her go and then walked around to the driver's side of the car, got in, and started the engine.

"Okay, buddy, let's go to the mall," I said to Isaac as I pulled onto Beverly Boulevard. "I hear Macy's has opened up a Rotund Petites department. I'm sure it's just chock full of fabulousness."

8

OUR SHOPPING TRIP was the exercise in humiliation I had come to expect from department stores. While my body had expanded well beyond a size ten, my eyes seemed to have gotten stuck at about a six. I took dress after dress off the rack and into the dressing room, only to find that they would fit provided I had time for a spot of liposuction. I seriously considered the plastic surgery before dumping my reject pile on a salesgirl who had been condescendingly watching my pathetic attempts.

"Ma'am, why don't you check out our large size collection? It's on the third floor, next to housewares."

I glared at her and stomped away. My dramatic exit was somewhat hampered by the fact that I got Isaac's stroller stuck on the corner of a display table. As I jerked it loose, I sent a pile of miniscule cashmere sweater sets flying.

"Sorry," I muttered to the salesgirl and hustled off across the store.

I was morosely making my way toward the escalator when my eye was caught by a mannequin wearing a pair of heavy satin pants in midnight black and an almost architectural shirt made of some kind of shiny gray fabric.

"Now, that's gorgeous," I said to Isaac. I wheeled him over to the mannequin and lifted up the price tag on the shirt. "Whew!" I gasped. The tag read $450. My first car cost less than that. The pants were a bargain at a mere $250.

"It's so hard to find something that fits when you're nursing, isn't it?"

I spun around to the source of the comment. An older woman in a beautifully tailored suit smiled at me.

"Impossible," I agreed. "Absolutely impossible."

"What's terrific about these pants is that they have an elastic waist. Very forgiving. The cut is slimming, too." She lifted up the shirt to show me the waistband of the slacks. "And the top is cut very full across the chest. Would you like to try it on?"

"You work here?" How could the same store that employed the snotty little twig who'd "helped" me earlier also have hired this lovely woman?

"Indeed, I do. In *couture*."

"Ah, *couture*," I said. That explained the price tag.

"Would you like to try it? If you decide you like it, we can shorten the slacks for you while you shop."

I paused for a moment. I had never in my life spent that much money on a single outfit, not even my wedding dress. I'd bought that at a sample sale for ninety-seven dollars. Ninety-seven dollars and the black eye I'd gotten when I yanked it out from under the sweaty fingers of another bargain-hunting bride.

"It *is* expensive," she said, reading my mind. "But it's beautifully made. It's a fabulous outfit."

She said the magic word. I was under strict orders to find fabulousness at all costs. "Okay, I'll try it."

Ninety minutes later, Isaac and I were on our way home, our trunk loaded down with the satin pants, gray shirt, and the astronomically expensive black sandals with silver buckles that I simply had to have to go with the outfit.

"I *am* fabulous, aren't I?" I asked my baby as we zipped through the streets of Los Angeles on our way to pick Ruby up at preschool.

That afternoon, I popped an Elmo video into the VCR for Ruby, mentally apologizing to the American Academy of Pediatrics, who had just informed me, via NPR, that I was doing incalculable damage to my child by allowing her to watch TV. I strapped Isaac into his Baby Bjorn and began to pace back and forth. As long as I was moving, the baby was quiet. I'd spent the day worrying more about my appearance than about Fraydle and I was feeling guilty. I was also certain that Fraydle's father was never going to find her, no matter how hard he was looking for her. I debated calling the police, but realized that without the Finkelsteins' cooperation, I wouldn't get very far. Chances were that she had just taken off, probably to avoid a marriage to someone she didn't love.

I needed to find her myself.

Even at the time, I knew my involvement with Fraydle was a little crazy; certainly it was out of proportion to how well I'd known the girl. But for some mysterious reason I felt a sense of responsibility toward her. Maybe she reminded me of myself at her age. Maybe her plight activated the do-gooder complex that had lain dormant since I'd left the federal public defender's office. Maybe I just needed to concentrate on something other than how utterly and completely exhausted I was.

I hadn't expected Yossi to call, and he hadn't surprised me. His evasiveness was certainly suspicious, but short of calling the cops and telling them that first of all I had a missing person to report and second of all I felt a little uncomfortable about the veracity of an Israeli friend of the disappeared, I wasn't sure what I could do.

I needed some advice and I knew just who would give it to me. I picked up the phone and, continuing to bounce Isaac up and down on my chest, called the federal public defender's office, my old stomping ground. The secretary to the investigators' unit put me on hold and I waited for Al Hockey to get off his butt and answer the phone. Al had been working as an investigator for the federal public defender ever since he'd retired after taking a bullet to the gut in his twenty-fifth year at the L.A. police department. Retirement hadn't agreed with him, and he always said that getting people out of jail wasn't all that different from putting them away, just a little bit harder. During my time as an attorney in that office, we'd been an unstoppable team. I owed every one of my "Not Guilty" verdicts to his tireless footwork. Al possessed the miraculous ability to pluck an alibi witness out of thin air.

"If it isn't my favorite private eye! Juliet Applebaum, how are your bullet holes?"

"Fine, Al. And yours?"

"Just fine. What borderline illegal activities do you have in store for me today?"

"Illegal? I'm outraged. Truly outraged. When have I ever asked you to do anything illegal? Unethical, maybe. Illegal, never."

"A rather fine distinction. What do you want now?" he asked.

"Missing person's case," I replied. I told him the story about Fraydle's disappearance.

"Sounds to me like she pulled a runner, Juliet."

"Yeah, that's what I think, too, but there's always the chance, however slight, that it may be more serious, and it makes me nervous that the cops don't know about it."

"You could always call them."

"I suppose so, but I'm worried about alienating the parents. I'm just wondering if there's a way I can unofficially find out if any girls have turned up."

"Turned up where, the morgue?"

That stopped me in my tracks. I suppose that's what I meant, but I hadn't put it so bluntly even to myself.

"Well, yeah. The morgue or a hospital or something. I suppose I could call every hospital in the city, and every morgue for that matter, but I figured you might know an easier way to do this."

He thought for a moment. "I could ask one of my buddies from the LAPD to check on any Jane Does."

"That would be wonderful. What do you need to know?"

"A general physical description, age, the neighborhood she lives in, that kind of thing."

I gave Al the information and made him promise to call me by the next day with whatever he'd found out. I'd done what I could that day. And anyway, Elmo was almost over.

9

I WAS DEFINITELY NOT ready to go out when Peter came home. In fact, Ruby and I were both covered in flour and Isaac was in his bouncy seat, looking like a little Abominable Snowman. We'd decided to bake cookies, but had never got past the dough stage. My mother had called in the middle of our project and I'd had to spend fifteen minutes explaining to her why it was that Peter and I couldn't put his project on hold, load up the kids, and hightail it out to Jersey for a week. Or two. Or six.

"Hey, family," Peter said when he walked in the kitchen.

"Hey, Daddy," Ruby and I answered, in unison.

"Is this fabulous enough for you?" I asked, pointing at my dirty sweatshirt.

He smiled. "No, but this is." He jumped across the room and wrestled me to the floor, pulling the sweatshirt off. Ruby, not one to be excluded from a wrestling match, leapt on top of us.

We rolled around the floor for a minute or two, laughing and shouting. Suddenly I noticed that Isaac was squalling.

"Party pooper," I said, as I got to my feet and picked him up. "We were just having fun, little guy."

"Hey, give him here," Peter said, getting up off the floor and brushing flour off his pants. "Come here, buddy. Say hi to Daddy."

Ruby began working herself into an apoplectic fit when she realized that her beloved father was actually paying attention to the usurper.

"Everybody, quiet!" I shouted. "Okay, you"—I pointed to Peter—"clean up the kitchen. You"— I looked at Ruby—"come help Mama get dressed for a party."

"I don't want to help you, I want to be with Daddy," she howled.

"Fine, whatever, Baby Electra. Help Daddy clean up. I'm going to take a nice hot bath."

AFTER MY BATH I slipped my new outfit out of the garment bags Macy's had so thoughtfully provided. No tacky paper shopping bags when you shop *couture*. The pants felt cool and slippery against my skin. The shirt looked, if anything, better than it had in the dressing room. I felt downright attractive for the first time in months. I carefully applied some makeup and put on my most expensive earrings, a pair of diamond studs Peter had given me when Ruby was born. I was admiring myself in the mirror when Peter and the kids walked into the bedroom.

"Wow," Peter said.

"You asked for fabulous."

"And that's what I got. You look great."

"Thanks, honey." I kissed him on the cheek and took the baby from him. He stripped off his shirt and put on a clean one. He brushed off his khakis and yanked a jacket out of his closet. I sighed. It's so much easier to be a man.

Angelika, the babysitter, showed up at the house with a bag full of colored paper, kid's scissors, glue, markers, and glitter. "I thought we could make our own greeting cards," she said. Ruby looked like she'd died and gone to heaven.

Peter and I left them engrossed in their project, with Isaac happily bouncing in his Johnny-Jump-Up.

"So what kind of party is this?" I asked as we drove down Beverly Boulevard toward Mysterious Mindy's Benedict Canyon house.

"What do you mean what kind of party?" Peter asked.

"You know, is this a normal people's party with, like, sour-cream-and-onion dip and a bunch of friends, or is this a Hollywood, catered kind of party with valet parking?"

"I dunno. It's dinner. It's a dinner party."

"Okay, well is it a 'come on over and I'll hand you a big bowl of chili and my grandmother's cornbread' kind of dinner party or is it a 'Suzette is serving our first course, Maryland crab cakes in a delicate saffron remoulade roux' kind of dinner party?"

"Look, Juliet." Peter turned to me. "Mindy is a friend of mine. And a colleague. My relationship with her means a lot to me. I'd really appreciate it if you'd lose the attitude."

"Professional or personal?"

"What?"

"Which means a lot to you, your professional relationship or your personal relationship?"

He looked at me for a minute and then back at the road. Neither of us said anything for a little while. Then I spoke. "Sorry."

"It's okay. I'm sorry, too." But it didn't really seem to be okay, and I didn't believe that he actually knew what he was apologizing for. Nor did I, in all honesty.

We pulled into the driveway of a 1940s bungalow that had obviously had a major face-lift sometime in the past few years. A line of young women in black vests emblazoned with the logo "Valet Girls" stood ready at the doorway. Peter handed the car keys to one and she leaped into the driver's seat and zipped off. So, it was that kind of a party.

The house was larger than it looked from the outside and decorated within an inch of its life. The style was a sort of eclectic Arts & Crafts with a few gorgeous old pieces that probably had the name Gustav Stickley carefully stamped under a drawer or behind a back panel. Each brightly colored kilim pillow and artful knickknack was in just the right spot. On the walls were a number of large black-and-white photographs in beautiful wooden frames. One, a photo of a pair of lovely young girls bathing in the ocean, looked to my untrained eye like a Sally Mann.

"This place is amazing!" I whispered to Peter.

"I know," he whispered back. "You should see the kitchen. It's gorgeous."

What the heck? How did he know what the kitchen looked like? I was getting ready to ask him, or punch him in the stomach, when the impeccably decorated owner of the impeccably decorated house glided up.

Magical Mindy was wearing a sleek black pantsuit and a white blouse with French cuffs that protruded from her coat sleeves and dangled over her fingers. She had on black stiletto heels that, in case we missed it, had the name Prada embroidered on the side. Her toenails were painted electric blue and her carefully tousled and highlighted hair fell in luxurious curls down her back. I hated her.

"Hello! Juliet! It's so wonderful to see you again. You look fabulous!"

I smiled, perhaps a bit grimly. "So do you, Mindy. Absolutely."

We stood there awkwardly for a moment, trying to think of something to say, and then Mindy turned to Peter. "Pete, listen, there's a kid here that I want you to meet. He's a hot new actor and I think we should consider him for one of the mid-season roles. He's hip-pocketed at CAA and I think he's about to shoot through the stratosphere."

"Terrific," Peter said. He turned to me. "I'll be right back, okay?"

"Sure, no problem." I answered, inwardly seething. Who, exactly, was "Pete" and who did he think I was going to talk to at this event?

I grabbed a glass off the tray of a passing waiter, plopped myself down on an overstuffed sofa, and sipped at my wine, feeling sorry for myself. Nobody talked to me, although who could blame them? I looked about as much fun as a colicky baby. After what felt like an hour but was probably no more than ten minutes, Peter came back. He sat down next to me.

"You're having a terrible time, aren't you?" he said.

"No, I'm having a great time. Really."

"Baloney."

"Okay, it's baloney. I'm sorry. It's just that I don't really know anyone. Everyone at this party is from TV or something. None of our friends are here."

"Why don't you try to meet some people? Make some new friends."

Like that was so easy.

I said, "You're right. You're totally right. Why don't you introduce me to some of the people you work with?"

Peter popped off the sofa and extended his hand to me. I took it and he hauled me to my feet. "Okay, let's go meet some folks."

"Okay," I said, not overly thrilled at the prospect.

After about twenty minutes I inwardly vowed that I would kill the next person who ardently shook my hand and said, "I am such a big fan of your husband's." Fan? Please. Those jaded Hollywood types hadn't been fans of anything since they had Shawn Cassidy's picture taped inside the doors of their lockers in sixth grade.

I was thinking up some snappy insult for the next "fan" when Peter leaned over and whispered in my ear, "Honey, you're leaking."

"I'm what?" Then I looked at my shirt. A large circle of damp was slowly spreading over the incredibly expensive fabric. I'd forgotten to put a breast pad in my bra.

"Oh, God," I said, and rushed out of the room. I couldn't find an unoccupied bathroom so I tore into the kitchen, dodging a caterer or two, and found a roll of paper towels. I tore off a handful and shoved them down my shirt.

"Are you okay?" I heard a woman's voice ask. I looked up into the dimpled face of the waitress who had served the kids and me at Nomi's, the Israeli restaurant. She was dressed in black slacks and a white caterer's jacket.

"I'm fine. Just leaking. You work at Nomi's, don't you?"

She plucked a dishtowel out of a pile of neatly folded cloths sitting on the counter and dampened it with San Pelligrino mineral water. "Try this," she said, handing it to me. "Seltzer gets out anything. Yes, I work at Nomi's. I also do catering jobs sometimes. For extra money. You came into the restaurant last night, right?"

I nodded and dabbed at the stain on my shirt. As far as I could tell I was just making a small wet spot into a larger one.

"You talked to Yossi," she continued.

"Yes."

"About his girlfriend."

My head shot up. Girlfriend? "You know her?" I asked.

The young woman shrugged her shoulders. "A little bit. One minute." She turned to the stove, a huge Viking range with an eight-burner cook-top and an oven that looked like it could roast six or seven Thanksgiving turkeys at the same time. Donning a pair of oven mitts, she reached into the oven and took out a cookie sheet of miniature *spanikopita* that she began to carefully arrange on a cut-glass tray.

"So, you know Fraydle?" I pressed.

"The Hasidic girl? I'm not her friend, but I have seen her sometimes."

"In the restaurant?"

"Oh, no. I don't think she would ever eat at Nomi's. No, in my building." She finished arranging the hors d'oeuvres. "I'll be right back," she said, and headed out the kitchen door.

I busied myself with my shirt, doing my best to dry the fabric. It occurred to me that the warm oven might help in that endeavor, so I opened the door and crouched down close to it.

"What are you doing?" the waitress asked as she came back into the kitchen.

"Just trying to get my shirt dry."

"Oh, good idea," she said. She squeezed by me and busied herself at the kitchen counter, taking the plastic wrap off a tray of sushi.

"You were telling me about Fraydle," I reminded her.

"Yes. The Hasidic girl. Yossi and I live in the same building, so I see her sometimes. Just passing in the courtyard, you know?"

Well, that certainly gave the lie to Yossi's claim about just seeing Fraydle "around the neighborhood."

"Are you friendly with Yossi?" I asked.

She shrugged. "Once. Maybe. I knew him from the army. You know, in Israel?"

"You were in the army?" She didn't look like a soldier. She looked like a typical Melrose Avenue babe.

"It's not such a big deal. We all go to the army in Israel. I was a secretary in his unit. So I knew him." There was something about her tone that bothered me.

"What kind of unit?"

"Excuse me?"

"What did you guys do in the army?"

She paused, and looked up at me. "Why do you ask that question?"

"No reason. I was just curious." And I wanted to find out if Yossi had any Israeli military training that would, say, allow him to spirit an eighteen-year-old girl out of her home without a trace.

"We were in the paratroopers."

"Wow. You jumped out of planes?"

"I jumped only once. But that's what the men did, yes."

Changing the subject, I said, "You know, we haven't even introduced ourselves. I'm Juliet Applebaum."

"Anat. Anat Ben-David."

We were quiet for a moment. I leaned out of the way as one of the other waiters grabbed a tray of wineglasses from behind me. Then I employed my trademark interrogation technique. The one where I blurt out the first thing that comes to mind. "So, Anat, I have to say, it doesn't sound as if you like Yossi all that much."

She didn't seem particularly taken aback by my comment. "Maybe I liked him once, but now I don't care about him at all."

That certainly sounded familiar to me. I'd felt that way about plenty of guys. Like maybe twenty or so before I met Peter. "So, did you guys go out, or something?"

She blushed a little and busily rearranged the already perfectly arranged sushi plate. "Something like that. A long time ago, I liked him very much. And he pretended to like me. For maybe a week. And then nothing. Until I saw him again here in Los Angeles."

"With Fraydle," I said.

"With the Hasidic girl," Anat agreed.

Giving up on my shirt altogether, I stopped my ineffectual blotting and leaned on the counter. "Were they seeing each other for a long time?"

Anat handed the sushi plate to a waitress who was hovering nearby. "Months, I think. I used to see her in the building all the time. I don't think she's been there in the past week or two. At least, I haven't seen her. We have a courtyard, you know? Like on *Melrose Place*?"

I nodded.

"So, if she's been there when I've been there, I would see her. The last time I saw her she was very upset. "She was crying or something. She looked awful. Almost . . . not ugly, but just . . . I don't know . . . bad. Like something really terrible had happened to her."

"Did you talk to her?"

"Oh, no. I mean, I said hello sometimes, but she just maybe nodded her head or something like that. She never talked to me. That last time she just ran by me."

"Do you think she knew about you and Yossi?"

"Maybe, but I don't think so. With Yossi, if he starts to talk about girlfriends, it would take a long time to finish the talk, you know?"

"Yeah, I've known guys like that. You know, you're probably lucky you only wasted a week of your life with him. Think how much worse it would be if you'd been with him for a year before you figured that out."

She smiled somewhat ruefully. "You know, you're right. I never thought of it that way."

"So, is there anything else you can tell me about Fraydle and Yossi?"

She pushed her hair out of her eyes with the back of her wrist. "I don't think so." At that moment, it seemed to dawn on her that she had no idea why I was asking her all these questions. "Are you a friend of hers?" she asked.

"No, not a friend," I replied. "Fraydle used to work for me. She's been missing for the past couple of days and I'm trying to help find her."

"Missing! Like she ran away or something?"

"Or something. Are you sure she hasn't been around Yossi's apartment?"

"I haven't seen her. But if we didn't come in at the same time, or if she just stayed in his apartment, I wouldn't necessarily know if she was there or not. I can give you our address. You can come over yourself and look." Anat picked up a pen and tore off a corner of a pastry box that was sitting on the table. She wrote out the address and handed it to me. "His apartment is on the bottom level, number four."

"Great, thanks, Anat. Here, take my phone number and call me if you think of anything or if you see her, okay?" I scrawled my name and number on another piece of the pastry box. She put it in her shirt pocket, said good-bye, and headed out of the kitchen holding the platter of raw fish.

As she walked out the kitchen door, Peter walked in. He looked relieved to see me.

"Hey! I've been looking all over for you. Are you okay? Did you get the stain out of your shirt?"

"I'm fine. My shirt is not so fine, however." I pulled at the fabric. It appeared that the milk had more or less rinsed out, but the fabric was bunched and crinkled where it had gotten wet. "Fabulous," I said forlornly.

"Oh, honey"—Peter crossed the room and took me in his arms—"you look beautiful. It doesn't matter if your shirt's a little wrinkled. Who cares? You're gorgeous."

I leaned into his chest and inhaled his familiar odor. Embracing him, I did my best not to cry. It had been a long time since Peter and I had just hugged each other. The combination of my postpartum moodiness and Peter's schedule had brought our relationship down to an unfamiliar low. It was hard to remember when we'd last had a conversation that didn't devolve into an argument.

Peter kissed the top of my head. "I love you, Juliet. You know that, don't you?"

"I know. I love you, too. I just seem to be soaking in some kind of perpetual hormonal bath. Ugh. The not sleeping isn't helping much, either."

"I'm so sorry, sweetie," he murmured. "I haven't been pulling my weight on that end, have I?"

I didn't answer. I didn't need to. I just buried my face a little deeper in his shirt.

"How about if I take baby duty two nights a week? I'll try to work it out on days when I don't have to be on the set, but I'll do it even if I have to work the next day. Okay?"

I leaned back and looked up at him. "That would be amazing, Peter. I think if I could get an uninterrupted six hours of sleep just two days in a row I would be in much better shape."

We smiled at each other.

"Look at the lovebirds hiding in the kitchen!" Maximum Mindy's voice rang out with a shrill falseness that was so obvious even Peter got it. He winced.

"Just a little breast-feeding accident," I said, glancing pointedly at her gravity-defying chest. "Let's go mingle, honey." I took Peter's hand and led him back out to the living room. Within a few minutes, I actually found someone with whom I enjoyed talking, another wife, this one married to an agent. She confided in me that she was ten weeks pregnant after three years of infertility treatments. By the end of the evening I knew all about her husband's low sperm motility and her endometriosis. We also talked for a while about her grandmother's recent Alzheimer's diagnosis and my two cesarean sections. Peter and the woman's husband discussed the Dodgers and their chances of winning the pennant.

It really is remarkable. Standing in line at a movie theater, I can learn more about a woman—her family, her academic background, and even her gynecological history—than my husband can learn about a man in five years of friendship. Women truly do share their lives with one another more easily than men. We confide and discuss, gossip and debate. I, for one, think that this willingness to let others in on our secrets is a source of our greatest strength. It is infinitely easier to survive a crisis, from a miscarriage to a husband's serious illness to a visit from your mother-in-law if you can turn to your friends, cry on their shoulders and gather energy, resources, and fortitude from their support. And, hey, if your friends aren't around, some woman you meet at a party can be almost as good.

It was almost eleven o'clock when Peter and I were ready to go. I hugged my new best friend, extended a warm if somewhat phony thanks to Miraculous Mindy, and went in search of Anat. I found her in the kitchen, washing dishes with another young woman in a caterer's jacket.

"Anat," I said. She turned to look at me. "We're heading home," I continued. "You have my number in case anything comes up."

"I have it," she replied. "Bye."

"Bye." As I was heading out the door I heard the second girl murmur something in Hebrew. Anat shrugged her shoulders in reply.

When Peter and I got home we found Ruby and Isaac asleep in their respective beds and Angelika lying stretched out on the couch. She jumped up when we came in.

"How were they?" I asked.

"Great! Really great," she answered. "Ruby's a doll. She worked on her project for the longest time and then she helped clean up everything without my even asking. She took a bath and didn't cry when I washed her hair. The baby slept for most of the evening, although he was up for the last hour or so. He crashed just about ten minutes ago."

Peter turned around and started walking back down the stairs.

"Hey!" I called. "Where are you going?"

"Home," he answered. "This is not our house."

"So, Angelika, what are you doing for the next, oh, eighteen years?" I asked.

I pressed some money into the girl's hand, over her strenuous objections. The only way I got her to accept it was by insisting that if she didn't take money from us I would feel uncomfortable asking her to babysit again. Peter walked her to her car and when he came back into the house, he found me lying in our bed. I'd somehow managed to cram myself into a black satin teddy he'd bought me as an anniversary present the year after we'd had Ruby. He crossed the room in about two steps and scooped me up in his arms. Then, we did something we hadn't done more than a couple of times since Isaac was born. And it was wonderful. Maybe, I thought, things were getting back to normal.

10

NSPIRED BY MY invigorating night, I decided that Isaac and I were going to get back into shape. I dressed him in his cutest outfit, a blue velour number with a purple collar and matching purple socks. I dressed myself in a less cute pair of leggings and a huge, ancient T-shirt of Peter's that said "Starfleet Academy" on the front and "Cadet" on the back. After dropping Ruby off at school, Isaac and I drove to Santa Monica to Yoga on Montana, the yoga studio where I'd done prenatal yoga during my pregnancy. I've always enjoyed yoga, particularly the position called *savasana*, which consists of lying on your back on the floor without moving, and I'd really meant to start doing it again as soon as the baby was born. The road to Weight Watchers is paved with good intentions.

I pulled into the parking lot and squeezed my Volvo station wagon in between a Mercedes wagon and a Land Rover. The Mercedes had a child's car seat in the back and a bumper sticker that read "My Child Made the Honor Roll at the Oakville School." The Land Rover sported a bumper sticker with the slogan "My Kid Beat Up Your Honor Student." In Los Angeles people sometimes just let their cars do their fighting for them.

I walked into the class with Isaac balanced on my hip. He stared around the room, which was filled with other babies and their mothers. His eyes widened and he began to giggle. I wasn't sure what exactly had tickled his fancy, but I didn't care. I was just relieved that we seemed to be getting off to a good start. Maybe we could do this exercise thing after all. Grabbing a yoga mat for myself and a blanket for Isaac, I found myself a place on the floor. I rolled one end of the blanket and propped Isaac up on the roll. He smiled at me and I smiled back. Then I looked around the room. All the good cheer drained out of me as I realized the truth. I was a hippo in a herd of gazelles.

Yoga on Montana is very popular with the Hollywood crowd. The classes are usually chock-full of actresses, agents, and studio executives. Looking good is a primary occupation for these women, so, unsurprisingly, each and every member of my prenatal class had looked like a toothpick with an olive stuck on it. Now it was obvious that they'd all managed to get back to their pre-pregnancy weight before they'd even left the hospital.

I tucked my stomach in and tried to refrain from doing a self-hating body-fat comparison with every woman in the room. It was a challenge. And I failed. But who can blame me? As soon as I sat down I heard a minuscule blonde a few mats down from me say, "My trainer measured the circumference of my thighs the day I told him I was pregnant. It was sixteen inches. We remeasured every week throughout my pregnancy, and if it went up at all, we modified my workout regime and carb intake to deal with it." She gave her perfectly dyed hair a toss and patted her perfectly flat, lycra-enclosed belly. Her baby, also blond and about two months old, chose that moment to belch. At least I knew someone in that family was human.

A gamine-faced redhead with a made-over nose sitting next to the blonde squealed, "What a totally awesome idea! I can't believe I didn't think to do that! What was your final measurement?"

The blonde looked confused. "Final? What do you mean final? I told you. We never allowed it to increase."

At this point I glanced down at my legs. My ankles had a circumference of sixteen inches. I moved a little so that my legs were out of the stick figures' line of sight.

A third woman, wearing a leotard and tights in an acid green that perfectly matched both her headband and her son's jumpsuit, leaned over excitedly. "My secret was to have a nutritionist work with our cook so that every morsel that passed my lips was carefully vetted for fat and caloric content. I'm still doing it. Before we go out to eat, I have the restaurant fax the nutritionist a menu so that she can decide what I'm going to order. It's been working out so well. I only gained fourteen pounds in my entire pregnancy and I lost that within two weeks!"

The two others positively cooed in admiration.

I was just about ready to gather up my baby and head for the nearest Dunkin' Donuts when the instructor walked into the room. Valerie was actually a human being, with a stomach and legs instead of the washboard and pencils that were de rigueur in her classes. She was certainly not fat, but her body had a heft to it. Her muscles were strong and obvious and her belly looked round and soft. She was incredibly sexy, although I was sure that the other women in the class probably couldn't see that, since their ideal of physical attractiveness hovered somewhere between Kate Moss and Bergen-Belsen.

"Hello, ladies; hello, babies. Let's start with a meditation."

Isaac and I had a terrific time, despite my generalized misanthropy and tremendous feelings of insecurity. I did my Downward Dog and Warrior Stance with a flexibility that surprised the heck out of me. Isaac stared happily around and chewed on his blanket. At one point, Valerie picked him up and perched him on a big rubber ball, gently bouncing him up and down. About twenty minutes into the class I managed to forget about the way I looked and just enjoy the feeling of having my body move again. My muscles felt sore and kind of achy, but in a good way.

After the class was over, I picked up an oversized smoothie made with blueberries and bananas and loaded Isaac into the car. I backed out of my parking space, missing the Mercedes in the next spot by a rather terrifying half an inch, and pulled onto Montana and headed for home. I'd been driving about five minutes when I began thinking about Fraydle again. Keeping my eyes on the road, or trying to, I groped in my bag for my cell phone. I spent a frustrating minute trying to remember what number I'd entered for Al Hockey on my speed-dial. I had no idea, but decided to take a stab at number 3. It seemed as likely as any other number. I got my mother instead.

"Hello?"

"Mom? Damn it."

"Juliet? What damn it?" she said, obviously a little confused about why her daughter would be calling and swearing at her.

"Nothing. I just meant to dial another number. I got you by accident."

"Of course. Why should you ever call your mother on purpose, God forbid?" Were we really having this conversation or was this a scene from a Woody Allen movie? My mother and I have always had a complicated relationship. We spend almost as much time talking to each other as we spend complaining about each other. I hold her responsible for all my various neuroses, and she holds herself responsible for all my good qualities. We fight constantly, but that never seems to keep us from being completely and totally wrapped up in each other's lives. I've been known to call her from a department store to describe an outfit so that she can weigh in on whether I should buy it. I never take her advice.

"Oh, Mom. Please. I call you all the time."

"When? When do you call me?"

"Yesterday! I talked to you yesterday."

"Yesterday? I called *you* yesterday. You did not call me."

"Oh what difference does that make? I talked to you yesterday. Anyway, Ma, I've got to go. I have to talk to Al Hockey."

"That nice man you used to work with? Why? Are you going back to work?" She sounded excited. No one had been more surprised than my mother when I'd quit work to stay home with my kids. For months she treated me to long, tearful conversations about my betrayal of everything she and her fellow bra-burners had suffered in order to make it possible for me to have the opportunities that I was throwing away so blithely. She reminded me of how she had always wanted to be a lawyer and had had to satisfy herself with a career as a legal secretary because she'd married so young and had to work to put my dad through school. She wept about my lost chance to make it to the United States Supreme Court.

"No. I'm not going back to work. Al is just helping me out with something."

"Helping you? With what? Oh, darling. Tell me you're not trying to get yourself shot again!" In the wake of the rather terrifying end to my last experience with private detection my mother had made me swear never to do anything like that as long as *she* lived.

"Give me a break, Ma. Okay? I'm not trying to get shot. I never tried to get shot to begin with. My babysitter ran away from home and Al is helping me find her. That's all."

"Your babysitter? Who knew you had a babysitter? I didn't, that's for sure. Why'd she run away?"

"I have no idea. Anyway, I have to go. I've got to call Al."

"When are we going to see you, Juliet? I wish we could come to California, but we can't leave Bubba."

"How is she?"

"Not so great. I don't think she's going to last long, honey. You should visit soon."

"I'm going to get there. I promise." I wasn't so sure that my grandmother wouldn't, in fact, live forever. She'd turned ninety-five the year before and gave no signs of throwing in the towel any time soon. "It's just a bad time for us, what with Peter's TV pilot. He's working all the time nowadays. There's just no way he can take the time off."

"So, *you* come. You come and bring my babies with you. It'll be a vacation for you. Daddy and I will take care of them, and you'll just relax. What could be better?"

"I'll think about it, Ma. Okay? I've really got to go."

"Okay, darling. I'll talk to you tomorrow."

I hung up the phone and sighed. I knew I should visit my grandmother. And it would be lovely to have my mother help me with the kids. I'd been pretty disappointed when she'd decided that she couldn't leave Bubba to come stay with us after Isaac was born. When I'd had Ruby, my mother had taken a leave of absence from her job and showed up in our apartment within hours of the birth. She cooked and cleaned for us for a solid month. It had been bliss and I'd really missed her this time around.

I gave up on my pathetic attempts to remember Al's number and called Directory Assistance. What is it about motherhood that causes women to get so dense? I used to be one of those organized people who could remember names, numbers, and even the occasional birthday. Now I was the kind of person who answered the door naked. It was as if every contraction had killed off a few hundred thousand brain cells. By the time both babies were out, I was left with the IQ of a ficus.

Al was out of the office when I called, but the receptionist put me through to his cell phone.

"Hey, Detective!" he greeted me.

"Cute. So, anything?"

"Nope. Nothing. One Jane Doe turned up in the past three days, but she's middle-aged and African-American. Not yours, I take it."

"Not mine. Mine's young and white."

"So you said. Anyway, I told my old sergeant to keep me posted if he hears anything. What else can I do for you?"

"Nothing right now, Al, but I might be calling you soon."

"I'll be expecting it."

At that moment I pulled into the intersection of Beverly Boulevard and Santa Monica. Home was to the right, but I continued straight and turned onto Melrose. I had an hour before I had to pick up Ruby. Just enough time to check out Yossi's apartment. Maybe I'd luck out and find Fraydle there.

I cruised down Melrose Avenue and started looking for a parking space as soon as I saw Anat and Yossi's building. After a frustrating few minutes, I pulled into the parking lot of a Baby Gap. I slipped on Isaac's Baby Bjorn and, after scraping off some mysterious yellow gunk that had managed to adhere itself to the front, strapped him into it facing outward. He immediately began fussing, so I slipped my pinky into his mouth. Sucking vigorously, he quieted down. I walked briskly by the sign informing me that cars belonging to those other than Gap customers would be promptly towed. I was about to head down Melrose Avenue when I heard a terrifying trumpeting sound.

"Isaac! Are you kidding?" I pulled my smelly son out of his Baby Bjorn and held him at arm's length. The little wretch had managed to burst through his diaper yet again. I looked back at the car. I'd remembered Barney tapes. I'd remembered diapers. I'd remembered wipes. I'd even brought the Baby Bjorn. But I'd forgotten a spare outfit. Once again, my place in the pantheon of bad mothers was assured.

Still holding Isaac out in front of me, I hustled into the Baby Gap and was immediately greeted by a smiling Gen-Xer. I responded to her "Hi! How are you?" with a wave of my malodorous child. She pointed to someone whose job actually consisted of helping people and not just welcoming them. I balanced Isaac precariously on my hip, trying to touch as little of his body as possible, reached into my purse, and tossed my credit card at the salesclerk.

"What can I get for you?" she asked.

"Something clean," I said.

She directed me to a bathroom where I stripped the baby down and washed him in the sink. I looked at what had once been my favorite baby outfit, now stained a horrifying shade of yellow, and debated throwing it out. I couldn't bring myself to part with it, so I shoved it into a sanitary napkin disposal bag and hid that in the bottom of my diaper bag.

Isaac and I found our salesclerk standing at the register holding a miniature pair of jeans, a rugby shirt, and matching socks. I dressed the baby, using my teeth to tear the price tags off. I handed the damp pieces of paper back to the be-pierced salesclerk, who gingerly scanned them into the register. We were in and out in less than five minutes. And we managed to spend less than seventy dollars. A miracle.

From the outside, the building where I hoped to find Fraydle hiding out was fairly nondescript. It was Spanish-style in the way that most Los Angeles houses of the 1930s are, that is to say it was stucco with wrought-iron railings. The façade was thickly covered in ivy that had been inelegantly hacked away from the windows. The entry was through an archway whose stone-faced interior walls were covered in brightly colored graffiti, some of it in Hebrew.

Isaac and I passed under the arch and into a courtyard. Once, it must have been beautiful. A stone fountain dominated the center of the yard. In its large oval pond, a mermaid balanced on her tail, her face raised to the sky. Her nose was chipped off, and there was a rusted pipe poking out of the top of her head. At one time water probably cascaded down in a lovely mist. Now, the bone-dry pond was filled with cigarette butts and the odd beer bottle.

The ground-floor apartments opened out into the courtyard, two on each side. The tenants of each of the eight apartments were obviously responsible for taking care of the area immediately in front of their front doors. One had decorated carefully, with colorful flowers growing in large tubs and a pair of Adirondack chairs. Most of the others had at least a folding lawn chair or two. One or two were barren of porch accessories.

In the back corner of the courtyard, I noticed a flight of stairs leading up to the second-floor apartments. These were accessible by a long exterior hallway, like a wrap-around porch, that circled the second floor.

Number 4 had in front of it a pair of beat-up lounge chairs with webbing that might have once been red but had faded to a rusty pink. There was a green window box propped against the wall next to the door and a tomato plant climbed out of the box and up the wall. I glanced down at Isaac. He had spat out my finger and was busily sucking on the folded front of his Baby Bjorn. I kissed the top of his head and knocked on the door to Yossi's apartment.

Within moments the door opened. Yossi stood there wearing only a pair of low-slung jeans. His bare chest was covered with a thatch of black hair that thinned down to a line as it crept down his flat stomach into the top of his pants. The button of his jeans was undone. It was everything I could do not to stare at him. It had been a while since I'd seen a bared twenty-something chest in the flesh. I looked up into his blue eyes. He didn't look particularly happy to see me.

"Hi," I said.

"She is not here."

"But she's been here before."

He looked me up and down for a minute. I hadn't bothered to change after yoga so I was still wearing nothing but a pair of leggings and a T-shirt. "You are a friend of Fraydle's parents?" he asked, sounding doubtful.

"She worked for me. I told you that at Nomi's, remember?"

"You are not Orthodox?"

I laughed. "Do I look Orthodox to you?"

He looked me up and down again, reading my T-shirt carefully as if trying to decide whether the Starfleet Academy was the flagship of a brand new chain of yeshivas. "Today, not so much. But at Nomi's you did."

"What are you talking about?" I tried to remember what I'd worn to the Israeli restaurant. And then I realized. A long black skirt, long-sleeved white shirt, and, most damningly, a beret to hide my hair. Of course he'd thought I was Orthodox. As soon as he'd seen me, Yossi had probably assumed I was a friend of Fraydle's parents or, at the very least, a member of her community. No wonder he wouldn't talk to me.

"Yossi. We need to talk. I'm not one of Fraydle's parents' friends. I'm not Orthodox. I'm just a woman that Fraydle worked for once who is worried about her. Just like I'm sure you are. She's missing and if there is anything you know that can help me to find her, you need to tell me. Her parents and aunt are out of their minds with worry."

He leaned against the door to his apartment for a moment and then, shutting it carefully behind him, sat down in one of the lounge chairs. He motioned me to sit in the other. I perched carefully on the edge, bouncing Isaac gently. I was afraid that if Isaac sensed I had actually gotten off my feet, he would start fussing. Miraculously, he seemed not to notice.

"Is Fraydle here, Yossi?"

He leaned back against his chair with a sigh and said, "No. She is not here. She is not with me. I wish she was with me. I asked her to come with me many times. But she always says no. Deep in her heart, Fraydle is a good girl. She does what her father tells her to do." This last part was said with bitterness.

"Yossi," I said, "was Fraydle your girlfriend?"

He scowled. "Can she be my girlfriend if she is not allowed to see me? Can she be my girlfriend if we never spend more than an hour or two together?"

"I don't know. Can she? Listen, Yossi, I know she left here very upset not long ago. What happened?"

He didn't answer.

"Tell me, exactly what are you and Fraydle to each other?"

He didn't answer.

"I know that you don't think this is any of my business, but maybe we can work together to figure out where Fraydle has gone."

He remained silent.

"Is it that you're afraid I'll tell her parents about you two? Is that it?"
Silence.

Finally, Yossi sighed. "It doesn't matter now." He took a deep breath as if to fortify himself for the story he was about to tell. Then he began: "Fraydle and I met about nine or ten months ago. I came to her aunt's store on my third day in Los Angeles. I was staying with an old friend of my mother's. This woman asked me to shop for her in the kosher grocery stores, so I came in with a long list and Fraydle helped me. She found everything on the list and even helped me to carry the bags and boxes to the bus stop. And she talked to me. Just for a minute. But she was so beautiful. Her eyes. You know how beautiful she is."

"Yes, her eyes really are quite remarkable. Violet, like Liz Taylor's," I said.

"Who?"

"Elizabeth Taylor? The movie actress?"

He shook his head.

"Okay, whatever—you met, you talked. And then?"

"And then not so much for a while. I came to the store every day, every two days. Sometimes she helped me. Sometimes she stayed in the back and her aunt helped me. And then, one day, I came to the shop and she was not there at all. I came only to see her, I needed nothing. I bought a chocolate bar just to buy something and I went to the bus stop to wait for my bus. Fraydle was sitting on the bench waiting also for the bus.

"At first I thought it was only a coincidence that we met, but she told me later that she waited for me. I sat down next to her and we talked. All the time we talked, she looked around to make sure nobody noticed that we were together. When the bus came, we got on. I sat down in a seat and she sat in the seat in front of me, not next to me, so no one would think we were together. We rode around the entire city. For two hours we rode the bus, talking and talking. She told me about her family, about the books she read. I told her about my family, about my military service, about Israel. We just talked. Finally, the bus made a full circle and we were back on Melrose and La Brea. We made a date to see each other again on the bus.

"For two months, that is all we did. Three, maybe four times a week we would see each other. I would get on the bus by the house where I was staying, and she would get on at her corner. We would ride for one full circle. Sometimes she had one of her baby brothers or sister with her. She would hold the baby and we would talk and ride the bus. Once or twice people got on with her, people from her synagogue or other Hasidim from the neighborhood. We always sat in different rows, so when that happened we just pretended to be strangers.

"After a while, we started getting off the bus in different parts of the city. We went to the La Brea Tar Pits. We went to the Los Angeles County Museum of Art. We went to cafés."

I interrupted him. "She ate at non-kosher restaurants with you?"

"No, never. She drank only water or tea. Once, she sipped my latte. She never ate."

"And that's all you did, Yossi? Ride the bus and tour Los Angeles?"

"For a long time, yes. And then I got a job. I work as a security guard. It's nights and weekends, mostly, but sometimes I have to work during the day. We saw each other less and less. One week, we missed altogether. That was very bad."

"So what did you do?"

He swallowed nervously and paused for a moment as if to decide whether or not to continue his story.

"I got this apartment. I took it because it was near her house. She would come here when she could get away, sometimes early in the morning, sometimes in the afternoon. I never knew when she would come, and sometimes I was at work so I missed her. But still, we met a few times every week."

"It's a little unusual for a Hasidic girl to meet a man at his apartment, don't you think?" I asked.

"We are in love!" he said. "I love her. She loves me. It is not like what you think."

"No, I'm sure it's not. I'm sorry," I said soothingly. "So when was the last time you saw her?"

He sighed. "A few weeks ago she came here, as usual, but afterwards she told me it was the last time. She told me that her parents had found a *shiddach*, a match, for her and that she'd accepted him.

"I knew they were bringing men to her. Each time before she rejected them. But this time, she said yes. I begged her, please marry me. I begged her, come with me back to Israel. She said no. She said she had to do what her father told her. Fraydle is always a good girl." He rubbed his eyes angrily. "So, that is our story. I saw her only once after that. I came looking for her at her aunt's store. I walked around the neighborhood, and I found her in the park with your baby. I asked her again to come with me. I showed her these." He reached into the front pocket of his jeans and pulled out a crumpled airline ticket folder. He handed it to me. Inside the folder were two TWA tickets to Israel. One was in the name of Yossi Zinger. The other read Fraydle Finkelstein. The flight had left at four o'clock the day before.

"All the money I saved these past months I spent on these tickets. You see, they are business class. Not coach."

I looked at the crumpled tickets. The tickets had cost $3,140.21. Each. "But she wouldn't go," I said.

"No. She said, 'I love you, Yossi.' But I know she loves her father more."

"Maybe she was afraid. She's a young girl; maybe the idea of leaving her home and her family was just too scary for her."

"Maybe. But she has left now, hasn't she? Where is she? Where is Fraydle?"

"I haven't any idea. Is there someone you can think of who might know? Did she have a friend, maybe someone outside her community to whom she would go?"

"Me. She had me."

"What happened the day she left here, crying?"

"What are you talking about?"

"One of your neighbors saw her leave your apartment in tears."

He looked intensely uncomfortable. "Nothing. Just . . . just a fight about her not wanting to come to Israel with me."

At that moment, Isaac began to howl. I stood up and started bouncing him up and down.

"Okay, honey. Just one more minute." I turned to Yossi. "Look, I have to go pick my daughter up at school and get this baby to bed. But we need to talk more. Is there a number where I can reach you?"

"You can call me on my cell phone," he said. Ah, L.A., where even illegal-alien security guards have wireless connections. I paced back and forth with my crying baby while Yossi went inside for a piece of paper and a pen to write down his number. I crammed the scrap into my purse and, with a quick good-bye, hustled out of the building.

11

$\mathcal{J}$ ARRIVED AT BETH El Nursery School to find Ruby sitting in the time-out chair. Brenda, my favorite of Ruby's teachers, was hovering around her, obviously at a loss. Ruby's arms were crossed over her chest, her shoulders were raised up to her ears, and she was scowling so hard her cheeks had turned white. Business as usual.

"Hey, Ruby. Hi, Brenda. What's up?" I was doing my best to come across as upbeat and cheerful, with just a touch of concern. I probably sounded just like I felt: embarrassed and wondering whether anyone would mind if I chose this moment to throttle my kid.

"Hello, Juliet. Ruby's having a hard time this afternoon." I'd never heard Brenda sound anything but sweet before. I'd never even known irritation was part of her repertoire.

"It sure looks that way," I said. "What happened?"

"Honestly, I wish I knew. She had to spend two minutes in the time-out chair because she bit Alexander, but that was half an hour ago. She's refused to get up."

"You bit Alexander!" I said, crouching down to Ruby's level. "What were you thinking? You know biting is a bad thing to do." I looked up at Brenda. "This really isn't like her. She's not a biter."

Brenda just smiled thinly.

"Ruby! Talk to me!" I said. "What's going on here?"

My daughter looked up at me, her grim little face screwed up in outrage. Clearly, it was too much that her mother had joined her oppressors. Tears gathered in her eyes and spilled over onto her cheeks. She collapsed into my arms with a wail. I stroked her back and murmured, "Okay, honey. Okay. It's all right. It's over now. Tell Mama what happened."

"It's not fair!" she sobbed. "Brenda is mean!"

"Brenda is not mean, Ruby. She's nice. You like Brenda. She put you in the time-out chair because you did a bad thing, not because she's mean. But kiddo, you could have been out long ago. You're the one who chose to sit here all afternoon."

She looked up at me. "Alex bited me first! I just bited him back. But Brenda didn't see him bite me. She only saw me bite him. But I bited him *back*. I told Brenda that I'm not getting up until she says she's sorry for giving me a time-out and not Alex."

That's my kid for you. Willing to ruin her own fun just to prove a point. Well, for all her sweetness, Brenda was too firm to give into the convoluted sense of justice of a three-year-old. But neither did I intend to spend the day, week, or month indulging this sit-down strike.

"Here's the thing, Ruby. Brenda didn't do anything wrong. She's not going to apologize. I'm going to get your lunchbox, and then Isaac and I are going to go home, get the stroller, and walk to the store to get a chocolate bar. You can either come with us, or stay here all day."

Ruby struggled for a moment, but finally gave in, as I knew she would.

By the time we'd reached our house Ruby had bargained her way into two chocolate bars and a bag of *gelt*. It remains a mystery to me how a person who could negotiate effectively with the nastiest and most powerful of federal prosecutors could fall entirely apart when faced with a wily three-year-old. It all probably comes down to the fact that I'd never gone into a negotiation on behalf of a client feeling bad because it had been weeks since I'd taken the prosecutor to the park or played Candyland with him. Guilt is a powerful thing.

When we wheeled our way into the kosher grocery, we found Nettie seated on a high stool behind the counter, leaning wearily on her elbows. Her face was crumpled and her wig looked uncombed. She'd aged years since the afternoon she'd first suggested that Fraydle work for me. When we came in, she roused herself to smile at Ruby and pat her red curls, but then sighed again. Isaac had fallen asleep in the stroller on the walk over to the store, so, once I'd hushed Ruby with her candy bars, Nettie and I were able to talk in peace.

"No news," I said, rather than asked.

"Nothing."

"Nettie, it's been three days. It's time to do something about this."

"I know. I know. I've been saying this to Baruch from the beginning. He must get help from outside. He must call the police."

"But he won't."

"No." She rubbed her brow.

"Nettie. You must see how this looks. It looks like he isn't interested in finding her. If he really cared, he would call the police!"

She shook her head. "You don't understand. Baruch is dying inside, I'm telling you. He does nothing but look for his child. But we are not like you. We have our own ways. We help ourselves."

"But clearly your ways aren't working! You haven't found her yet. And every day that passes makes it less likely that you will."

"I tell my brother every day, please call the police. But he won't. He is a stubborn man, Mrs. Applebaum. He is a stubborn man."

"What about Mrs. Finkelstein?" I asked. "Do you think she might be willing to talk to the police? Just to report Fraydle missing?"

"I don't know. I don't think so."

"Well, have you talked to her about it? Have you suggested calling the police?"

Nettie leaned over the counter and grabbed my hand. "You do it!" she said. "You talk to her. Maybe she'll listen to you."

I disengaged from her hot, dry grasp. "Nettie, your brother won't even talk to me on the phone. He's certainly not going to let me into his house."

"He's not home!" she said. "He's out looking for Fraydle. He's out driving night and day. You go now, you'll find just Sima, my sister-in-law. Go now! It will take you only a moment. I'll watch your children."

I looked at her doubtfully for a moment. But the truth was, I felt guilty. I hadn't told Fraydle's parents about Yossi, and I wasn't planning to. The least I could do was try to convince them to report their daughter's disappearance to the police.

"Okay." I agreed. I checked on Isaac, who was still sleeping, and told Ruby I'd be right back. She opened her mouth to protest, but snapped it shut and smiled at Nettie, who was dangling a little mesh bag of gold coins in front of her eyes.

"Oooh. *Gelt*," Ruby breathed.

"You like chocolate, *maydele*?" Nettie said, unwrapping one and handing it to Ruby. Ruby crammed it in her mouth and held her hand out for another. "One at a time, darling." Nettie stroked her hair and cupped a palm on her cheek. She turned to me. "So go already," she said.

I left the store by the back door and walked over to Fraydle's house. I opened the creaky little gate and found two little boys around Ruby's age or a bit younger playing at the top of the long flight of steps leading to the front porch. Their mouths opened in round O's as I came up the stairs. One of them, the older, shouted something in Yiddish and ran inside the house. The younger popped his thumb in his mouth and sucked it, all the while backing carefully away from me. I smiled at him, but his eyes just grew bigger and he moved a little more quickly.

I reached the front door just as Sima Finkelstein walked through the doorway. She was holding a dishtowel in one hand and another little boy on her hip. Her long skirt was covered with a flowered apron.

"Yes?" she said.

"Hello, Mrs. Finkelstein. I'm Juliet Applebaum. I was here a couple of days ago?"

"Yes. Yes, of course. You have news about Fraydle? You know where she is?"

"No. No, I'm terribly sorry. I haven't found her. Could I come in for a moment?"

She hesitated, but then stepped back and motioned me through the door. I walked quickly into the house and back to the kitchen. She followed me. There was a baby asleep in a bouncy seat on the kitchen counter and Sarah, Fraydle's sister, stood at the sink washing dishes. She looked up when I walked in the room, but blushed and looked down again when I said hello.

Sima motioned me to a chair. She set the little boy down on the floor and he toddled off. She sat down next to me. "Can I get you something? A glass of tea?" she asked.

"That would be lovely."

"Sarahleh. Put the kettle on for tea."

The girl obeyed, filling the dented metal teakettle from the sink.

Suddenly, there was a crash of crockery. The shock of the noise made me jump in my chair. The baby woke with a cry and Sima stood up and rocked the bouncy seat. Sarah stood at the sink, stock-still.

"Sarahleh, what happened? Did you break something?" her mother asked.

"No, no. I just dropped a plate. It's fine. See?" The girl held up a blue saucer with small white flowers. Her mother nodded and sat down again. The baby stopped her cries and settled down. Sima closed her eyes, as if exhausted. I looked over to Sarah in time to see her surreptitiously slipping the broken pieces of what looked like another saucer into the pocket of her skirt. When the girl realized that I had seen her, her face turned ashen and she looked at me, wide-eyed. I smiled in what I hoped was a reassuring way. She took a breath and turned back to the sink. I shook my head at the thought of a house where the consequences of breaking a plate were so terrifying.

I turned back to the girl's mother. "Mrs. Finkelstein, I'll be perfectly honest with you. I came here to try to convince you to report Fraydle's disappearance to the police."

Sima shook her head. "That is my husband's decision, Mrs. Applebaum. He will decide if that is appropriate. For now, we are looking for her ourselves."

"I understand that, Mrs. Finkelstein. But I also know that the longer you wait, the harder it will be for the police to find Fraydle once you do go to them. The trail will be colder. Do you understand what I mean?"

The woman nodded her head slightly and stared down at her hands. They were work-roughened and red and the nails were bitten almost to the quick. Her cuticles were torn and chewed. She grasped her right hand with her left, twisting her wedding ring.

"Mrs. Finkelstein. Sima," I said, "please, we must do something here. What if she hasn't run off? What if something really happened to her? Every minute you wait makes it less and less likely that you'll find her."

The rabbi's wife looked up at me, gathered herself together, and spoke. "I know you are trying to help. But this is not your business. My husband will find Fraydle. He does not need the police or any of you to help him." She rose from her chair and walked out of the kitchen. Grudgingly, I followed her. I walked out the front door that she held open for me, down the steps, and out the gate.

This family, these people, were a mystery to me. Like my own grandparents, theirs had probably come to America from a *shtetl*, a tiny, Jewish village in Eastern Europe. The isolationist life steeped in tradition and religious observance that Fraydle's family led in the heart of Los Angeles was not much different than the lives led by our respective great-grandparents in Poland, Lithuania, or Russia. My assimilated life, with my non-Jewish husband, was two or three or ten worlds apart. How was it that people from the same place, brought up in the same religion, ended up so entirely different?

I trudged back to Nettie's store and found her crouched on the floor, blowing soap bubbles for Isaac, whom she'd propped up into a sitting position. He was giggling hysterically as Ruby chased the bubbles around the store. The few customers who'd arrived in my absence did not seem to mind having to wait to make their purchases. All of them older women, they leaned against the counter and smiled at my children.

When Nettie noticed me, she hoisted herself up off the floor with a groan and busied herself checking out the line of waiting women. When they'd all left, she turned to me.

"And? What did she say?"

"She refused to consider it. She said her husband knows best."

Nettie snorted derisively.

"Nettie, tell me about this match of Fraydle's."

"The Hirsch boy? A wonderful match for Fraydle. An important family. And wealthy."

"Yes, you told me that. Did Fraydle agree to the match?"

"Everyone agreed. Baruch is thrilled. The Hirsch family is happy. The boy likes her. It's all set."

"And Fraydle's mother? What does she think?"

"Ah, Sima." Nettie shook her head. "Sima wants Fraydle to choose for herself. Sima is a big believer in love matches. Don't ask me why; hers certainly wasn't one. Her parents chose for her and that was that. And Sima and Baruch have been very happy. Happy enough. Anyway, they have a lovely family."

"Did Fraydle choose what's-his-name, Hirsch?"

Nettie looked uncomfortable. "Ari Hirsch. The boy's name is Aharon, but they call him Ari."

"Did she choose Ari Hirsch for herself?" I was getting insistent.

"Not specifically," Nettie replied.

"What does that mean? Not specifically? Did she say she would marry him or not?"

Nettie shrugged her shoulders. "She didn't agree, not exactly. But she didn't reject him, either. She told Baruch she needed more time. She said she would do as her parents asked and marry, but she needed more time to decide if she wanted to marry Ari Hirsch."

A thought occurred to me. If this marriage was so important to her father, and if she had refused to obey him, would he, could he, have tried to force her?

"Nettie, I have a question for you. I don't want you to take this the wrong way, but what would your brother have done if Fraydle refused to marry the boy? Would he have made her do it anyway?"

Nettie looked at me. She shook her head firmly. "Baruch, maybe he would have tried to make Fraydle marry Ari Hirsch, but Sima wouldn't stand for it. I told you, she always insisted that the girl be allowed to make a free choice. She would never have let my brother force a match on her daughter."

A possibility was beginning to occur to me.

"But let's say somehow Rabbi Finkelstein got Fraydle to do it. Would Sima object to the marriage once it had happened?"

"A marriage is a marriage. Once it's done, that's it."

"Look, Nettie, there's got to be a reason your brother is refusing to get the police involved in the disappearance of his child. Maybe he's unwilling because he knows where she is. Is it possible that your brother sent Fraydle to the Hirsches, maybe against her wishes, and without Sima knowing about it?"

Nettie looked at me. To my surprise, she did not seem at all shocked at my question. "Anything is possible," she said.

12

BY THE TIME Peter walked in the door at ten o'clock that night, I'd already decided what I was going to do. He came into the bedroom and found me standing over Isaac's changing table, which we'd moved into our room once we'd realized he wasn't going to be sleeping in his and Ruby's room any time soon. I was holding my nose and dabbing at the mess in front of me.

"Hey, honey," Peter said, kissing me on the cheek. "That's gross."

"I know. Totally disgusting," I agreed. "Why is it *green*? I swear this kid did not eat anything today that was this particular shade of fluorescent green."

"Here, you take a break, I'll deal with this."

I handed over the box of wipes and, after washing my hands, stretched out on the bed.

"Listen, Peter, my mom's been bugging me to go visit her and my dad in New Jersey."

"I can't possibly get away right now."

"No, I know that. I was thinking of just me and the kids."

"Okay."

And that was it. No *Please don't leave me*. No *I'll be lost without you*. Nothing.

When I told my mother that we'd decided to come out and visit, she positively crowed with delight. She inventoried all the baby items she needed to borrow or buy and almost hung up on me in her eagerness to get started setting up the kids' room. I managed to get plane tickets for the next redeye to New York. Thank God for frequent-flyer miles. I debated using another 25,000 miles to get Isaac a seat of his own but decided to risk having him on my lap. After all, how many people would be flying to New York in the middle of the night in the middle of the week? I packed three suitcases full of everything I could imagine ever needing, including a breast pump, ten changes of clothing for the kids, every infant medication known to humankind, and an assortment of toys, games, rattles, and dolls. You would have thought we were setting out for a year at the South Pole, rather than a week in Northern New Jersey, the shopping-center capital of the world.

The next evening, Peter drove us to the airport and insisted on parking and taking us to the gate, even though I'd offered to martyr myself at the curbside check-in. He schlepped my sixty pieces of carry-on luggage for me and entertained Ruby while I gave Isaac one last preflight diaper change. When the preboarding announcement came, he grabbed me and wrapped me in a bear hug.

"I'm going to miss you guys," he croaked, resting his face on the top of my head.

"We'll miss you, too." I reached up to kiss him, but Ruby wriggled in between us, forcing me to step back and out of his arms. He gave her a kiss good-bye and then transferred all the various bags to me. I walked down the ramp pushing Isaac in his folding stroller, holding Ruby's hand, with Isaac's car seat in the other hand, the diaper bag around my neck, a flight bag full of snacks and toys hanging from each shoulder, and my purse clenched in my teeth.

The flight was every bit as horrific as I'd expected, and then some. While it had certainly occurred to me that Isaac might spit up all over himself, I forgot that a goodly portion could land on me. I'd brought plenty of changes of clothing for him, but none for myself. By the time we got off the plane we were a sight to behold.

My parents swept us up in their arms and packed us into their massive Chrysler. We stopped at my grandmother's nursing home on the way to their house, and my parents entertained the kids in the solarium while I held my grandmother's hand. She didn't recognize me. My mother had prepared me for that, but it came as a shock nonetheless.

Once we got back in the car, I fell asleep immediately and barely woke up to walk into my parents' house and crawl up the stairs to my old room. Hours later, when I'd slept enough to recover from the flight, I ambled downstairs to find my children happily playing in the kitchen in which I'd grown up. The radio was, as usual, earsplittingly loud. My parents' radio is perpetually tuned, full blast, to a news station. Until I started spending time at friends' houses in grade school I'd assumed all families carried out conversations over the blare of a radio announcer yelling, "You give us ten minutes, we'll give you the world."

I walked across the room and turned off the radio. I rubbed my eyes and smiled at my mother and father.

"What time is it?"

"Two in the afternoon," my father answered. His hair had grown even more Einstein-like in the months since I'd seen him. It stood up in soft white peaks all over his head. His blue eyes looked out of a crinkled face and his cheeks were slightly reddened. I kissed his bald spot.

"Hi, Daddy. I've missed you."

"We've missed you, too, *mamaleh*. Ruby here is teaching me how to color a rainbow." Ruby was perched on his lap, a red crayon gripped firmly in her hand. Next to my tiny girl, my father looked even older than his seventy-five years. Sometime in junior high school I realized that my parents were much older than those of my friends. My mother had me when she was forty, long after she'd given up hopes of having a child. My younger brother came along just two years later. Back then, before the dawn of the age of Pergonal and Chlomid, that was decidedly rare.

My parents came from a different generation than the other parents they saw at ballet recitals and Little League. Their Brooklyn accents and the *yiddishisms* peppering their speech gave them a vaguely Old World air. They cared more about politics and social justice and less about material acquisitions than most of the other grownups I knew. As an adult, I grew to be proud of them and glad to have been raised in a house where Woody Guthrie songs were sung at bedtime and a McGovern poster hung in our window well into the mid-seventies. As a child, I'm ashamed to admit that they embarrassed me.

I walked around the table to where my mother was sitting, holding Isaac. She was feeding him a bottle full of yellowish liquid. It gave me a moment's pang of concern. The only thing he'd consumed thus far in his life was breast milk.

"I'm giving the boy some chamomile tea," my mother said. "It says in that book over there that it's good for them." She pointed to a brightly colored tome on the kitchen table. I pulled it over and read the title: *The Holistic Baby*.

"Wow," I said.

"Listen, alternative medicine is a perfectly legitimate thing. Don't be so dismissive," she said. My mother has always been willing to jump on any new philosophical bandwagon, especially if the word "alternative" can be used to describe it. She was a beatnik, a hippie, an ardent feminist (that one stuck) and now, apparently, she was into the New Age. But she always looked exactly the same. Like a Jewish grandmother from Brooklyn.

"What dismissive?" I protested. "How am I being dismissive? I just said 'Wow.'"

"It was your tone."

"What tone? There was no tone."

"Ladies, ladies," my father interrupted. "Could we please have five minutes of peace and harmony before the fighting begins?" That's my father's job. Mom and I argue, and he steps in and referees.

"Mama and Grandma are fighting?" Ruby said, sitting bolt-upright on her grandfather's lap.

"Nobody's fighting," I said. And we really weren't. We were just bickering, like we always do.

"Hi, Ma." I kissed her on the cheek. She handed the baby over to me. He immediately began rooting around my shirt front, so I sat down and took out a breast to nurse. My father blushed and began closely studying Ruby's drawing.

"So, Ma, are you taking time off while we're here?" I asked.

"Of course," she said, nodding her head vigorously, the tight gray curls of her perm bouncing like so many little antennae. My mother's undying loyalty to the hairstyle she'd chosen in the mid-seventies is a source of mystery to me. Every three months she spends two hours in Hair-o-matic, having her steel-colored locks tightly wound up in pink rods. Because she's rail-thin and about four foot ten, she looks decidedly like a Q-tip. In fact, when I was in my senior year of high school, she greeted trick-or-treaters wearing a white tunic and tights, with her hair dusted in baby powder. I was the only one who got the joke. The other kids all thought she was supposed to be a nurse.

I popped Isaac off my nipple and propped him on my shoulder where he promptly let loose with a tremendous belch. My parents burst into a round of applause. You would have thought he'd just hit the winning run in the World Series.

"So, Ma, Daddy, do you know any Hasidic Jews in Borough Park? Preferably Verbover," I asked.

My father wrinkled his brow and tapped his chin with one finger. "Margie, didn't the son of one of your Russian cousins become a Hasid?" he asked my mother.

"What *tsuris* that family had. They weren't here six months before Anatole, the father, had to have bypass surgery. They were burned out of their first apartment, and the insurance company wouldn't pay off. Then, that terrible thing with the daughter's baby. It was born d-e-a-d."

"And the Hasidic son?" I reminded them, just in case they'd forgotten that I had actually asked for something other than a litany of familial tragedy.

"What was his name, Gene? Do you remember?" my mother asked.

"It was something Russian. And then he changed it to Jewish. Like Sasha to Schmuel. Or Boris to Binyamin. Like that," my father answered.

I rolled my eyes. Getting a straight answer out of my parents was harder than getting Isaac to sleep through the night. I bounced the baby on my knee, trying not to express my impatience.

"I remember!" my mother shouted. "Josef. That's his name."

"What's Russian about that? Or Yiddish for that matter?" I asked.

"Nothing. Who knows where your father got that. He's senile. Ignore him."

"What senile? It's spelled with an *F*, that's Russian."

"This Russian Josef, do you think I could call him?" I asked.

"I don't see why not," my mother said. She picked up the phone and riffled through her ancient Museum of Modern Art address book. She found the number and dialed it on the telephone stuck to the wall next to the fridge. My mother's hair isn't the only seventies throwback in my parents' house. They don't own a cordless phone, but rather make do with a couple of ancient appliances that they used to rent from Bell Telephone. The one in the kitchen has an extra long cord that is still twisted in the knots I made while talking endlessly to my high school girlfriends about whether Larry Pitkowsky did, indeed, like me or if Maxine Fass was his dream girl. They also have a couple of old TVs, one of which has a pair of rusty pliers permanently attached to it in place of the channel dial. I think the dial got lost sometime when I was in elementary school. Back then the set only reliably received two channels, PBS and some religious station out of upstate New York. My mother used to insist that that was precisely enough TV. PBS gave us a little culture and the religious station allowed us to understand the true soul of America. Or something like that.

My mother mouthed "machine" at me and waited for a moment, then said, into the phone, "Josef, this is your cousin Margie. Margie Apple-baum. Remember my daughter, Juliet? The one who went to Harvard Law School? She's in town and would love to talk to you. Give us a call." She left the number and hung up. There are an infinite number of ways to work the words "Harvard Law School" into a sentence, and my mother has mastered them all. I've heard her respond to an innocuous comment about the weather with a declamation on how her daughter had suffered through the bitter Cambridge winters while attending law school.

"Not home," she said.

"So I gathered," I replied.

I sat quietly for a while, sipping at the coffee my father had poured for me while my mother was on the phone. I could think of only one other Hasidic Jew who might be willing to give me a little insight into their community. She might even know the famous Hirsches of Borough Park.

Libby Bernstein nee Barret, my freshman-year roommate at Wesleyan University, was a daughter of a Daughter of the American Revolution and member of the Mayflower Association, who had somehow ended up an Orthodox Jew. Her husband, Josh Bernstein, was a couple of years ahead of us at college. They'd begun dating at the end of our freshman year. After he graduated, Josh moved to Brooklyn. He'd started out as a run-of-the-mill, assimilated Jewish kid, but as he got older he become more and more interested in religious Judaism. After graduation, he joined the Verbover Hasidic community. After a while Josh must have realized that he couldn't be an Orthodox Jew and date a *shiksa*. He broke up with Libby, and she was utterly devastated. She spent two weeks crying on the shoulder of every one of her friends, me included, and then took off for Brooklyn herself. She begged Josh to take her back and promised she would do whatever it took to be with him.

Libby never came back to college. She moved in with a Hasidic family and began to study for conversion. Her host family had nine children; Libby was an only child from a WASPy New England family. The contrast between her silent home and the apartment stuffed with children must have been astonishing. Libby's mother had died when she was in high school and the woman of the house became a second mother to her. I know Libby had longed for a mother-daughter relationship, and I'm sure it felt wonderful to have a woman take care of her, and teach her.

When I'd call Libby on the phone from college she would wax rhapsodic about Yaffa, her "mother." She told me they spent hour after hour in the kitchen, drinking tea, cooking, talking. There was an endless amount of work to do in that house, what with all the children, but Libby said Yaffa never seemed overwhelmed. Every day had its schedule, its activities, and Libby and Yaffa did them together. Yaffa would quiz Libby on her Hebrew and on Bible studies while they kneaded dough or chopped onions.

Libby's conversion was complete within two years, and, with the Verbover *rebbe*'s permission, she and Josh married in a traditional ceremony. It was kind of a trip for the few of us who came down from Wesleyan for it. We women were kept strictly separate from the men. We sat by ourselves, ate by ourselves, and even danced by ourselves. But it was pretty incredible. People were so full of joy, whirling and twirling to the *klezmer* band. And Libby seemed genuinely delighted with the life she'd chosen. I remember dancing the hora at the wedding, feeling as if I were part of something ancient, exciting, and beautiful. People, my people, had danced to this music for hundreds of years. It was so compelling and wonderful that it made someone like Libby desperate to be a part of it, of us. When Peter and I were married people danced the hora; they even raised us up on chairs, but somehow it wasn't the same. It felt almost hollow, and I don't think anyone was sorry when the DJ changed the record to the Rolling Stones.

Libby and I kept in touch for the first few years, but then life kind of gobbled each of us up. Last I'd heard, she'd had a couple of sons and was still living in Brooklyn.

I decided to give her a call. Handing Isaac back to his grandmother, I went out to the front hall, where my father had left my bags. I dug my Palm Pilot out of my purse and looked up Libby's number. Peter had given me the little electronic organizer for my last birthday. Initially, I was disappointed that the box it came in didn't contain the sapphire earrings I'd had my eyes on, but I'd quickly grown to love it. It kept all my addresses and all my appointments current and available at the touch of a button. True, I didn't actually *have* any appointments, other than the kids' doctor's visits, but if I *had* had somewhere to go, I'm sure my Palm Pilot would have helped me get there on time. I found Libby's number and went upstairs, where my voice wouldn't have to compete with the shrill giggles of my children.

Libby was home.

"Libby! You'll never guess who this is!"

"Juliet Applebaum!" she said.

I was flabbergasted. "How did you know? We haven't talked in what, seven years?"

"I think it's closer to eight. I have no idea how I knew it was you. I just recognized your voice. How are you? Where are you? Are you married? Do you have kids?"

"I'm great. I got married about five years ago. I have a daughter named Ruby, she's three, and a son named Isaac, who's just about four months. And you? I remember you had two sons. Any more kids?"

"Well, you know about Yonasan and Shaul. And then I had three more, all boys. David is five, Yiftach is three, and the baby, Binyamin, is a year and a half old. And I'm pregnant."

"Wow. Libby, that's incredible. Five boys. And another one on the way. You must be absolutely exhausted. Do you know what you're having?"

"Well, I'm a little tired, but mostly I'm just very happy. The boys all keep each other busy. I don't know what's coming this time, but I'm hoping for a girl. I think Josh would be happy if we had six more boys, but it would be lovely to have a little girl. You're so lucky. Is Ruby just a doll?"

"She's great, really, but she's hardly a doll. Unless Mattel has come out with a new extra-bossy Barbie. Ruby's a lovely kid, but she sure knows what she wants."

"My Shaul is the same way. He's under the impression that he's in charge of all the others. He even bosses his older brother around. Yonni is such a gentle soul that he does whatever Shaul tells him to."

"I imagine with five you must be home with them?"

"Of course. I haven't worked since I was pregnant with Yonni. I wouldn't want to miss any of this time. It's just so magical, don't you think?"

Magical? Well, sometimes. And a lot of the time it's boring and stressful.

"Definitely," I said aloud. "So, listen, Libby—do you live anywhere near Borough Park?"

"If right in the middle counts as near, then yes."

"Oh, wonderful. That's great. Here's the thing: I'm trying to track down a family in Borough Park. Maybe you know them, the Hirsches?"

"The head of Yeshiva B'nai B'chorim?"

"Yes, I think that must be him. I wasn't sure of the name of the yeshiva, but I know he's the head of one."

"Of course I know the Hirsches. Everyone knows the Hirsches. Or, at least, everyone knows of them."

"Do you know them or just know of them?"

"I've never met Rav Hirsch, but I actually do know his wife, Esther. Our boys are in *cheder* together."

"*Cheder*?" Libby's glottals were better than mine and I'd spent my entire childhood in Hebrew School.

"You know, like nursery school for little boys. David and her son are in the same class. I've even been to her house a few times for tea. What do you want with the Hirsches?"

"Well, it's kind of a long story. How about if I invite myself over to your house and I tell you all about it there?" Once I was ensconced in her home, maybe I could persuade Libby to introduce me to her friend.

"I'd love to see you." She sounded a little doubtful, obviously worried about what it was I was after.

I decided to just go ahead and be pushy. "Are you busy tomorrow morning? Do you think I could stop by at around, say ten thirty or so?"

"Sure," she said, getting over whatever concerns she might have felt. "That would be fine. I would love to see you, Juliet."

"Great! I'll see you at ten thirty."

Before I could hang up, Libby quickly said, "Um, Juliet, remember to dress appropriately, okay? You know, modestly?"

Luckily, I'd brought along the outfit that had convinced Yossi that I was Orthodox. "No problem. I'll be so modest, you won't recognize me."

13

I HAD EXPECTED BOROUGH Park, the capital of American Hasidic Judaism, to look something like the pictures I'd seen of Manhattan's Lower East Side at the turn of the century. Crowded tenements, scores of black-hatted men in sidelocks rushing to and fro. I probably wouldn't have been surprised to see the odd pushcart. Instead, as I drove my mother's car down Thirteenth Avenue, I found a bustling, commercial district like any other in the city. There were stores everywhere. Some looked like discount clothing outlets, but others were decidedly upscale. Granted, the men were wearing their black hats and coats and many did have long beards. But the women were dressed to the nines. If I didn't know that laws of modesty required them to cover their own hair with wigs, their perfectly styled coiffures would not have given them away. While there was the occasional matron in a dowdy dress, most of the women wore flattering and elegant suits with gorgeous, matching hats. They pushed huge strollers of the most expensive makes; Apricas and Peg Peregos. My neighbors back in Los Angeles looked provincial and old-fashioned by comparison.

Libby's apartment building was a huge, concrete-and-metal structure built probably in the mid-1950s. I parked in the pay lot across the street and carried Isaac into the building. I'd left Ruby in New Jersey with my parents. The lobby had a sitting area with pale pink couches, darker pink carpeting, an elaborate silk flower arrangement, and a doorman. I gave him Libby's name and apartment number and he buzzed her for us.

"A Mrs. Applebaum for you, Mrs. Bernstein," he said into the intercom. He paused for a moment and then turned to me. "Please go ahead, seventh floor."

Libby's apartment was pleasant and large. The front door opened into a living room with an oversized brown corduroy sectional couch wrapped around two walls. A large television was set into a sturdy wall cabinet, surrounded by bookshelves spilling over with titles in both Hebrew and English. The set was tuned to *Teletubbies*, and three little boys were stretched out on the floor, eyes glued to the screen. Libby turned from the door she'd opened for us and called out, "David, Yiftach, Benny, look, it's Mama's friend Juliet." The boys looked up and smiled good-naturedly but immediately turned back to their show.

"Teletubbies, feh!" Libby said. "It's one of the only shows I let them watch, so they're just crazy about it."

"Ruby loves it, too," I said.

Libby smiled and gently tapped the older boy on the behind with her foot. He giggled, and swatted her away.

I almost didn't recognize my college roommate. In fact, if I'd bumped into her on the street I might have walked by without more than a faint feeling of having seen her somewhere before. In college, Libby had been beautiful, in kind of a horsy way. She'd had long blond hair that fell to her shoulders and had always been swept back in a headband: denim for every day, velvet for special occasions. She was tall, probably five foot eight or so, although I'm so short that anyone over five foot two seems like a giant to me, and leggy. Now, Libby had covered her blond hair with a brown wig teased into a puff at the top of her head. She was still thin, and carried her pregnancy like a basketball stuffed under her shirt. She wore a plain navy maternity dress, and heavy support hose covered her beautiful legs. Libby looked almost exactly like your typical Hasidic matron. But she couldn't cover up the long, narrow nose that one of her ancestors had schlepped over on the *Mayflower* and proceeded to hand down to every generation of patrician New England WASPs that sprang from his loins.

"Juliet! You look exactly like you did in college!" she said.

"Yeah, exactly," I replied, "except now my hair is red, and I've gained thirty pounds. Other than that, I look exactly the same. You, on the other hand, haven't changed a bit. Well, except for the clothes. And the hair. And the pregnancy."

She patted her wig absently. "It's actually kind of ironic that I have natural blond hair that I cover with a brown wig. Half the women in the neighborhood cover up their mousy brown hair with luxurious blond wigs.

I'd never do that, though. It sort of defeats the purpose of dressing modestly in the first place."

Libby led me into the kitchen. It was a bright room painted a soft yellow with children's drawings taped to the walls. There was a large white table pushed up against one wall, surrounded by eight chairs made of blond wood with woven straw seats. I sat down at the table, cradling a sleeping Isaac in my arms. Libby leaned over me and touched him gently on the cheek.

"What a sweetheart," she said.

"I hope you don't mind that I brought him. I haven't had a chance to pump any breast milk and he's never had formula."

"Not at all, not at all. What a little sleeper he is!"

"Hardly," I said. "He's only just started napping in the past week or so. And, he still wakes up all night long. Last night at my parents' he woke up every hour and a half."

"That's the time change. And the unfamiliar crib. He'll adjust," Libby reassured me.

"Were your guys good sleepers?" I asked.

"Oh, we're so lucky. They all slept through the night at about six weeks."

My mouth dropped open. "I'm trying not to hate you," I said.

Libby smiled. "It has nothing to do with me, I promise you. My boys just came out like that. They're all pretty easygoing. Well, all except Shaul. He's my challenge. He's smarter than the rest of us and knows it."

We chitchatted for a while longer and then fell silent. I took a cookie from the platter that Libby had put on the table.

"So, Juliet. What's all this with the Hirsches?" she asked.

I chewed for a moment before answering. The Finkelsteins didn't want the Hirsches to know about Fraydle's disappearance because they felt that that might jeopardize her match with Ari. It was certainly not my place to give away that secret. On the other hand, what if my speculation was right? What if Fraydle's father had, despite her opposition and his wife's support of her right to make a free choice, shipped Fraydle off to the Hirsches, knowing that once the marriage took place, neither Fraydle nor her mother would do anything about it? If that was the case, and if I could find Fraydle before the wedding, then I owed it to her and to her mother to do something.

First I swore Libby to secrecy. She promised to tell no one what I was going to tell her. Then, I told her the whole story. When I finished, I looked up at her. Her face was white, except for two spots of color, high on either cheek.

"Juliet, you have some nerve," she said.

I was taken aback. "What? What are you talking about?"

"What do you think we are? Do you think we're some barbaric tribe of people? That we kidnap our children and sell them in marriage?"

"No, no—I just—"

She cut me off. "You just assumed that this man, this learned rabbi, would smuggle his child out of her mother's house and send her to be with a man she doesn't love."

That was true, I had to admit. "I know it sounds terrible, but you have to understand, Libby, the man is acting very strange. His daughter has been gone for days, but he refuses to call the police."

"Maybe because he knows her. Maybe because he knows that she ran away and he is trying to save her from herself. If the police find her and arrest her as a runaway, do you think any self-respecting man would marry her? Her father is trying to salvage a future for her out of the mess she made."

"Libby, you don't know that, any more than I know that he sent her out here. Neither of us knows what he's capable of."

"Maybe so. Maybe I don't know him. But I do know Esther Hirsch. And I know she would never harbor a kidnapped girl, no matter how much she approved of the match. I know she'd never let her son marry a girl who didn't want to be his wife."

I didn't know what to say. Libby slapped her hand on the table. "You know what? I'm going to introduce you to this woman. I'm going to let you see for yourself whether or not she's a white slaver. But so help me, Juliet, don't you dare open your mouth about your crazy ideas. You just come with me to drop David off at *cheder*. We'll tell Esther you're an old friend. You'll meet her and you'll see that she's just a loving mother and not a criminal."

"I never accused her of being a criminal," I said weakly.

Libby just glared at me.

14

LIBBY LENT ME a stroller for Isaac, and I helped her get her boys ready to go out. We walked the few blocks to the school in silence and arrived before most of the other mothers. Libby kissed David goodbye and sent him into the classroom. After a few minutes, the other boys began arriving, and Libby introduced me to their mothers as an old friend from college. Esther Hirsch and her son Nosson came a few minutes late. She was a woman in her forties, no taller than I, and quite plump, with a prodigious shelf of a bosom. Her merry brown eyes were surrounded by laugh lines and she greeted me with a smile and a kiss on the cheek.

"Welcome. It's so lovely to meet you. Your friend Libby is very dear to me, you know!"

Libby looked surprised at the warmth of Esther's greeting but blushed happily.

Just then, Isaac woke up from his nap and began fussing. I lifted him out of the borrowed stroller and jiggled him up and down, to no avail.

"I'm afraid I'm going to have to nurse him," I said to Libby. "Is there somewhere I could go?"

"There's the ladies' room," she said doubtfully. "But I'm not sure how clean it is."

Esther put her arm around me, and squeezed. "Don't be ridiculous. You don't want to nurse in the ladies' room. Come to my house, we live right next door. You'll nurse and we'll have a cup of tea and some cake. I made a sour cream nut cake this morning. It's still warm."

I happily agreed. Libby shot me a worried look, but she couldn't beg off without insulting her friend. The three of us gathered our assorted babies and headed off down the block.

Libby and I made ourselves comfortable at Esther's kitchen table, a lovely piece of antique pine. As I pulled out a breast for my hungry son, it occurred to me that I'd sat around more oversized kitchen tables eating kosher baked goods in the past week than I had during the course of my entire life. Esther bustled about the large kitchen, pulling china plates and cups out of the French country–style cabinets and cream out of the massive, double-door, Sub-Zero refrigerator. She cut the cake on the marble countertop and carefully laid the slices on a cut-glass serving dish. Finally, she sat down with a contented grunt, and served us each a generous slice of cake and a large cup of tea.

"So, Juliet, dear. Tell me about yourself. Where do you live? Are you observant? How many children do you have?"

I neglected to mention that my husband wasn't a member of the tribe. I started by describing Ruby's Jewish preschool. Once I'd thoroughly detailed the *succah* Ruby's class had constructed in the yard of the synagogue, I pressed Esther to tell me a little about her own kids. She happily told me all about her three sons and one daughter. They ranged in age from little Nosson up to Shira, the daughter, who, at twenty-six, was her oldest.

"Shira's married, with three of her own. My grandson Ya'akov is the same age as Nosson!" Esther said proudly.

"And your oldest son, what about him? Is he married?" I asked.

Libby ground the heel of her shoe into my foot. I plastered a smile on my face to cover my wince of agony.

"Ari's engaged," Esther said. Her tone changed just a bit. She was still smiling, but there seemed to me to be something forced about it.

"Congratulations!" I said. "When is he getting married?"

"This year," Esther said. "The girl lives in Los Angeles, like you, and she needs to prepare herself for the move. I hope that the wedding will be in four or five months. Certainly before six months."

"And is he excited about the wedding?" I asked.

"Of course," Esther said, a little too quickly. "He's thrilled. What boy wouldn't be thrilled? She's a beautiful girl from a good family. He's thrilled. Just thrilled." As if by saying so she could make it true. Had the Hirsches heard something about Fraydle that was giving Ari second thoughts about the match?

I was preparing myself to probe a little deeper when Isaac gave a contented belch and popped off my breast.

"Well, we'd better be off," Libby said hurriedly. "We don't want to keep you."

Esther smiled, but she didn't protest. There wasn't any way I could keep us there short of out-and-out rudeness, so Libby and I gathered our things, made our thank-yous, and left. As we walked down the block toward her house, Libby seemed disturbed.

"Well, there's clearly *something* going on there," I said.

"It's not what you think."

"What do you mean, it's not what I think? What is it?"

"It has nothing to do with Fraydle."

"You don't know that, Libby."

"Yes I do. Trust me, I do."

"Okay, enough of the cryptic comments. Just what the hell, er, heck, do you know?"

Libby didn't answer.

"Libby!" I stopped in my tracks. "I'm not walking another step until you tell me what's going on."

She turned back to me and sighed. "I hate doing this. It's pure *lashon hora*, evil tongue, malicious gossip. I shouldn't say anything, but I can't bear for you to think badly of that lovely woman. As if she could ever do what you think she did."

"I didn't ever say I thought she did anything knowingly."

"She didn't do anything, knowingly or not."

"Come on, Libby. What do you know?"

She paused for a minute and then, roughly scratching at her wig, said, "I'll tell you, but not here on the street. Come back to my house."

I walked as quickly as I could back to Libby's apartment with her lagging behind me. I was obviously more interested in having the conversation than she was. When we got there, she tortured me further by first settling her sons down for their nap. By the time she returned to the living room, I was going out of my mind with impatience.

She plopped down on the couch next to me and reached out for Isaac. I passed the baby to her and she held him on her knees, facing her. She kissed him a couple of times on the nose. Finally, I burst out, "Libby! Talk!"

"Okay." She handed Isaac back to me and settled herself on the couch. "Before I say anything, I want you to understand that nothing I'm telling you can go beyond this room."

"I can't promise you that, Libby. If anything happened to Fraydle, then I'm going to have to talk to the police."

"This has nothing to do with the girl!" Libby insisted. "What I'm going to tell you is about Ari."

That intrigued me. "All right, I'll tell you what. I won't tell anybody anything, unless I absolutely have to. Okay?"

That satisfied her. She nodded and began: "Josh heard a rumor about Ari from some of the other men at the *shul*, the synagogue. Last year, Rav Hirsch had a mild heart attack. It wasn't any big deal, he only stayed overnight at the hospital and then they sent him home. But the scare got people talking about who would take over the yeshiva once Rav Hirsch couldn't lead it anymore. The obvious choice is Ari. He's something of a Talmudic scholar in his own right, and he hasn't shown any interest in going into his mother's brothers' business. As soon as his name was mentioned, however, the men began talking about how he would be an "inappropriate" choice. Josh pressed them, but all they would say was that since Ari was unmarried he wouldn't be suitable. Well, at the time, the boy was only twenty-three years old. Hardly an old bachelor. Later, when they were alone, one of Josh's good friends, also a *chozer b'tshuvah*, told him what the men were talking about."

"What's a chozer b'whatever?" I interrupted.

"A *chozer b'tshuvah*. A Jew who, like Josh, comes to Orthodoxy after being raised in a secular family. It means, literally, one who returns to the answer. Since they are both *chozrei b'tshuvah*, Sam and Josh have a lot in common. Sam joined the community ten years before Josh and I did and he's been sort of a mentor to Josh. Anyway, Sam told him that there are rumors that Ari might be . . . well, that he might not like women."

"Ari's gay?" I asked.

"I don't know that," Libby said quickly. "All I'm telling you is that some of the men say that about him. It could be nothing. Maybe it's just because he's a delicate boy. You know how men are."

"Oh yeah, those rough-and-ready yeshiva *buchers*. The most macho crowd outside a tubercular ward. I can see how they'd turn on a sissy."

"That's not fair, Juliet. Just because a man is learned doesn't mean he's necessarily effeminate. Look at Josh, for example."

Now, maybe Libby was right, and maybe all male intellectuals aren't weenies, but the example of her husband, who weighed in at about ninety-eight pounds, did not lend particularly strong evidence to her claim.

"I'm not saying that they're effeminate," I explained. "I'm saying that, as a group, they aren't particularly, well, *butch*. And most of them are straight. So, it really doesn't make sense for them to have spread rumors about Ari just for being, what did you call it? Oh yeah, 'delicate.' There's got to be something more. Did Josh's friend say where the rumors started?"

"No, he didn't know. I only told you that story so you would understand why Esther might be reticent on the topic of her son's marriage. Maybe she knows people are talking about him. Maybe she has her own concerns. Whatever it is, it has nothing to do with Fraydle."

"Maybe, maybe not. What would happen if Fraydle or her family got wind of the rumors about Ari?"

"I don't know. That would depend on them. If they believed the rumors, they might call off the match. But maybe not. It depends."

"What?" I asked. "You mean they might go ahead and let her marry him?"

"Well, they would probably ask Ari to reassure them that he wasn't gay, or that if he was that it wouldn't be a problem in the marriage."

"Uh, Libby? Exactly how could that not be a problem?"

"I don't presume to know everything about homosexuality, Juliet. But I do know that if it's true that ten percent of people are homosexual, like the Queer Alliance at Wesleyan told us, then it stands to reason that there are a decent number of homosexual Hasidic Jews. But the vast majority of us marry and have children. Obviously, there are homosexual people who manage to suppress their sexual urges in favor of the rewards of family, community, and religion."

"Or else they're just deeply in the closet."

"Maybe, but what's so wrong with that? If they feel content with their family lives and happy in their community, then who's to say they're not happy? Sex isn't really that important, anyway."

"It's not just sex, Libby. Being gay isn't just a matter of who you like to sleep with. It's about who you are. How can you say that someone can be happy denying his identity solely because his community won't accept him? How do you know that those people you're talking about aren't absolutely miserable, pretending to be something they're not?" I asked.

"You're right, Juliet," Libby said. "I have no idea what they might feel. For all I know, the vast majority of gay people leave the community rather than figure out a way of being both gay and Hasidic. I don't know. I guess it's just that I'm so happy, I can't imagine that everyone wouldn't want exactly what I have: a wonderful family with beautiful children and a community in which I feel loved and protected."

"You know, Libby, that's probably all that the vast majority of gay people want, too. They want a wonderful family and a supportive community that accepts them for who they are."

"Juliet, I know that. I'm not some homophobic person. I *agree* with you. I'm just saying that for us it's more complicated."

My mind was spinning with the possibilities raised by what Libby told me. I had no idea what it all meant, or if it played any role in Fraydle's disappearance. But I definitely needed to know more.

"Libby, what you told me could be important. I'm going to need to find out more about it."

"Why? Why can't you just leave it alone?"

"Because Fraydle is missing and I have to find her."

"You? Why you? You barely even know this girl. She babysat for you all of one time, for goodness' sake. Why do you need to disturb this poor boy's life for someone you barely know?"

That brought me up short. Libby was right, of course. I didn't know Fraydle. The truth was that none of this was any of my business. Just like the murder of Abigail Hathaway hadn't been any of my business. But you know what? I'd never been very good at minding my own business, and I wasn't particularly interested in learning how at this late date. And it wasn't like there was someone else in New York looking for Fraydle.

"I just have to, that's all. Libby, I can do this with or without you. I can try snooping around on my own, but I can't promise to be very discreet. I don't know anyone around here, and the only way for me to get information is to ask for it. And if I'm asking strangers, that's not discreet."

"It sure isn't." Libby was scowling.

"But if you and Josh were willing to help me, then maybe I might be able to get my questions answered without causing too much of a fuss." I know, I know. Blackmail. Unpleasant, but certainly effective.

Libby sighed. "What do you want me to do?"

"I want to meet Josh's friend. The one who told him about Ari."

Libby didn't say anything.

"Libby?"

She slapped her hands on her knees. "Fine. Come to dinner tomorrow night. I'll make sure he's here."

"Libby, you're a champ." I leaned over to kiss her on the cheek. She pushed me away, at first, but finally shrugged her shoulders and rolled her eyes.

"Juliet Applebaum, you haven't changed an iota, have you?"

I shook my head and then looked down at my watch. It was getting on in the afternoon. If I wanted to miss the bridge traffic going home, I had to get started right away.

"I'd better get going," I said, picking up Isaac and standing up. Libby walked me to the door and we hugged.

I held her tight for a moment, trying to understand what was making me so sad. Suddenly, I realized that I wasn't sad for Libby. She was happy. I was sad for myself. Whatever she had, whatever it was that made her so satisfied with her life, was missing in my mine. "You know what, Libby?" I said, "I'm jealous of you. You've found a place in life where you can really be content. I don't think I know anyone who is as happy as you are."

"I know just how lucky I am, Juliet. I *am* happy. Really happy. I have a loving husband, beautiful children, and a supportive community. I have found my place. But what a funny place for a card-carrying member of the Daughters of the American Revolution!"

I laughed and said, "See you tomorrow."

"You'd better be on your best behavior, Juliet."

"I will. I promise."

She rolled her eyes again and shut the door after me.

15

THE NEXT MORNING I sat at breakfast mulling over the events of the previous day and braiding Ruby's hair. Libby was right. Esther Hirsch didn't seem like the kind of person who could participate in anything nefarious. But appearances can be deceiving. It was at least possible that Fraydle's disappearance had something to do with Ari Hirsch.

"Sit still!" I said to my daughter, just barely resisting the temptation to yank on her braids. "I can't braid your hair if you keep bending over like that."

"My foot itches!" Ruby said indignantly.

My mother scooped a squirming Ruby out of my lap and held out her hand for the comb and elastics. I handed them over, relieved. I've never been much of a hairstylist. My mother sat down with Ruby, who suddenly decided to become a contender for best-behaved preschooler.

I got up to get myself another cup of coffee.

"Every drop of caffeine you drink goes directly to your breast milk," my mother said.

"Thank you, Madame La Leche, but I need coffee this morning. I'm exhausted. Your grandson was up all night, in case you hadn't noticed."

"Of course he was up. Why should he sleep? You're chock full of caffeine."

"Ma, I am so *not* going to fight with you this morning. Where's Isaac?"

"His grandfather took him for a walk. Okay, Rubileh, go look in the mirror. You look like a princess." My mother had made two braids on either side of Ruby's face. For a total of four. She looked like a lunatic.

"Just like a princess," I agreed. I leaned back and put my feet up on the kitchen table.

"Listen, Ma. I'm going to have to go back to Libby's for dinner tonight, okay? You don't mind watching Ruby again, do you?"

"Of course not, but why don't you leave Isaac, too?"

"I can't. I haven't pumped any milk for him and I really don't want him to have any baby formula."

"So pump. You brought that horrible machine. Why don't you use it?"

True, why not? I went to the pile of suitcases and pulled out my breast pump. I stripped down to my nursing bra, set the machine on the kitchen table, and attached the hoses and bottles. The first time I'd used this pump I'd had the pressure turned on full blast. It had taken a good minute and a half to extricate my nipple from the grip of the machine. A minute and a half spent screaming both in pain and in horror. Who knew my nipple could extend to a cool seven inches in length? I carefully adjusted the vacuum to the "medium" setting and settled in for a wait. Pumping has never been easy for me. I can sit for hours like some pathetic heifer and end up with a measly two ounces of milk sloshing around in the bottom of the bottle.

Today wasn't any different. I closed my eyes and imagined that the sucking and hissing of the machine was really my darling baby boy. I visualized. I meditated. And half an hour later I had three ounces of milk.

"Is that enough?" my mother asked.

"I hope so. It's all I've got."

"Here. Give it to me and I'll put it in the fridge." My mother reached out to take the bottle. I waved her away.

"Don't worry, I've got it."

"No, give it to me. You're still hooked up to the milking machine."

We wrestled for the bottle and, inevitably, watched it crash to the floor between us.

"*Oy,*" she said, as the milk spilled in a tiny little pool on the floor.

"I guess the baby is coming with me tonight."

"I guess so."

"HERE'S MY QUESTION for you," I said to Libby's husband's friend. "If Ari Hirsch is hiding the fact that he is gay, what would happen if that information were made public?"

We were sitting around Libby's kitchen table. Libby's children were sleeping and she was leaning against the counter, holding a dozing Isaac in her arms. She'd made roast chicken and Brussels sprouts, and we'd eaten the meal awkwardly, waiting to have this conversation. Josh's friend Sam Kramer had come to dinner somewhat reluctantly. I could tell he suspected my motives for asking questions about Ari Hirsch. Josh wasn't any happier to see me.

After a moment, Sam answered my question.

"I don't really know. Maybe his family would disown him. Maybe they wouldn't talk about it and hope it would just go away."

I raised my eyebrows.

"Mr. Kramer, maybe you can just give me some background here. Do you know if there are any gay Hasidic men? Are being gay and being religious mutually exclusive?"

Sam carefully wiped a crumb of strudel from the corner of his fleshy mouth. He leaned back and crossed his hands over his corpulent belly. "The way I see it, there are basically three routes open to the gay man who is also a religious Jew," he said. "First of all, he can get married and do his best to suppress his sexuality. He can fake being a heterosexual man."

"But do you think that's really possible?" I asked.

"What do I know? I imagine it's possible. If the man concentrates on the holiness of his life and not on his own needs, he might be okay."

This was more or less the scenario Libby had described. "Do you know men who live like this?" I asked.

"Not really. It's sort of a necessary corollary to that lifestyle that a man keep it all a secret, don't you think? But once I met the rabbi for the gay Jewish center in the Village. They run workshops and have meetings there. He told me they even have a group of gay yeshiva students that meets regularly."

"Really?" I was surprised.

"Really."

I thought for a moment. "It seems like Ari's parents are hoping he'll do just what you're talking about: get married and ignore it, hope it'll go away. If the rumors are true, that is."

"If he is gay, then that's probably what they want, but we don't know that he is, do we? Whatever he is or isn't, he could make the most wonderful, loving, and sensitive parent. He could be a perfect husband." Sam belched softly.

"Maybe," I said doubtfully. "You said there are three options. You described one. What are the other two?"

"He could break with the strict Hasidic community altogether. There are Modern Orthodox synagogues on the Upper West Side that would probably accept him. He might find a community there. That's more or less what that gay rabbi I told you about did. He's from a strict Orthodox family. He came out of the closet when he was in rabbinical school. You can imagine what his family thought of that. Needless to say, he's not really Orthodox anymore."

"And the last option?"

"Lastly he could remain in the community, but be on his own. He would never get married. He would live alone, or even with a man if he did it very discreetly. He would be isolated from the gay community, but he would still be a member of the religious community."

All this was very interesting, but how did it relate to Fraydle?

"Ari was getting married, so he was clearly choosing the first path. What would have happened if Fraydle's family found out?" I had asked this question of Libby, but I wanted to see if Sam's answer was any different.

"That depends. They might cancel the match. Or they might ignore the rumors and go forward. It depends on how important the match was, and on how suited the two were for each other in other ways."

Could Fraydle and her family have heard about the rumors? Perhaps her father had pushed her to go forward despite what they'd heard. Maybe that had been her reason for running away.

"Listen, Juliet, if I were you, I'd be careful," Josh said.

"Excuse me?" I said.

"The Hirsches are an important family. And Ari's uncles on his mother's side are, well, powerful."

"I know. I heard about the rich uncles who own half of Borough Park."

"Those uncles have their own reputation. They're . . . they're not so easy to deal with."

"Josh," Sam said, a note of warning in his voice.

"What do you mean?" I pressed.

Josh looked at Sam and shrugged his shoulders. "Nothing really. It's just that they're real estate guys. They collect their own rents."

"What? Like they're Jewish mobsters or something?"

"No! No! Nothing like that. All I'm saying is that you shouldn't mess around with these guys. They might not like someone asking questions about their nephew."

I looked at Josh for a moment, wondering if he was serious. Was he really telling me to watch out for a couple of old Hasidic men? I thanked him for his warning and assured him I would be careful. I almost told him that after being shot once, I wasn't likely to put myself in that position again, but I decided that I didn't have the time for the explanations that comment would require.

What he said did make me think of something else, however. Maybe Fraydle had found out about Ari and threatened not only to call off the match, but also to tell people why she was doing it. How far would the uncles have gone to ensure her silence?

"I need to talk to Ari Hirsch. Can you arrange that for me?"

Libby, who had been silent throughout our conversation, interrupted. "No. That's ridiculous. Why do you need to talk to this boy? Why do you need to bother him? You'll just scare him with this."

"Look, Libby, all I know right now is rumor and innuendo. I need to know the truth, and I need to find out what Fraydle knew. The only way that I can think of to do this is to talk to Ari."

"Ridiculous," Sam blustered.

"Not ridiculous at all," I said. "The other option is to ask Fraydle's family. Which do you think would bother Ari more?"

The three looked at one another for a moment. Finally, Josh spoke. "I can't promise he'll talk to you. But I can tell him who you are. The rest is up to you."

16

OSH AGREED TO speak to Ari the next day. Libby handed Isaac to me and stiffened when I hugged her. She did not return my embrace. I hoped I hadn't lost a friend.

I found Ruby still awake and waiting for us at my parents' front door.

"Hi, kiddo," I said. "Did you have fun with Grandma and Grandpa? Did you go visit Bubba in the nursing home?"

She nodded, but, with a trembling lip, whispered, "I miss Daddy."

I handed Isaac to my mother and scooped Ruby up in my arms. I kissed her on the cheek. She buried her face in my neck and started to cry.

I said, "I know, honey. It's hard to be away from Daddy. I miss him, too. Should we give him a call?" We'd already spoken to Peter about three hundred times in the two days we'd been gone, but another call wouldn't hurt. I settled her on one hip and reached for the phone. I dialed Peter's cell phone number, since I was pretty sure I'd find him on the set.

It rang twice and then a female voice answered, "Hi!"

I felt a wave of intense jealousy crash over me, utterly obliterating all the good feelings generated by our loving moments at Miserable Mindy's party and at the airport. Now, I know that my husband is crazy about me, and I know that he would never cheat on me. But there's something about being postpartum, even four months postpartum, that makes you feel vulnerable. The problem isn't that you're still carrying around that extra pregnancy weight, although that doesn't help. It's not even that sleep deprivation has etched permanent black smudges under your eyes and in your mood. The real problem is that the very last thing in the universe you feel like doing is touching any human being other than your baby, and that includes your husband. When you're a nursing mother, your body belongs to someone else. You are perpetually available to satisfy the physical demands of your

THE BIG NAP 271

baby. The idea of satisfying another person's physical desires, no matter how much fun that might end up being for you personally, is just too much. At least that's how I felt. There I was, a woman who loved her husband desperately but who had about as much interest in sex as in skydiving; less, in fact. And there she was, whoever she was, with her breathy little "Hi!"

"This is Juliet. Is my *husband* there?" Icicles dangled from my words.

"Juliet! It's so wonderful to hear from you! We were just wondering how you and your adorable kids are doing!"

We? "Who is this?" I asked, not defrosting in the least.

"Oh, I'm sorry. This is Mindy Maxx."

"No, *I'm* sorry," I replied. "I thought I dialed Peter's cell phone. I must have gotten your number by mistake."

Mindy and I both knew that I didn't know her cell phone number. Obviously, I couldn't really believe I'd miraculously dialed it instead of Peter's. She would have had to be a total moron not to understand how angry and suspicious I was.

She wasn't an idiot. "Juliet, I just picked up Peter's phone. We're in the production trailer going over the rushes and I just picked it up off the table where he left it. Honestly."

There was a scuffling noise and then Peter's voice came on the line.

"Hey, honey!" he said. "Sorry about that. Mindy just grabbed my phone as a joke."

"Ha ha ha," I said.

He paused, as if he was trying to figure out why I was upset. Are all men this clueless? "Let's talk about this later, okay?" he said.

"Whatever. Your daughter wants to talk to you." I handed Ruby the phone and walked out of the kitchen, tears in my eyes. I grabbed Isaac from my mother and sat down on the couch and buried my nose in his soft little neck. He giggled deliciously.

"*You* love me best, don't you?" I whispered in his ear.

He grabbed a clump of my hair and shoved it in his mouth. I listened while Ruby chatted animatedly with her father. That little girl sure loved her Daddy.

"What's wrong, *mamaleh*?" my father asked, leaning forward in his chair. He patted me on the knee. "Did Peter say something?"

"No," I sighed. "I'm just jealous of Mindy, his new best friend."

"What are you jealous for? You're a beautiful woman. You're the mother of his children. What do you care if he has some friend? He loves *you*!"

"I know. It's just that things haven't been very much fun around the house lately. I can't blame him for enjoying her company more than mine. At least she doesn't smell like spit-up. And I'm not beautiful, by the way." Now I was fishing.

"Yes, you are. You're gorgeous. Lovely. A little *zaftig*, maybe, but that's very attractive. Who wants to sleep with a bag of bones?"

Great. Even my own father thought I was fat.

"For God's sake, Gene," my mother said, whacking my father on the back of the head with a magazine. "She's not *zaftig*! What are you saying? *Zaftig*. You idiot."

"Stop hitting me!"

"What hitting? I tapped you on the head. I should show you hitting."

By now I'd stopped crying and was just laughing. My parents, the Jewish Honeymooners. I handed Isaac to my dad and went back into the kitchen. I took the phone away from Ruby, unwinding her from the cord she'd managed to wrap around her neck and waist.

"Hi. Sorry," I said.

"Me, too," Peter said. "Why don't you come home so we can fight in person? That way we'd at least get to have make-up sex."

"We could have make-up phone sex," I suggested.

"Hmm. Maybe. Where are your parents?"

"Right here."

"Never mind."

"We're coming home soon."

"I know. I love you, Juliet."

I started to cry again. "I know. I love you, too."

"I love you too, too."

"I love you too, too, too."

"Oh, for God's sake," my mother said, pushing past me into the kitchen. "What are you, a couple of teenagers? You miss him so much, you should go home."

"I don't want to go home. I want to stay here and watch you and Daddy hit each other with newspapers."

"It wasn't a newspaper! I tapped him with a magazine. You and your father. The two of you should go down to City Hall and get yourselves a restraining order."

I laughed. "Hey, Peter? Have I ever told you how insane my parents are?"

"I figured that out all by myself," he said. "Listen, I'd better go. We're in the middle of something."

"Okay, honey. I'll talk to you tomorrow."

We hung up.

My mother was pulling covered dishes out of the refrigerator. "I'm heating up leftover chicken for a little late-night snack," she said.

"Sounds fine to me."

"You should go visit Bubba tomorrow morning."

"I will."

"So how did it go today? Did you find your girl, what's her name? Fruma?"

"Fraydle. No, I didn't. I don't think she's in New York." I recounted my conversation with Sam.

"Sounds to me like you need to speak to that boy," my mother said.

"I thought of that myself. I asked Josh, Libby's husband, to call him for me."

"Why not just call him yourself?"

"That's a terrible idea, Mom. What am I going to say, 'Hi there, Ari. Are you queer and did you make your fiancée disappear by any chance?'"

"Don't be ridiculous. Why don't you just ask him if he'll meet you for a cup of coffee? Then you can delicately ask him about Fraydle."

"Right. Like this yeshiva *bucher* is going to meet some strange woman for coffee."

"Fine. Don't take my advice. What do I know? I'm just an old woman. You're the detective."

"I am *not* a detective."

"No. You just solve murders in your spare time."

"Exactly. I mean, no! I don't solve murders. I did solve that one before Isaac was born, but this isn't a murder. I don't even know if Fraydle is dead!"

"Who's dead? Daddy?" Ruby asked, soundly bizarrely unperturbed at the thought.

"Nobody's dead! Daddy's fine! He's just in California!"

"Don't yell at me! Yell at Grandma, not me!"

I knelt down and gave her a hug. "Sorry, honey." I kissed the top of her head. Then I walked over to my mother, put my arm around her, and kissed her on the cheek. "Sorry, Ma."

"What sorry? You don't need to be sorry. Don't be silly."

17

THE NEXT MORNING I woke up late and found my mother sitting in the living room, holding the telephone receiver up to a gurgling Isaac's mouth.

"What are you doing?" I asked.

"Isaac is talking to his daddy," she said.

"Sounds like a scintillating conversation. Here, give me the phone."

I took the receiver out of her hand and made myself comfortable on the couch. Isaac immediately started nuzzling me, and I settled him across my lap.

"Hi, honey," I said, into the phone.

"Hi, baby. I'm glad I caught you."

"Isaac not enough of a conversationalist for you?"

"Not at all. He's great. He burped twice and I swear he said 'Dada.'"

"He did not. He's only four months old."

"Well, all I know is what I heard. What are you wearing?"

"What?"

"What are you wearing right now?"

I laughed. "Um, my father's green flannel nightshirt."

"Underneath?"

"Peter!"

"C'mon! Tell me."

"I can't. My mother's sitting right here."

My mother shook her head, sighed dramatically, and hoisted herself off the couch. "I'm going upstairs," she said, and stomped away.

"Okay, she's gone. Nothing."

"Mmm. Come home."

"Where are you? It's six in the morning California time. Are you at home?" I asked.

"No, I'm in the production office. I've been here all night."

"Is Mindy there?"

"Oh, for God's sake, Juliet! You really are insane. Of course she's not here. Would I be talking to you about your naked body if Mindy were here?"

I didn't say anything.

"Juliet. When are you going to figure out that I love *you*? You're the one I'm dreaming about. It's *your* body that I'm thinking about."

I sighed. "I know. I'm sorry. Again. As usual. I'm always sorry." And I was, really, it just seemed like Peter and Mindy were spending so much time together. "Listen," I said, "let's not talk about Mindy, or my body for that matter. Let me tell you about yesterday."

After I told Peter about everything I'd discovered I asked him what he thought my next move ought to be.

"Well, if I were writing this as a screenplay," he said, "I'd want to know what your motivation was. What do you want to know? What information are you missing?"

I thought for a minute. "I guess what I need to know now is if Fraydle knew about Ari, and if she did, what, if anything, she did about it. Was she planning on going forward with the marriage? What did her parents know? Were they planning on going forward?"

"Well, you can't ask her, because she's still missing. She *is* still missing, isn't she?"

"I assume so. Nettie has my number here. She promised to call if Fraydle came home or if anything else happened." I didn't say what the anything else was, but Peter and I both knew what I meant: if she turned up dead.

"Okay, so you can safely assume she's still missing. So you can't ask her. Her father isn't likely to tell you."

"And I know Nettie would have told me if she knew anything about it. At least, I think she would have."

"So who does that leave? The mother?"

"She won't talk."

"Then who?"

"Ari Hirsch."

"So call Ari Hirsch."

"God! You and my mother. That's just what she suggested that I do. I'll tell you what I told her: I asked Josh to call him for me."

"Don't wait for Josh. Do it yourself."

And I did.

I found Ari's parents' telephone number by using my keen detective skills and calling directory assistance. Once I reached Esther, I claimed to be a clerk at a store where Ari had placed an order and asked to speak to him.

"What kind of order?" Ari's mother said.

"It's a gift order, Mrs. Hirsch," I replied. "Mr. Hirsch specifically asked us not to tell what it was. Are you his wife?"

"No, his mother."

"Well, then I certainly can't tell you, can I?" As soon as the words left my mouth I felt horribly guilty, imagining Esther waiting day after day for the surprise gift from her son, which would never arrive.

"He's at the yeshiva all day today."

A boy's high-pitched voice answered the phone at the yeshiva.

"Can I speak to Ari Hirsch, please?" I asked.

"I'll transfer you to the rabbi's office. He's in there, studying."

A moment later a soft voice answered the phone.

I swallowed, a little nervously. I've had conversations with bank robbers, drug dealers, and even the worst scum of the earth, confidential informants, but for some reason this particular conversation, with a young man I imagined to be skinny and acne-covered, hunched over his sacred texts and doubting his sexuality, made me tense.

"Is this Ari Hirsch?"

"Yes, who is this?"

"Mr. Hirsch, Ari, my name is Juliet Applebaum. I'm a friend of Fraydle Finkelstein."

"Yes. I know about you. Josh Bernstein spoke to me this morning in *shul*."

So Josh had come through.

"Ari, is there any way we can meet? I have some questions to ask you and I'd rather do it in person."

"Meet?"

"This is very urgent. Very. Please trust me. I must talk to you about Fraydle. It's an emergency."

He didn't respond.

"I'm taking my kids to the Museum of Natural History today," I said. "Would you meet me there? We can talk for just a moment or two?"

The mention of my kids seemed to reassure him. He said, tentatively, "It is urgent, correct?"

"Very."

"I must study this morning. I can meet you this afternoon at three o'clock."

"Terrific," I said. "In the elephant room. Right under the tusks of the lead elephant. I'll be there with my two small children, a baby and a little girl."

"Under the elephant," he said, and hung up the phone.

When I hung up I looked up at my mother. She was standing over me, smiling complacently.

"What?" I said.

"A ridiculous idea," she said.

"What was?"

"Calling him. Ridiculous, you told me."

"Okay. Not ridiculous. A good idea. A very good idea. So, do you want to come into the city with me?"

"No. I have to go to the office for a few hours. Myron has a petition for certiorari due this afternoon and I can't trust the temp to get it right. You only have one chance, you know. If it's late, it's late. The Supreme Court doesn't take excuses."

"I know, Ma. I filed a few of those while I was the federal public defender."

"Of course you did," she said, clearly mourning my lost days as a professional.

"Maybe Daddy will want to come along."

"Sure he will. He loves the museum."

WHEN WE GOT to the Upper West Side we parked the car and unloaded the kids. My father insisted on putting Isaac on his own chest in the Baby Bjorn. I was sorry I hadn't brought my camera along to catch the two of them waddling down the street with Ruby skipping along next to them, her little hand buried in her Grandpa's furry paw.

It was one of those perfect New York City autumn days. The air was cool and crisp and the sun shone brightly. The city looked new and polished and smelled like apples and the streets were so clean, the asphalt seemed to sparkle. Even the homeless people looked a little more cheerful than usual. I gave Ruby a couple of dollars to distribute among them on our way down the block. My usual rule is that I give money only to women, and then only if they don't seem visibly intoxicated, but today I let Ruby hand out the bills to whomever she pleased. I wasn't sure I should be letting her play Lady Bountiful this way, but I figured it wouldn't hurt for her to understand that since she was lucky enough to have money, she had an obligation to share some of it with those who weren't as fortunate.

We walked into the beautiful old Museum of Natural History and made our way to the huge hall where the herd of elephants stands, massive and imposing, in the center of the room. I sat down on a bench under the looming tusks of the lead elephant. Ruby came up and, leaning against me, stared up into the behemoth's face.

"These elephants are all dead, right?" she asked.

"Yup," I said.

"Somebody killed them," she stated.

"That's true."

"Even the baby?"

"Even the baby."

"Why?"

"Well, Rubes, a long time ago, people didn't know that it was bad to kill animals. When these elephants were shot, people didn't really understand that if you kill lots of animals, there won't be any left."

"They'll be stink."

"What?"

"Stink. Like the dinosaurs."

"Right, exactly, *extinct*. People didn't understand about extinction and endangered species back when these elephants were killed."

"But now we know that's bad, right?"

"Right."

"And nobody kills elephants anymore. Cuz it's bad."

I wasn't about to get into a discussion of wild animal poaching and the insatiable Asian market for things like elephant tusk and rhino horn, particularly since one of my last clients was a Chinese bear-bile smuggler. So I just said, "Right."

Ruby scampered off to play with her grandpa, and I looked up. Across the room I saw a young man dressed in the garb of a Hasidic Jew. He wore a fedora, a dark suit, and his *tzitzit* hung outside his trousers. His long sidelocks were tucked behind his ears and a patchy, light brown beard covered his chin. His cheeks were reddened with acne and pitted with scars. For all that, he wasn't unattractive. He had big blue eyes with long lashes and a straight nose. His full lips looked almost bruised under the mantle of his moustache.

I lifted my hand in a sort of half wave and he walked over to me.

"Ari Hirsch?" I asked.

"Yes. And you are Mrs. . . . uh, Mrs. . . ."

"Applebaum."

"Yes, of course. Mrs. Applebaum. A friend of Fraydle's." He stood awkwardly, a few feet from me.

"Would you like to sit down?" I motioned to the bench on which I sat. He perched at the far end, carefully maintaining a respectable distance from me.

"Did Josh Bernstein tell you why I asked you to meet me?"

"Why don't you tell me yourself," he said, his voice soft.

How was I going to do this? One of the reasons I was here was my suspicion that Ari and his family might know something about Fraydle's whereabouts. But what if he didn't? Fraydle's family was adamant about keeping her disappearance a secret from the Hirsches. How could I ask him if he knew where she was without giving away their secret? How could I ask him whether she knew about his sexual orientation without making him aware that *his* secret was out? I could do neither.

I've always believed that it's secrecy that causes the most difficulties. If you are honest and open about your problems, then nobody can hurt you by disclosing them. I didn't believe that either the Finkelsteins or Ari were doing themselves any favors by being so reticent. Now, maybe that decision wasn't mine to make, but I decided to act as if it were. For the purposes of this conversation, at least.

"Ari, I don't know how much Josh told you, but Fraydle has disappeared. Her parents don't want your family to know; they're afraid your parents will call off the match. But she's been gone for almost a week now, and I am very worried."

"Gone? What do you mean, gone?"

"Gone as in she's not at home and nobody knows where she is."

"Could she have been kidnapped? What do the police say?"

"For the time being, Rabbi Finkelstein is conducting the search on his own."

"No police?"

"No."

"So she has just run away? Nobody has . . . has hurt her?"

"Nobody knows where she is, Ari. That's why I asked you here to talk to me. I wonder if you might know if she has run away and if so, why."

He shook his head vigorously. "I know nothing. I have met her only a few times. I don't really know her at all."

I took a breath. "Ari, there's no easy way for me to ask this. Did you tell Fraydle that you might be a homosexual?"

The blood drained from his face. He looked at me for a moment, stricken.

"Ari? Did you tell her?"

He reached his hand to a sidecurl and tugged at it nervously.

"Ari?"

"How do you know? What did she tell you about me?" he whispered.

I said nothing. I felt guilty about letting him think that Fraydle was the source of my suspicions, but I'd promised Libby and Josh that I would keep their confidence.

Ari shook his head, as if to clear his ears of my words.

"I'm not . . . not . . . I'm not what you said," he murmured.

"Ari, I'm not judging you, and I'm not going to tell anybody what I found out. All I need to know is whether you told Fraydle anything."

He remained silent for another moment, winding his hair around his finger. Finally, he turned to me and said, "Fraydle knew everything there is to know. I told her about my doubts about . . . about myself. We talked about it and we decided that with her help, and God's, I could overcome this."

That was a surprise. I guess I'd been expecting to hear that he'd told Fraydle, and her shock and her fear of marrying a man who would rather be with another man had made her run away from home. I hadn't expected to hear that the two of them had discussed the issue openly and nonetheless reached an agreement to marry.

"She agreed to go forward with the wedding?"

"Not at first. She was upset at first. But she didn't reject me right away. She told me she needed some time to think."

"Then what happened?"

"I went back to New York. She called me on the telephone, a few days later. She told me that she had thought about it and that we should marry."

"Ari, did she tell her parents?"

He shook his head. "No. We agreed to keep the secret between us."

"Are you sure she kept this agreement?"

"Yes. She promised not to tell her parents. I don't think she would have broken her promise."

"Did she tell you anything about herself, of her own doubts about marriage?"

Ari didn't take his eyes off the long thin fingers knotted in his lap. He shook his head.

It surprised me that despite the fact that her fiancé had been so honest with her, Fraydle had failed to confide in him about Yossi. However, the truth was that none of this helped me at all. If Fraydle and Ari had worked this out between them, there was no reason for her to run away. A chill ran across the back of my neck. Since the first days of Fraydle's disappearance, I'd done my best to think of her as a runaway. But I'd always known that the odds were good, and getting better with each day, that she hadn't run anywhere. It was all too possible that someone had taken her, had done something to her. Maybe that someone was sitting next to me under the elephant tusks. Or maybe that someone was in Borough Park or back in Los Angeles. I had to get on a plane to Los Angeles as soon as possible. I needed to see the Finkelsteins and convince them to go to the police. And if the rabbi refused, I would make the report myself.

The young man interrupted my thoughts. "What are you going to do?" he asked.

"Don't worry, Ari. I'm not going to tell anyone about you. I'm just trying to find Fraydle."

"You must call me as soon as you know anything."

"I will. Of course I will. Thank you for talking to me."

"No, thank *you*. Thank you for telling me. You said you are a friend of Fraydle's?" He looked at me, obviously not understanding what I, a non-Hasidic woman in a pair of overalls, could have to do with his wife-to-be.

"She was my babysitter." It was, I knew, a ridiculously thin connection. Not a friend. Not a member of my family. Just a girl who watched my baby one morning. So that I could take a nap.

"Ah, yes. Well, good-bye," he said.

"Good-bye, Ari."

I rushed off to where my father was standing with the kids, looking at a diorama of the African veldt.

"Look, Mama," Ruby said. "A Thompson's gazelle."

I looked at the sign next to the exhibit box. Lo and behold, it was, in fact, a Thompson's gazelle.

"How do you know what a Thompson's gazelle looks like?" I asked.

"The Kratt Brothers told me!" she replied. Thank goodness for public television.

I hustled the three of them through the rest of the museum as fast as I could, zipping by the dinosaurs and the giant blue whale. I wanted to get back to New Jersey and call the airline. The fates were conspiring against me, however, and we ended up stuck on the West Side Highway, creeping slowly north toward the George Washington Bridge. It took almost ninety minutes to get home. Luckily, Isaac fell asleep in the back of the car, after he'd screamed for an hour at the top of his lungs.

When he finally crashed into slumber, my father looked at me and said, "For a minute there I thought he'd shatter the windshield."

18

BY THE TIME we pulled into my parents' driveway, it was dark. As my father and I unloaded the kids from the car, I noticed a big black Cadillac pulled up in front of the house. The car stuck out like a sore thumb in a neighborhood where my parents' Chrysler was the only American car that wasn't a sports utility vehicle.

I lumbered up the porch stairs with a sleeping Isaac draped over my shoulder and Ruby wrapped around my leg. A group of Hasidic men stood waiting outside the front door. All wore hats, but only a few were bearded. They did not look particularly friendly.

"Hello? Can I help you?" I asked. My father, who had been coming up the steps behind me, said, at the same time, "Who are all these people?"

A large man with a big belly stepped forward. He pointed a finger at me. "You are Juliet Applebaum," he said, rather than asked.

"Well, you're ahead of me, sir. You know who I am, but I don't know who you are," I said, trying not to show how nervous I was. I did a quick head count. There were six men standing on the porch. I decided to pretend this was a social call.

"Why don't we go inside so I can get the baby out of the cold." I walked by the man who'd spoken to me and unlocked the front door. My father followed me, reaching out for Ruby's hand.

"What's going on?" he whispered as he walked past me into the house.

"I have no idea," I answered, in a loud, clear voice.

I held the door open and the men filed in, one by one. I walked into the living room area and sat down on the couch, still holding the baby on my lap.

"Daddy," I said, "why don't you go set Ruby up with a video upstairs."

He nodded and led her away. Meanwhile, the men had followed me across the floor and stood in a little huddle in the center of the living room. I looked them over. There were two older men, the big one who'd spoken to me and another of about the same size, but with a long, grizzled beard. The four other men were much younger. Two looked to be about my age, and two seemed no more than boys. One of the younger men, with short blond hair, a trimmed beard, and broad shoulders, looked vaguely familiar. Where had I seen him before?

"Please sit down," I said.

They all looked at the leader of the pack, who shook his head angrily. "We are not staying in this house. We came only to warn you, Juliet Applebaum. Stay away from the Hirsch family. You are not welcome."

Ah. The uncles.

"You must be Esther Hirsch's brother. It's a pleasure to meet you," I said. Here's the thing about having been a public defender: After a while, scary guys just don't scare you anymore. My clients had almost all been scary guys. They were gangbangers with elaborate tattoos, jittery bank robbers with thousand-dollar-a-day smack habits, car-jackers with arsenals of Glock 9mm semi-automatics. As their lawyer, and often the only person who really cared about what happened to them, I almost always became their confidante, confessor, and even their friend. I'd learned to look behind the crime and see the man. And the person standing in front of me, for all that he looked intimidating and even dangerous, was just a man. An old Jewish man. Like my father, but with a fur hat.

"Who I am is not important!" my rude visitor bellowed. My father came running downstairs at the sound of the shout.

"Daddy, please go up and stay with Ruby," I said.

"But—" he began.

"Daddy! I need you to stay with her. I don't want her to be scared." Though clearly reluctant, he headed back up the stairs.

I turned to the spokesman, who was pointing a finger in my face. "Stop shouting," I said. "You'll wake the baby."

The blond man, the one who looked familiar, stepped forward. "We are here to ask you to refrain from prying into the affairs of Ari Hirsch. That is all." He spoke with a faint accent.

"Ask nothing!" the leader shouted. "We are telling you! Mind your own business, you *churva*!"

At that moment, the front door opened and my mother walked in the door.

"*Churva*?" she said. "Did I hear someone say the word *churva* in my house? What's going on here?" She looked at me, and at the group of men still standing in the middle of the living room. "Josef?" she said. "Josef Petrovsky, what are you doing here? What is your mother going to say when I tell her your friend called my daughter a whore?"

19

Y MOTHER'S SCOLDING seemed momentarily to take the wind out of the sails of my second-cousin-twice-removed and his cabal of hostile Hasidim. Then the leader raised his fist. "This is a warning," he bellowed.

The older man with the grizzled beard, who had been silent up until then, put a restraining hand on his cohort's arm. He turned to me and, in a voice made somehow more ominous by its softness, said, "We are a close family." I didn't answer. "We protect each other."

"That's nice," I said. "But what does that have to do with me?"

He smiled thinly. "You should know this about us, that is all."

"Listen, you," my mother squawked. "What do you think you are, the Jewish Gambini family? I want you out of my house. All of you. Out now, or I'm calling the police."

The quiet man ignored her and looked at me. I stood my ground.

"I think you should leave," I said.

"Out, out!" My mother grabbed the young man closest to her by the arm and began pushing him in the direction of the door. He shook her off with a rough jerk and she stared at him, her mouth open.

"Please leave," I repeated.

"Yes," the soft-voiced man said. "And you, of course, will no longer make my nephew a subject of your conversation." I said nothing. "Good. That is settled. Thank you for your time." He nodded once and walked to the front door. He waited for a moment for one of the young men to open it for him, and then walked out the door, followed by the others. My cousin was the last to leave. He walked over to my mother but she pushed him away. "Out of my house, Josef Petrovsky. You are no longer welcome here!" He slunk out the door.

"Humph!" my mother said.

"Yeah, no kidding. Hey, Ma?"

"Yes, darling?"

"What the hell was that about?"

"You're asking me? You're the one out raking muck. You tell me what happened."

"First of all," I said, "muckraking is investigative journalism. I'm not raking muck. Second of all, what was cousin Josef Petrovsky doing in our house? And why was he with Ari Hirsch's uncles?"

She shrugged her coat off her shoulders and tossed it over a chair. "First of all, that sure looked like muck to me. Second of all, I haven't any idea what Josef was doing with those horrible men."

"But you know why he was here?"

"I talked to Bella Petrovsky, Josef's mother, this morning. You've met her, darling. At Tante Tsunya's funeral years ago, when you still lived in New York. For that matter, that's where you met Josef for the first time."

I gritted my teeth in exasperation. "Ma! What did you tell her?"

"I told her you needed Josef's help."

"That's all?"

She busied herself with picking lint off her skirt.

"Ma!"

"So maybe I told her that you thought that this boy, Ari Hirsch, was a homosexual and did she ever hear any rumors about him from her son, about whom, incidentally, I've always had my doubts."

"Oh, for God's sake, Mom."

"Look, darling, how was I supposed to know that Josef knew Ari Hirsch's uncles? What, all observant Jews know each other now? Josef manages apartment buildings, for God's sake. What does he know from rabbis?"

"Oh, Mom. Ari's *father* is a rabbi. His uncles are in real estate. Josef probably works for them."

My mother put her hand to her throat. "You think?"

"Yeah, I think. Here, take the baby." I handed Isaac to her. "I'd better go upstairs and make sure Daddy and Ruby haven't barricaded themselves into a closet."

I found Ruby happily watching *101 Dalmatians* perched on my father's lap, his arms crossed protectively over her chest. He jumped about three feet into the air when I walked into the room. "All clear, Pop," I said.

"Oh, thank God. What a nightmare. Were they armed?" he asked.

"Oh, Daddy, don't be ridiculous. They were not packing heat."

"*I'm* ridiculous?" He put his hands over Ruby's ears. "I'm not the one who's been shot, young lady." Ruby squawked and batted at his hands.

"I can't hear!" she shrieked.

"Sorry, *maydele*," he said, taking away his hands and kissing the top of her head. She settled back against his chest.

"It's okay, Grandpa. I still love you," Ruby said.

I left the pair to Cruella de Vil and went to the telephone. I wanted to warn Ari Hirsch that his uncles knew that I had been looking for him. When I told him, he seemed resigned rather than upset, and I hung up the phone wondering if my search for Fraydle had accomplished anything other than making a confused young man's life that much more difficult. I then called the airline and managed to book us on a flight for the next morning. We were going to have to make two transfers and the trip would take us thirteen hours door to door, but we'd be home by tomorrow night. My parents weren't surprised at my decision, although they did extract a promise from me that we'd be back again in a couple of months. When I called Peter, he sounded overjoyed and promised to pick us up at the airport.

About the trip home I won't say anything other than that babies cry most when planes take off and land because of the change in cabin pressure. And we took off and landed six separate times. If I'd had any doubts about Isaac's lung capacity before the trip, they were entirely dispelled.

20

THE MORNING AFTER we got home was a Sunday. Upon waking, Ruby begged to be taken to the Santa Monica Pier and Peter happily agreed to drive her. Isaac and I unpacked and then headed out to Nettie's store. I needed to find out what was happening with the search for Fraydle and if Fraydle had told Nettie anything about Ari.

Nettie was behind the counter, as usual. She shouted my name when she saw me and rushed out to hug me.

"Did you find anything?" she whispered in my ear, eyeing her waiting customers.

"Maybe. I don't know," I replied.

"Wait!" she said, and hurried back around the counter. She quickly checked out her customers, virtually chasing out one or two who were lingering in the aisles. Then she locked the door and turned the CLOSED sign around.

"Come! To the back!" Nettie motioned me toward the storeroom. I wheeled Isaac's stroller through the narrow doorway and she shut the door behind us.

"Now. Tell me."

"First of all, you tell *me*. I take it Fraydle hasn't come home."

Nettie shook her head, her wig jiggling back and forth with the motion.

"Has Rabbi Finkelstein called the police?"

"Not yet. If she's not home by *Shabbos*, he will. That's what Sima says. She says they must call by Friday afternoon."

"Nettie, today is only Sunday. Friday is a long way off."

"I know, I know. I'll talk to him again today. I'll try to convince him to call."

"Good."

"Juliet, did you see the Hirsches? Have they heard from Fraydle?"

"I met Esther Hirsch, and I'm pretty confident that she doesn't know anything about Fraydle's disappearance. I also met her brothers and, frankly, they are a couple of nasty guys. And I met Ari. That's what I want to talk to you about, Nettie. Did Fraydle ever tell you anything about Ari?"

"What do you mean?"

"Did she ever tell you she didn't want to go through with the marriage?"

"At the beginning, yes. She didn't even want to meet Ari Hirsch. I was worried she would reject him like she did the others."

"And she didn't?"

Nettie paused. "No, not really. I remember she asked her father if she had to marry. She asked him about the match and he told her how important it was for the family. And then she agreed to meet the boy. After they'd met a few times, she agreed to marry him."

I didn't want to give away Ari's secret to Fraydle's family. On the other hand, it seemed that Nettie was Fraydle's closest confidante.

"Nettie, did Fraydle ever confide in you any concerns she had about Ari? About his . . . um . . . his suitability as a husband?"

She paused and looked at me. "What do you mean?" she asked.

"I heard some rumors about Ari. Rumors that he might be gay."

"Gay?" she asked, confused.

"Homosexual."

"*Oy yoy yoy*!" Nettie exclaimed. "That is what she was talking about!"

"What? Did she say something to you?"

"She asked me what it meant for a man to lie with another man like it says in the *Tanach*. She asked me if it was true that some men had feelings for other men. She asked me if I knew men like this."

I leaned forward eagerly. "And what did you tell her?" I asked.

"I told her that sometimes men are like this, but that it is an abomination in the eyes of God."

She said the last so matter-of-factly.

"What did Fraydle say to that?" I asked.

"She asked me if those feelings were permanent, or if a man like that could become normal if he chose to."

"And what did you tell her?"

"Well, I thought maybe she saw something, or maybe she heard someone talking, maybe one of the young boys. So I told her that I had heard that sometimes the yeshiva *buchers* did things like that, but that it was very wicked. I told her that grown men, married men, never did that. I told her that as soon as they married, all that stopped."

I looked into Nettie's face. She looked almost defiant. "Nettie, do you really believe that?"

She shrugged her shoulders. "Why should a young, innocent girl hear about such things? Why shouldn't I reassure her?"

"Well, Nettie, do you really think she would be happy in a marriage to a homosexual man?"

"Why not? If he was a good father, and a good husband? If he could give her children? What difference does it make what he feels in his heart, as long as he follows the law?"

Never before had I felt the gulf between Nettie and me so deeply. Our beliefs were completely at odds. There was no point in arguing over this issue.

"Did you tell Fraydle's parents about your conversation?"

"No! Of course not. The girl confided in me. I wouldn't tell. Anyway, I had no idea she was talking about Ari. I'm telling you, I thought she maybe saw something or heard something," Nettie said.

I left the store, puzzling over what I'd learned. I had confirmed what Ari had told me. He'd been honest with Fraydle and she'd been reassured by her aunt. Fraydle had agreed to the match and made peace with it. So why had she disappeared? What had happened to her?

21

RUBY AND PETER were waiting for us when Isaac and I got home. I fed the baby and, when he fell asleep, carefully transferred him from my arms to his bassinet, holding my breath, hoping against hope that he wouldn't rouse. For a moment it looked like he was about to wake up, but with a grunt and a wiggle, he settled himself back to sleep.

Peter and Ruby were in the living room, playing a game called Newborn Babies. It consisted entirely of the pair of them wailing like infants.

"Mama! Let's pretend you're the mommy and I'm the baby!" Ruby shouted when I walked in the room.

"You know what, kiddo? I *am* the mommy. It's not really very much fun to pretend to be what you already are."

My daughter looked at me, puzzled, and, with a shrug of her shoulders, turned back to her father.

"Daddy, you be the daddy, and I'll be the newborn baby."

"Okay," Peter said. "Newborn baby, it's time to sleep." She collapsed on the ground and he tucked one of Isaac's blankets around her. "Night-night, newborn baby," he said.

"Waaaa," she wailed softly, and then began to pretend-snore.

Peter and I settled back on the couch and I nestled my head against his shoulder.

"What did the aunt have to say?" he asked.

I told him about Fraydle's conversation with Nettie. "I'd like to know if Yossi knew about this," I said.

"What difference would that make?" Peter asked. "Even if he knew, that doesn't put you any closer to finding out if he or anyone else did her harm."

"It's possible that she confided in Yossi and that he convinced her that her aunt was wrong."

"But then wouldn't she have gone away with him? Why would he still be hanging around L.A.?"

"True. And he did have those plane tickets to Israel that they never used. Still, I want to talk to him again."

"Call him."

"I will. In a minute." I snuggled up to my husband again. "I missed you."

"I missed you, too," he said, kissing me. Suddenly, thirty pounds of outrage landed in our laps.

"Hey! Stop it!" Ruby shouted, wriggling her way in between us. She held up her face to her father. "Kiss me instead!"

Peter kissed her on the nose. "You know, I'm allowed to kiss *both* my girls." He leaned over the top of her head and kissed my nose, too.

Ruby placed a hand on either side of his face and kissed him, over and over again. "This is *my* daddy," she said.

"Okay, Baby Electra." I hoisted myself off the couch. "I'm going to make some phone calls."

Yossi was home when I called. When I told him I had news about Fraydle he agreed to let me come over. I left Peter with the kids and headed out the door. I considered the nightmare of parking on Melrose Avenue—especially on the weekend when all the kids from the Valley pour into the city in their SUVs to buy platform shoes and artfully torn jeans and get their tongues, lips, navels, and other parts punctured—and decided to walk the half-mile or so to Yossi's house.

Without my stroller or a jogging suit as an excuse, I stuck out like a sore thumb as I marched up La Brea. I walked by Nettie's store without even glancing in and made it to Melrose in no time at all. It was a bit tougher going on the trendy avenue itself, as I had to keep dodging giggling clumps of teenage girls and whizzing herds of skateboarders. After staring at what seemed like three million bared midriffs, I had just about decided that I was the fattest person in the Los Angeles basin when two Harley Davidsons roared by, piloted by a pair of massive women with long hair streaming out of tiny pink helmets. Who knew they made leather clothes that big?

Those women obviously looked and felt gorgeous. There they were, tricked out in their leather pants, squealing down Melrose Avenue, wordlessly shouting, *We're here, we're gigantic, get used to it!* And there I was, a few pounds overweight, skulking down the same avenue, wordlessly shouting, *I'm fat, I'm ugly, ignore me!* What was wrong with this picture?

I had a husband who loved me—belly, thighs, and all. My body had just produced and was giving sustenance to a big, healthy baby boy. Why wasn't I able to feel better about myself?

I thought about my little daughter, with her gorgeous potbelly and lovely soft skin. If I didn't get over this obsession with my weight, and soon, my contagion would spread to her. The last thing I wanted was for her to be one of those pathetic eight-year-olds, complaining about their weight and guzzling Diet Coke.

In the midst of this reverie, I arrived at Yossi's building. I walked into the courtyard which, on that sunny Sunday afternoon, was populated with the tenants of the apartments, lounging in their deck chairs and sitting on the edge of the fountain. Rap music blared from a speaker propped in an open window. Yossi's door was open and he stood in the doorway, leaning against the doorjamb. He was smoking a cigarette and wearing a flannel shirt with the sleeves cut off. His feet were bare and his jeans looked at though they hadn't been washed in a while.

I walked across the courtyard, followed by the curious gazes of his neighbors. At thirty-three I was probably the oldest person there. Yossi lifted his hand in a halfhearted gesture of welcome and, with a nod at me to follow, turned back into his apartment. I walked in and shut the door behind me.

The entire apartment was one large room, with a kitchenette at one end.

"Please, sit down," Yossi said, pointing at a futon-bed covered with an unsavory looking Indian-print bedspread. "Can I get you some coffee? All I have is café *botz*."

"*Botz*?" I asked, perching on the very edge of the bed.

"Mud. Like Turkish coffee. In Hebrew we call it mud coffee."

Delicious. "Oh. Sure, mud sounds great."

He walked into the little kitchenette, and I watched as he scooped what I thought looked more like dirt than mud into two coffee mugs and poured in boiling water. He added two heaping teaspoons of sugar to each cup and gave them a brisk stir. Handing me my mug, he said, "Let it sit for a minute so your mouth doesn't get full of grounds."

Even more delicious.

He pulled a folding chair away from the card table that stood against the far wall of the room and sat down backwards in the chair, his legs straddling the seat and his arms leaning on the back.

"Did you find Fraydle?" he asked.

"No, I didn't find her. I did find out some things, though."

"What? What did you find out?"

"I found out that she was going to marry Ari Hirsch."

"I told you that," he said. "I told you that she decided to be a good girl and do what her father told her."

"I also found out that Ari Hirsch may be gay."

"Gay? Like a *faygeleh*?"

I winced. "Gay like homosexual, yes." I took a sip of the hot, sweet coffee. It *was* delicious.

"She can't marry him now! She'll never marry him when she hears about this!" he crowed.

"She knows."

"What do you mean? She knows? But you said you didn't find her. Did she find out before? Oh my God, is that why she is gone? Did she find out about him and he did something to her?"

"I don't know, Yossi. But I don't think so. Ari says that they discussed it and decided to go forward with the marriage anyway."

"What are you talking about? That is ridiculous." He stood up and pushed the chair away. It fell to the floor with a crash and he angrily righted it. "Why would she marry a *faygeleh*? She would not want a pretend marriage—a life without sex."

"I don't know, Yossi. Maybe she thought that once Ari was married he would change. I take it that you don't know anything about this. Fraydle never told you about Ari?"

"No! Of course not! If I knew about this do you think she would be missing? I would never have let her go forward with this marriage. I would have taken her away!" He seemed to realize what he had just said. "I didn't do anything!" he bellowed, and then let loose a stream of Hebrew.

Suddenly, he rushed over to me. "You!" he said, grabbing my arm and dragging me roughly to my feet. "I don't need you here in my house, accusing me of this. You get out! Get out!" He shoved me toward the door. I scooped up my purse with one hand and shook off his arm with the other.

"I'm leaving," I said, in as dignified a tone as I could muster. "I'm not accusing you of anything, Yossi. I'm just trying to get to the bottom of this. All I want is to find Fraydle. Isn't that what you want, too?" He looked at me angrily, and then his shoulders sagged and he slumped, defeated.

"Yes," he whispered.

"I'm going now."

He nodded and let go of my arm.

"You have my number, right?"

He nodded again.

"You'll call me if you hear anything."

He nodded a third time.

I strode out the door and shut it firmly behind me. I stood in the court-yard for a minute, taking a breath to quiet my racing heart. I sure was getting good at pissing people off. Oh, let's be honest; I've always possessed that particular quality in spades.

A voice rang out from above. "Hello! Juliet!"

I looked up, and saw Anat, the waitress from Nomi's. She waved at me and shouted, "One minute! I'll come down."

She ran down the stairs.

"Have you found her? Yossi's girlfriend?"

"No." I shook my head. I glanced back to Yossi's door to make sure it was still closed. "Anat, did you remember anything more about her, about them?" I asked, not particularly hopefully.

"Maybe," she said, in a conspiratorial whisper. "You want to get a cup of coffee? We can talk."

I hadn't actually managed to have more than a sip of the mud Yossi had prepared for me, and I needed a shot of caffeine.

"Is there somewhere we can go?"

"For coffee? On Melrose?" she asked, incredulous. We walked out of the courtyard. It took us a minute or two to choose which of the seven coffee shops on the block we would find the most comfortable.

We settled for a Starbucks on the opposite side of the street. "It'll be more private," Anat said. "None of the people on the courtyard buy coffee there."

We walked into the café and up to the counter. I ordered a mochaccino, which I once heard has the calories of a milk shake. I dumped in a rather ludicrous packet of Equal and shook an inch-thick layer of chocolate flakes onto the top of the foam. Anat got a triple espresso. No wonder she looked so thin. And wired.

We made our way over to a couple of comfortable armchairs and sat down. Say what you will about the Starbucks-ing of America, the stores sure are cozy. And, I've always liked the somewhat watery brew. I like a cup of coffee I can sip, not chew. Except for the chocolate flakes.

"I've been thinking about the last time I saw Yossi's girlfriend," Anat said to me. She was obviously relishing the prospect of gossiping about her ex. "Maybe two weeks ago, maybe a little less, I saw her here one day after the next. Both times she was upset."

"Upset?"

"The first time, she looked furious. I noticed her because she slammed his door so hard that I came out of my apartment. She was pale, like a sheet. But you know, she still looked beautiful. Like a movie star. Those big eyes."

"And then you saw her again?"

Anat sipped daintily at her espresso. I gulped my frothy, fat-filled festival of chocolate. "Yes," she said. "She came back the next morning. I was sitting out on the balcony and I saw her run into the courtyard. Something was wrong. She looked terrible. She knocked on his door and when he answered it she pushed into the apartment. It was like he didn't want to let her in, but she pushed by him. I waited on the balcony, watching, and then maybe ten minutes later, she flew out. This time she was crying hysterically. She ran out of the courtyard. And that was the last time I saw her."

"Could she have come back when you weren't around?"

"It's possible, but I asked the others and nobody saw her there, either. A lot of us noticed her when she made those two dramatic exits, but nobody I talked to saw her come back ever again. If she did, it was when none of us were home."

I leaned back in my chair. Yossi had told me that they'd argued, but he certainly hadn't told me that she'd left him once in a rage and once weeping. This seemed like information critical to Fraydle's disappearance. I realized that Anat wasn't the most reputable of witnesses. She herself had a motive to do away with Fraydle. She was obviously still in love with Yossi. Nobody is that interested in an old boyfriend unless she still cares.

By now I was convinced that something very bad had happened to Fraydle. It was time to tell Fraydle's parents about this. And it was time to call the police.

22

"I TOLD YOU, JULIET, if they hear nothing by *Shabbos*, Sima will insist they go to the police. Before that, I can do nothing."

I leaned on the counter at the front of Nettie's market, where I had rushed immediately after leaving Starbucks.

"Listen, Nettie, I don't think Fraydle ran away. I think that something has happened to her. Friday is too long to wait. By then, it might be too late."

Nettie drew back, anxiously knotting a cloth in her hands. She shook her head. "I can do nothing. Nothing."

"Nettie, Fraydle had a boyfriend. An Israeli boyfriend. Not religious. I'm afraid he might have hurt her because she was getting married."

Nettie shook her head furiously. "What are you talking? A boyfriend. That's ridiculous."

"She went to his apartment. I talked to him, I talked to his neighbors."

Nettie gasped, "*Mein Gott.*"

"It's time to go to the police."

She nodded. "You go talk to Sima." She glanced around the store as if looking for something. "Listen, this is what you'll do. I'll call her and tell her I'm sending you to get something from the garage. And then when you go get the box, you'll talk to her."

"What?" I asked, confused.

"I use her garage for storage. My storage area is so small and they have lots of room. It's their *Pesach* kitchen, their kosher-for-Passover kitchen, and during the rest of the year they don't use it. So I put my things there. I'll tell her I need a box from the garage, and while you're there, you'll talk to her."

"Nettie, I'll just go over to talk to her. I don't need an excuse."

Nettie shook her head. "She's not going to talk to you. She won't even let you in the house. Baruch told her not to talk to you anymore."

"What? Why?"

Nettie shrugged her shoulders. She picked up the phone and dialed.

"Listen, Sima, I'm sending someone over to pick up a case of"—her eyes scanned the empty shelves—"a case of tuna fish. I'm out. I can't come myself because the store is full of customers. They won't leave me alone today." She gestured wildly around the empty shop and hung up the phone.

I rolled my eyes at this unnecessary subterfuge. Nettie obviously didn't want to be there while I coerced Sima into going to the police. I walked quickly out the back door, down the alley, and to the Finkelstein house. Fraydle's younger brothers were once again playing on the porch. I climbed the steps, smiled reassuringly at them, and knocked on the door.

Fraydle's mother came to the door. When she saw me, she began to shake her head.

"Please," I said. "I just need to get a case of tuna for Nettie."

Sima looked at me for a minute, and then shrugged her shoulders. "Come," she said, leading me into the house and to the kitchen. The little boys trailed after us. I stood awkwardly for a moment and watched as one of the youngsters crawled onto a kitchen chair. He reached out for the sugar bowl sitting in the middle of the table and sent it flying to the ground, shattering in an explosion of sugar and porcelain. Remembering Sarah and the broken saucer, I flinched. Sima, however, didn't react the way I'd expected her to. She merely kissed the top of the boy's head, and reached for a broom and a dustpan to sweep up the fragments and spilled crystals.

"The garage is down those stairs." She pointed toward a door in the wall next to the stove. I opened the door and walked down the steep wooden stairs into the gloom of the garage. There was a rickety banister that I didn't dare touch for fear it wouldn't support even the weight of my hand. The garage was entirely taken up by boxes piled against walls and by a complete kitchen set up in one corner. There was a small stove, an old refrigerator, a metal sink, and an ancient chest freezer.

I walked toward the piled-up boxes and began searching for a case of tuna. A low hum filled the garage. I lifted my head and looked around. The hum seemed to be coming from the freezer. I walked over and put my hand on the top. It was cold. This was, Nettie had said, the Passover kitchen. The holiday wasn't for months. I heard my grandmother's voice in my mind, "*Aroysgevorfen* electricity!" A waste of electricity. My mouth grew dry. I grasped the handles of the freezer and gave a tug. With a hiss, the top lifted up, and I screamed.

Fraydle looked as though she were asleep, except she was very white. She was curled up in the freezer, with her legs up against her chest. Her eyes were open just a crack, enough to see that they had rolled back in her head. Frost crystals had formed over her eyes and mouth. Her head rested in a pool of something frozen and black. Blood.

Suddenly I became aware of the thumping noise of footsteps coming down the stairs. I dropped the lid of the freezer and backed away from it.

Sima rushed down the stairs, the little boys close behind her. When she saw me she stopped dead in her tracks. "What? What?" she asked, her face pale. Her hands reached out and grabbed the boys by their collars, not allowing them to cross the floor toward me. Sima stood motionless, her white knuckles gripping the backs of her sons' shirts as they wriggled, trying to escape her grasp. She looked into my face.

"Fraydle?" she whispered.

"Yes."

"Where?"

I looked at the freezer and she moaned. She knelt down and scooped the little boys into her arms, burying her face in their necks. Great, rasping sobs shook her body, and the boys grew silent and pale at the sight of their mother's tears. I stood there with the wailing woman and her children for what felt like hours, but was surely not more than a moment or two. Then I led them up the stairs to the kitchen and shut the door at the top of the stairs behind me. I sat them at the table, lifted the phone, and, finally, many days after I should have, dialed 911.

23

BY THE TIME they let me go home, I had leaked though my breast pads and soaked my shirt. It was only the sight of me dripping all over myself that convinced the police officers to allow me to leave. Before I made my escape, a detective interviewed me in the little room where I'd nursed Isaac the first time I was at Fraydle's house. I told the investigating officer, a woman of about my age with close-cropped brown hair and horn-rimmed glasses, everything I knew, including Yossi's name and address. I even disclosed Ari's sexual orientation. At this point I knew I could hold nothing back. The police needed to know everything so that they could find out who had done this horrible thing.

I walked the few blocks from the Finkelsteins' house to my own quickly, desperate to see my husband and kids. My eyes were dry, which surprised me, as I'm a woman who can be reduced to tears by a television commercial. I hadn't cried once since we'd discovered Fraydle's body. It was as if I couldn't lay claim to tears in the presence of Sima and the rabbi, who had walked into the horror on the heels of the police. Their mourning was so complete and total that my tears would have been a pale and inappropriate shadow.

The scene I left behind me in Sima's kitchen was quiet and miserable. Fraydle's father leaned against the counter, his body folded and almost shrunken in despair. Nettie, whom I'd called after I'd spoken to the police, and Sima sat at the kitchen table, each kneading a dishtowel and, periodically, using it to wipe their streaming eyes or noses. Fraydle's littlest brothers were huddled in a corner of the kitchen. Sarah sat in a chair next to her mother, shaking and weeping, gripping Sima's hand in her own. The older boys stood around the edges of the room, eyes wet with tears and faces pale.

When I reached my house, I unlocked the door and ran up the stairs into my apartment. I found Peter in the rocking chair, feeding Isaac a bottle. Ruby was watching television.

"Juliet! Where have you been? It's been almost four hours! I was completely freaking out!" Peter shouted.

I ran across the room and, kneeling beside his chair, put my head in his lap next to Isaac's warm body. The baby spat out the bottle nipple, grasped a piece of my hair in his little fist and shoved it into his mouth. Only then did I start to cry.

Peter stroked my hair with his hand. "What happened, honey? What happened? Are you okay?"

I hiccupped and sat up. I looked over at Ruby, who was so enraptured by the dancing purple dinosaur on TV that she had not even noticed my tears.

"Fraydle's dead," I whispered.

Peter didn't look surprised. "I was afraid of that," he murmured. "How?"

"I don't know. Peter, I found her body." I was still whispering.

He looked at me, his mouth open and his eyes wide.

I told him about how I had found poor Fraydle shoved into the freezer.

"What's a Passover kitchen?" he interrupted at that point in my story.

"At Passover you can't eat any bread, only matzo. Really strict Orthodox won't even cook in the same kitchen that bread was ever prepared in. So they keep an entirely separate kitchen to do their Passover cooking. They never let anything that's not kosher for Passover into that kitchen so that it will never be spoiled."

"Oh," he said. The two of us were silent for a moment, thinking about the horrible despoiling of the Finkelsteins' kosher kitchen.

I continued: "When I was in the garage, I heard the freezer humming. It didn't make sense that there would be something in the freezer, because Passover is still months away. I just walked over and opened it." My eyes filled with tears again.

"Hey! Why are you crying?" Ruby shouted. She had momentarily looked up from Barney.

I quickly wiped my eyes. "It's nothing, honey. I'm just tired." I turned to Peter. "What's the baby drinking?" I asked.

"Formula."

"What?"

"Juliet, you weren't here and he was going nuts. There wasn't any breast milk in the freezer. I found that sample can of formula that they gave us at the hospital. He seems to like it fine."

I shrugged my shoulders, too exhausted by the events of the afternoon to argue. Also, I realized that I couldn't expect Peter to share my obsession with keeping my nursing infant pure of the contamination of baby formula. I wasn't really sure, myself, why I felt so strongly about it. I took the baby from Peter's arms and nestled him in my lap on the couch. He rooted madly as I freed a breast for him. He gave a contented sigh as he latched on.

"Oh, I almost forgot," Peter said. "You got a message from Barbara Rosen."

"Who?" I asked. "I don't know anyone named Barbara Rosen."

"She said she's Jake's mother."

"Jake who?" I asked.

"Jake Rosen, I assume."

"I don't know any Jake or Barbara Rosen."

"Mama!" Ruby shouted. "Jake in my class!"

"Oh, right. Jake's mommy. What did she want?"

"She said she just called to remind you that *The Boys From Syracuse* is tomorrow afternoon."

I'd forgotten all about our plan. "Oh, right. Her older son's play. She thought it would be fun if we took the kids to see it."

"I wanna go, Mama!" Ruby said.

"Okay, honey," I said, thinking that sitting through a children's production of a Rodgers and Hart musical was a little more than I could handle right at that moment.

"I wrote down all the details," Peter said. "She'll save seats for you and Ruby."

"Do you want to go instead?" I asked hopefully.

"Do you need me to go?" Peter asked.

"No, I guess not."

"Good, because I'd rather have root canal. But have fun."

THE POLICE CAME by again later that day. The female detective who'd spoken to me at Fraydle's house was accompanied by an older man in an

ill-fitting navy suit with the unmistakable sheen of polyester. She introduced her partner, Carl Hopkins, and herself, Susan Black.

Peter took the kids out to play in the yard and I sat at the kitchen table,
hands wrapped around a steaming cup of chamomile tea and, once again,
and in more detail, told the officers everything I knew about Fraydle's
death.

"How well did you know the victim?" asked Detective Black.

"Not well at all. She babysat for me once, and then didn't show up
the next day. When I went looking for her, that's when I found out that
she was gone."

"And when was that?"

"A little over a week ago."

"And why didn't you call the police then?" Detective Hopkins interrupted.

I turned to him. "It wasn't my place to. I couldn't report her as a missing person. Only her parents could have done that."

"That's not exactly true, ma'am," Detective Black said. "You couldn't
have filed a report, because we would need a member of the family to
verify that the girl was actually missing, but you certainly could have
alerted us to her absence."

I nodded my head and softly said, "I could have, and in retrospect I
should have."

Once we'd gone over the details of my search for Fraydle, Detective
Black gave me her card and asked me to call her if I heard anything new.
Then she leaned back in her chair, looked at me intently for a moment,
and said, "Ms. Applebaum, I used to work with Detective Mitch Carswell
of the Santa Monica Police Department."

I swallowed, not a little nervously.

"I understand that you were helpful to him in solving the Hathaway
murder."

Helpful? If single-handedly finding out who killed Abigail Hathaway,
the headmistress of Los Angeles's most selective nursery school, qualifies
as helpful, then I suppose I was.

"Yes," I said.

"I understand that you were shot by Ms. Hathaway's killer."

I looked into Detective Black's face. Her expression was absolutely
impassive.

"Yes," I said.

"Ms. Applebaum, we at the Los Angeles Police Department take our work very seriously." She paused, as if waiting for me to say something. I didn't. I just looked at her. Detective Hopkins stared at me balefully.

Finally, Detective Black continued. "This is *my* homicide investigation, Ms. Applebaum. I am the primary detective on the case. I expect you to provide me with any and all information you possess."

"As I have," I said.

She held up her hand as if to still my voice. "And I expect that you will do nothing else. No more trips to New York. No more interviews with witnesses. Nothing. Do you understand?"

I considered defending myself and explaining to her exactly why I'd investigated Fraydle's disappearance, but decided it wasn't worth the effort. I wasn't going to convince the two detectives that they needed the services of a crime-solving soccer-mom-in-training to track down Fraydle's killer. All the same, I felt a niggling sense of irritation. Why couldn't the woman just say thank you and assure me that she would competently carry out the investigation? Why did she feel the need to warn me off, as if I were some recalcitrant adolescent mucking up her turf?

I nodded my head once, and rose from my chair. "If there's nothing else, Detective, I'd like to get back to my husband and children," I said.

"Do you understand me, Ms. Applebaum?" Detective Black asked again, also rising from her seat.

"Of course, Detective. Let me see you and your associate out."

I hustled the two of them out the door, then turned and walked through the apartment to Peter's office, at the back of the house. Leaning out the window overlooking the back yard, I shouted "All clear." As my family came clomping up the back stairs, I looked around Peter's office. Every available shelf was covered with toys. Action figures, mostly vintage and all in near-perfect condition. Peter, an avid collector, was in for a rude awakening. Ruby had never paid Peter's toys the slightest attention, but at some time in the near future Isaac was surely going to wake up to the bounty in Daddy's office and tear that Major Matt Mason right out of its original 1969 blister pack.

24

I DECIDED TO STUDIOUSLY ignore the police detective's instructions and make some phone calls. I had promised both Ari and Yossi that I would let them know if I heard anything definitive about Fraydle. Her death was something pretty definite. I had my suspicions about Yossi, but I was fairly convinced that Ari was innocent of the murder. I couldn't say the same about his uncles, however. I managed to find Ari at the yeshiva, and as gently as I could, I told him about his fiancée's death. He was shocked into silence for a few moments. Finally, he spoke, "Perhaps this is a message to me."

"Excuse me?" I said.

"Perhaps *Ha Shem* is sending me a message that I should not be a married man."

"Ari," I said, "I don't think God is sending you any kind of message. What I think is that some evil person killed Fraydle. I also think that you had better be prepared to tell the police everything."

Ari didn't seem surprised that I'd ratted him out to the cops. On the contrary, he insisted that he wanted to help in any way that he could and asked me for the detective's phone number so that he could call her right away. I had a sense that I didn't need to worry about this young man. While confused, he seemed to have a deep sense of right and wrong. He was not only able but willing to take responsibility for his own actions. I had no idea what path he would choose, but I felt that he would ultimately lead a life he could be proud of.

I couldn't get through to Yossi, and decided to call Al Hockey instead, to give him an update. His wife told me that he was out at the municipal golf course but gave me his cell phone number.

"Hockey!" he bellowed, by way of hello.

"Hi, Al, it's Juliet."

"Juliet? What the hell are you doing calling me on the golf course? Are you trying to ruin my swing?"

I could always count on Al's bluster to improve my mood. I told him about Fraydle's death and my part in the discovery of her body.

"Want me to make some calls, see what I can find out?" he asked.

"That would be great," I said. "I have a feeling the cops aren't going to be particularly forthcoming with details of their investigation." I recounted my experience with Detective Black.

"I know the woman. She's a real ball-buster."

"Al," I said, warningly. The guy was anything but politically correct.

"Hey, don't get your panties in a twist. All I meant was that the two of you have a lot in common. I'll call you later." He hung up.

AL CALLED WITHIN an hour and offered to come over after dinner and tell me the little he'd found out. I was surprised at his willingness to drive all the way from Westminister, the small city on the way to Orange County that he called home, to my house in Hancock Park, but I was happy at the thought of seeing him in the flesh. It had been a while.

When he arrived, my old investigator and my husband greeted one another a little uncomfortably. It wasn't that they didn't like each other. It was just that they were two different species. Al didn't know quite what to make of my nerdy husband with the shaggy hair and sensitive-guy glasses who made his living writing movies about cannibals, homicidal androids, and teenage succubae. Peter hadn't spent much time around middle-aged men with brush cuts and Marine Corps tattoos whose libraries contained pirated copies of the Zapruder tape and books with titles like *The Trilateral Commission Exposed*. The two men shook hands and made a few awkward comments about the Dodgers' chances next season. Whatever would men talk about if it weren't for sports?

Turning to me, Al said, "So where are those kids of yours?"

"Ruby's asleep, or at least in bed. Isaac's over there in his Johnny-Jump-Up.

"Johnny-what-up?" Al said.

"You know, that jumpy thing. Haven't you ever seen one of those? It's a kind of harness that hooks in a doorway and lets the baby jump up and down. He'll stay quiet in there for hours."

As if to illustrate my point, Isaac sprang up and down a few times and laughed.

"Interesting contraption," Al said, walking over to Isaac.

"You know," I told him, "if you'd let your daughters get married, you might have a grandchild to buy one of those contraptions for." Al was legendary for driving away potential mates for his three girls, all of whom still lived at home although they were well into their twenties.

"Yeah, well, soon as one of 'em brings home a man instead of a degenerate pile a crap, excuse my French, I'll be slapping down my checkbook for a caterer and a band. But honestly, Juliet, you should see these guys. Earrings. Nose rings. *Nipple* rings, for crying out loud!"

Peter self-consciously covered his pierced left earlobe. "Um, honey, I'd better get to work, if you don't mind," he said.

"Sure, babe. Hey, Peter, why don't you show Al your bellybutton stud!"

Al blanched and Peter rolled his eyes. "I do *not* have a stud in my bellybutton. Very funny, Juliet." He walked out of the room.

"Does he?" Al asked, obviously horrified.

I smiled mysteriously.

Suddenly, I remembered why he was there. "I can't believe we're sitting here joking around. Tell me what you found out about Fraydle's death."

Al plopped himself down on the couch and swung his feet onto the coffee table.

"Make yourself comfortable. Can I get you something to drink? Coffee? Tea?"

"Tea?" he asked, incredulous. "How about a beer? Something American."

"I'll check." Rooting around in the fridge, I managed to locate an ancient bottle of Sam Adams from a party we'd had no more than a year before. I popped the top off and brought the bottle out to Al. "How's this?" I asked.

He took a long swallow, burped, and said, "Fine."

"What did you turn up?" I sat down in an armchair opposite him. I glanced over at Isaac, who was contentedly gnawing on one of the hanging straps holding him in the air.

"I talked to Fat Rolly Rollins, a detective in the division that includes

Hancock Park. He's an old buddy. Obviously they have no official cause of death yet, but the M. E. on the scene said the girl had a broken neck. She also suffered some kind of blow to her head."

"Which of those killed her?" I asked.

"No way for them to tell now, although Fat Rolly did say it looks like she could have died by falling down the stairs and hitting her head on the concrete floor."

"Falling down the stairs? And then what? Conveniently landing in the freezer, which then plugged itself in?"

"Maybe she was pushed."

"Could someone have hit her on the head?"

"I suppose so. All I can tell you is what Fat Rolly heard from the officers on the scene. The M.E. said it looked like a fall to him."

"Okay, what about time of death? Did the medical examiner have an estimate?"

"Not even a tentative at the scene. He couldn't guess at anything, because of the freezer."

"Did Fat Freddy—"

"Rolly. Fat Rolly."

"Did Fat Rolly tell you if they had any suspects?"

"No, but Juliet, in cases like this they look to the family."

I knew that. Most murder victims die at the hands of someone they know, and the circumstances of Fraydle's death seemed to point particularly to the members of her family. Her body had been found at home. Her parents had failed to notify the police of her disappearance. It certainly looked damning.

I told Al about Ari and his uncles and filled him in on my latest experiences with Yossi.

"So what do you want to do now?" Al asked.

"I don't know. Nothing, I guess."

"Yeah, right."

"No, really. I'm going to let the police figure this out."

Al snorted. "Whatever you say, Detective. I'd better get going. I'm going to be late."

"Late? Where are you going?"

"You think I drove all the way to this cesspool of a city just to see you?" Al asked. "No way. I've got a meeting."

"What meeting?"

"Southern L.A. Basin Chapter of the Freedom Brigade," he said proudly.

"A militia! Are you out of your mind?"

"Listen, missy, last time I checked, the Constitution of this great nation still guaranteed us the right to a well-regulated militia. I'm just doing my bit to keep that alive."

How could such a warm, loving guy with such an astute investigative mind be such a nut case?

"Just promise me that you're not a white supremacist, Al," I said.

He gave me a disgusted look. "Juliet, have you ever seen my wife?"

I thought for a moment. "No, I don't think I have."

"But you've seen pictures of my kids, right?"

"Of course." Al's office was covered with pictures of his three, dark-haired, beautiful daughters.

"Ever notice that my girls are biracial?"

"What? Really?" I hadn't.

"My wife's African-American, Juliet."

I blushed. "Oh, wow. I'm sorry about the white supremacist comment."

"Whatever. Us freedom fighters, we have to deal with that kind of ignorant nonsense all the time. Just because we don't swallow every word the federal government says doesn't mean we're a bunch of racists. I'll have you know that my chapter is full of all kinds. Black, white, Asian, Latino, you name it."

I was just about to comment on how nice it was that his particular department of the lunatic fringe was an equal opportunity employer when I decided to give it up. You just can't win with Al. Every time I wind up in one of those conversations with him, I swear to myself I'm never again going to mention Roswell, David Koresh, or the United Nations.

I got up and gave Al a kiss on the cheek. "Thanks for the information, Al. I really appreciate it."

He blushed. "No problem, girlie. I'll talk to you." He hoisted himself out of the couch and left.

25

RUE TO HER promise, Barbara Rosen had saved us seats at the performance of *The Boys From Syracuse*. Ruby and Jake sat next to each other, holding hands and giggling. I settled Isaac in my lap and tried to nurse him to sleep, much to Barbara's horror. Apparently, baring the breast, even under cover of a shirt and a draped baby blanket, is just not done at the better Los Angeles private schools. What could I do? It was either get the kid to sleep, or listen to him cry through the entire performance.

While the baby nursed, and Barbara tried very hard to look as if she was not utterly humiliated to be seen with us, I checked out the mobbed auditorium. The attendees were mostly mommies, although there were a number of daddies who'd managed to escape from the office. Virtually all the daddies were watching the play through the eyepiece of their video cameras. Every second person was holding a bouquet of flowers, as if this were opening night at the opera rather than a junior high school production. The smell of roses was thick and heady.

The lights dimmed and the orchestra struck up an almost recognizable version of the play's overture. I looked down at Isaac, who had thankfully dropped off to sleep, and settled back in my chair, determined to try to enjoy the show.

It actually wasn't awful. The sets and costumes were almost professional, and there were some hysterical moments when the young boy playing the duke took off his hat with a flourish, inadvertently releasing into the air huge clouds of the baby powder that had been used to whiten his hair. I even found myself humming along to the songs. It was in Act I, as I was tapping my feet to "This Can't Be Love," that I began to get the beginnings of an idea. As I watched the preadolescent Dromios get hit over the head and an Adriana in braces drag home the wrong Antipholus, it became clearer in my mind. By the time Dromios shrieked, with a rather endearing lisp, "Shakespeare!" I knew who had murdered Fraydle.

I sat through a full twenty minutes of standing ovations before I could finally bear it no longer. I whispered a hurried good-bye to Barbara and Jake and, carrying Isaac and dragging an unwilling Ruby, ran out to the car.

"But I don't want to leave!" Ruby wailed, as I buckled her into her car seat.

"I'm sorry, honey," I said. "But the play is over and Mama has an errand to run."

I drove much too quickly down Santa Monica Boulevard, dialing Peter's cell phone as I whipped through yellow lights. I reached his voice mail. Cursing, I tried his assistant. Voice mail again. I wasn't going to be able to unload Ruby and Isaac. I turned onto Melrose Avenue and drove to Nomi's restaurant. I parked in the last spot in the lot, yanked the kids out of the car, and hustled them into the almost-empty restaurant. Anat sat at a table, reading a Hebrew newspaper.

"Hi! What's going on?" she asked.

"Anat, I have a question for you. You told me that the last time you saw Fraydle she looked weird. What did you mean by that?"

She shrugged and wrinkled her brow. "I can't explain it. She just looked different."

I leaned forward and looked at her intently. "Could you have seen someone else, someone who looked like Fraydle, but wasn't Fraydle?"

Anat looked at me, puzzled. "I don't think so. It was her. Same hair, same clothes. She just looked—I dunno, different."

"Like less pretty?"

"Exactly!"

"Could it have been someone who looked like Fraydle, but wasn't as pretty?"

Anat looked skeptical. "I guess so," she said, not sounding particularly confident.

I thanked her, gathered up the kids and ran out the door of the restaurant to the car. I buckled them into their car seats for the millionth time that day, and headed back up Santa Monica Boulevard. As I drove, I thought once more about Anat. The fact that Fraydle's body had been found in her own parents' home seemed to rule Anat out as a suspect. I couldn't imagine the Hasidic girl inviting Anat into her house. And besides, I knew who killed Fraydle. I just needed someone to tell me why.

I pulled into the Gap parking lot and jumped out of the car. I stuck Isaac in his stroller and convinced Ruby to postpone her tantrum with the promise of an ice cream reward. I didn't even bother to pretend to be visiting the store, but just walked right up the block into the courtyard of Yossi's apartment building and knocked on the door. After a few moments it opened a crack. Yossi grimaced when he saw me and tried to close the door in my face.

"Yossi!" I said. "You have to talk to me. Please. I know what happened with Fraydle."

Now, I didn't *know* anything. I merely suspected. However, I was sure that the only way to get Yossi to tell me the truth was to pretend that I already knew it.

He opened the door slowly. His face was unshaven and he looked pale and ill. I pointed to Isaac, who was sitting in his stroller chewing on his fist, and to Ruby, who was throwing sticks and pebbles into the fountain.

"I have my children with me," I said. "Let's sit out here so I can watch them."

He looked at me for a moment, and then walked out of his apartment and sank into one of the two lawn chairs in front of his door. I perched on the other one and made sure that Ruby was far enough away that she couldn't hear our conversation.

I sat silently for a minute, and then I said softly, "You were sleeping with Fraydle's sister Sarah."

He didn't deny it. He didn't even look surprised. He simply said, in a hoarse whisper, "Has she told the police?"

"I don't know," I answered.

He looked up at me. "I didn't kill Fraydle. I loved her. I still love her."

I nodded. "Tell me what happened, Yossi."

"It was after Fraydle told me about Ari Hirsch. She came one day and we were together, like always. Then, afterwards, she kissed me and said good-bye. She said she had to marry Ari, that her father insisted and that it was important to the whole family. She said her father needed the alliance with the Hirsch family. She told me she loved me but that she had to take care of her family."

His eyes filled with tears.

"Go on," I murmured.

"I begged her not to leave me. I promised her that I would take care of her family. I even promised to *chozer b'tshuvah*, to become Hasidic. She wouldn't listen. She just said that it had already been decided. She had accepted him. And then she left. She just got up and left.

"For days I tried to talk to her. I looked for her at the store. I walked up and down the streets looking for her. I couldn't find her anywhere. It was like she had disappeared. Finally, one day, I saw her sister Sarah, walking home from school. I stopped her and begged her to take a message to Fraydle. She said she knew all about Fraydle and me. She said she knew we'd been together, that she'd followed Fraydle to my house. She promised to help me, to talk to Fraydle for me. She told me to wait at my house and that she would come to me after she'd talked to Fraydle.

"Sarah came that evening, right before dark. She sat down on my couch and told me that Fraydle didn't love me. She said that Fraydle wanted to move to New York, that she wanted to be with Ari Hirsch. Sarah said that Fraydle told her she was tired of me and was glad of the excuse not to be with me anymore.

"I didn't know what to say. I just sat there, in shock. And then Sarah came over to me, and kissed me. She kissed me, and she took off her clothes and . . . and . . . "

"And you slept with her," I said.

He nodded. "She looks so much like Fraydle," he whispered. "I closed my eyes and it was like being with Fraydle." He paused. "Look, I know it was terrible. I know it was unforgivable, but you have to understand, Fraydle had left me and I needed her so much."

I couldn't give him the absolution he craved. "Did you see Sarah again?"

"No, I mean, I saw her but we didn't—we weren't together again."

"What happened?"

"After she left, I just went to sleep. I woke up the next day to someone banging on my door. It was Fraydle. She came into the room and she was smiling. She looked so happy! But then she saw Sarah's sweater. Sarah had left her sweater on the chair. Fraydle stopped talking and picked up the sweater. She looked confused and asked me what it was doing there. I lied to her. I told her that it was hers, that she'd left it there, but she shook her head. And then she looked at the bed."

"The bed?" I asked.

"I woke up to answer the door. The bed wasn't made. She saw . . . the blood."

"Sarah was a virgin."

He nodded.

"What did Fraydle do?"

"She picked up the sweater and she walked out the door. She slammed it so hard, plaster fell from the ceiling."

"Did you follow her?" I asked.

"No." He shook his head. "I didn't know what to say to her. I was so ashamed."

"What did you do?"

"Nothing for a while. I just sat there. Then, I went to the travel agent and I bought the plane tickets. I wanted to prove to Fraydle that I loved only her and wanted only her. I was sure I could convince her that I'd only been with her sister because I missed *her*, because I wanted to be with *her*. I was sure if I bought the tickets, she would understand how much I loved her and she would come with me. Come to Israel and marry me."

"Did you see Sarah again?"

"She came the next day. I went to find Fraydle in the morning. That was when you saw me outside your house. Fraydle was angry, furious at me. She said she wouldn't go with me and to leave her alone. I came back here. I just lay on the bed, trying to figure out what to do. And then Sarah showed up. She knocked on the door, and I told her to go away. She pushed her way inside. She came up to me and tried to kiss me, but I pushed her away. I just snapped. All the pressure building inside me just exploded." He looked ashamed. "I said terrible things. I told her to go away, that she disgusted me. I told her that she was a whore."

"What did she do? What did she say?"

"Nothing. She just started to cry, and ran away. That's the last time I saw her."

"Did you ever see Fraydle again?"

"No. But I think she must have wanted to come with me. I think she was going to come, and that's why she was killed." His voice rose sharply. Ruby turned around at the sound.

"It's okay, honey," I reassured her. "Mommy is just having a talk. Everything is fine."

She turned back to her game and I looked at Yossi. "Yossi, what do you think happened to Fraydle? Who do you think killed her?"

He didn't answer. Instead, he just buried his head in his hands.

"I want you to come with me to Fraydle's house," I said.

He shook his head, not bothering to lift it up.

"I want you to come with me to confront Sarah and her family. I know that your relationship with Sarah is why Fraydle died."

Yossi raised his head and then, to my surprise, agreed to come with me. I didn't trust him enough to put him in my car and, besides, I really didn't want my kids along for this ride anymore. Dragging them on an investigation was one thing. Putting them in danger was something else entirely. I told Yossi that I'd meet him at the Finkelsteins' home in an hour and bundled the kids back down the block and into the car, which, thankfully, had not yet been towed. I drove as fast as I could down Melrose Avenue, dialing Peter's number. Of course he wasn't answering. His assistant, however, picked up her phone. She told me that Peter was on his way back to the set from a meeting off the lot. When I informed her that it was an emergency, she promised to tell him that I was coming and to call the security booth so that they would let me in.

The kids and I tore through the studio lot in the direction of Sound Stage #6 where they were shooting the interiors of Peter's show. I parked in a spot clearly marked No Parking and once again unloaded my children. We walked brazenly through the Authorized Entry Only door and onto the cavernous sound stage. On the far end was a perfect replica of a 1970s-style kitchen. Ruby looked over at the stage and then let loose with a piercing shriek that brought the bustling crowd to a standstill. A remarkably lifelike corpse lay in a pool of blood on the baby-blue, vinyl-tiled floor, a hatchet lodged comfortably in its forehead.

I clamped my hand over her eyes and crushed her face to my stomach. "It's just fake, Ruby. Pretend. It's just a picture." I tried to sound jovial and reassuring, but that was made a bit difficult by the fact that fifty or sixty people had stopped dead in their tracks and were staring at me as I stood there holding a screaming toddler and pushing a stroller containing a now-wailing infant.

"Um, excuse me," I said to the room at large. "I'm looking for Peter Wyeth."

"Juliet! How wonderful to see you." I turned in the direction of the voice and found myself staring into the perfectly made-up face of the ever-lovely Marvelous Mindy Maxx.

"Peter's not here, Juliet," she said. "He's on his way back from a meeting with the special effects guys in Burbank. He's on the road, but he should be here any minute. Can I help you with something?"

I was ambivalent for a moment, but a glance at my watch decided me. "Listen, Mindy, sorry to do this. Sorry, everybody," I called out. I turned back to my husband's producing partner. "I really need to be somewhere. It's an emergency. Is Angelika around? Can I leave the kids with her?"

Mindy paused for a second, obviously mulling over my request. The various sound, film, and props folks whom I'd disturbed turned back to their work.

"Why don't you leave the kids with me? I can watch them until Peter gets here," she said.

"No, that's okay. I'll wait." I looked around for an out-of-the-way place to deposit the children and myself.

"Really, Juliet. I don't mind."

"Really, Mindy. It's fine. I'll wait." I knew I sounded hostile, but I was too distracted by what I had to do to cover up my feelings. The truth was, I *felt* hostile toward this impeccably dressed woman who was spending way more time with my husband than I was.

Mindy shrugged her shoulders and turned away. She walked a few steps and then turned back. "We need to talk," she said.

I felt my stomach tie itself in a knot. Was this true confessions time? Was she about to tell me that she and Peter were desperately in love? Mindy took my arm and led me a few steps toward an empty corner of the sound stage. I rolled the stroller along.

"Listen, Mindy, I can't do this now. I have my kids with me. We can't have this conversation in front of my children."

"I think we can."

"Well, you're not their mother. I am."

"I *know* that, for goodness' sake. Look, Juliet, I'm not an idiot. I know what you think is going on."

"Oh, you do, do you?"

"Yes, I do. And it isn't. Nothing is going on. We work together, that's it."

"Well, pardon me for thinking that you guys are just a little more intimate than that. I've worked with plenty of people and never been so, how shall I put it? Close."

"But you've never produced a TV series. It's a totally different level of stress and time commitment. Peter and I are forced to spend fifteen hours a day together."

"Neither of you seems to be objecting."

"Because we *like* each other. Because we're friends. Don't you know how much Peter would rather be with you?"

"Look, Mindy, I don't know what you're after here. But I don't have time for this. I have something really important I need to do. And I can't do it with my kids. I need to find Peter and get the hell out of here."

"I said you should leave them with me."

"No."

"Juliet. I'm gay."

I stared at her. "What?"

"I'm gay. I'm a lesbian. You see that woman?" She pointed toward a tall athletic woman with close-cropped blond hair bent over one of the cameras. "That's my girlfriend. I'm not having an affair with your husband. I'm having an affair with *her*."

My mouth dropped open. I didn't know what to say. "God. I *am* an idiot, aren't I? I am so sorry, Mindy. I don't even know how to begin to say how sorry I am."

"You're not an idiot. You're a new mother married to an incredibly sexy man who hasn't been able to spend much time at home lately. You're normal. You were just wrong."

"That's for sure. Why didn't my lunatic husband *tell* me this?"

"I don't know. Maybe he figured it was my business. Or maybe it just never occurred to him that you would be jealous. Maybe he loves you so much he can't even imagine that you'd ever think he'd cheat on you."

Suddenly I remembered where I needed to be.

"Mindy, can you really watch the kids for me? Just until Peter gets back."

"Sure. I'd love to," she said and smiled.

"Terrific." I turned to Ruby and crouched down next to her. "Hey, kiddo, are you all right?"

"Yup," she announced. "I was just surprised by the dead guy. It's okay. It's just a show. Like a comic book."

"Right. It's not real. Listen, Ruby, Mama needs to go somewhere real quick. You're going to stay here with Mindy. It'll be so fun!"

Ruby looked unconvinced.

Mindy leaned over and said, "How'd you like to go to the makeup room and have your face painted?"

Ruby nodded.

"Okay, honey. That's a great idea. Daddy will be here in a few minutes." I handed Mindy Isaac's diaper bag. "Thanks, Mindy. This is terrific of you. Just tell Peter I'll be home as soon as I can. And I'm sorry. Really."

She waved me away with a smile and walked away with the stroller. I watched them for a second, and then tore off the sound stage and leaped into my car. As I careened down Melrose Avenue, I dug in my purse for Detective Black's card. I found it and dialed the number. Voice mail. Of course. I left a message and my cell-phone number as I pulled up in front of the Finkelsteins' house.

Yossi had arrived before me and was waiting on the corner. He stood nervously, his hands shoved into his pockets. I parked my car in a commercial loading zone and together we walked toward the house. The two little boys were in their seemingly permanent position on the porch and Nettie sat on the steps, watching them. She was wearing a dark dress and a pair of fabric slippers. Her face was blotchy and pale but she smiled wanly when she saw me. The smile dried up when she saw Yossi. I marched up the steps. At my approach, the boys ran inside.

"Nettie, this is Yossi, Fraydle's boyfriend," I said.

Nettie paled and muttered something in Yiddish.

Yossi, who'd followed me, shook his head vehemently and replied in the same language.

"You speak Yiddish?" I asked him.

"My grandmother taught me," he said.

"What did Nettie say to you?"

"She says maybe I killed Fraydle. But I told her that is not true. I told her I loved Fraydle. I wanted to marry Fraydle. I would never have killed her."

Nettie turned to me. "What do you want? Why did you bring him here?"

"Nettie, we're going to talk to Fraydle's parents. We're going to get to the bottom of this."

She shook her head.

"Nettie. Please," I said softly. She looked at me silently for a few moments, and then shrugged her shoulders. "She is dead. What else matters?"

"Finding out who killed her matters."

"That might be true. But it might also be a terrible thing to find out."

"Maybe. But don't you think we owe it to Fraydle to find out who did this to her?"

Nettie shrugged her shoulders again and stood up with a soft groan.

"Come," she said, leading the way into the house.

26

FRAYDLE'S PARENTS' HOME was full of people. The men were in the living room, standing around in small groups, most of them holding plates heaped with food. A tall candle burned on the hall table. Through the open door to the kitchen I could see the women in their accustomed place. The soft buzz of conversation stopped entirely as Yossi and I walked inside. As we entered the room I noticed a large, dark cloth covering what I assumed was a mirror over the mantel. Jewish law requires that during the seven-day period of mourning all mirrors in the house must be covered. The furniture had been moved out of the living room. Fraydle's father and the older boys sat on low chairs pushed up against the walls. Their vests and shirts were torn to signify their mourning.

As I walked in the room, Fraydle's father lifted a hand and waved me over. I walked over to him and stood quietly, waiting for him to speak. He wept openly, as did Fraydle's brothers.

"Thank you for coming," he said.

"I am so terribly sorry for your loss, Rabbi Finkelstein."

"My sister tells me that I have misjudged you, Mrs. Applebaum. She says that you have tried very hard to find out what happened to my daughter." A fresh stream of tears streaked down his reddened cheeks.

I didn't know what to say. "I just wanted to help, Rabbi. I didn't know your daughter very well, but she was a lovely girl."

At that moment, Sima came in from the kitchen. She was also weeping. She held Sarah firmly by the hand. The girl had an expression of complete panic on her face and she sank into a low chair. I followed her gaze to Yossi, who stood, head bowed, behind me.

"Rabbi, there is something I'd like to talk to you and your wife about. In private."

The rabbi looked, for a moment, as though he was going to say no. Then, with a wave of his hand, he motioned to the crowd of men and said something in Yiddish. Within two minutes the house was empty of everyone except Fraydle's family, Yossi, and me.

As the men left the house, followed by their wives, mothers, and daughters, I watched Sarah's face grow paler and paler. The only sound that came from her was the rasping of her breath.

"Rabbi Finkelstein, Mrs. Finkelstein, this is Yossi Zinger. He was a friend of Fraydle's. And of Sarah's," I said.

The rabbi looked confused. "What are you talking about? A friend?" He turned to Yossi. "Who are you? How do you know my daughters?"

Yossi stepped forward and said, in a far firmer voice than I imagined he would be able to muster, "I was Fraydle's boyfriend, Rabbi. I wanted to marry her."

"Boyfriend? Boyfriend?" Sima interrupted. "What do you mean? My daughter was engaged to marry Ari Hirsch. She had no boyfriend." Sima looked at Sarah's stricken face. "Sarahleh, what is this man talking about? Do you know him? Did Fraydle know him? What is happening here?"

Sarah jumped to her feet and in a quavering voice began to talk. "It's not my fault. Fraydle went with him. She went to his house. She told me she was with him. She was proud of it!"

"What are you saying?" her father roared. He turned to me. "Is this true?"

I nodded.

"And did he kill her? Did you kill my daughter?" His shout made the walls of the house shake.

"No! I did not kill her," Yossi said. "I loved her. I wanted to marry her."

"But she didn't want you!" Sarah wailed. "She said she was going to marry Ari. That *Abba* and *Ema* wanted her to. That's why I went to you! Because she didn't want you anymore, so I could have you!"

Sarah's parents fell silent. Her brothers looked as if they were melting into the chairs on which they sat.

"Papa. It wasn't on purpose. She said she was going to marry Ari. So that meant I could have Yossi."

"But then she changed her mind," I interjected softly.

Sarah nodded. "It wasn't my fault. I wasn't going to tell her that Yossi was mine until she was married. But then she changed her mind. She decided not to marry Ari; she decided she loved Yossi. So she went back to Yossi. And when she was there she saw my sweater and found out about us. She was so angry. She didn't understand that it wasn't my fault. I only did it because she decided to marry Ari Hirsch. I went to Yossi because she didn't want him anymore. It was my turn. She was supposed to marry Ari Hirsch and that meant I could have Yossi."

"Sarah," I said, "What happened?"

"It wasn't on purpose," the girl repeated. "She found out about Yossi and me. And then he didn't want me anymore. I was so angry. I just slapped her, not hard or anything. But she slipped. She just slipped and fell down the stairs. It was so loud. Such a loud crash. I ran down after her, but it was . . ." Sarah paused and waved her hands in the air, as if she were pushing something away. "It was so messy. Her head was wet and bloody. Her neck was all crooked."

"Did you put her in the freezer?" I asked.

"Yes."

"Why?"

"I had to put her away. It was so messy." Sarah's voice was affectless and flat. "She fit in there just right. Once I had her in I just plugged the freezer in. So she wouldn't get spoiled."

At that her parents, who had been staring silently, erupted in loud, anguished sobs. Nettie stood against the wall, her hand clamped over her mouth, her eyes wide with horror. Yossi crumpled onto the floor, kneeling with his head bowed and his eyes streaming.

I remembered the broken saucer hidden away in a pocket. At the time, I thought that Sarah had so carefully hidden her misdeed because she was afraid of her parents. I assumed that Sima or the rabbi had terrorized her into feeling that she couldn't make a mistake. But now I realized that, like some of the sociopaths whom I'd represented, this deeply disturbed girl was simply unable to respond in anything resembling a normal manner. She hid her broken saucer. She hid her broken sister.

"No," Fraydle's father said suddenly, shaking his head. "This did not happen. Some stranger did this. You!" He pointed at Yossi. "You did this! Not my daughter. No."

Yossi shook his head wordlessly, tears spilling out of his eyes and down his cheeks.

"Rabbi," I said, "the police will figure it out. They'll find evidence, maybe Sarah's fingerprints or something else. You must get a lawyer right now and go to the police. She's a minor; she's clearly disturbed. The lawyer will be able to help you figure out a strategy."

"No!" he shouted again.

"Rabbi, they will never believe that a stranger did this."

"So I will tell them it was me! It was me." He wasn't shouting any longer, but his voice was loud.

"No, Baruch," Sima whispered, through her tears. Her voice grew firmer. "You will not do this. You will not take responsibility for this. We will do what Mrs. Applebaum says. We will find a lawyer to help Sarah."

"But—" he began.

"No," she said.

27

I LEFT FRAYDLE'S FAMILY with the lawyer, a Hasid, who had come as soon as the rabbi called. They didn't need me anymore. I left quietly. I stood for a moment on the front steps of the house, looking out at the street where the Finkelsteins' community had gathered. A few men looked at me, and I lowered my eyes. I felt a hand on my arm and turned to find Nettie. She reached an arm around my shoulders and whispered, "Thank you."

"Thank you? For what?" Ruining her life and the lives of her family even more than they'd been ruined before? After all, what good had I done? I hadn't saved Fraydle; she was gone. And because of me their other daughter was lost to them forever.

"Oh, Nettie, you were right. The truth is a terrible thing. I'm so sorry for what I did," I said.

"For what *you* did? You did nothing wrong. What, you think you had something to do with this? Don't be silly." She squeezed my shoulder.

"If I hadn't gotten involved, you might never have found out about Sarah."

"Juliet, with or without you, our darling Fraydle, *aleha ha shalom*, would still be dead. With or without you, we would have found her body. And then, with or without you, Sarah's guilt would have come out. The only thing you did was spare us months of uncertainty."

I nodded, embarrassed at my own self-centeredness. Was I really looking to *her* to comfort *me*?

"If you need anything, call me, okay?" I said.

She patted me on the arm. I put my arms around her and we hugged for a moment. I kissed her on the cheek and walked down the steps and through the crowd, which parted for me as if I were Moses and they the Red Sea.

When I pulled into the driveway of my house, I sat for a moment in my car, thinking about the Finkelsteins. They would not need to bear this tragedy alone. I knew that moments from now Sima's kitchen door would open and women would begin to stream through, their arms laden with casseroles of *tsimmes* and thick soups of chicken and barley. They would pile the *babkas* and the sponge cakes on the counters and prepare the first of endless cups of tea. The low murmur of their voices would fill the room and the air would be redolent with the smell of talcum powder and food and the warmth of women. Their husbands would pour into the living room like a sea of dark coats and hats. Some would rock back and forth in prayer. Others would simply stand in the corners of the room, talking in soft, deep voices. Or perhaps they would be quiet—not sure what to say to a family burdened with such incalculable pain. The Finkelsteins' house would fill to bursting with the members of their community. The compassion and support of the men in their long beards and dark clothes and of the women with wigs so carefully covering their shorn heads would give to Sima and Baruch the strength they needed to get through the horrible and harrowing weeks, months, and years ahead.

Suddenly, I thought of my own family. Those three people I loved most in the world. I wanted to be with them, to be surrounded by them. *They* were my community. Peter, Ruby, and Isaac were my universe. I got out of the car and walked up the stairs to my apartment. I could hear Ruby's bubbling laugh. I started to run, desperate to see them and to be back in the center of my own little world. I burst through the back door and found them sitting around the kitchen table. Peter held Isaac in his lap and Ruby sat across from them, a pile of chocolate chip cookies in front of her and her face painted with a milk mustache.

"Mama!" she shouted when she saw me. I leaned over and kissed her milky, chocolatey face.

"Hi, sweet girl."

Peter reached out with his free arm and grabbed me around the waist. He squeezed me to him and I leaned on his warm, strong shoulder.

"Tell me," he said.

A PLAYDATE WITH DEATH

To Sophie, Zeke, and Ida-Rose

ACKNOWLEDGMENTS

Many thanks go to Susanna Praetzel who gave me critical information about Tay-Sachs disease; to Julie Barroukh, Sandra Braverman, Lauren Cuthbert, Ginny Dorris, Clare Duffy, Allison Kaplan Sommer, Carlie Masters William, Saundra Schwartz, and Karen Zivan for being ever-present companions and ever-useful sources of information; to Mary Evans, Jeff Frankel, and Sylvie Rabineau for working so tirelessly on my behalf; to Sue Grafton, an inspiration and a role model; and to Michael, my best friend.

1

ISAAC SHOT ME two times in the chest. With his toast.

"You're dead," my two-and-a-half-year-old son said, biting off a chunk of his Glock 9mm semiautomatic pistol.

"Mama doesn't like that game, Isaac. You know that. Mama doesn't like guns." I ruffled his hair with my hand, planted a kiss on the top of his older sister's head, and turned to my husband. "Don't cut his bread on the diagonal anymore."

"Why not?" Peter asked over the top of his coffee mug. His hair stuck out in wiry spikes and his gray eyes were bleary with exhaustion.

"Because he chews out the middle and turns the crust into a gun."

"Maybe if he had a *toy* gun, he wouldn't need to fashion weapons out of his *breakfast*."

I gave my husband a baleful glare and poured my own coffee. I leaned against the kitchen table and slurped. Ruby turned to me with a conspiratorial air made only slightly ridiculous by the fact that her uncombed curls stood up all over her head. She looked like a dandelion puff.

"Isaac has been playing guns all morning, Mama. And Daddy let him."

"Oh really?" I said.

"Don't be a tattletale, Ruby," Peter said.

He was right. Telling tales is a dreadful habit. Nonetheless, I was glad of an ally. I was becoming heartily sick of Isaac's never-ending game of "bang bang you're dead." Honestly, what *is* it with boys? Before I had one of my own, I would have sworn up and down that gender differences were cultural constructs and that it was possible to raise a boy who defied stereotypes by being more interested in dolls than trucks and in arts and crafts than weapons. Then Isaac was born. And he *was* interested in dolls: Superman dolls. Batman dolls. And he *loved* painting and sculpture;

they were wonderful tools with which to make the weapons I wouldn't buy for him.

I took away the Play-Doh, the modeling clay, and all cylindrical objects. We stopped eating food that could be easily chewed into the shape of artillery. I banned all remotely aggressive videos and television, including most of the Disney movies the kids liked; Peter Pan spends way too much time sword-fighting and that Sea Witch would inspire anyone to violence. I refused to be swayed by the fact that Isaac was chafing under a diet of *Teletubbies* and *Barney*. Mindless pap was better than warfare any day. I bought him a succession of gender-neutral toys and videos, played house with him, changed his dolls' diapers, and taught him every single Pete Seeger song I could remember. So far, my efforts had borne exactly no fruit.

My mother attributed Isaac's gun obsession to the fact that I'd been shot the day I gave birth to him, but that's just blaming the victim, as far as I'm concerned.

"What fabulous thing are you guys going to do today?" I asked. I'm afraid I didn't do a terribly good job of concealing my glee at the thought of being excluded from my family's plans for the morning. Peter, a screen-writer, had just finished two long months of shooting on his latest work of art, *The Cannibal's Vacation*. The director had demanded his presence on the set, apparently worried that without Peter there to rewrite various exclamations of horror, the film would never wrap. To compensate me for having been alone with the kids while he lounged away the days and nights on Lomboc, a lesser-known tropical island in Indonesia, my husband had been doing solo kid duty for a week or so.

"We're going fishing for dinosaurs," Isaac announced.

"Really?" I asked.

"We are *not* going fishing." Ruby reached across the table and pinched her brother, who squealed in protest. I inserted myself between them and frowned at her.

"Ruby, watch it, or you won't be going anywhere," I said.

"Yes I will. Because Daddy promised to take us to the La Brea Tar Pits, and you're going to the gym, so I am *too* going."

The mouth on that kid. But you couldn't argue with her logic.

I didn't bother answering her, just picked Isaac up and buzzed him with my lips. "I'm going to miss you guys today," I lied.

"You could come if you want." Peter's voice was a hopeful squawk.

"No thanks. Ruby's right, I'm going to the gym."

I plopped Isaac on the floor and finished my coffee with a gulp. I took a Powerbar out of my stash hidden in the back of the pantry, waved gaily at my family, and headed out the door.

"I'm taking your car!" I shouted, all too happy to leave Peter with my station wagon bursting with car seats, baby wipes, and broken toys, and haunted by a mysterious odor whose origin lay in some long-lost tube of fluorescent yogurt. I slipped into his pristine, orange, vintage BMW 2002, popped the car into gear, and zipped off down the street, reveling in my hard-won freedom.

I'm the first to admit that I'm a somewhat unwilling stay-at-home mom. Not that I didn't choose the role. I did. Before I'd had my kids, I'd been a public defender representing indigent criminals in federal court. My particular specialties had been drug dealers and bank robbers, but I'd happily handled white-collar cases and even the odd assault on a national park ranger. I had never expected to leave work. I'd planned for a three-month maternity leave, imagining that I'd toss Peter the baby to take care of while I happily continued my twelve-hour-a-day schedule. I even tried it after Ruby was born. I went back to work when she was four months old, skipping off with my breast pump in one hand and my briefcase in the other. Ten months later, I was back home. I couldn't stand being away from her for so much of the time. By the time I realized that I wasn't any happier at home all day than I'd been at work all day, I was already pregnant with Isaac. That pretty much put the nails into my professional coffin. The past couple of years had passed in something of a blur, punctuated by car pool, endless loads of very small laundry, and the occasional murder.

I pulled into the parking lot of my gym and slipped into a spot. For my last birthday, Peter had given me a series of training sessions at a glitzy Hollywood health club. I had decided to view the gift not as a passive-aggressive comment on the magnitude of my ass but rather as the expression of a good-hearted wish to see me fit and healthy. I'd been having a terrific time, despite my usual loathing of all things physically active. There is something remarkably pleasurable about having your very own personal trainer hovering over you, expressing apparently sincere interest in your food intake and exercise concerns. I, like the majority of women I know, am certain that the rest of the world finds every detail of my calorie neuroses and body image obsession as scintillating as I do myself. I skipped into the gym, ready to confess to Bobby Katz the grim tale of the four Girl Scout cookies and half pound of saltwater taffy I'd eaten the night before.

Instead of the collection of almost familiar Hollywood faces in brightly colored Lycra, straining under Cybex machines and hefting free weights, I found an empty gym. There were no trainers shouting encouragement, no beautifully sculpted and perfectly made-up starlets grunting and groaning. The machines glinted forlornly in the sun shining through the windows, and the place echoed with a silence made all the eerier because I'd never before walked in without being subject to a blaring retro-disco beat.

It took me a few minutes to track down the denizens of my snazzy workout studio. They were huddled around the juice bar behind the locker rooms. The trainers, deltoids shining with carefully applied moisturizer and abdominal six-packs peeking from skintight tops cropped at the midriff, wept noisily. The clientele, a bit more concerned with the exigencies of eye makeup and foundation, dabbed their eyes with Kleenex. The owner of the gym, an oversized Vietnamese bodybuilder named Laurence, opened his arms to me and pressed me to his sweaty chest.

"Oh, darling. You poor darling. You don't even know, do you? You just came here to see him, and you don't even *know*," he wailed.

"Laurence, calm down. Tell me what's happened," I said as I attempted to extricate myself from his damp embrace. His nipple ring was poking me in the cheek.

"It's *Bobby*. He's *dead*. They found him this morning in his *car*. He *shot* himself."

I gasped, and now leaned against Laurence despite myself. "What? What are you talking about?"

"Betsy just called. He didn't come home last night, so she called the cops. They found his car parked on the PCH, just north of Santa Monica. Bobby was inside. Dead. He shot himself in the head."

I led Laurence over to a stool and sat him down. Then I asked him, "How's Betsy?"

"She's a mess, of course. Oh my God, I can't stand this, I can't *stand* this," Laurence wailed, burying his face in his hands.

"Oh for God's sake, Laurence. Quit crying. This is not *your* opera, girlfriend." I turned to Jamal Watson, one of the other trainers. He was dressed, as usual, in a vibrant shade of pink. His dark-brown leg muscles strained at his micro-mini shorts, and his top stopped a good six inches above his bellybutton. He looked back at me and said somewhat abashedly, "I mean, really, Bobby was my friend, too. Laurence here is acting like he's the only one who's devastated. We all are."

I turned back to the weeping gym owner. "Laurence, honey. You're upset. You should close up shop for the day." The other trainers and clients began to protest. They were sad, very sad, but not quite sad enough to sacrifice a morning's worth of crunches and leg lifts.

"No. No." Laurence heaved himself off his stool with a sigh. "The show must go on. Back to work, all of you. Back to work. That's what Bobby would have wanted." He waved everyone onto the gym floor and turned back to me. "Shall I give you a referral? Luzette's got some free slots, I think."

"No, no, that's okay. Maybe later. Can you give me Betsy's address? I want to see if she needs some help or if she could use a shoulder to cry on."

I could have used one myself. I'd been working out with Bobby Katz only for about six months, but in that short period of time, we'd gotten strangely close. Or maybe it wasn't so strange, considering the fact that we spent three hours a week together, most of that time filled with intimate conversations about our lives, loves, and the shape of my thighs. As a teenager, Bobby had made the thirty-mile leap from Thousand Oaks in the Valley to Hollywood, convinced that his sparkling azure eyes, flaxen hair, and laser-whitened teeth would garner him instant fame. It hadn't taken him long to realize that there were at least 7,200 other kids who looked just like him auditioning for all the same parts. He'd had some success. He'd gotten a couple of fast-food commercials and even a role in an Andrew Dice Clay movie. Unfortunately, his part in that work of cinematic genius was so small it could only be appreciated using the frame-by-frame viewing feature of a VCR.

He'd become a personal trainer as a way to supplement his acting income; it had soon become his career. And if I'm anything to go by, Bobby was good at what he did. I'd gained over sixty pounds with my second pregnancy, and despite the fact that Isaac was now well over two years old, before I met Bobby, I hadn't managed to lose more than half of it. He'd put me on a kooky diet that involved eating a lot of egg-white omelets and set me on a workout program that was having remarkable results. I could actually see my feet if I looked down. And craned my neck. And leaned a bit forward. Anyway, it was working for me. But that's not why

I kept coming back. Before Bobby, I'd quit every exercise regime I'd ever begun, despite the fact that they all showed at least some results. I kept seeing Bobby because I liked him. He was a sweet, gentle man with a ready hug and an arsenal of delightfully dishy Hollywood gossip. He remembered everything I told him and seemed genuinely to care about what I'd done over the weekend or how Isaac's potty training was progressing. He was interested and attentive without being remotely on the make. He gave me utterly platonic and absolutely focused male attention.

A few months before that horrible morning, Bobby had asked for my advice as a criminal defense lawyer. He was a recovered drug user and an active member of Narcotics Anonymous, where he'd met his fiancée, Betsy, and he'd asked me for help on her behalf. She'd fallen off the wagon and tried to make a buy from an undercover cop. The good news was that she never actually got the drugs. The bad news was that she found herself in county jail. I was thrilled at the opportunity to help Bobby after all he'd done for me, and I'd gotten them in touch with a good friend of mine from the federal public defender's office who had recently hung out her own shingle. Last I'd heard, Betsy's case had been referred to the diversion program. If she remained clean for a year and kept up with NA, it would disappear from her record.

Betsy and Bobby's place was in Hollywood, not too far from my own duplex in Hancock Park. I gave a little shudder as I climbed the rickety outdoor staircase up to their apartment. The building was made of crumbling stucco held together with rotted metal braces. The doors of each unit were dented metal, spray painted puce. The floor tile in the hallway was cracked, and large chunks were missing. Given the Los Angeles real estate market, they probably paid at least fifteen hundred a month to live in this dump.

Betsy opened the door and fell into my arms, a somewhat awkward endeavor since she was at least six inches taller than I. I led her inside and found myself face-to-face with two police officers. The cops took up much more space than it seemed they should have. The instruments hooked on to their black leather belts—the guns, billy clubs, radios, and other accoutrements of the LAPD—seemed to blow them up all out of human proportion. They were planted on the electric green carpet like a couple of bulls in a too-small pasture. I squeezed by one of the pneumatically enlarged officers and lowered Betsy onto the light beige leather couch, where she folded in on herself like a crumpled tissue.

I turned back to the men. "I'm Juliet Applebaum. I'm a friend of Betsy and Bobby's."

One of the officers, a man in his late twenties with a buzz cut so short and so new that his ears and neck looked raw, nodded curtly. "We're here to escort Betsy on down to the station so she can give a statement."

I turned to the weeping girl. "Betsy, honey? Do you want to go with the officers?"

She shook her head, buried her face in her hands, and slumped over on the couch.

"I don't think Betsy's quite ready for that," I said in a firm voice.

The officer shook his head and, ignoring me, leaned over Betsy's prone form. "It'll just take a few minutes. The detectives are waiting for you." He managed to sound both menacing and polite at the same time.

Betsy just cried harder and jerked her arm away from the officer's extended hand. I sat down next to her and slipped an arm around her shoulders.

"Officer, why don't you let the detectives know that Betsy's just too distraught right now." The cop started to shake his head, but I interrupted him. "Am I to understand that you are placing her under arrest?" I asked. I felt Betsy quiver under my arm, and I gave her back a reassuring pat.

"No, no, nothing like that," the other officer spoke up. He looked a bit older than the one trying to get Betsy up off the couch. "We just need her to give a statement to the detectives."

"Unless you're planning on arresting her, Betsy's going to stay home for now. You can let the detectives know that they can contact her here. And if there's nothing further, I think Betsy would like to be left alone."

The police officers looked at each other for a moment, and then the older one shrugged his shoulders. They walked out the door, leaving behind a room that suddenly seemed to quadruple in size.

I patted Betsy on the back for a while, and then got up to make some tea. Bobby had introduced me to the wonders of green tea, and I could think of no time when I'd needed a restorative cup of Silver Needle Jasmine more than at this moment. I opened the fridge in the little galley kitchen off the living room and sorted through the jars of protein powder and murky green bottles of wheat grass juice until I found a little black canister of tea. I dug up a teapot and ran the faucet until it was hot. I poured some water over the leaves and let them steep for a moment. By the time I came back out to the living room holding two small cups of tea, Betsy had gathered herself together and was wiping her eyes and blowing her nose.

"Thanks," she said. "You still know how to be a lawyer."

"What? Making tea?"

"No, no." She smiled through her tears. "Getting rid of the cops."

"Don't mention it. Pissing off cops is my specialty. Are Bobby's parents on their way?"

Betsy shook her head.

"Do they know?"

She nodded and said, "The police called them this morning and told them. I tried to call, too, but they aren't answering the phone. I just keep getting the machine."

That surprised me. "You mean you haven't talked to them at all?"

"I haven't talked to them in months. Ever since . . . ever since that whole thing happened. When they found out about it, they tried to get Bobby to break up with me. They told him that I was a bad influence and that I'd drag him down. Which I guess I did." The last was said in a sort of moan, and more tears dripped down her cheeks.

I wrapped my arm around her and handed her a tissue and the cup of tea. "Drink," I said. "It'll make you feel better." She took a few sips and then blew her nose loudly.

"You weren't a bad influence on Bobby," I said, although I have to admit that at the time of her arrest, I'd taken the same line as Bobby's parents, albeit a bit more delicately. I'd just suggested to Bobby that since he had worked so hard to kick his addiction, he might want to put a little distance between himself and Betsy, just until she got her act together. Bobby had thanked me for my advice and gently informed me that he loved Betsy and planned to stand by her. I'd been chastened and never mentioned my reservations again. I had still had them, though. Bobby was the poster child for twelve-step programs. He'd stopped using methamphetamine five years before and hadn't missed a weekly meeting since. Before he'd gotten sober, his addiction was so bad that it was costing him hundreds of dollars a week, just to stay awake. He'd turned his athlete's body into a husk of its former self. The damage he'd caused to his heart from years of drug abuse was permanent. Despite the great shape he'd managed to return himself to, he still had an enlarged heart and a severe arrhythmia. Bobby had once told me that methamphetamine was so toxic to him nowadays that even holding the stuff and having it absorb through his fingers could trigger a heart attack. The risks to him of falling off the wagon were astronomical. I'd been terribly worried that Betsy's weakness would be contagious. But, in the end, he'd proven me wrong. He'd gotten her back on the program and never fallen off himself. So I had believed, until that morning.

"Betsy, why were the police here? Did they tell you why they need you to make a statement?"

"No. They just said I have to."

"But it's a suicide, right? Bobby killed himself?"

"I don't know. I mean, that's what they told me this morning. They said they found him in the car with a gun in his hand, and that he'd shot himself in the head."

"Was it his gun?"

She shook her head. "I don't think so. I mean, he doesn't have a gun. At least I don't think he does."

"And just now, when the cops were here, did they tell you they were considering other things? Like maybe that someone had killed him?"

She sniffed loudly and wiped her nose on her sleeve. "They didn't tell me anything."

"Betsy, do you think Bobby killed himself?" I asked flat out.

She shook her head and wailed, "I don't know. None of this makes any sense. I mean, why would he kill himself?"

"I don't know," I said. "But then, I don't know him as well as you do. Had anything happened between you two? Had you guys been getting along?" The truth was, I didn't expect Betsy to confide in me. I didn't know her that well, and for all I knew, Bobby had told her that, like his parents, I'd encouraged him to break up with her.

"Things were great. Great," she said firmly, rubbing the tears away from her eyes. "We'd set a date for the wedding; we'd even picked a rabbi."

"A rabbi? But you're not Jewish, are you?"

"Bobby's parents really wanted us to have a rabbi. Their guy said that he'd do it, if we went to premarital counseling and if Bobby did all the tests and stuff."

"Tests?"

"Yeah, you know. Genetic testing for Tay-Sachs. The rabbi says he makes all Jews who he marries get Tay-Sachs testing. Just in case."

Tay-Sachs disease is a birth defect that is carried by something like one in thirty Jews of European descent. If two carriers have children together, they have a one in four chance of giving birth to a baby who will die of Tay-Sachs. Tay-Sachs is always fatal; generally, children die by age five after being desperately ill for most of their lives. Nowadays, there's a simple blood test to determine if you are a carrier. Most Jewish couples automatically get tested, but Peter and I hadn't bothered, since Peter wasn't Jewish. Both of us would have had to be carriers for there to be any danger, so we'd never even considered it.

"Bobby had it," Betsy said.

"Had it? You mean Tay-Sachs? He was a carrier?"

"Yeah. We found out a few months ago, right before my . . . my arrest. I mean, it's no big deal that he had it, because of course I don't have it since I'm not Jewish. I mean, it *wasn't* a big deal." She sniffed. "I guess none of that matters anymore."

I didn't answer.

"What am I going to do?" she asked, turning to me and peering into my eyes.

I shook my head helplessly. "I don't know, Betsy. Get through every day, one day at a time, I guess."

"One day at a time? You sound like my goddamn sponsor," she said. "You sound like Bobby."

I sat with Betsy for a while longer, leaving only when her Narcotics Anonymous sponsor and a few other friends from the group arrived.

2

WHEN I GOT home from Betsy's, I found my kids and my husband hurling themselves around the living room wearing pink tutus; Peter's was around his neck. Ruby had a collection of tulle, lace, and ribbon that rivaled that of the Joffrey Ballet. From the moment she was able to make her sartorial preferences known, she'd begun lobbying for frills and ruffles. If she'd had her own way, she'd have had a pastel-colored confirmation gown for every day of the week. We compromised on cute little patterned cotton dresses and a costume box fit for a drag queen.

As soon as Isaac was born, she'd begun stuffing him into leotards and draping feather boas around his neck. He was only too glad to oblige his idolized older sister and happily participated in her endless stage productions and ballet recitals. Lately, he'd begun adding his own accessories, and it was not uncommon to find him, as I did that day, wearing a pink tutu, a purple ostrich feather tucked behind his ear, and a sword and scabbard belted around his waist.

"Mama! I'm a Princess Knight," he announced. Then he whipped out his sword and clocked his sister on the head with it.

"Damn it, Peter, I put that sword away for this very reason. Why did you take it out?" I said.

"Because you can't be a Princess Knight without a sword."

"Why does he have to be a Princess *Knight*? Why can't he just be a princess? Or a prince? A nice prince. Who kisses the princess instead of hacking off her head."

Peter sighed dramatically and reached out his hand. "Okay, sport. Hand over the sword. Mama says no more fencing."

Isaac began to wail and didn't stop until I'd popped a video into the

VCR. The child development experts can shake their heads all they want. TV is an essential tool of the modern parent. How else can two adults have a conversation during the day? I'm all for stimulating my children's tiny little developing brains, but sometimes you just need them to sit in one place and be quiet. My kids are going to have to be couch potatoes when I have something I absolutely must do. Like tell their father that I'd stumbled across yet another suspicious death.

"He killed himself?" Peter asked.

"I guess so. I mean, it looks that way with the gun and everything, but it seems so unlikely. He was such an upbeat kind of guy."

"Aren't methamphetamine addicts sort of by definition upbeat? It's called speed for a reason."

"He wasn't an addict. I mean, he was, but he wasn't using anymore. He'd been in recovery forever."

"How can you be so sure?"

"What? That he wasn't using?"

"It's not like he'd necessarily admit it to you if he *was* using. And you did always talk about how hyper he was."

"Hyper in a *good* way. Like a trainer is supposed to be. Not like some whacked-out speed freak. I think I'd know the difference," I said. I certainly should know the difference. In my career as a federal public defender, I'd spent plenty of time with people addicted to all different sorts of substances. I'd had heroin-addict clients to whom I'd needed to give at least twenty-four hours' notice that I was planning to drop by the Metropolitan Detention Center if I didn't want them to be completely stoned when I had them brought down to the visiting room. As a young lawyer, it had taken me a while to figure out that they were wasted, not because they weren't acting high, but just because I was so naive that it never occurred to me that the federal jail would be such an easy place to score. It turns out you can get pretty much anything at the MDC, and the prices aren't much more than out on the street. Don't ask me how they get the drugs into the jail. I suppose a cynical person might suggest taking a look at the fine display of automotive splendor in the prison guards' parking lot.

I'd represented my share of methamphetamine dealers, mostly Mexican guys who brought the precursor chemicals in over the border and cooked them up in labs out in the wilds of Riverside, or aging bikers who kept themselves in Harley parts doing the same. I knew a speed freak when I saw one, and by the time I met Bobby Katz, he wasn't using. I was sure of it.

"He wasn't using," I said firmly.

"Okay. Well, maybe he just did a good job of hiding how depressed he was. Maybe that whole thing with his girlfriend was harder on him than you thought. Maybe *she's* using again, and he couldn't stand it anymore."

"Maybe," I said doubtfully. "But isn't it a bit more likely that he'd just leave her?"

Peter shrugged. "When is the funeral?"

"I don't know. I guess that depends on when they release the body. If they decide it's a suicide, I'm sure it will be soon. Bobby's Jewish, and that means his parents will want to bury him as soon as possible."

3

"WHY IS IT that wearing black to a funeral seems ostentatious?" I said to my pint-sized companion. "I mean, you're supposed to wear black. That's the traditional color of mourning. Unless you're Buddhist. Not that white would be any easier. I mean, I own literally nothing white except panties and bras."

"Wear this, Mommy. It's black," Ruby said, pulling my one full-length gown out of its dry cleaner bag.

"I don't know, honey. Sequins on a Sunday morning?"

Ruby nodded. "They're *black* sequins."

"Let's try something less formal, shall we?" I waded to the back of my closet where I'd consigned my business attire. I pulled out a charcoal pantsuit and brushed the dust off the shoulders. I pulled on the slacks, exhaling while I zipped. "Ruby, hand me one of your hair elastics, would you?"

She pulled one out of her ponytail, and I picked the clump of red hair out of it. I hooked one end around the button at the waistband of the pants and the other through the buttonhole. With that extra couple of inches, I could get away with the pants. Just. I found a pale gray cotton knit sweater and shrugged on the suit jacket.

"So? What do you think?" I asked my four-year-old daughter.

"Gorgeous. But a little fat."

I gave her the stink eye and pinched her on the tush. "Go tell your daddy I'm leaving."

The L.A. county coroner had released Bobby's body a week after he died. Jewish law requires that a body be buried as soon as possible after death, within a day or two, so his parents arranged for him to be buried the day following the body's release. Sometimes *halacha* has to give way to the exigencies of the criminal justice system, but all things considered, I thought the county had done a pretty good job of finishing their work expeditiously. It probably helped that they didn't need to worry about what the body looked like; we're not allowed to have open caskets, so no one besides the undertaker was going to see whatever remained of poor Bobby Katz.

The turnout for Bobby's service was impressive, considering that it took place all the way out in Thousand Oaks. I got there early enough to take a strategic place in the back and watch people as they came in. Bobby's friends from work were sitting in the first few rows. I noticed that none of them had had my doubts. To a one they were impeccably turned out in absolute, unremitting, pure black. The women wore severe dresses and suits that were just a shade too tight, and the men all seemed to have bought the same Armani funereal attire. I thought the midnight ties were a bit overkill, but then I had an elastic band around my waist, so who was I to comment?

Behind them were a couple of rows of what had to be friends from Alcoholics and Narcotics Anonymous. They were a diverse bunch: old and young, nicely dressed and decidedly sloppy. It took a moment for me to realize that Betsy sat among them. I could just see the back of her bent neck leaning against the shoulder of an overweight woman whose thick gray ponytail was tied with a piece of red yarn. I considered getting up and paying my respects but decided to wait until after the ceremony. Older couples—most likely friends of Bobby's parents—took up the rest of the seats. I couldn't see anyone who looked like his family.

After a few more minutes, a door opened, and Bobby's family filed in. They sat down in a few rows of chairs set up to the side of the hall, and one of the ushers drew a large wooden screen in front of them, effectively shielding them from view. Odd, I thought, but then I hadn't been to that many funerals.

The service was quick; the rabbi spoke briefly about lives cut short before their time. A man who identified himself as Bobby's brother described their bucolic life as children. He told us about Bobby's earlier high school drama successes and his struggles in Hollywood. Bobby's brother said how proud he and the rest of the family had been when his younger sibling had ultimately found professional satisfaction. Except that he described Bobby as a physical *therapist*, not a trainer. I suppose Bobby might have gone to school and been certified as a physical therapist, but somehow I didn't think that was something he'd keep a secret from his clientele. He'd certainly never mentioned that to me.

After Bobby's brother sat down, a beefy man in an ill-fitting blue blazer rose to his feet and looked as though he might begin to speak. He was sitting with the AA crowd, and they all raised their faces to him expectantly. He opened his mouth but then caught sight of the rabbi. The rabbi shook his head vigorously and frowned. The man blushed and, appropriately chastened, sat back down. The rabbi launched into a final prayer, and then it was all over. The usher rolled back the screen, and Bobby's family walked back out of the room. I caught a glimpse of his dark-haired mother, her face drawn and gaunt. Her narrow, colorless lips were pinched in a thin line, and she leaned heavily on the arm of a younger woman with similar coloring, whom I imagined must have been Bobby's sister. As soon as they'd gone, I squeezed past the exiting guests in the direction of Betsy and her friends.

"Hi, Betsy," I said.

"Oh, Juliet," she wailed and fell out of her friend's arms and into mine. "Did you see that? They wouldn't even let me *sit* with them. The funeral director wouldn't let me into the *room* with them. He said, 'Family only,' and threw me out."

I patted her back and murmured a few comforting words.

"It's disgraceful, is what it is," said the gray-haired woman. "Betsy's the *widow* for crying out loud." The other friends and supporters who'd gathered around us murmured in agreement.

"Did you talk to Bobby's parents, Betsy?" I asked.

She nodded, her face pressed against my shoulder. Then she sniffed and picked up her head. "Oh, sorry," she mumbled. "I got your jacket all wet."

"Don't worry about it. I have two kids, remember? I'm used to having snot on my clothes."

She smiled wanly.

"Have you spoken to his family?" I asked again.

"Yeah," she said. "His brother came by a couple of days ago to tell me that they were going to *let* me stay in the apartment until the end of the month. Like they have a right. It's my home. They can't throw me out."

This was worse than I thought. "And his parents?"

"They won't even talk to me. I finally got through to them, and his dad said that their *lawyer* told them not to talk to me. Can you believe that? I mean, Bobby and I were *engaged*. We had a date and *everything*. The *rabbi* is talking to me. Why can't they?"

"What did the rabbi say?"

"He came by the same day as Bobby's brother. He said he wanted to see how I was doing, but who knows why he was really there. She probably sent him to make sure I hadn't stolen the TV set or something."

"She?"

"Bobby's mother. God, I hate her."

The gray-haired woman put her hand on my arm. "We're having a potluck after the burial. Since none of Bobby's AA family is welcome at his parents' home, we're hosting our own reception at Betsy's house. You're welcome to join us."

"Thanks," I said. I followed the group out of the hall and down a long, winding path of crushed white rock to the burial site. I stood with the AA contingent on the outskirts of the crowd and watched as the members of Bobby's family gathered around the grave. The coffin was perched on a hydraulic lift over the gaping hole. There was a pile of earth covered in a large piece of what looked like AstroTurf to one side of the open grave, and the air was redolent with the meaty smell of soil and grass. The rabbi began to sing the prayers in his deep, atonal voice, and a few of the onlookers joined him. Dredging up the Hebrew words from somewhere deep in my memory, I murmured along with them. The deeply familiar prayers brought tears to my eyes, yet I found them soothing and peaceful. So slowly that it seemed almost imperceptible, the coffin began to sink into the grave. It landed with a faint and final thump, and, one by one, each member of Bobby's family took a small trowel full of dirt and spilled it onto the coffin. After the last of them had gone, Betsy pushed forward and took the trowel out of the pile of earth. She dumped the dirt into the grave and cried, "I love you, Bobby. We'll be together someday. I promise you."

I glanced over at Bobby's parents in time to catch his mother's face pinch into an angry scowl. Bobby's father reached an arm around his wife and drew her away from the scene. The two of them, flanked by their children, walked back to the waiting limousines.

SINCE THE BAN on the presence of recovering addicts at Bobby's parents' home after the service obviously did not include me, I decided to head over there with the rest of the guests. I got the address from Laurence, Bobby's boss, and found my way to a large Mediterranean-style home set far back from the road on a block of almost identical houses. Bobby's parents had put out quite a spread, and it was a little while before I could pry myself away from the buffet table. Finally, having gorged myself to a rather embarrassing degree on blintzes, whitefish salad, and those fruit minitarts that are ubiquitous at every L.A. event, be it a funeral or a movie opening, I made my way through the crowd in the direction of Bobby's family.

They were making a fairly symbolic effort at sitting shivah, the traditional Jewish mourning ritual. They sat on low chairs, but they all wore their shoes and had on little black polyester scarves that they'd torn at the corner, instead of rending their own garments. I know that's not unusual, that only the ultra-Orthodox still tear their clothing, but still, it seemed somehow to belie the sincerity of their mourning, like they were sad, but not sad enough to ruin a good shirt. I stood in a line of people and finally reached Bobby's mother.

"I'm so sorry for your loss," I said, echoing everyone else. What else is there to say?

"Thank you," she murmured and looked beyond me at the next person.

"Um, I was a client of Bobby's," I said, trying to keep her attention. "Oh?"

"He was a wonderful trainer. So knowledgable."

She didn't answer, just nodded politely and reached out her hand to the woman standing behind me.

"I'm so sorry for your loss," the other woman said.

I wandered through the line, expressing my condolences to the rest of the family. His two sisters and brother all looked quite a bit older than he'd been, the oldest sister by as much as a dozen years. But then, Bobby might have been older than I thought. His business did require a certain youthful appearance.

I stood for a while in a corner of the room and then caught the eye of a short man with a hairline that had receded to the purely hypothetical. He sidled over to me.

"Were you a friend of Bobby's?" he asked.

"A client. And a friend. I'm Juliet Applebaum," I replied.

"I'm Larry. He was my brother-in-law. I'm married to Michelle."

"Bobby's sister?"

"The younger one. Over there, that's Lisa, she's the oldest. And that's her husband, Mitch." He pointed to the dark-haired woman seated next to Bobby's mother and to a tall, stooped man with an oversized nose sitting on the couch and leafing through a magazine.

"Did he just have the one brother?"

"Yeah, David. Dot com David."

"Excuse me?"

"Didn't you know? David is Cyberjet. The Internet portal? He's worth like a hundred million dollars, even after the crash."

"Wow," I said, delighted to have found someone at once close to the family and indiscreet.

"Wasn't Bobby getting married?" I said. "Where's his fiancée?"

Larry snorted. "Betsy? No way Arthur and Leslie would ever let her into the house. She's a drug fiend. And, anyway, *I'm* betting she had something to do with Bobby's death."

"Really?" I asked. "I thought it was suicide."

"Who's to say she didn't drive him to it? Anyway, the cops haven't ruled out murder."

That explained their insistence on getting a statement from Betsy. "Do the police consider the fiancée a suspect?"

"Probably. At the very least, she drove him to it. That's what Arthur and Leslie think, anyway. Like I said, she's a drug fiend."

"Didn't Bobby and Betsy meet in recovery?"

He snorted. "I wouldn't mention that around here if I were you. We're not allowed to talk about Bobby's little problem. The most Arthur and Leslie will admit is that he had a period of 'youthful indiscretion.'"

At that moment, Larry's wife joined us. She, like her mother, was slim and dark-haired. Her mascara was smudged and her nose tinged with red. She looped her arm through her husband's and smiled at me wanly.

"I'm Juliet. I was a client of Bobby's," I said.

"Thanks so much for coming. It really means a lot to my parents, to all of us, that so many of Bobby's colleagues and clients came today," she said.

"He was a lovely guy," I told her, feeling my eyes fill.

"He was. He really was." The tears flowed freely down her cheeks. "He's always had just the biggest heart. He was the kind of kid who brought home stray cats and lost dogs."

Larry shook his head. "Gee, your mom must have just loved that."

Michelle smiled through her tears. "Oh, she went ballistic. He'd hide them in his room until one of the cleaning ladies would find them and tell my mother. Once he hid a rat in his closet for like a month. And not a white rat, either. A big gray street rat. Then, one day while he was at school and Lisa was home from college, she was digging around his room for something or other, and she opened up this plastic shoe box with holes punched in the top. She started screaming and ended up kicking the box over and the thing got loose. My mother had the exterminators in within an hour, and there was rat poison all over our house for days. They never caught the rat, though. He's probably still living in the basement."

We made small talk for a while longer, during the course of which Michelle told me what Bobby had already told me months before: Their parents were both doctors. Their father was a surgeon and their mother a pathologist on the faculty at UCLA. The girls had followed in their footsteps. Lisa, the older sister, and her husband, Mitch, had an obstetrical practice in the Valley. Michelle, a research scientist with both an M.D. and a Ph.D., was a statistical geneticist with Biogenet, a biotech company that specialized in creating disease-resistant seed.

"Wow," I said. "A doctor, a scientist, and an Internet entrepreneur. It can't have been easy competing with you guys."

"No," she admitted, "but then Bobby didn't really try to compete. He wasn't academically inclined. From the time he was a little kid, he said he was going to be an actor. That's all he really wanted. He didn't even go to college."

"That must have been something of a disappointment for your parents."

"I guess so, but then they never really expected that much from him. I mean, not academically. He wasn't like the rest of us. He just didn't have that kind of brain."

She sighed and leaned against her husband. "I should go sit next to Mom. Are you okay on your own, Larry?"

"I'm fine. Juliet's keeping me company. Aren't you?" he said with a leer.

Michelle didn't seem to notice her husband's wolfish expression. She nodded distractedly and left us.

"Intense family dynamic," I said to Larry.

"You don't know the half of it," he whispered.

"Really?" I leaned closer to him and raised my eyebrows.

He was obviously flattered at the attention and altogether too happy to be dishing his in-laws to an encouraging ear.

"It can't hurt to talk about this now. I mean, the poor guy's dead. Arthur and Leslie never expected much from Bobby because they're big believers in the heritability of intelligence."

"Excuse me?"

"They expected their kids to be brilliant because they think they are such perfect genetic specimens. But not Bobby."

"Why not?"

"Because Bobby wasn't theirs. He was adopted."

"Really?" This shocked me. Bobby and I had had long talks about our families. He'd never mentioned this.

"You want to know the really messed up thing?"

I nodded.

He glanced over his shoulder and motioned me closer. I leaned in, and he said in a low voice, "They never told him."

"Really?" I matched his whisper. "That's so strange. Why not?"

"They said it was because they didn't want him to feel inferior. But David, Lisa, and Michelle all knew. Michelle's the baby, and she was eight when they brought him home, so of course they knew. The whole family kept it a secret from Bobby."

"He *never* knew?"

"No. I mean, he didn't know until recently."

"And how did this suddenly come out?"

"Totally by accident. It had something to do with his being a Tay-Sachs carrier. David knows. He's the one who told him."

BECAUSE IT WAS some time before I could corner Bobby's brother, David, I had to satisfy myself instead with reinvestigating the buffet table. I was strategically placed to take advantage of the tray of tiny pecan tarts that made their late appearance on the arm of a white-jacketed server. I was wolfing down my third when I saw David start to walk out of the living room. I wiped my mouth and slipped out after him. I found him slumped in a cracked leather armchair in a library, away from the noise of the crowd. I smiled at him as I entered the room, then gazed admiringly at the walls of books.

"What a beautiful room," I said.

"Yeah. My parents keep all their medical texts in here. When Bobby was little, I used to get the dermatology ones down and scare him with pictures of pustules and varicella and the like."

"Gross."

"He loved it. He'd squeal and shriek and then say, 'Show me another one.' We really liked the V.D. pictures."

I lowered myself into the matching armchair opposite Bobby's brother. "You gave a lovely eulogy."

"I guess. I didn't really know what to say. I mean, what do you say when your kid brother dies?"

The question was rhetorical.

"Were you two very close?"

"No. I mean, we got along, but, you know, I was twelve when Bobby was born. I left for college when he was six. I didn't come home much after that."

"Still, it sounds like you loved him very much."

David shrugged and wiped tears from his eyes with an angry fist. "Yeah," he croaked.

"I'm Juliet. I was a friend of Bobby's. And a client."

He shook my hand perfunctorily.

I didn't really know how to ask David what it was that I wanted to know, but it's always served me well just to open my big mouth, so that's what I did. "I hope you don't think I'm prying, but I was wondering, well, what you make of Bobby's death. I know it's not really any of my business, but Bobby didn't seem at all depressed to me, and I saw him pretty regularly. Do you have any idea why he would have killed himself?"

David looked at me for a moment, as if surprised at my audacity. Then he said, "No. Honestly, I don't. I mean, I thought for a while it might have been because . . . well, because of something that happened, but then he didn't seem depressed at all to me, either, even after everything, and I just didn't think it could be . . . that."

"You mean Bobby finding out that he was adopted?"

"You know about that? He told you about that?" David sounded surprised.

I nodded, figuring I was answering the first question, not the second.

"I thought it might be that at first," David said. "But you know, I don't really think it could be. I mean, he freaked out when I told him, but he was mostly pissed off at Mom and Dad for keeping it a secret. He didn't seem depressed about it. On the contrary."

"On the contrary?" I asked.

"Well, you know Bobby. He never really felt like he fit in this family. He always felt like an intellectual failure around here. He seemed almost relieved to find out that he wasn't biologically related to the rest of us. He even said to me something like, 'So I'm not a freak of nature; I'm just a regular person.'" David sounded as if he were trying to convince himself rather than me.

"He found out because of the Tay-Sachs diagnosis?" I asked.

"Yeah. I guess you know that I told him."

I nodded.

"The rabbi made him do genetic testing before the wedding. Bobby called me after he got the results of his Tay-Sachs screen. He came to me because he knew that Lisa and Michelle would have had to be tested when they got married. But I'm not married. He wanted to tell me that he was a carrier and that I might be, too. I told him I wasn't worried about it, but he, you know, pressed me. So then I finally told him. I mean, why not? I never thought it *should* be a secret. I never agreed with Mom and Dad that we should pretend he was just like the rest of us. I mean, he had a *right* to know. Didn't he?" He held his hands out beseechingly. I wanted to make him feel better, to reassure him that he'd done the right thing. I had a feeling that, his protestations notwithstanding, David was terrified that he'd done something awful by telling his brother about the adoption. Deep inside, he was probably desperately afraid that what he'd said had driven Bobby to suicide.

"I certainly think he had a right to know," I said. "How did your parents react to his finding out?"

David grunted in disgust. "They were furious with me. My dad still isn't speaking to me. My mother just gave me one of her trademark 'I'm so disappointed in you' speeches. Neither of them was really willing to talk about it with Bobby. They confirmed it, and that was that. We weren't supposed to speak about it ever again."

"And did you speak about it again? Did Bobby?"

He heaved a sigh and ran his fingers through his hair. "He tried, I think. But you have to understand, once my parents decide to dig their heels in, that's pretty much it. I know Bobby was hoping to get information about his birth family out of them, but it's like getting blood from a stone."

Poor Bobby. I could imagine him trying to find out about himself, eager for any scrap of information. "Do you know if Bobby ever did learn anything about his birth family?"

At that moment, David seemed to decide he'd confided enough in a stranger. He just shook his head and got up out of his chair.

"I should be getting back." He opened the door to the library and waited for me to follow him.

4

I WANTED TO MAKE an appearance at Betsy's gathering. It was the decent thing to do, and it would give me the opportunity to find out more about Bobby's adoption. Finding out that fact about himself had surely resulted in a considerable amount of personal turmoil. Perhaps it had even been enough to lead him to kill himself.

I called Peter from the car to let him know I'd be out for longer than I'd expected.

"There's someone here who has something to say to you," he said.

Then I heard a high-pitched squeak. "Mama?"

"Hi, Isaac. How are you doing, buddy?"

"I want to nurse. Come home right now, and bring me my breasts."

Peter got back on the line.

"I suppose you think that's funny," I said.

"He's been bugging me all day. When are you going to wean this kid?"

"I'm *trying*. You know I'm trying." And I was. I'd been trying to wean Isaac since he was eighteen months old and announced, in a loud voice in the middle of a restaurant, "This side empty. Other side, please." But the kid clearly had other plans, and they included breast-feeding his way through college. Whenever I tried to hand him a bottle, he would fling it across the room and dive-bomb my shirt front. Nine times out of ten, I would give in, if only to quiet the shrieking. Peter thought I was way too much of a softy, but he'd never experienced the humiliation of sitting on an airplane next to a toddler screaming, "Give me my breast *now*!" at the top of his lungs.

While the quality of the food at Betsy's wasn't quite up to that of the Drs. Katz, the ebullience of the crowd made up for the hodgepodge of a buffet. The room was packed with people weeping, laughing, and sharing reminiscences of Bobby. I greeted a few of those I'd met at the funeral and made my way over to Betsy, who was sitting on the living room couch, smiling through tears at a story told by a muscular man with a shaved head.

"And then I was like, 'I'll go first,' and Bobby was like, 'Okay.' And then as soon as I start screaming, he decides, no he doesn't want to get his tongue pierced, he's never going to get his tongue pierced, and goddamn it if he didn't check himself into rehab two days later. When I got sober, we started telling people that it was fear of this"—the man stuck out his tongue, revealing a large silver stud—"that got Bobby on the wagon."

The small crowd of people huddled around Betsy and the bald man groaned and laughed. I slipped in between them and put a hand on her shoulder.

"Hey," I said. "How are you holding up?"

She shrugged. "Okay, I guess. I'm just glad Annie arranged for all this. I couldn't have dealt with being on my own after that horrible funeral."

"I went to the Katzes," I said. "I found out a few things that I'd like to talk to you about."

"What's going on?"

I looked around at the crowd of interested faces. "Is there somewhere we could go to talk?"

Betsy led me down the hall to the bedroom. She flopped on the bed, and I sat on the edge of a sling back chair, doing my best not to fall through the torn seat.

I told her briefly about my conversation with David. Betsy started to shake her head.

"What are you talking about?" she asked, her brow wrinkled and her eyebrows raised in shock. "Adopted? Bobby was adopted?"

"Didn't he tell you?" That floored me. Bobby hadn't told his fiancée about what was surely one of the greatest surprises of his life?

Betsy shook her head. "I can't believe this. I mean, I'm really surprised. Not that he's adopted. I'm just surprised he didn't tell me. I thought we told each other everything."

"You're *not* surprised that he was adopted?"

She shook her head. "It makes sense; I mean, how could *that* woman have given birth to a wonderful, sweet, generous guy like Bobby?" She sniffed.

"Were you guys doing okay?" I chose my words carefully. "I know you'd had some difficult times lately."

"You mean when I got busted, right?"

I nodded my head.

"Yeah, well, Bobby really helped me through all that. He stood by me and even went along with the wedding plans, in spite of everything. In spite of his parents trying to convince him to dump me."

"And you don't have any idea why Bobby might have committed suicide?"

She shook her head. "No. And, honestly, it doesn't make sense to me. Not a bit. It's just not something that Bobby would do. He's not that kind of person. I mean, I was supposed to be the pessimist in our relationship." She barked a hoarse, sad laugh and then started crying again.

At that moment, I realized that I wasn't going to be able to just walk away from Bobby's death. Call it compassion, call it an inability to leave well enough alone, call it plain old-fashioned nosiness. I couldn't live with myself without at least trying to find out why Bobby Katz had died and who, if anyone, was responsible.

I sat down next to Betsy and took her hand. "Would you be willing to let me look into things a bit, maybe do a little investigation? I've got some experience with this kind of thing. Maybe I can help figure out what happened to Bobby."

She looked at me curiously and said, "I don't mind. I mean, it's not like the police are doing anything, as far as I can tell." Her face brightened momentarily, and it seemed to me that she liked the idea of having an ally, of having at least one other person in her corner, trying to figure out what had happened to the man in her life.

"Would you mind if I look through some of Bobby's things? His papers or his computer? It could give me an idea of what was going on with him, maybe lead me in the direction of whatever was bothering him or even whoever might have wanted to hurt him," I said.

"I guess that would be okay. The cops took a lot of stuff, but they left his laptop. Do you want to see that?"

"That could be useful."

Bobby had turned their second bedroom into a small home office. He had a computer table set up against one wall and a four-drawer filing cabinet in the corner. I shut the door of the room against the sound of

Bobby's friends, who had begun singing versions of his favorite songs—he must have been a big Billy Joel fan—and started rifling through the filing cabinet. The cops had pretty well cleaned it out. I could see where he had a folder with each of his clients' names printed across the top, but the contents of the individual files were missing. I found my own and couldn't resist checking, but it, too, was empty. They'd left the drawers full of articles on weight control and fitness innovations pretty well alone, but I didn't think those would be particularly useful to me. I was impressed with how carefully Bobby organized his information files, though. He was a man who took his work seriously and clearly tried to keep up in the field.

I turned my attention to the computer, hoping that the cops hadn't wiped the hard drive. Luckily, they'd either ignored it or perhaps had made a copy of it for themselves. I felt vaguely guilty searching through Bobby's files. A person's computer is as intimate as his underwear drawer, and it reflects his character even more. Bobby's hard drive was as tidy and orderly as he was. He had carefully organized his files; his folders were all divided into subfolders. In a folder named "Work," I found a client list with phone numbers and addresses that I printed out on the inkjet printer cabled to the laptop. I clicked my way through his various folders, hoping I might find a diary of some kind. No luck. I was about to open a folder temptingly called "Correspondence" when my purse started ringing.

"*Oy*, Peter, I totally lost track of time. Is everything okay?"

"It's fine," my husband said, "but the kids are asking for you. I'm about to start dinner, and I need to know if you plan to make it home."

"Oh God, is it that late?"

I promised I'd be home right away and went to find Betsy. Most of her friends had gone home, and she sat in the living room with the last few. When I walked in, she looked up from the photo album she'd been leafing through.

"Did you find anything?" she asked listlessly.

"Not really. Not yet. Listen, Betsy, would you have any objection to my borrowing Bobby's computer? I'd copy the hard drive here, but I'm afraid it would take me hours to get everything."

She shrugged her shoulders. "Go ahead and take it. I don't care. If his brother comes around, I'll tell him you have it. Otherwise, he'll probably think I pawned it or something."

5

OVER BREAKFAST THE next morning, I decided that if I was going to investigate Bobby's death, I would need some expert advice. I don't know what I'd do without Al Hockey. Never in my life would I have imagined that I could rely so unreservedly on someone who collected semiautomatic weapons for pleasure. Al and I are about as divergent politically as two people can be, but in some strange way that neither of us understands, we're friends. Al is an ex-cop who retired from the force after taking a couple of ounces of lead in the belly. He'd been working as a defense investigator at the federal public defender's office for a few years when I got hired, and we hit it off almost instantly. He'd investigated all my cases for me and had saved me from many an embarrassing mistake. He's been a terrific source of information, both legal and less-than, ever since.

"What do you want?" he growled when I called him. "I'm packing."

"Packing? What do you mean packing? Are you moving?"

"No. Quitting. Today's my last day at the office. You're lucky you found me here."

That came as a shock to me. Al's retirement from the LAPD had lasted all of six months before he'd taken the public defender job.

"You're not retiring?" I asked him.

"Please. I'm going to go freelance."

"Freelance investigation?"

"Yeah. A couple of weeks ago at the Dodger's game, I bumped into Vinnie Hernandez, a guy I knew from the LAPD. Turns out he retired two years ago. Now he's making six figures."

"Freelancing?"

"Exactly."

I poured a sippy cup of orange juice and handed it to Isaac, who had his legs and arms wrapped around my leg.

"Like a private eye?" I asked.

"Vinnie's billing out at a hundred bucks an hour, working for private criminal defense attorneys. The guy's a complete idiot, and in twenty hours a week, he's making twice what I do in forty."

"So you decided to quit."

"You bet. I'm no fool. I'm sick of babysitting public defenders. I'm going to hang out a shingle, print up some business cards, and start living large."

I mopped up the sippy cup's worth of orange juice that Isaac had just expertly spilled all over the floor and opened a cupboard full of pots and pans.

"Does that mean that now I have to pay you a hundred bucks to get you to make a call for me?" I said.

"That depends, Juliet of the black leather miniskirt." Was he never going to let me live down my youthful indiscretions? Why oh why had I ever thought that skirt was an appropriate thing to show up in on my first day of work?

Isaac went to work on the pots and pans, drowning out Al's next question.

I put a finger to my ear and shouted, "What?"

"Do you want to go into business with me?" Al replied, also shouting.

At that moment, Isaac grabbed a wooden spoon and smacked me with it on the shin, as hard as he could. I grabbed his fat little hand and wrenched the wooden spoon out of it. "No!" I yelled.

"That's pretty definite," Al said.

"What? No. I mean, I don't know. Wow. What an offer. You're really asking me to become a PI?"

I could swear I heard him roll his eyes. "I'm not talking *The Rockford Files* here. I plan on doing your basic criminal investigation. Skip tracers. Maybe some death penalty work. That kind of thing."

"Wow," I said again, not particularly articulately.

"Don't answer me now. We'll get together sometime soon and talk about it. What did you call me for?"

I filled him in on Bobby's death.

"What is *with* you, Juliet?"

"Excuse me?"

"You're like some kind of human Ebola virus or something. How many dead people do you trip over in the course of a week?"

"Funny. Ha ha. So, will you call up your friends at the LAPD and find out what's going on with the investigation? Mostly, I want to know if they're considering it a murder or a suicide."

"Yeah, I'll make some calls. Give me a day or two, okay?"

"Great. Thanks, Al."

After I hung up the phone, I scooped Isaac up, disengaged him from the drum kit he'd made out of the set of Magnalite cookware I'd gotten from my mother as a wedding present, and went in search of his older sister. I found her in her bedroom, carefully pasting bits of colored paper, yarn, and other scraps to a large sheet of poster board.

"Get him out of here!" she shrieked, draping her body over her art.

"Oh, Ruby, don't be so melodramatic. He's not going to do anything."

The words had barely left my mouth when Isaac grabbed a plastic bottle of Elmer's glue and squeezed a huge white puddle out on the carpet.

"Oh my God! No, Isaac! No!" I shouted.

"You see! You see! He ruins everything!" Ruby echoed my yell. I mopped up the spill, yanked her squirming brother out the door, and shut it firmly behind me.

"Well, clearly you're not going to be playing with Ruby this afternoon," I said. "Look, kid, I need to do some work on the computer. Your daddy's going to be home from his meeting in about an hour. Can you think of something to do by yourself until he gets home?"

"TV?" my angelic child suggested with a bat of his eyelashes.

"Right. Fine. As a special treat."

He ran to the couch and scrambled up. I sorted through our bedraggled video collection until I found a copy of *Color Me Barbra*, a Barbra Streisand TV special from some time in the 1960s. Ruby loved it because she was obsessed with show tunes. Isaac liked it because La Streisand does half the numbers inside of a tiger cage. With real tigers.

I set Bobby's laptop up next to my computer and connected it to our home network with an Ethernet cable. Now I could freely copy documents and files from it onto my own hard drive. I went back into his correspondence folder and spent the next half-hour skimming through letters to clients and friends until I found something. I had a feeling about it even before I opened it, because the document wasn't titled like the other letters in the folder, with the recipient's name and the date. It was just called "Letter #1."

The letter started out somewhat cryptically. Underneath Bobby's stan-

dard letterhead—an old-time circus strongman holding up his address—
the salutation read simply, "Hello."

> *I don't even know how to address this letter. Dear Mom seems
> wrong; I already have a mom, and you probably wouldn't want
> me to call you that. Calling you by your name seems so formal.
> So, maybe I'll just leave it blank. I guess you've probably figured
> out who this letter is from. My name is Bobby Katz, and I'm your
> birth son. I was born on February 15, 1972. I was placed for
> adoption on that very day through Jewish Family Services.*
>
> *I've had a pretty happy life. My adoptive family gave me the best
> of everything, and any problems I have had were my fault, not
> theirs. I didn't even know I was adopted until I had some genetic
> testing done in preparation for my wedding (I'm getting married in
> six months to a wonderful girl named Betsy). Once I found out
> about myself, I registered with the State of California Reunion
> Registry. I was hoping that you might have done so, too, and was
> pretty disappointed to find that you hadn't. I understand, though,
> that it's pretty common for birth parents not to be registered—most
> people don't even know the registry exists!*
>
> *I won't tell you how I found you—I don't think it would be
> fair to the people who helped me. But I did find you. And I'm
> hoping you'll be willing to write or E-mail me or maybe even to
> meet me.*

The letter went on to describe Bobby's job and interests, and he closed
with another plea to his birth mother to write or E-mail him.

I leaned back in my chair, touched by the hope with which Bobby had
sent this letter to someone who, for all he knew, had no interest in establishing any kind of contact with him whatsoever. How must it have felt
to find out, as an adult, that you weren't who you thought you were? Or,
at the very least, that some of the basic tenets of your life and sense of self
were lies? Had Bobby's mother refused his attempts at contact? Had he
responded to that rejection with despair? Had he even *sent* the letter? Why
wasn't there an address?

My reverie was interrupted by my growing consciousness of a suspicious
sound: silence. My house was never silent, except when my children were

either asleep or engaged in some act of nursery terrorism. I hustled out to the family room, where I found Isaac sitting, slack-jawed and glassy-eyed, staring at Barbra's flaring nostrils and purple boa. I tiptoed away. I put my ear to Ruby's door. She was singing softly to herself; the tune seemed to be her own version of "Bohemian Rhapsody," which her father had for some reason considered it not merely appropriate but desirable to teach her.

It was a miracle. My children were actually giving me a period of uninterrupted peace.

I went back to my desk and sat for a minute, tapping my finger against the keys. The police had confiscated the contents of Bobby's filing cabinet, so there was no way for me to see if he'd ever gotten a reply from his birth mother. However, I could check to see if he'd gotten an E-mail. I'd already noticed that Bobby kept careful track of his paper files and the documents on his computer. It stood to reason that he would do the same with his E-mail records.

He didn't disappoint me. His E-mail program had a carefully organized archiving system. Unfortunately, because I didn't know his mother's name or E-mail address, it was going to be a challenge sifting through the hundreds of messages in the "Personal Correspondence" archive to find which one might have come from her. Using the program's Find command, I started searching by E-mail subject heading. "Birth Mother" came up with nothing, as did "Mother." "Mom," however, led me to a series of E-mails from Bobby's sister Michelle, complaining about how their mother had criticized Michelle's new living room furniture. Apparently, Michelle had bought it at IKEA, and Dr. Katz felt constrained to point out that in Sweden, where the chain had begun, and which the good doctor had recently visited to deliver a paper on "Fluorescent In Situ Hybridization," IKEA was considered about as classy as Wal-Mart. Michelle had written to Bobby seeking reassurance 1. That IKEA was a reasonable place to buy a couch, and 2. That their mother was a bitch. I searched through Bobby's "Sent Mail" file and found that he had responded to both in the affirmative.

Subject headings "Adoption," "Adopt," and "Adopted" led nowhere. Finally, I decided I had to find a more efficient way to search. I launched Bobby's Internet browser and looked up his favorite sites. The California Reunion Registry was listed, but I already knew that Bobby hadn't found his mother through that site. Nothing else in the favorite sites list looked promising, so I clicked down the Go button, hoping he had given his browser a large cache. He had. The browser allowed me to track the last two hundred websites he'd visited immediately before he died.

Bobby had searched a medical site for a cure for athlete's foot (I made a mental note not to shower at the gym) and bought a Palm Pilot online. He'd posted a review of the new John Grisham on Amazon.com (he liked it okay but wasn't thrilled) and bid on a set of golf clubs on eBay. None of these activities, I thought, was that of a man about to kill himself. As of a day or two before his death, Bobby had planned to be around long enough to monitor a five-day online auction and receive a package that would take three to seven days to arrive. If he *had* committed suicide, it had been a spur-of-the-moment decision. I wondered if the police had come across this information.

Bobby had also, I noticed, checked his I-Groups home page over and over again. I-Groups is one of the many sites on the web that allows people with similar interests to join up in E-mail circles. The site has hundreds of different groups, some open to the public, some open only to those approved by the members of the group. Being part of an E-mail circle through a service like I-Groups lets members send messages to the group as a whole, instead of having to cc each individual member. I was part of a couple of these circles myself. Friends from college and I had been E-mailing for quite some time. When I was pregnant with Ruby, I'd joined a list for mothers due in the same month and spent a very self-indulgent and satisfying nine months comparing stretch marks and hemorrhoids. For a while, I'd participated in an I-Group for "recovering attorneys" but found the "support" I got a bit over the top. I mean, it wasn't like I'd weaned myself off heroin; all I'd done was quit my job.

I held my breath as I selected the I-Groups link in Bobby's Go menu. If he hadn't saved his password as a cookie to be entered automatically when the page came up, there would be no way for me to check his I-Groups home page and access the archives of posted messages.

I was lucky. Like me, Bobby was not particularly security conscious. His home page showed just one I-Group. It was called Parentfinder@I-Groups .com. I clicked over to the archive and began sifting through the messages. Bobby had joined the group almost three months before. His initial message informed the other members that he was an adoptee looking for his birth parents, who were not registered with the California Reunion Registry. He asked for advice about alternative ways to find them. And boy did he get it.

As I scrolled down through the many replies to Bobby's initial posting,

I was interrupted by the scourge of the work-at-home parent: her children. Ruby and Isaac wandered into the room. Isaac was naked from the waist down.

"Isaac! Where are your pants?" We'd only recently convinced Isaac to lose his diapers. It had taken about forty pounds of M&M's doled out one by one as a reward for each successful bathroom excursion.

"They're in the toilet," Ruby said as if I were an idiot for even asking.

"Oh, no. Did you go to the bathroom, Isaac?" He nodded happily, sucking on the two middle fingers of his left hand. I stifled my gag reflex and hustled him back to the bathroom. I fished his pants out of the toilet and briefly considered throwing them directly in the trash. They were from Baby Gap, however, and not even a toilet full of poop justified tossing out a thirty-dollar pair of toddler jeans. Instead, I dumped them into the washing machine. As I scrubbed my disgusting yet adorable boy from tush to fingertips, I wondered, not for the first time, if I'd still be wiping the kid's behind when he was in graduate school. Probably not. Probably by the time he had his bar mitzvah, he'd be able to handle his own potty needs.

I'd clearly ignored the kids for long enough. I gazed longingly at the TV, but guilt won out over my desire to keep reading Bobby's E-mail. Instead, I spilled a load of blocks and miniature cars on the carpet. I groaned softly as I sat down. I know there are some mothers who love nothing more than spending hours finger painting and making Play-Doh castles. I'm not one of them. Don't get me wrong, I adore my kids. I love them with a combination of ferocity and obsession that can be overwhelming both to them and to me. But playing with them can be skull-crushingly tedious.

Ruby and I played with the blocks while Isaac zoomed his Hot Wheels around us. I did my best to convince her not to bellow in protest when he dared approach our construction site. I was less successful at getting him to stop talking about how his cars were going to shoot and kill each other. We compromised by agreeing that the red Formula One could beat up the other cars, as long as he gave their booboos kisses afterward.

After half an hour or so, my garage built out of blocks was teetering dangerously, and I wasn't sure if I had the energy to rebuild. Luckily, Peter showed up just as I was beginning to lose focus. As soon as he'd gotten down on his hands and knees and begun renovating my structurally unsound building, I slipped back to my computer.

Within an hour, I'd made a long list of potential means of finding a birth parent who didn't want to be found. Bobby's E-mail pals had provided him with names and numbers of private investigators, online search services, and a few organizations dedicated to furthering an individual's access to his or her biological and familial history. According to his E-mails to the group, Bobby had contacted the organizations first, so that's what I did. I checked out their websites. By and large, they seemed fairly innocuous, mostly providing the same kind of support that Bobby had gotten from his I-Group.

One was a little more intense. This site, called www.righttoknow.net, was dedicated to assisting people whose birth parents were not just unknown but were actively keeping their identities secret. The site offered more arcane investigative services, including instructions on performing skip traces and credit card searches. It offered the names of investigators who specialized in "fugitive parents." At the bottom of the home page was an E-mail address. I copied it and then clicked over to Bobby's E-mail program. I searched his archives for any message from that address. Pay dirt.

Over the past couple of months, Bobby had been E-mailing with someone named Louise, the founder of Right to Know. From her E-mails, I pieced together that Bobby had contacted her through the website and asked for help with finding his birth mother. Early on in their correspondence, she told him that she, too, lived in Los Angeles, and that she had sources for finding parents in the area. Louise sent Bobby E-mails almost daily. I read through a pile of them before I found one that sounded promising. In it, Louise told Bobby that she had "good news" and "information." She asked him to meet her where she worked, at the Starbucks across the street from the Westside Pavilion, a mall in West L.A.

I copied all the important information onto my computer. It had taken me all of an afternoon to get within one step of Bobby's birth parents. The Internet seems to have been designed to allow people to spy on one another. It certainly has made the private detective's job significantly easier. I found this somewhat troubling, although I was less concerned with the death of privacy than with the possibility that Al would find a significant portion of his new business usurped by a website's offering to find anything about anybody at bargain basement rates.

6

THE NEXT MORNING, after I'd dropped Ruby off at preschool, Isaac and I headed out to the Westside Pavilion. I guess it probably says something about my approach to detective work that before I went to question Louise, I did a little shopping. I had never actually bought new clothes for Isaac. He'd spent the first two and a half years of his life wearing Ruby's hand-me-downs. Suddenly, however, as if in concert with his burgeoning interest in firearms, he'd begun to refuse to allow me to dress him in her old pink overalls, flowered T-shirts, and pastel leggings, although for some reason he was still perfectly happy to sleep in her Little Mermaid nightgown.

Isaac and I stocked up on navy blue shirts, royal blue pants, and indigo sweatshirts from the sale racks in the various baby stores. I hung my purchases over the handle of his stroller, and we rolled out of the mall onto Pico Boulevard at the corner of Westwood Boulevard. There, directly across Pico from us, was a Starbucks. Across Westwood, and at the other end of the block, was another Starbucks. Now, granted, Westwood is a busy street, and they were at either end of a fairly long block, but still—was there really enough latte business for two identical coffeehouses?

"Shall we flip a coin, buddy?" I asked Isaac.

He looked up at me quizzically. "Okay," he said.

"Heads we go to the one down the block, tails we go to the one on the other side of the street."

It came up tails. Isaac was fascinated. "Do it again," he said.

"Okay." It came up heads.

"Third one breaks the tie, buddy." Tails.

I waited for a pause in the traffic and then, shopping bags flapping in our wake, jaywalked as fast as I could across the street. Isaac shrieked delightedly at both the speed of our run and the fact that we were very clearly breaking the "cross at the corner" rule I'd so carefully drilled into his head.

I walked up to the counter and ordered a tall, fat, skinny, wide something or other and asked the pierced young thing behind the bar if Louise worked at the store. A dark-haired woman with bad skin, who was studying the foaming action she was getting from her steam-valve machine, lifted her head at the sound of my voice. I smiled at her, sure that I'd found my Louise.

The boy with the studded eyebrow to whom I'd asked my question said, "No, I don't know any Louise."

"Are you sure? I know there's a Louise working either here or at the Starbucks down the block. Is your manager around? Maybe I could ask him or her?"

The boy shrugged his shoulders and jerked his head toward the woman. The thick ring in his nose jiggled with the action, and he reached up a hand to steady it. God help me if my children decide to have themselves pierced. Peter swears that the fad will be over by the time Ruby is a teenager, but I am convinced that will only be because they will have come up with something worse, like voluntary amputation, or recreational trepanning.

The dark-haired woman came over to me, her face blank. Her cheeks were pitted and scarred, and a few angry pimples covered her chin and nestled in the corners of her mouth. "I'm the supervisor. Can I help you?"

"I'm looking for someone named Louise. Does she work here?"

"We don't have anybody by that name," she said.

"Oh. Well, maybe it's the Starbucks at the end of the block. I'll try there."

"Don't forget your latte," the pierced boy called. I went back for the cup and balanced it on the handle of the stroller as I tried to open the door. I couldn't manage to hold the coffee, open the door, and push the stroller through at the same time, and neither employee seemed particularly interested in helping me. Finally, I tossed the latte in the trash and, holding the door open with one hand, pushed Isaac and his stroller out with the other. I'd get a coffee at the next Starbucks.

Isaac and I reenacted our dangerous and illegal asphalt traverse and headed to café number two. The next Starbucks was a slightly larger version of the first, with a few extra tasteful banquettes and little round tables. This time, the person with the nose ring who took my order was female. She shook her head immediately at my question about Louise and handed me my extra-foamy mocha with a smile that seemed much too sweet for her severe haircut and jewelry. I pulled Isaac out of his stroller, handed him a madeleine, and fed him the foam from my coffee.

I turned to ask the coffee girl if she was sure that there was no Louise when Isaac's bellow of rage made me spin around in my chair.

"What happened?" I asked, checking him over for broken bones.

"My cookie!" he wailed.

"What about your cookie?"

"It got in your coffee!"

"How did it get in my coffee?"

"I tried to scoop the foam, but it melted my cookie!"

I tried to comfort him, but finally just got him another cookie. His face broke into a grin to rival that of the Cheshire Cat. It had been an elaborate ploy to weasel another madeleine out of me.

"Okay, cookie boy, let's go."

We wandered back down the street toward the mall and our car. As we got closer to the other Starbucks, I kept thinking of the supervisor with the bad skin. I was sure that when I'd first said the name Louise, she'd raised her head in recognition. I mentally kicked myself in the pants for being so dense. A pseudonym. It was entirely possible that the name Louise was merely an alias. Given the fact that some of the "suggestions" on the website seemed a bit on the gray side of legality, it was reasonable that "Louise" might not want to be directly associated with it. She would want to avoid liability, not to mention the wrath of parents whose identities she'd given away over their objections.

Once more I hauled Isaac back across the street. I walked into the store and up to the front of the counter, without waiting in line.

"Hey! There's a line here, you know," a voice snarled at me. I ignored the muscle-bound man in the shiny suit who'd yelled at me and caught the dark-haired woman's eye.

"Hi," I said. "I'd like to talk to you."

She flushed and shook her head. "Sorry, we're busy."

"I'll wait," I said and leaned against the counter. Isaac started kicking the glass pastry case. Helpful child.

She glared at me and then, finally, shrugged her shoulders and motioned for another young employee to step into her spot at the register. She ducked out from behind the counter and led me to a table in the far corner of the café.

I pulled a few board books out of the basket of the stroller and settled Isaac on a bench not too far from where the woman had sat down. Between the books and the sugar packets on the table, he was set for a few minutes at least.

"Hi, Candace," I said, reading the name tag pinned to her chest.

She didn't answer.

"I think we have a friend in common."

"Yeah? Who?" She sounded like she didn't think it was very likely.

"Bobby Katz."

Her face flushed again, and she looked down at her fingernails. They were bitten red and raw.

"You know Bobby?" she murmured, the harshness gone from her voice.

I realized at that moment that she hadn't heard. I dreaded being the one to tell her. I reached out my hand and grasped hers.

"I'm so sorry to have to tell you this," I began.

She jerked her hand out of mine. "What?" Her voice was a hollow croak.

"Bobby died ten days ago. I'm so sorry."

Her skin seemed to gray before my eyes. The acne and scars stood out crimson against the ashen pallor. "What? How?"

I took a breath before launching into the ugly details. I also lowered my voice so that Isaac wouldn't hear. "It's not real clear. What we know for now is that he was found dead in his car along the PCH, just south of Santa Monica Canyon. He was holding a gun, and it looks like it was probably a suicide."

"No!" The people standing in line for coffee looked our way at the explosive sound of her voice.

Isaac whined softly, "Mama?"

"It's okay, honey," I said. I walked over and gave him a hug. He was making neat stacks of sugar, Equal and Sweet'N Low, alternating the white, blue, and pink packets. "You keep playing, okay?"

He nodded, and I went back to Candace. Her face was buried in her hands, and she was worrying the pimples on her forehead with her fingers.

"I couldn't figure out why he hasn't been answering my E-mail. I've been writing like ten times a day for over a week," she said.

I realized then that I'd been so busy reviewing his archives that I hadn't thought of checking Bobby's E-mail account for *new* messages that had come in since his death. I made a mental note to log on from his laptop once I got home and download all his pending messages.

"Candace, I'm hoping you can give me some information."

She looked at me suspiciously.

"I'm doing a little checking around for Betsy, Bobby's fiancée. We're trying to figure out what was going on with Bobby in the last couple of months of his life."

At the sound of Betsy's name, Candace's jaw tightened.

"I can't help you."

"I think you can. I know Bobby found you through Right to Know's website. I know you were helping Bobby find his birth parents. Can you tell me a little more about your organization?"

She leveled a suspicious gaze in my direction. "Like what?"

"Well, for example, you're an organization for adoptees looking for their birth parents, right?"

"Not only. We have some birth parents, too. Anybody who's looking for information. But, yeah, it's mostly lost children."

The term surprised me.

"What kind of information do you provide?"

"RTK is really a clearinghouse, more than anything else. We pool information, get ideas on where and how to look. That kind of thing."

"And you started it?"

"I got the idea after I spent two years tracking down my birth mother. I ended up finding my family through the Lost Bird Society. They help lost and stolen Indian children find their way home. I'm Lakota. Part. My birth mother is half-Indian. Her mom lived on the rez her whole life."

Now that I looked closely, I thought I could see a trace of American Indian; maybe it was just the dark hair, or the not-quite-prominent cheek-bones.

"Did you find your birth mother?"

Candace shrugged her shoulders. "Yeah, but she didn't want to have anything to do with me. She'd really been co-opted by the dominant culture, you know? But my grandmother, her mother, she was great. I got to know her pretty well before she died. Meeting her was like coming home. If I hadn't been stolen from my people, I might have grown up on the reservation, instead of in Newport Beach."

I resisted the urge to point out that to many people, it might be preferable to grow up in an exclusive beach community rather than a pre-casino-era Indian reservation rife with unemployment and substandard schools and health care. But, then, what did I know about the spiritual vacuum experienced by American Indian children growing up away from their tribes?

"You founded Right to Know to help others in your situation?" I asked.

"Yeah. The thing is, nobody really cares about the kid in all this. Everybody is so worried about the rights of the birth mother and about the adoptive family. But nobody considers that the kid has a right to know who she is, even if her birth mother is trying to hide from her."

"Why?"

"Why what?"

"Why does a child have a right to know? If the birth mother gave her up and doesn't want to be contacted, why should the child be told who the mother is?"

Candace glared at me, furious that I'd questioned her orthodoxy.

"Well, the most obvious reason is medical. I mean, look at Bobby. If he hadn't gotten tested, he might have ended up having a baby with that horrible genetic disease, what's it called?"

"Tay-Sachs."

"Yeah, Tay-Sachs. He's lucky; he got tested. But what if he hadn't?"

"Well, his fiancée would have had to have been a carrier, too. But I understand what you're saying. There are lots of genetic diseases that people should have information about."

"You can't imagine what it's like to go get a physical. The doctor starts asking you for all this information about family history, like cancer or diabetes. And you have nothing to say except 'I don't know.' It's terrible," Candace said, banging on the table to punctuate her words. "Why should adopted kids be deprived of medical history information that could save their lives?"

The intensity of her emotions surprised me, and I inadvertently drew back from her. She noticed my reaction and blushed.

I didn't want to make her uncomfortable, so I said in my most reassuring voice, "That's a good point. I've never really thought of that. But couldn't we solve that problem by requiring birth parents to provide medical histories when they relinquish their babies?"

She pushed herself back in her chair and shook her head vigorously. "You don't get it. It's not just the medical stuff. It's about your identity. I'm an Indian. You know what that means? That's the reason I never felt at home in the white man's world." She waved angrily around her at the benches, the carefully selected prints and posters, the little wooden tables, the white coffee drinkers. "My whole life I felt like I didn't belong. And if my birth mother had had her way, I'd have never known why. Well, now I know. I'm a Lakota woman. And nobody can keep that from me. Not even my mother."

She banged her fist on the table, again, hard. Isaac looked up, frightened, and I motioned him over with my hand. He ran up to me and I scooped him into my lap.

"Thank you so much, Candace," I said. "I hadn't thought of these issues before, and I appreciate your taking the time to educate me." We both knew I was buttering her up, but I smiled my sweetest smile anyway. "Betsy, Bobby's fiancée, is desperate to figure out what was happening with him. I understand that you found out something important for Bobby, and that he met you here at the store. I need you to tell me what it was that you told him."

"Why should I tell you? I don't know you. I don't even know Betsy." The name sounded like curdled milk on her tongue.

"Please, Candace. I'm not trying to get you in any trouble. I'm just trying to track Bobby's actions for the period before his death. We need to find out why he killed himself. *If* he killed himself."

She looked at me with narrowed eyes. "Do you think someone murdered him?"

Did I? That seemed even less likely than that the cheerful, optimistic man had committed suicide. "I don't know. That's one of the things I'm trying to find out."

"What are you, some kind of a detective?"

I paused at that. How much easier it would have been to say, "Yes, right. A detective." Instead, I shook my head. "I'm just a friend. Candace, please. What did you find out?"

"How do I know you're not trying to pin all this on me?" she said, crossing her arms over her shelflike chest.

That brought me up short. Pin what on her? Bobby's death? I shook my head. "I'm not trying to pin anything on anybody. I'm just trying to find out if Bobby ever found his birth parents. And I know you can help me."

"Mama," Isaac whimpered. The tone of our conversation was obviously frightening him. I couldn't continue this in front of him. I wrapped him in my arms and gave him a kiss. Then I dug around in my bag for one of the business cards Peter had made up for me the previous Christmas. They were a pale moss green with my name, telephone numbers, and E-mail address engraved in a darker shade of the same color.

"Here's my number. Call me if you decide you're willing to talk. In the meantime, you'll forgive me if I turn your name over to the detectives investigating Bobby's—" I looked down at Isaac in my lap and bit off the last word of my sentence.

"No!" Candace said. Then, seemingly embarrassed at her own vehemence, she continued, "I'd prefer not to be involved. For the sake of Right to Know."

She paused for a moment and then, leaning forward, whispered, "All I can tell you is that Bobby was born at Haverford Memorial Hospital in Pasadena. That's all I know. But it should be enough for you to find his mother."

7

*A*L'S NEW OFFICE turned out to be a phone line, a card table, and a dented filing cabinet shoved into one corner of his garage in Westminster, a small city just south of downtown L.A.

"Nice digs," I said.

I'd called him on my way home from meeting Candace to ask his advice on how to find the names of all the babies born at Haverford Memorial Hospital on February 15, 1972. I'd also asked him what he'd heard from his friends on the force.

"It looks like a suicide," he had said.

"But they're not sure?"

"There are some ambiguities."

"Like what? Explain to me what they look for when they're evaluating a suspicious death to determine if it's suicide or murder."

"A variety of things. The presence or absence of a weapon."

"And they found a gun in the car."

"In his hand, actually."

"Right, in his hand. What else?"

"They look at the trajectory of the bullet. You know, could a person have shot himself at that particular angle."

"Did they do that in Bobby's case?"

"Yup, but it didn't get them very far. The trajectory is consistent with suicide, but that obviously doesn't rule out murder."

"Anything else?"

"Sure. The presence or absence of fingerprints in the car."

"And?"

"And there were fingerprints. Lots of them. Your friend had a lot of passengers."

I sighed. "Anything conclusive? What about residue on his fingertips? If he had fired the gun himself, wouldn't there be gunshot residue?"

"You're getting good at this, girl. Sure, there would."

"And was there?"

"Some."

"Some?"

"Some. Not as much as you might expect, but enough to be consistent with suicide."

"Basically, what you're telling me is that there's not enough conclusive evidence either way."

"Right now, the forensic evidence could lead to either conclusion: suicide or death by person or persons unknown."

"Well, where does that leave the cops? What do they do next?"

"That depends. There was no note, so they could treat the death as a murder, investigate the family, that kind of thing."

"And will they?"

"Maybe. It depends how many other murders the detectives have on their plates."

I told Al about Bobby's online purchases. "Why would someone contemplating suicide buy a Palm Pilot?" I asked. "It doesn't make sense."

"You're right. It does seem unlikely. But maybe it was a spur-of-the-moment kind of thing. I'll tell you what I'll do. I'll call my friend and suggest that someone check into Bobby's credit card bills in the days before his death. They've probably already done it, but it's worth a word."

"Thanks, Al."

"No problem. I'll let you know what I find out about the hospital, too."

Al called two days after our telephone conversation and invited me over for a "consultation." I'd left Isaac with Peter—they had big plans to check out the new titles at Golden Apple Comics—dropped Ruby off at preschool, and headed down to Westminster.

I sat down in a white vinyl chair Al brought out from the kitchen for me.

"So, how's business?" I asked.

"Getting there. Listen, have you given any more thought to my idea?"

"You mean about joining you in this flourishing endeavor?" I asked, waving my hand around the garage.

"Hey, this is only temporary. Pretty soon I'll be able to afford office space, but until then, the wife said if I'm going to be home all day, the least I can do is get out from under her feet."

"I don't know, Al. It looks like a one-man operation to me."

"This is just the beginning. Like I told you, I'm going to start doing defense investigation, maybe some death penalty work. I could really use someone like you—someone whose legal experience would complement my investigative skills. It would be worth your while, Juliet. At a hundred and fifty bucks an hour, the money's going to be rolling in."

I nodded, not wanting to rib him anymore when he clearly had such faith in me. "Why would my legal experience be useful to you? I don't know much of anything about investigation. That's why I'm always bugging *you* for information."

He leaned back in his chair and propped his feet up on the card table. He was wearing pale blue Sansabelt slacks with a slight flare, a gold shirt, and navy socks with white clocks. His shoes seemed to have been made out of the same material as my chair. I wondered if they came as a set.

"Because you're a defense attorney. You know how to put together a case. You know what kinds of things to investigate, what's relevant, what's not."

"But the lawyers you're working with will tell you what they want investigated. They'll put together their own cases."

"True. But having that added expertise would give us an edge on the competition. And how many times have I heard you say that two-thirds of the criminal defense lawyers out there don't know their asses from their elbows? Just because they're paying us doesn't mean they have any idea what we should be doing."

That made sense to me. "But I'm not licensed."

"You don't have to be. That's the beauty of it. I'm a licensed private investigator. You work for me. We call you a defense specialist, or a mitigation specialist if we're doing a death case, and then you don't need to take the investigator's test or do the obligatory hours. Or, if you want to, you can apply for your license, take the test, and then do your hours with me."

The idea did have a certain appeal. Since I'd quit work, I'd found myself increasingly bored and frustrated with staying home. I'd left my job because I thought raising my kids myself was more important than working, but sometimes it was difficult to imagine that my sighing, listless presence around the house was really doing Ruby and Isaac any good. The only time I'd been really happy over the last couple of years was when I'd been doing what amounted to investigative work. Only then did I feel like I was taking advantage of my skills and my intelligence. At the same time, however, I wasn't ready to give up and go back to work even if pushing a stroller might not have been doing it for me.

"The whole point of quitting the defender's office was that I wanted to be home with my kids. If I wanted to go back to work, I'd go back to being a lawyer."

"Aren't your kids in school by now?" Al asked.

"Ruby's in preschool. But Isaac's just a baby. Almost. He's two and a half."

"He'll be in school soon, too. What are you going to do with yourself while the kids aren't home? Are you planning on going back to the defender's office then?

He'd hit the nail on the head. What was I going to do when Isaac started school next year? Going back to a public defender's rigorous schedule didn't appeal to me. Someone had to pick the kids up every day after school, and Peter's schedule was just too unpredictable. If I went back to my job, I wasn't going to be able to be there when the kids came home. I'd show up in time for dinner, like I'd done when Ruby was a baby. I hadn't wanted to do that then, and it wasn't looking any better to me now. On the other hand, I wasn't one of those people who could while away the school day at aerobics classes or volunteering at the local hospital. I was going to have to find something else to keep my mornings busy.

The idea was sounding better all the time. But was I really ready? I didn't think so. "I don't know, Al. I'll think about it. Anyway, are you going to charge me a hundred and fifty bucks an hour to tell me how to find the mothers who gave birth at Haverford Memorial on February 15, 1972?"

Al smiled. "Nope. You're still on the discount plan."

"Thanks. So, how do I go about tracking down the mothers?"

"You read this list." He swung his feet off the table and pushed a sheet of paper across to me. On it were the names of seven women.

"What's this?"

"The mothers who gave birth at Haverford Memorial Hospital on February 15, 1972."

"No way! How'd you get this?"

He smiled mysteriously. "Secret of the trade, I fear. Available only to other investigators."

"C'mon, Al!"

"Come work for me and find out."

I kicked his ankle, hard.

"Okay, here's what I did. It wasn't that difficult. The hospital keeps records of births, obviously. Nowadays, those records are all computerized, and if you're allowed access, or if you can somehow get into the system, the records are there at a touch of a button. However, because of patient confidentiality, it's a challenge, to say the least, to get into the system. We were lucky, though, and Haveford Memorial never bothered to computerize its old records. I figured right off the records probably wouldn't be stored at the hospital—they take up too much space. I called a few of the larger document storage facilities and found the one the hospital uses to store its old records. It wasn't too far from here, so I just took a little drive on over."

"And they let you in to look at the documents?"

"Well, let's just say that a well-placed gratuity did the trick. You owe me a hundred bucks."

I got out my checkbook and wrote him a check, which he pocketed with a gracious "Thank you."

"No, thank *you*," I said.

"Lucky for us the records were very well-organized. I found the births recorded by day and date."

Together we went over the list. Four of the women who had given birth to babies on Bobby's birthday had had girls. The mother of one of the three boys was named Michiko Tanazaki. I figured I could safely rule her out. That left two women, a Brenda Fessler who in 1972 was nineteen years old and a Susan Masters, who was twenty-six.

Al promised to run a skip trace on the two and happily accepted the check I wrote him to cover the costs of the search. Then the two of us went inside to say hello to his wife.

Jeanelle Hockey was a lovely, dark-skinned woman with perfectly ironed hair who favored twin sets and knee-length skirts. In many ways, she seemed an unlikely mate for Al, who, with his golf clothes and military haircut, was the last man you'd imagine in an interracial marriage. The two had met in the late 1960s, when he was a uniformed police officer, and she a civilian employee of the Los Angeles Police Department. They'd been married almost thirty years and had three daughters in their twenties.

When we walked in from the garage, Jeanelle was going over Al's gun collection with a pink feather duster. I'd only been to Al's house a few times, and the sight of the racks of shotguns and cases of handguns and vintage pistols still made my skin crawl. He could tell I was nonplussed, perhaps because of the grimace on my face and the loud retching noises I made.

"Want to hold one?" he asked, deadpan.

"No! What is it with boys and guns? Isaac's as obsessed with them as you are. Why? Can you explain this to me? Is it a phallic thing?"

Jeanelle smiled and said, "If it's phallic, then I don't know what that says about me. I've been a target shooter for years. And our youngest, Robyn, is nationally ranked in the biathlon. She was an alternate for the Olympic team."

"Wow," I said. "What's that? Shooting and biking?"

"Shooting and skiing," Al said. "Robyn's an incredible athlete. She's at Cal State Northridge now, but she's thinking about Quantico."

"The FBI?"

"Yup. She'd make a great cop."

Jeanelle handed me a large photograph of a beautiful, carefully made up young woman aiming a rifle. Her curly brown hair was held off her face with a tortoiseshell clip, and her nails were long and painted a brilliant shade of aquamarine.

Al's daughters were all gorgeous and successful. And unmarried. A glance at the artillery around the room made it all too obvious why. Their father probably blasted a hole in any guy who dared show up at the front door.

WHEN I GOT home from Al's, I found my house empty and the light flashing on the answering machine. The first message was from Peter, telling me that he and Isaac would pick Ruby up from school and then go to the zoo at Griffith Park. I heaved a sigh of relief at having been spared the trip to that grim place with its tiny cages and palpable air of animal desperation.

The rest of the messages were from Betsy. She'd left four, and by the last one she was hysterical. By replaying her messages a few times, I managed to figure out that David Katz had come by for Bobby's things and had been upset to find the computer missing. I tried to call her and had the eerie shock of getting Bobby's voice, asking me to leave a message at the tone. He sounded absolutely like himself, down to the trademark instruction to "make the most of" my day. The hair on the back of my neck stood up. For a moment, I was surprised that Betsy had left his voice on the machine, but then I considered what I would have done under the same circumstances. I didn't think I could have borne to erase Peter's voice, either.

I debated leaving a message but decided to go to the apartment instead. Betsy had sounded so distraught that it wouldn't have surprised me if she were immobilized in bed.

She was anything but. I found her standing in the middle of her living room with the apartment door wide open. She was swigging water from a bottle and pacing frantically back and forth.

"Betsy?" I said.

"Oh God! Thank God it's you. Tell me you have the laptop. Do you have it? Did you bring the laptop? Is it with you?" Her words tumbled out of her mouth in an agitated rush.

"I have it." I held up the computer.

"Oh, thank God. I was really freaking out. You have no idea. I mean, that creep was over here basically screaming at me—telling me that if I didn't come up with the laptop he was going to, like, sue me or something. I hate that whole family. Honestly I do. You have no idea. I hate them."

I looked closely at Betsy. She took a mouthful of water and then brushed her hair away with an angry jerk of her hand.

"What are you on, Betsy?" I kept my voice soft and neutral.

She snapped her head in my direction. Her lower lip trembled. "What are you talking about? What are you accusing me of? You're just like them. You're all the same."

I walked over and put my arm around her, and to my surprise, she let me lead her to the couch. She sat down, her leg twitching, and then her face crumpled. She sagged into me and began to cry.

"I'm sorry. God, I'm so sorry. I didn't mean to do this. I just . . . I just couldn't help myself. I was so freaked out by Bobby's brother. I mean, he really scared me. I called you!" She glared at me accusingly.

"I'm sorry. I was out."

"Yeah, well I called you. And I called my goddamn sponsor. Everybody was out. I mean, what am I supposed to do? My boyfriend is dead, goddamn it. I mean, if that didn't make me fall off the wagon I wouldn't be *human*."

"What did you take?"

"Nothing. A couple of pills. Like barely anything. Just to feel a little better. A little hopeful. I mean, what's wrong with that? Do you know how long it's been since I felt good? I'm not even asking for good, goddamn it. Just the, like, absence of pain would be nice for a minute."

I was disgusted with Betsy, despite myself. I know addiction is a disease—one that's difficult and often impossible to cure. Bobby had done it, however, and so had she, at least for a while. It seemed an utter betrayal of his memory and the faith he'd had in her for her to be using. "Maybe it's time to try your sponsor again," I suggested.

She whirled around. "Are you *nuts*? Are you totally insane? What am I going to say? 'Hi, Annie, I'm wired out of my mind. Wanna come over and play?'"

"No, but you can ask for help. Do you want to go back on the meth?"

She stuck her chin out defiantly.

"Do you want this to be the end of your sobriety? Do you want to go to jail? You're still on probation. If your drug test comes up positive, they're going to take you out of the diversion program and send you right back to court. If that happens, you and I both know that there is a very good chance you'll have to serve some time."

Her lip trembled again. "I don't want to go to jail." She began crying in earnest and pointed to a corner table. I walked over and found Annie's pager number taped to the wall above the telephone. I dialed the number and hung up the phone. It rang almost immediately.

THE GRAY-HAIRED, MATRONLY woman from the funeral was in the living room within half an hour. She held Betsy in her arms while the young woman wept. I sat watching them for a moment and then took the laptop back into Bobby's office. I hooked up the modem and launched his E-mail program and web browser. I went to Yahoo.com and set up an E-mail account with a pseudonym for myself. It didn't hurt to be cautious.

I downloaded all his new messages to his laptop and then forwarded the contents of his in-box to my new Yahoo E-mail address. Now I had the messages, and I was the only person who knew I had them.

I found Betsy and Annie still huddled together on the couch.

"This has to get to Bobby's parents," I said, lifting the laptop that I'd zipped into its case.

Annie nodded.

"I don't think she's in any shape to take it over," I said.

"No, I don't think she is."

"Should I do it?" I asked.

Annie nodded, and Betsy just cried harder.

8

OBBY'S BROTHER, DAVID, answered the door of the Katzes' house. It took a moment for him to remember me from the funeral. He invited me in somewhat warily and directed me to the large living room where the shivah had taken place. His mother was sitting on a sleek brown couch, her legs tucked up under her and her spectator pumps carefully lined up on the carpet, under the coffee table. She looked up from the medical journal she was reading and made a halfhearted attempt to rise. Motioning for her not to bother, I sat down in a tweed armchair opposite the couch. The room was entirely furnished in shades of brown and taupe. The carpet was discreetly patterned in various browns, the furniture was all soft earth shades. Even the paintings on the walls were mud-colored. A large, dark landscape of a dry hillside hung over the fireplace, and a series of small oblong prints in tones ranging from a rich cream to an almost black brown hung along the wall over the couch. Dr. Katz herself was dressed in an off-white cashmere turtleneck and a brown wool skirt. She matched her décor perfectly.

"Hello?" she said, doubt in her tone, obviously wondering what I was doing there.

"I'm Juliet Applebaum, a friend and client of Bobby's. I met you at the funeral, although you probably don't remember me."

"Yes, yes, of course." She arched an eyebrow expectantly.

"What can we do for you, Juliet?" David asked.

I lifted the computer bag off the floor an inch or two. "I'm returning Bobby's computer for Betsy. She asked me to bring it to you; I understand you came by their apartment looking for it."

David flushed a bit, as though he were for the first time considering what an outsider might think of his stripping Bobby's fiancée's home of all of its valuables.

"We, um, we just wanted to make sure that Bobby's things were taken care of. Given Betsy's . . . problem."

I handed him the computer. I wasn't going to tell him that I understood his actions, although in a way I guess I did. Betsy's relapse might or might not have had to do with David's visit. I could certainly understand how Bobby's family would be angry with her and suspicious of the role her drug use might have had in his death. On the other hand, given how much money these people obviously had, did they really need to be prying knick-knacks and small appliances out of Betsy's hands? What difference would it make to them if she kept the computer—or sold it to buy methamphetamine for that matter?

"Why didn't she just give me the computer when I was there picking up Bobby's other stuff?" David asked.

"Because I had it," I said, wondering exactly how I was going to explain why.

The two looked at me quizzically. I thought of lying for a moment, telling them that I'd borrowed the computer before Bobby's death, but like I tell Ruby whenever I catch her stretching the truth, there's really nothing quite as embarrassing as when a lie comes back and bites you in the butt.

"I asked Betsy if I could look through Bobby's files."

"Excuse me?" Dr. Katz's voice was sharp. "You were going through my son's computer files?"

"What the hell is this about?" David asked, leaning forward in his chair.

"Betsy and I were hoping that there might be something in Bobby's computer files that would give us an idea of why he killed himself. Or if," I added, trying to sort of slip it in.

Dr. Katz's eyes narrowed. "If?"

I nodded. "It's my understanding that the police have not made a final determination as to suicide or . . . or murder."

Bobby's mother closed her eyes for a moment. "Forgive me, Ms. . . . Ms. . . ." she murmured.

"Applebaum."

"Ms. Applebaum, I'm afraid I still don't understand why you were going through Bobby's personal belongings, or why you imagined that you had the permission to do so."

This time it was my turn to blush. "Betsy gave me permission. As Bobby's fiancée and the cohabitant of his apartment, I felt she had the right to do so." My language was getting as stiff and formal as hers.

"Are you some kind of investigator?" David interjected.

If I had just taken Al up on his offer, I could have simply said "Yes," and that would have been that. "No, but I'm an attorney, and I specialize in criminal law. I've done some . . . some freelance investigation in the past. Informally. I'm doing the same for Betsy."

"What exactly is it that you are doing? And why did you need Bobby's computer?" Bobby's mother asked.

The two looked at me, Dr. Katz's face stern and haughty, her son's heavy with grief and confusion.

"I read through some of Bobby's E-mail, trying to discover whether his search for his birth parents might have something to do with his death."

Dr. Katz's face tightened.

"You should have told him, Mom," David muttered.

She glared at her son. "This is not the time, David," she snapped. Then she turned to me. "And," she said, "did it, in your opinion?"

"Excuse me?" I said.

"Did Bobby's misguided search for his 'birth mother'"—she wrinkled her nose as she said the words—"have anything to do with his death? In your opinion?"

"I don't know yet," I said. "Did Bobby talk to you about his birth mother? Did he tell you whether or not he had found her?" I didn't tell the Katzes that I had all but tracked her down by myself. First I wanted to find out what they knew.

"I was not interested in discussing the issue with my son. Nor am I interested in discussing it now, with you. Bobby told me that he was looking for this woman. I discouraged him. I told him that as she had not been concerned with his welfare when he was an infant, it was unlikely that she'd want any contact with him almost thirty years later. I also told him that neither I nor his father would participate in any further discussion of this adoption nonsense."

"Oh for God's sake, Mom," David said.

She turned on him. "What? For God's sake what? This is your fault, David. Had you just had the decency, the *intelligence*, to keep your mouth shut, none of this would have happened. Before you took upon yourself the role of truth-sayer, Bobby was perfectly happy, as were we all."

"Right. Perfectly happy. He was a drug addict, Mother. A drug addict."

"Addiction is a disease. A disease, what's more, with a strong genetic component."

David jumped out of his seat. "Sure, Mom. None of this is your fault. Bobby took crank because he's genetically inferior. Not because of anything you did. It has nothing to do with the fact that you made him feel like a failure his entire life. It has nothing to do with the fact that you never even bothered to expect him to succeed. No, that's not why the poor schmuck got high. It has nothing to do with *you*."

He pounded out of the room and through the front door, slamming it behind him.

Dr. Katz sat still in her chair for a few moments. Then she turned to me. "I apologize for my son's behavior."

I didn't say anything. I didn't know what to say.

"David is upset. He feels responsible for Bobby's death. He knows he should never have told Bobby about the adoption."

"Why did you keep it a secret, Dr. Katz?"

She paused, as if considering whether to answer. After a moment she said, "We saw no reason to tell him. Bobby was our son. Our feelings for him were in no way different than our feelings for our other children. Highlighting for him the difference would only have hurt him. And hurt him it did. All of this has only served to prove to me that I made the right decision."

"If you don't mind my asking, why did you adopt Bobby?"

"I don't mind," she said, sounding surprised at her own willingness to discuss this with me. "My husband and I had always planned to have four children. But, after my third Caesarean section, my obstetrician discouraged me from undergoing the procedure again. He claimed it was dangerous. I understand now from my daughter that this was unnecessarily conservative advice. Had we known that, Arthur and I would have gone on to have another child of our own."

The regret in her voice was unmistakable.

I didn't know how to respond to this, and she seemed immediately to regret having so clearly indicated how she felt about being forced to adopt when she would rather have given birth to her own baby. We sat silently for a moment. I fidgeted a bit with my feet, crossing and uncrossing my ankles. She sat perfectly still, the only visible motion in her body the slight flare of her nostrils as she inhaled.

Finally, she said, "If there's nothing else I can do for you . . ." Her voice trailed off.

I rose quickly to my feet. "Would you like me to keep you apprised of what I discover?" I asked.

"So you intend to continue to . . . to investigate?" She sounded as though the very word made her skin crawl.

I nodded. "I'm sorry."

She shook her head slightly and then, rising to her feet, led me to the front door.

9

THAT EVENING, PETER announced that he wanted to have a celebratory dinner but refused to tell me what we were celebrating. The four of us went to Giovanni's, an Italian restaurant located in a strip mall not too far from our house. Giovanni's is our favorite restaurant, and we've been regulars for years. Despite the unprepossessing surroundings, the food is fabulous—simple and delicious.

The kids went straight back to the kitchen, where they knew the chef and his mother were sure to slip them some before-dinner *panna cotta* or almond nougat. Peter and I took our usual table and ordered our usual bottle of Chianti.

"What are we celebrating?" I asked, raising my glass.

"Two things. First of all, Parnassus agreed to Tyler's counteroffer. I'm going to do *The Impaler*. And they're already talking about a twenty-or thirty-million-dollar budget."

"Wow! That's fabulous. And they caved on your quote?" Hollywood screenwriters spend their lives trying to raise their "quotes," the amount they are paid per picture.

"Not by as much as Tyler asked, but by enough. Definitely enough. We're a little closer to buying that house."

"Peter! I'm so proud of you." I was dying to get our family out of the duplex apartment where Peter and I had been living since we moved to L.A. Every time we put aside enough money for the down payment on a house, however, real estate prices shot a little higher. By now they were stratospheric, and I was beginning to lose hope. This was very good news.

"Yup, I'll be bringing home some bacon now," my husband said.

"You're amazing. Really." I kissed him on the cheek. "Without you, we'd be in the gutter." Without him, I would probably have stayed at my fancy law firm and be raking in the high six figures by now. But I wouldn't have been happy. Not for a minute.

"So what's going on with this thing with your trainer?"

I brought Peter up to date on what I'd found out. I described the complicated situation with Bobby's adoption and how I had narrowed down the list of possible birth mothers to two. I also told him about Candace and her crusade.

"Pretty intense," Peter said.

"No kidding."

"You know, sometimes I wonder. If you have kids, and you adopt another, is it really possible to love the adopted kid as much?"

"I suppose it must be. For some people. I don't think the Drs. Katz succeeded very well, though."

"It must be hard. I mean, think about how much time we spend talking about how much Ruby looks like you, or about how Isaac has my ability to focus on an issue."

"Focus? I think *obsess* is a better word for it."

"Semantics. Anyway, we're always talking about how much they're like you, or like me. How many times have you said that Isaac looks like your dad? Isn't that a big part of why we love them so much?"

I took a sip of wine and considered that. "I don't know. I think it might be part of *how* we love them, but not *why*. With an adopted child, you just have a different *how*, if you see what I mean. You don't love him any less. Just differently, the way we love each of ours differently."

Peter shrugged. "Maybe. I guess we'll probably never know. Anyway, it sounds like you think the adoption might be related to Bobby's suicide."

"If it was a suicide."

"Is there still any doubt? What are the cops saying?"

"I'm not sure, but I think they're still considering it a suspicious death." I told Peter about Bobby's online purchases, and he agreed that the behavior didn't sound like that of a man about to kill himself. "Al made another call to one of his friends. I'm hoping he can prod the cops into looking at Bobby's case a little more closely."

"How is Al? How's his new business?"

"Okay, I guess. Oh. Ha. You'll never believe this. It's the most ridiculous thing. He wants me to go into business with him."

Peter looked at me seriously. "Why is that so ridiculous?"

"What? Me, go into business as a private eye? Like Hercule Poirot? Or Cordelia Gray? Or Matlock?"

"I don't think it's such a nutty idea for you to team up with Al to do some investigation. It's clear you have a knack for it, don't you think? Without you, the cops would never have solved Abigail Hathaway's murder or the Fraydle Finkelstein thing. Why *not* turn this skill of yours into a career?"

"Because I *have* a career. Or had one. I don't want another. Anyway, I'm supposed to be home raising the kids, remember?"

He shrugged. "You decided that you couldn't be a half-time public defender. Maybe you could be a half-time investigator."

"It would never work. What would I do? Sit around Al's empty garage helping him polish his gun collection? I have better things to do with my time."

"Like?"

"Like car pool! Like playdates!"

"That reminds me," he said. "Since I'm getting back to work, you get to take Ruby and Isaac to Ari's birthday party tomorrow. I've got a meeting with the studio executive assigned to my project." He reached into his pocket and handed me an invitation printed with a pattern of mottled green, brown, and black.

"Tell me this isn't *camouflage*," I said.

IS IT ONLY in Los Angeles that people would do this? Or is it because Ruby's classmate Ari's parents were from Israel, where they take for granted that the army is a part of life? Whatever the reason, the party was like something out of a movie: *Rambo* or *The Guns of Navarone*. Isaac had never been so happy in his entire life.

The playroom of the birthday boy's house was decorated in brown and green streamers. The party hats perched jauntily on the children's heads were little green berets. G.I. Joe himself was there, though he was actually more of a G.I. Jacob. Ari's uncle, who had recently mustered out of the Israeli army and immediately immigrated to Los Angeles to work in his brother's chain of electronics stores, wore what looked like an Israeli army uniform, complete with sergeant's stripes and a webbed belt cinched tightly at the waist. He had a black plastic toy Uzi submachine gun hanging on his shoulder (at least I hoped it was a toy), and dark red combat boots. His dark, curly hair peeked out from under a burgundy beret that was close in color to his full, pouty lips. He had longer lashes than I did.

The kids marched around the living room in formation for a while, then had a water pistol fight in the backyard. I concentrated my attention on the soldier uncle and did my best to keep from licking my lips. What is it about a man in uniform? No matter how much all of the guns and pageantry of it bothers me, I still find something strangely compelling about a set of cute buns swathed in military green.

At the same time that I was drooling over the soldier, I was feeling pretty damn disgusted about the whole gun thing.

Thank God Stacy was there. Her son Zach was quite a bit older than the birthday boy, but as he went to school with Ari's sister, he'd been invited to join in the festivities. We leaned against the kitchen counter talking softly.

"Can you believe this?" I asked.

She rolled her eyes and flicked back her thick blond hair. Stacy is one of those women who were born to make others feel jealous. She seems beautiful, although she's the first to point out that it's more a result of careful preparation and judicious spending than any natural physical perfection. Her hair is always carefully cut in a classic modification of the style of the moment, and I haven't seen her without makeup since we graduated from college. Her life seems perfect, too. She has a math-whiz son, a handsome husband, and she is one of the rising stars at International Creative Artists, Hollywood's biggest talent agency. Unfortunately, what with her husband, Andy's, infidelities, sustaining that image of impeccable contentment requires as much work and artifice as does keeping up her physical appearance. She and Andy have been in and out of divorce court and couple's counseling, trying for years to deal with the fact that she earns more money than he does and that, for some reason, that fact instills in him the urge to buy expensive cars and even more expensive women.

"I just don't get it, really I don't. Why are boys so infatuated with guns and soldiers?" I said, keeping my voice low.

"I don't know. Probably because their parents are," Stacy said.

"Are they? Do you really think these people are gun owners?" I waved at the collection of Hollywood and almost-Hollywood parents. The women all looked like they were trying to be Stacy, and the men had that self-satisfied air they tend to acquire when their incomes keep pace with their toy-buying whims.

"You'd be surprised," my friend said.

"Am I going to have to start asking whether there's a gun in the house before I send Ruby and Isaac out on playdates?"

"It's not a bad idea. But, then, Ruby's been over to my house thousands of times. It's never bothered you."

My jaw dropped. "You have a gun?"

She nodded. "Just a little one. I got it last year after Andy moved back home."

"Are you kidding me? Why?"

"Remember last's year's bimbo?"

"Who could possibly keep track?"

Stacy rolled her eyes. "I know, I know. Anyway, she was the craziest of them all. After he broke up with her, she started calling the house at all hours. We changed our phone number, and then she started calling me at work. I kept imagining that scene from *Fatal Attraction*, you know, where Glenn Close puts the bunny in the pot? I wanted to be prepared in case she came after Zach's gerbil."

Was I the only person in the city of Los Angeles who wasn't packing heat?

The pièce de résistance of the party—I swear I'm not making this up—was a piñata shaped like a two-foot-long pistol. The kids thwacked at it happily, while Ari's parents beamed and scrupulously videotaped every minute of the festivities. When the piñata finally burst, after a good half hour of feeble strikes by the children and one good whack with his machine gun by G.I. Jake, a rain of tiny plastic soldiers, water pistols, and foil-wrapped chocolates in the shape of rifle cartridges showered down on the children's heads. God knows where they got the candy bullets.

After cake and ice cream, I gathered my two and put them in the car.

"That was a *gun* party," Isaac announced, beside himself with astonishment and glee.

"Yes, it was. Did you like it?" I asked them.

"I didn't," Ruby said loyally. "We don't like guns, do we Mama?"

"No. No, we don't."

"I do," Isaac said. "I love guns. I *love* them. And I loved that party. That's the kind of party I'm going to have, okay?"

"Over my dead body," I said, thinking of Bobby Katz and what a gun had done to him.

"No!" Isaac wailed.

"What, honey?" I asked, leaning into the car where I'd just buckled him into his car seat.

He wrapped his soft, plump arms around me and kissed me on the cheek, hard. "I don't want you to have a dead body."

I kissed him back. "That's just a saying, honey. My body is fine. It just means I don't want you to have a gun party."

"But why not?" he whined.

"I've told you a million times, baby. Guns are bad; they kill people."

"Real guns are bad. *They* kill people. Play guns are just pretend. They just pretend to kill people."

I looked at him, surprised. Did he, at his age, really understand the difference between real and pretend? "Even pretending to kill people is bad, Isaac."

His lower lip pooched out a bit and his eyes filled with tears. "Am I a bad boy?" he whispered.

"No! No, of course not." I covered him with kisses. "You're a very good boy. You're the best boy."

"Mama?" Ruby interrupted.

"What, sweetie?"

"Well, you always tell Isaac guns are bad. So maybe that's why Isaac thinks *he's* bad. 'Cause he loves something so much, even though it's so bad."

I stared at her. Then I turned to him. "Is that true, Isaac? Do you think you're a bad boy because you love guns and I tell you guns are bad?"

He burst into tears and buried his head in my neck.

10

HAT NIGHT I finally got around to reading all the E-mail Bobby had received after his death. There were a couple of messages from clients, obviously written before they knew what happened to him. The rest were from Internet contacts who were not aware that he'd died. There were messages from his online adoptee support group. There were piles of spam—junk mail from mortgage brokers and pornography web sites and the like. Mostly, however, there were messages from Candace.

The first of Candace's messages began with a plaintive lament about his failure to contact her. Apparently, it had been a long time since she'd received an E-mail from him. She begged him not to cut her out of the "loop of his life." The rest of the message had to do with the letter Bobby had written his birth mother. Candace urged him to ignore the woman's failure to respond and to contact her. Candace's tone was almost nagging. Clearly, she'd been giving him this advice for some time. At one point she even threatened to "drive out there" and talk to the woman herself. I didn't think she was serious, the words were followed by a keyboard ;), but the threat didn't strike me as entirely idle.

In her next message, Candace apologized for "haranguing" Bobby and asked him to call her or come by the café. After that came a string of short messages. A couple begged him to call and apologized again and again for "being so bossy." Finally, she grew angry and called him cruel and selfish for excluding her from "the most important moment of your life—the culmination of your very existence."

There followed twenty or so one-line messages along the lines of "Where are you?" and "Why aren't you answering me?"

The last message began with the words, "You know I love you." It went on from there. She told him that long before they'd met in person she'd realized that she wanted to dedicate herself to him. She insisted that their shared tragedy brought them together. She berated him for his unwillingness to consider a relationship with her, his obvious "soul mate." Finally, she wrote, "I know you say that the reason you don't want to be with me—in every sense of the word—is because you consider me your 'soul sister,' and not your lover. But we both know that's not true. You're allowing your guilt about Betsy to keep you from realizing your true destiny. The Lakota don't believe that you can hide from your destiny. You can't remain shackled to that stoned and destructive soul, not when mine cries out to you."

I leaned back in my chair with a sigh. Poor Candace. Poor Bobby. The truth was, he seemed an unlikely object of such passionate devotion. Bobby had been handsome, sure, but in a kind of bland, blond way. His good looks were strained, blurred, somehow, as a result, I'd always assumed, of his methamphetamine use—speed wreaks havoc on the skin. Bobby was, of course, in good shape. It was his job to be. He wasn't, however, bulky and overly defined. He had a pleasantly strong and firm body, and his stomach was less of a washboard than a solid countertop. But really what made him seem something less than a Lothario was his easygoing, almost innocuous manner. He was pleasant and cheerful. He was ready with an encouraging word or an inspiring quote from one of his AA manuals. But he wasn't passionate. He wasn't ardent or fervent. He was calm and pleasant and decidedly un–soul mate–like. But then, who am I to say? My soul mate spends most of his days playing with vintage action figures and writing about serial murder, cannibalism, and human sacrifice.

THE NEXT MORNING, Al called me with the news that he had, basically, no news. His sources at the LAPD weren't saying much about Bobby's death.

"Let me put it this way," Al said. "It could be suicide. Or maybe not. I get the feeling they're thinking that if it was a homicide, it was a drug hit—you knew the guy was an addict, right?"

"Recovered."

"Whatever. Once an addict always an addict, that's what I say."

I rolled my eyes at the phone. "How original, Al."

"Anyway, the gun wasn't registered to him or to anyone else, but there's no evidence it was an illegal weapon. It was most likely purchased through a gun show, in which case there would be no records about who bought it."

"Why not? Don't gun sellers have to do background checks?"

"Not at gun shows."

"Why not?"

Al didn't answer for a moment. Then he said, "Honestly, I've never really understood that myself. Anyway, a background check wouldn't do us much good. Those records are destroyed after the person passes the check."

"What?" I was shocked. "Why? Why destroy the record of who bought the gun?"

"Haven't you heard of privacy, girlie? You want the United States government keeping track of its private citizens' every move?"

"I sure as hell want the government keeping track of the gun buyers!" I said.

I could feel Al seething on the other end of the line. Finally, he said, "Listen, you tree-hugging feminist, I'm just *not* going to have this fight with you. And, anyway, maybe you should be *thanking* me instead of *yelling* at me."

I was suitably rebuked and decidedly chastened. "You're right. Thank you so much. Really. Don't be mad, okay?"

He sighed. "No sweat. It's not your fault. You're confused. Anyway, I got the skip trace results back on the two women from the hospital. I'll fax them over to you."

"Thanks. Really. I owe you one."

"Don't owe me. Come work with me."

I laughed.

"I'm not kidding," he said.

I'D ALREADY FIGURED that the younger woman, Brenda Fessler, was the mom. I knew that Bobby had been adopted through Jewish Family Services, and Fessler sounded like a Jewish name. Moreover, I thought a nineteen-year-old was more likely to put up a child for adoption than a twenty-six-year-old. The skip trace had turned her up in Reno, Nevada. I tried the telephone number but found it disconnected. I tapped my fingers on the table for a moment, irritated at the dead end. Then, figuring what the heck, I could afford the ninety cents, I called information. There was no Brenda Fessler listed, but there was a Jason Fessler. I decided to give it a whirl. The phone rang once and was picked up by a jaunty voice. I wasn't really expecting much, but when I asked for Brenda the man yelled out, "Hey, Ma! Now you're getting *phone calls* at my house! Here, give me the baby."

"Hello?" The voice was as bright and cheerful as the man's, and I hoped that this might be the woman I was looking for.

"Hi. I hope you can help me. I'm trying to track down the mother of a baby boy born at Haverford Memorial Hospital on February 15, 1972."

"Again?"

"Excuse me?" I asked.

"A nice young man called me about this very thing a month or so ago. He was born on that date and was trying to find his mother. Are you calling about the same baby?"

"Yes, I am."

"Well, I'll tell you what I told him. Much as I wish I could help him, he's not mine. My Jason was born at Haverford Memorial on February 15, 1972, and he's right here. You called his house, actually. And I'm holding his son, Jason Jr., who's six months old. And a doll. Aren't you? A big precious doll?" I thanked the happy grandmother for her time and hung up.

It had to be Susan Masters. The skip trace had turned up a woman whose maiden name was Susan Masters but whose married name was Sullivan. The fact that confused me was that the date of her name change was 1968, a full four years before Bobby was born. The birth date and the social security number matched, however. For some reason, Susan Sullivan had used her maiden name when she checked into the hospital. Perhaps because she planned to give her baby up for adoption and hoped for some anonymity.

The Sullivans still lived in Los Angeles. Their address was in the Pacific Palisades, a beautiful little community north of Santa Monica. I dialed the number, and a woman's voice answered almost immediately.

"Hello, I'm looking for Susan Sullivan."

"This is she." Did I imagine a whiff of suspicion in her tone?

"Mrs. Sullivan, I'm trying to track down the mother of a baby boy born in Haverford Memorial Hospital on February 15, 1972—"

The phone clicked before I'd even finished my sentence. I was talking to empty air. I tried again, hoping that we'd just been disconnected, but the phone rang and rang. Susan Masters Sullivan did not want to be found. But found she was. I was determined to talk to her and see if she had any information about Bobby's death, whether she wanted to see me or not.

Unfortunately, I also had to go pick Ruby up from preschool. Isaac, who'd been napping while I made my calls, didn't even stir when I hoisted him out of bed, flung him over my shoulder, and hauled him out to the car. The boy had slept about twenty minutes in the entire first four months of his life, turning me into a blithering idiot and putting a strain on my marriage the likes of which we'd never experienced before or since. Now a brass band wouldn't wake him up.

I was only seven minutes late picking up Ruby, a personal record, but nonetheless I found her tapping her foot, arms folded across her narrow little chest. I ignored her irritation and said, "Let's get moving, kid. You and Isaac need to go home and play with Daddy."

"Why? I want to play with *you*."

"Sorry, Ruby. I'm busy this afternoon."

"What are you doing?"

I certainly wasn't going to say, "Investigating a murder." So I settled for, "I've got a playdate."

That seemed to satisfy my daughter.

I don't know why, but I was expecting Susan Sullivan to live in one of the cute little bungalows on the tree-lined streets in Pacific Palisades. I knew once I saw the address that her house was going to be worth something, but even those little cottages sell for a cool million bucks in today's overinflated real estate market. What I didn't expect, however, was a mansion. I didn't expect a house set so far back off the street that its driveway had a Private Road sign. I didn't expect a curving drive of crushed pink gravel, lawns and gardens as far as the eye could see (at least up to the boundary rows of fragrant eucalyptus trees), or the glimpse of a marble-bordered pool peeping out from behind one wing of the salmon-stuccoed villa. I cringed as the wheels of my Volvo station wagon crushed the carefully combed stones and marred the manicured perfection of the circular driveway.

Rich people make me nervous. I rummaged around in my purse for some makeup, found an old lipstick, and carefully applied it. I looked for something to cover the triangle of pimples that had taken up residence on my chin, cursing yet again the acne gods who didn't even allow a single moment of bliss between blemishes and wrinkles. I'd gone from having one to having both with nary a day of smoothness in between.

I fluffed up my cropped curls, relieved that at least I'd remembered to have my roots done, and firmly averted my eyes from the chocolate milk stain down one leg of my khaki capri pants. I was ready to see how the other half lived.

I rang the bell, listening to the chimes echo throughout the house. The door was answered by an older Mexican woman in a plain gray smock.

"Yes?" she said.

"Buenos días. Estoy buscando la señora de la casa, Mrs. Sullivan."

The woman flashed me a huge smile brightened by at least four silver teeth along the side of her mouth and, with a cascade of Spanish far beyond my limited skills, ushered me through the door and into a round entry hall. The ceiling was easily twenty or thirty feet tall and opened into a massive, round skylight of leaded stained glass. Little oblongs of brightly colored light glowed on the polished marble floor and up the circular staircase along the back wall.

Within a few moments, the maid returned, following behind a tall blond woman wearing a white tennis dress with mint-green piping. Her bobbed hair was colored strawberry blond, as if she were matching the hair color she'd had as a girl. She looked like a blonde. Not a tanned, California surfer-girl kind of blonde but a pallid, English-lass kind of blonde. She had the faded prettiness so common in women of that coloring. She might have once been beautiful, but her skin had crumpled, and her chin seemed to have slipped back into her neck. Her nose, though, was sharp and defined. Her close-set, pale blue eyes glanced at me nervously, as if she knew me and had anticipated my arrival with trepidation.

"Can I help you?" she said. She sounded as though what she really wanted to do was throw me out of her house.

"Mrs. Sullivan, I don't mean to cause you any trouble, and I'm terribly sorry for bothering you. But my friend Bobby Katz is dead, and I think you can help me."

Susan looked quickly at the maid, who kept her eyes firmly affixed to the floor.

"That will be all, Salud," Bobby's birth mother dismissed her maid, her voice just the tiniest bit hesitant, as if asking the older woman's permission to assert the authority her status ought to have made natural to her.

"I bring you some *limonada,* Mrs. Susan? Some ice tea?" Salud asked.

"No. No, thank you," Susan said. Salud left, and Susan finally met my eye.

"We can't talk out here. Come into the living room," she murmured.

The living room was a vast open space reached through two oversized doors of heavy carved wood. The long gallery opened along one side to a flagstone patio that ran the length of the house. The many sets of French doors were closed against the late-afternoon chill.

She sat down on a button-back armchair and motioned me toward the matching leather sofa. The buttery soft skin felt delicious against the backs of my legs. I introduced myself and told her how I knew Bobby.

"You said he's dead?" she asked in a soft voice.

"Yes. I'm sorry. He died a couple of weeks ago."

"How?"

"It's not clear at this point. He was shot, but the police have not determined yet whether it was suicide or . . . or murder."

She nodded and then began fiddling with the diamond and gold tennis bracelet on her wrist.

"Mrs. Sullivan, I believe you met Bobby," I said.

"He contacted me. As you did. It was you who called, wasn't it?"

I nodded.

"He contacted me. But I told him what I'll tell you. I didn't give birth to a baby in 1972. I'm not his mother. He made a mistake."

I considered that possibility. Could the skip trace have led to the wrong person? It had been known to happen. But if that were the case, why was she so very nervous?

"There doesn't seem to be any doubt, Mrs. Sullivan. The woman who gave birth to Bobby had your name and used your social security number and birth date."

She kept her eyes on her bracelet, catching bits of light with the diamonds and sending them skittering across the walls.

"There's been a mistake. I'm sorry," she insisted.

I didn't say anything.

Suddenly she stood up and crossed the room. "See," she said, grabbing a double frame with pictures of two young blond men. "These are my boys. P. J. was born in 1969, and Matthew in 1974. I was married in 1968. Why ever would I have given my baby up for adoption?"

I looked at the pictures of the young men. They were both blond and blue-eyed. And they looked quite a bit like Bobby.

I raised my eyebrows at Susan. We both jumped when a shrill ring pierced the silence like a siren. Moments later, Salud came into the living room, holding a cordless phone.

"It's Mr. Patrick, Mrs. Susan," she said.

"Excuse me." Susan took the phone from her and walked quickly out of the room.

"Can I get you a *limonada*, miss?" Salud asked.

"That would be lovely," I said, and she followed Susan out the door.

I got up and started looking over the photographs perched on the grand piano and on the many bookcases and end tables. I crossed the room to get a better look at a large, glass-enclosed cabinet. In it, I found photographs of men in uniform, fatigues, and camouflage hats. A few of the photos showed soldiers holding large machine guns, the sun beating down on their shirtless backs. Vietnam.

A small glass case resting inside the cabinet held a medal. I looked closer. A Purple Heart. I wondered exactly when it was that Patrick Sullivan had served in Southeast Asia. Had he been over there in, say, June of 1971, nine months before Bobby was born?

I heard Susan's voice in the hall. "Take the phone, Matthew."

A petulant male voice said, "No. I don't want to talk about it."

"Matthew. Your father wants to talk to you. Take the phone."

"I said no. I don't need to hear what he has to say. He's been yelling at me for, like, two days. Anyway, I have to get to work."

"Matthew, honey. Please," she said, plaintively.

"Screw him. And screw you, too."

The front door slammed, and Susan walked slowly back into the room.

She immediately realized that I couldn't have helped but overhear what she'd said. "My son Matthew," she explained. "He and his father are having a disagreement."

I did my best to smile sympathetically. "So, Mrs. Sullivan, was your husband in the military?"

"Yes. He was an Air Force pilot. An Academy graduate," she said, as though by rote.

"He served in Vietnam?"

"Yes. I'm sorry about your friend. Really. But I can't help you. I'm afraid I have to go now. I'm late for my match." She walked quickly out the door and across the hallway. She opened the door and stood, waiting. Unable to think of a way to make her talk to me, I gathered my bag and left. As I walked out, I saw Salud walk out of a door in the back hall holding a tall tumbler, its sides dewed and a sprig of mint carefully balanced on the top. The maid caught my eye, shrugged, and then took a long sip from the glass.

11

MAJOR PATRICK SULLIVAN had served two tours of duty in Vietnam in the early seventies. In September of 1972, he'd been shot down over North Vietnam but had managed to work his way back to friendly territory, despite suffering two broken shoulders and severe burns on his hands. He was discharged not long after. The archive of the *L.A. Times* was full of stories describing his triumphant return, including one photograph of a much younger Susan Sullivan, wearing a pink pillbox hat and crouching next to two small boys as Major Sullivan ran across the tarmac toward them.

A little more searching in online news files showed stories about the Sullivan family of Los Angeles and Santa Barbara, going back as far as the archives would take me. One piece, an obituary of a Patrick Sullivan who died in 1980 at the age of seventy-three, was most instructive. Patrick Sr., Major Sullivan's dad, had been, like his son after him, a pilot in the United States Air Force. He himself was described as a scion of an old California family that had earned its money during the gold rush and later on as real estate barons. He was an intimate friend of Archbishop Timothy Manning and an important member of the Catholic community. He was survived by his son Major Sullivan and his two grandsons, Patrick Jr. and Matthew, and by his brother, Father Edward Sullivan, provost of Saint Ignatius University. His will included a bequest described as "generous" to that Jesuit institution. A wing of the physical sciences building had been named in his honor.

With a husband away at war and the reputation of a prominent Catholic family to consider, no wonder Susan Sullivan had, when she found herself pregnant, given birth in secret and given the baby up for adoption. It was curious, however, that she gave the baby up to a *Jewish* adoption service.

The next morning, I stopped by Betsy's house. She was home, and I got the feeling that that's pretty much where she'd been since I'd seen her last. She wasn't high, or at least she didn't seem it. I found her watching television, wearing a pair of sweatpants that were clearly much too big for her and a man's flannel shirt. Her hair stood up in odd clumps on her head. She had a huge mug of something steaming in her hand.

"Want a mocha?"

"Sure," I said. I wheeled a snoozing Isaac into the living room and put him in a corner, far away from the blaring television. I'd schlepped him, strapped into his stroller, up the stairs to the apartment. Despite the few times I'd clunked him against the banister, and despite Jerry Springer's theme music, he slept on, blessedly still wedded to his morning nap.

I watched as Betsy puttered around the galley kitchen. She poured a packet of hot cocoa mix and a heaping teaspoonful of instant coffee into a mug, drowned the mess in milk, and microwaved it. She garnished it with a dollop of Cool Whip. I gagged as I took my first sip. I didn't see Betsy having a career at Starbucks in her future.

"Mm. Delicious," I said.

"It's my idea of comfort food. I've been pretty much living on these for the last couple of days. Ever since I took those . . . those . . . you know. That day you saw me. Eating kind of makes me sick, but I'm desperate for sugar. And I need the caffeine. I already sleep like twelve hours a night, even with, like, eight of these a day." Betsy spoke in a listless monotone. She looked and sounded like the before character in a TV commercial for Prozac.

"Honey," I said. "I don't mean to pry, but have you considered seeing someone? Maybe a grief counselor? It sounds to me like you're pretty seriously depressed."

She shook her head. "The last thing I need is some shrink raking through my private business."

Now why would that be? "Well, have you been to a meeting since you took the pills?" She might not be able to say the words, but I sure could.

She shrugged, slurping loudly from her cup. "Not really, but they're kind of coming to me. Every reformed drunk and stoner I know keeps dropping by to tell me to 'hang tough.' Like they have a clue. Losers."

I set my mug down on the coffee table where it joined four or five other encrusted cups. "Betsy, don't you think that those people might be just the ones who *do* have a clue? Some of them must have experienced the challenge of staying sober in the face of tragedy."

She rolled her eyes.

"What about work? When do you have to go back?" I asked.

"I'm not going back."

"What?"

"I quit my job. I've always hated it, and I don't see why I should bother now. Even though Bobby's family stole all my stuff and is tossing me out of my home, I was smarter than they were about at least some things."

This kind of belligerence was a side of Betsy I hadn't seen before. I tried not to be judgmental. I tried to remember my Kübler-Ross. Wasn't anger a stage of grief through which everyone passed?

"Really?" I said, in a neutral tone.

"Yup. Like our wedding account. Even though we always kept our money separate, we had a joint account set up for wedding expenses. Bobby's parents didn't know about it, because I guess they thought my parents were going to foot the bill for the wedding—like that would ever happen. As soon as I realized those cheapskates were going to Je—bleed me dry, I emptied the money out of that account."

Had she really been about to say "Jew me?"

"How much was in it?" I asked. The question was clearly none of my business, but that didn't seem to bother Betsy.

"Almost fifteen grand. And the best part is that most of it wasn't even mine. I mean, when we first set up the account, I put in about five thousand, but then I had to use that to pay for that fancy lawyer you sent us to. So that whole fifteen thousand came from Bobby's savings, and I got every dime of it. Which is exactly what he would have wanted. I know it." She took another slurp of her concoction, looking very satisfied with herself.

To people like Bobby's parents, fifteen thousand dollars was a fairly meaningless amount of money. But it was enough cash to convince Betsy that she could take some time off work.

Betsy drained her cup and looked over at me. There was a smear of chocolate on her upper lip, and I could barely resist the urge to reach into my purse for a baby wipe and clean it off.

"What have you found out? Did you get any dirt on the creepy Katzes?"

I was getting more and more uncomfortable with the vitriol Betsy was spewing in the direction of her would-have-been in-laws. Granted, they hadn't behaved very well toward her. But, at the same time, she seemed to be almost enjoying her anger at them. "No," I said. "But that really wasn't the kind of thing we were looking into, was it?"

She shrugged again.

"I think I found Bobby's birth mother, though."

That perked her up. "Really? Who is she? Did he meet her? What's she like? Is she married? What does her husband do? Do they seem like they've got money?"

Now Betsy was really making me uneasy. Why was she interested in Bobby's mother's financial situation? I was loath to tell her more than I absolutely had to. I told myself that she wasn't technically a client of mine; I didn't owe her any kind of duty, fiduciary or otherwise. I was just a friend of Bobby's looking into his life to see if I could shed some light on his death.

"Why don't I check things out a little more, and when I'm sure it's really her, I'll let you know, okay?" I said.

"Whatever," Betsy said, seeming to lose interest.

ISAAC WOKE UP as I bumped him down the steps to the curb, and he started whining as soon as I loaded him into his car seat. Not even his favorite tape, *The Coasters' Greatest Hits*, calmed him down. I decided to strike a bargain. I promised him half an hour at the playground if he promised to behave afterward and let me take him with me on a grown-up playdate.

As soon as we crossed from sidewalk to sand, Isaac made a beeline for the tire swing. Since the little girl who was sitting in it didn't want to give up her perch, he shoved her off. I ran over, scooped her up, and handed her to her mother, who snatched her out of my arms. I put Isaac in a time-out, which he didn't seem to mind particularly. I released him on condition that he figure out a way to "share." He did. He "shared" another child's shovel by wrenching it out of the little boy's hands, aiming it at his head, and shouting, "Bang, bang, you're a dead man!" Then he poked the kid with the shovel. Hard.

Within two minutes, my precious boy and I were relegated to a sandy patch of unpopulated lawn on the far corner of the playground. I smiled pathetically at the mothers whose scowls had precipitated our segregation and called, "I have a really well-behaved daughter." I swear it wasn't my fault my son was behaving like a testosterone-poisoned member of the World Wrestling Federation. The mothers shot me final, disgusted looks and formed themselves into a protective circle around their perfectly behaved children, many of whom were boys, no doubt raised by more competent mothers who could effectively resist gender stereotypes.

Meanwhile, my monstrous son had crawled into my lap and was placing firm but gentle kisses all over my face.

"You are my darling," he said to me.

"You're my darling, too, but I wish you wouldn't attack the other kids." I sighed, kissing him back. His cheeks and neck still had the doughy softness of infancy, and I buried my nose in them. He giggled while I made snuffling noises and buzzed at his soft skin with my lips. How could something so delicious be so wretchedly behaved?

We played in our corner for a while and then made our way over to the slide. Two mothers promptly grabbed their little girls and carried them to the other side of the park. Isaac, blissfully unaware of his pariah status, clambered up the ladder and whizzed down the slide with a bellow of joy.

Was it really just a matter of gender? For all her stubborness, for all her temper and propensity to willful behavior, Ruby was, by and large, an obedient child. Sure she had her moments, but they'd never included socking a kid on the head with a piece of playground equipment. Isaac, who had once seemed so tractable and still amazed me with his loving sweetness, had an exuberant, aggressive streak about the length and breadth of the Mississippi River—with the same tendency to overflow. I'm convinced that neither Peter nor I treated them any differently from one another. So what was it? The mysterious Y chromosome? Or maybe it was just Isaac. Maybe that's the way the kid was, and all my efforts at forcing him to be something else, forcing him to be more like his sister, were not only hopeless but ultimately destructive. Maybe instead of trying to beat and berate out of him that wonderful sparky personality that gave me such joy when it wasn't being unleashed on unsuspecting children, I should have been helping him figure out how to direct it more appropriately. Like at inanimate objects.

At the end of our agreed-upon half-hour, Isaac was happy to leave, the attractions of solitary play having worn thin. I strapped him back in the car seat, popped the ubiquitous Coasters into the cassette deck, and set off for the Palisades. It never occurred to me not to bring Isaac on this errand. First of all, I had nowhere else to put him. Peter had spent the entire night working on *The Impaler* and probably wouldn't wake up until the sun was dipping back down in the horizon. Equally important to me, however, was a somewhat less innocent motive. There is something about a mother and toddler that inspires the sharing of confidences. Any woman who's ever taken a baby to the playground can attest to that. Mothers tell things to one another even when they've never met before. I can't count the number of times I've been made privy to a virtual stranger's innermost secrets while our children cavorted on the swing set. I'll admit that with the Ninja Toddler around, I'd been less often the sounding board for other women's intimacies than I had been with a sweet-faced Ruby on my lap, but since Susan Sullivan didn't have a little boy for Isaac to torment, I figured I was safe.

Either Bobby's birth mother lived in tennis whites, or it was just a coincidence that I'd caught her on her way to the courts once again. This time Salud didn't ask me in but made Isaac and me wait on the doorstep. Susan herself looked as though she were about to send me packing, but her face softened when she saw Isaac's tousled head. He didn't have his sister's dramatic red ringlets, but his sandy blond hair still highlighted his deceptively cherubic face.

"Why don't you come round to the back?" she said. "There's a swing set out there. It belonged to my boys when they were young, and I've never had the heart to take it down. I guess I'm saving it for grandchildren."

She led us around the side of the house. As we walked across the lawns, I was conscious of my clogs sinking deep in the lush, damp grass. The back yard was expansive and as perfectly groomed as the front. Flower beds flanked a large grassy area edged with blue and gray stones. A green climbing structure, complete with swings, tree house, and sandbox, stood in a generous patch of playground bark. As soon as he saw it, Isaac took off for it at a run.

"He won't hurt himself," Susan said. "The bark is about a foot deep. I still replace it every spring."

She led me to two Adirondack chairs set at the edge of the huge flag-stone patio, and we watched Isaac in silence for a moment or two. He was in heaven, climbing up the rope ladder, sliding down the firefighter's pole.

"You came back," Susan said finally.

"Yes," I replied.

"Why?"

"Your husband was stationed overseas, in Vietnam, when Bobby was born."

She didn't answer, simply rolled her diamond tennis bracelet around and around her wrist.

"I imagine it must have been very difficult, finding yourself pregnant under those circumstances, especially considering who his family was." I kept my voice gentle, but I don't believe it was my tone, or anything I said or did, that made Susan Masters Sullivan finally speak. She told me her story because she desperately wanted to talk to someone. Her son was dead, and whether or not she'd ever known him, she felt some kind of grief, and she needed someone to share it with.

"I'm sorry he's dead. I really am," Susan said, without looking at me. Her voice had a huskiness to it, and I wondered if she was suppressing tears.

"Yes," I said. "We all are. He was a lovely man."

"I didn't know him well enough to tell. You see, we met just the once."

I didn't speak. I was afraid that if I did, she would stop talking. I realized that I was holding my breath, and I let it out as quietly as I could.

"I was twenty-six years old when I had him. I had been married for almost three years. My family . . . well, they weren't much. My dad moved us out here from Chicago because of Santa Anita. You know, the racetrack? He'd been a groom at a racing stable in Saratoga, New York, and he thought he'd make a career out of horse training. But anything he earned at the stables, he'd lose at the betting window or drink up on his way home at night. My mother supported us. She was a dispatcher for a taxicab company."

Susan glanced at my face and looked away almost immediately.

"I'm not telling you my hard luck story because I want you to feel sorry for me. It's just that all this had a lot to do with what happened. You see, when I met my husband, it was like meeting a prince from a completely different world. And I was Cinderella. He was home from the Air Force Academy for Christmas. We met at a fraternity party at USC, and for the longest time he thought I was a student there. I didn't ever really lie, I just didn't correct his misunderstanding. When he graduated and began his service, he came home so rarely . . . I guess I sort of stopped thinking about what he knew or didn't know. We got married, in kind of a hurry. For the usual reason. It was only then that he found out that I wasn't a college girl but . . . some other kind of girl. But it was too late.

"I think his parents always knew that I wasn't what I seemed to be. They never liked me. Not back then, and not after the kids were born. They set me up in a little house in Beverly Hills while Patrick was overseas. They paid all my bills. Mary-Margaret even took me to her very own obstetrician. They hired a baby nurse for P. J. I almost felt like Mary-Margaret was teaching me how to be a Sullivan—like she was training me to be the kind of wife she wished Patrick had married.

"I suppose I felt smothered. Or else I was lonely. It's funny, that you can feel so oppressed by people's expectations and demands, but still so desperately alone."

I nodded in sympathy. I'd felt something similar when I'd first had Ruby. Sometimes I thought that having a baby was the most lonely thing in the world. There you are, constantly at another person's beck and call, never by yourself for even a minute, but utterly isolated and alone.

"I met Bobby's father at Papa Bach's Bookstore. I used to hide out there, sometimes, when the nanny came. I was terribly intimidated by her. She so clearly disapproved of how little I knew about being a mother. I just know she was telling Mary-Margaret everything I did wrong. Anyway, I was there one morning, and this nice young man kept watching me. After a while he asked me out for a cup of coffee. I don't know why I went. Like I said, I guess I was lonely. Anyway, we had coffee and talked. He was a doctor. A pediatrician. He was handsome—I mean, not like Patrick, not blond and gorgeous—but kind of dark and moody looking. He was a Jew, and I hadn't really known many Jews. I went to Catholic schools through high school, and I never really did go to college.

"Anyway, we met at Papa Bach's a few times, and then, one afternoon, I went home with him. I don't know why. I never could figure out why. I just did. It was stupid. But it was 1971. People did things like that. Or at least, I thought they did. It would have been nothing, I would have forgotten all about it." A deep red flush crept up her neck and into her cheeks. "The . . . the rubber broke," she whispered.

I nodded again.

She paused for a moment, cleared her throat, and continued in a stronger voice. "And there I was. Pregnant. I really didn't know what to do. I thought for a while about trying to lie to Patrick and his family. Mary-Margaret and Pat Sr. had flown me out to Japan for a week a month or so before all this happened so that I could meet Patrick for his leave. I suppose I could have pretended I'd gotten pregnant then. But, you see, I knew that chances were I'd be found out. I just knew it."

"Why?" I asked. "Why were you so sure?"

She flushed again and looked out across the yard to where Isaac was lying on his stomach on the bark, digging a pit with his toes. "Well, for one thing, the dates would have been all wrong; the baby would have ended up coming a whole month late. Although he ended up coming a week or so early, so I guess I could have worked it out somehow. Maybe I could have gone away to have him and just lied about his age by a couple of weeks. But there was something else."

"What?"

"Well, like I said, the man was . . . Jewish. And he looked Jewish. You know. Dark."

I was waiting for her to remark on the size of her lover's nose, but she refrained. I suppose it had occurred to her at some point that Applebaum wasn't exactly a WASPy name.

"You didn't think you'd be able to get away with it?"

"No. I thought for sure Patrick would be able to tell."

"It's ironic," I said.

"What is?"

"Well, that Bobby was so blond. He looks just like his half brothers."

She nodded. "He did, didn't he? They all three favor me. But, then, I couldn't be sure that he would. Favor me, that is. What if he'd looked like his father?"

I nodded.

"And thank God I did it, given what happened," she said.

"Excuse me?"

"You know, that Tay-Sachs. The Jewish disease. Even if I'd been able to keep it a secret from Patrick, he would have found out, because Bobby had that Jewish genetic disease."

"Well, chances are that you wouldn't have found out about the Tay-Sachs," I said.

"Why not?"

"Bobby only got tested because he was Jewish. If he'd been brought up as your child, there never would have been a reason for him to be tested. Unless he married a Jewish girl."

"I doubt a son of mine would do that," she said and then stiffened as if suddenly remembering who or what I was. "I mean, they don't meet many Jewish people. They went to Catholic schools. Like my husband and I did. But even so, we would have found out."

"How?"

"Because we were all tested for it a few years ago."

"Excuse me?" I was flabbergasted. She'd have had no reason in the world to be tested for Tay-Sachs.

"My sister's granddaughter has cystic fibrosis. Her doctors at UCLA asked the entire family to participate in a genetic study. We were all tested."

"What do you mean? What does being tested for cystic fibrosis have to do with Tay-Sachs?"

"Because the test they gave us was what they call a panel. It looked for three diseases at once, cystic fibrosis, Tay-Sachs, and something else, caravan? Canavan? I can't remember the name. Anyway, they used that panel for the entire study, and even though we weren't in a risk group, we had to be tested like everyone else. My test came back positive for cystic fibrosis, P. J.'s and Matthew's tests were negative. Of course none of us had the Tay-Sachs gene or the one for that other Jewish disease. If Bobby's had come back positive for Tay-Sachs, then Patrick would have found out he wasn't his child, that his father was someone else, someone Jewish."

"I guess you're right, then. You were lucky." I glanced over at Isaac, who was digging a hole in the wood chips. He looked happy, so I turned back to Bobby's mother. "How did you keep your pregnancy a secret?"

"It was surprisingly easy. Even though P. J. was already a year and a half old, I was still carrying quite a bit of my pregnancy weight. I just kept wearing the same clothes and tried not to eat too much. I didn't end up gaining more than twenty pounds or so."

I stared at her jealously. *Twenty pounds? I gained that much in the first trimester!*

"No one really noticed," she continued. "At the end, I stayed in bed a lot. I told the nanny that I was having migraines. Mary-Margaret made me go to her doctor, and I was terrified that the jig would be up, but he didn't look at me past my neck. He just prescribed some sleeping pills and sent me home. It was only in the very last month that it was really obvious that I was pregnant. I sent P. J. off to Mary-Margaret and Pat Sr. I told them I was going to Arizona to a spa to try to lose weight once and for all before Patrick came home on leave again. They bought it. I think they were glad to have me gone for a little while.

"Instead, I went home to my mother in Pasadena and had the baby at Haverford Memorial Hospital. I registered as Susan Masters, and that was that. I gave the baby to Jewish Family Services and went home."

"Why did you go through Jewish Family Services and not through one of the Catholic agencies?"

"My mother wanted me to go through a Catholic charity. In fact, she tried to convince me to go to Saint Anne's Maternity Home, this home for unwed mothers in Los Angeles. But I wasn't unwed. I didn't belong there. And I had to give the baby to the Jews."

"Why?" I asked again.

"The baby was half-Jewish, wasn't he? It didn't seem fair to try to give a half-Jewish baby to a Catholic family."

"Fair?"

"Well, because they were sure to assume he was from a Catholic family, because of me, because of my name. But he'd be part Jewish."

I didn't get it. "So what?"

"Well, they'd end up with a Jewish baby. That wouldn't be right."

I stared at her for a moment, not sure what to say. Was she really saying that she couldn't stomach the idea of foisting off a Jewish baby on an unsuspecting Catholic family? As if they'd be getting inferior goods?

My discomfort didn't seem to register on Susan in the slightest. She gave me the name of Bobby's birth father, Dr. Reuben Nadelman, and told me that she'd given it to Bobby, too, but had never found out whether Bobby had contacted him.

While I was writing Bobby's birth father's name on a scrap of paper, I heard Isaac squeal. I looked up, and my heart caught in my throat. For a moment, I thought that the handsome blond young man pushing my son on the swing was Bobby. Susan Sullivan followed my gaze.

"My son Matthew," she said fondly. "I remember when he was small, like your boy. I used to push him on that very swing."

"He and Bobby look so much alike," I said.

She smiled faintly, and her lip trembled. "Like brothers," she murmured.

"Well, I guess that only makes sense," I said. I felt bad as soon as the words escaped my lips. It seemed cruel to remind her that Bobby had been hers, her son just like this man was. Something about Susan Sullivan inspired me to want to protect her, she seemed so delicate, so fragile. And yet, this was a woman who felt such clear distaste for who I was.

As Isaac and I drove away from the Pacific Palisades, I felt a kind of listless disgust. As the most assimilated of Jews, married to an indeterminate Protestant of vaguely Anglo-Saxon heritage, I gave little thought in my life to anti-Semitism. I'd never been called a kike or a hebe. As far as I knew, I'd never failed to get a job or make a friend because I was a Jew. My life had been blessedly devoid of prejudice. So much so, in fact, that I'd sort of forgotten that there were people in my own country, my own city, for whom my status as a Jew meant something more than that I hung a few Stars of David on our Christmas tree. Susan Sullivan had given away her baby because his father was a Jew. Despite the fact that a conveniently scheduled leave in Japan meant that she might have been able to convince her husband and his family that he had impregnated her, she gave her baby up for adoption. She was *that* sure that his Jewish blood would give him away, that it would mark him, as surely as a pair of horns on the top of his head. I angled the rearview mirror so that Isaac's sleeping face was reflected back at me. Did he look Jewish? Half the blood that flowed through his veins could be traced back to the Jewish Pale in Poland, and farther, if the biblical stories are true, to the rocky, desert sands of Israel. Did his face bear indelible traces of generations of hook-nosed moneylenders?

My son's sand-colored hair stuck to his damp, sweaty forehead. His blue eyes were closed, and his thick lashes rested on round, pink cheeks. His soft lips formed the shape of the nipple he was probably dreaming of. If I were totally honest, I would allow that his nose was perhaps a little large for his tiny face. But the fact was, he had inherited that from his father, whose own visage bore the craggy sail of an oversized schnoz that could easily have graced the pages of a Nazi caricature. And there wasn't a Jewish bone in Peter's body.

My grandmother, who'd lived long enough to see us married, had wept at our wedding. I'd assumed it was because Peter wasn't Jewish, and I'd gone up to her after the ceremony at my mother's urging, prepared to promise to raise our children Jewish.

"What a waste!" she'd cried, hugging me to her breast. "Your tiny *piskela* of a shiksa nose, all for nothing."

ISAAC AND I left the Palisades and drove crosstown to Ruby's Jewish preschool. It was something of a relief to be back in the world I understood, where even the goyim knew when to call someone a schmuck and how to eat a pastrami sandwich.

On the way home, my cell phone rang. I fumbled for it, coming dangerously close to swerving into the next lane.

"Hello?" I shouted over the freeway noise and the crackle of static.

"Hey! Mama! It's dangerous to talk on the phone and drive. Daddy says so," Ruby bellowed from the backseat.

I ignored both her voice and that of my conscience and continued my conversation.

"Hello?" I said again.

"Hi. This is Candace. You know, Bobby's friend."

That was something of a surprise. I hadn't expected to hear from her again.

"How did you get this number?" I asked, sounding ruder than I'd intended.

"Your husband gave it to me. I called the number on your business card, and he told me you'd have your cell phone. I hope it's all right. I can call back if it's not a good time."

"No. No. Now's fine," I said, quickly.

"I was just calling to see how you're doing. I mean, with Bobby's case and all."

I flinched. I didn't have a "case" or a client. All I had was a rather unhealthy curiosity.

"Okay. Fine. Is there anything *you* can tell me, Candace?"

"Me? No. I mean, I don't really know anything. I was just wondering if you'd found out more about Bobby's family. His mother. That kind of thing."

I paused for a moment, trying to figure out exactly what the woman was getting at. The last time we'd spoken, she'd been unwilling to tell me anything other than the name of the hospital where Bobby was born, and that was only to keep me from mentioning her involvement to the police. What was she after now?

"I spoke to Bobby's birth mother," I said.

"Really? What's she like? Did he talk to her before he died? Did she know anything about his death?" The questions poured out of her mouth in a frantic tumble.

I didn't answer any of them.

"Candace, did Bobby mention anything to you about his birth father?" I asked.

"His father? No. Why? Did he find him, too? What is his name? Did Bobby contact him?"

I decided not to be forthcoming with her. "I'm not sure. Was there any other reason you called?"

"Actually, there was," she said. The tone of her voice changed—it became conspiratorial. "I've been thinking a lot about Bobby and his suicide. At first I didn't think it was possible that he'd killed himself, but the more I think about it, the more sense it makes to me."

This caught my attention. This was the first time anyone who knew Bobby had said that it was possible that he'd want to kill himself.

"Really?" I asked. "What makes you say that?"

"Well, you know, Bobby and I were very close. Intimate really." She giggled. It was an unpleasant sound. "He confided in me things that he'd never tell to anyone else."

"Like what?" I asked.

"Like how unhappy he was in his relationship. Like how he wanted to leave Betsy but felt like he couldn't."

I slowed down, not wanting my piqued interest to cause me to get into an accident.

"Why couldn't he leave her?"

"Because she was a junky. He felt like if he left her, she might start using again, or worse."

"Worse?"

"You know, like kill herself or something."

"But why would that make *Bobby* kill *himself*?"

"I don't think you really knew Bobby. Not like I did," she said, her voice oily.

"That's probably true. So maybe you can explain to me why Bobby and Besty's problems, if they were having any, would cause him to kill himself."

"Bobby was a special soul. A sensitive soul. We were very alike in that way. That kind of emotional blackmail makes someone like us feel very . . . very trapped. And anxious. I'm sure that is what Bobby was seeing. He lost sight of himself. He lost sight of the others in his life who could give him peace and joy. So he killed himself."

Everything about what Candace was saying rubbed me the wrong way. She and Bobby didn't seem at all alike, and I doubted that their "special souls" had much in common. Furthermore, the woman was clearly in love with Bobby. Of course she would blame Bobby's lover and fiancée for what had happened to him. But did she have a more nefarious motive for her phone call? Was she trying to steer me in the wrong direction? The E-mails she had sent to Bobby after his body was discovered seemed to absolve her from any knowledge of, or involvement in, his death. On the other hand, even though they'd had the ring of honesty to them, it wasn't impossible that they were part of a ruse to establish her ignorance and innocence.

"So you think Bobby killed himself," I said.

"I think it's possible. Although, of course, there's another possibility, too."

"What's that?"

"That Bobby finally decided to leave Betsy once and for all. And that she killed him rather than let him have his freedom."

12

"DO YOU THINK cannibals would ever eat their own young, and if so, how would they reproduce?"

It's a mark of the state of both my marriage and my husband's career that Peter's question didn't faze me in the slightest. "I suppose the mama cannibal would only nosh on her own offspring if no other food sources were available," I said after some thought.

"Hmm. Interesting idea. The possibility of a famine-inspired infanticide could lend the second act just that added level of tension that I've been looking for."

We were lying with our legs tangled together on the couch, recuperating from the effort of putting our children to bed. I'd come close to strapping Ruby in with her jump rope or the utility belt from Isaac's Batman costume, but she'd finally consented to lie still and listen to a tape. The strains of "There's No Business Like Show Business" from *Annie Get Your Gun* were just barely audible. She had a big thing for show tunes; her Ethel Merman imitation was almost as good as her dad's.

"I could spend my entire career writing nothing but cannibal movies." Peter sounded absolutely thrilled at the idea.

"Career. What's that?" I said. He poked me in the side with his toe. I noticed that it was sticking out of his sock. "You need new socks."

"I always need new socks. Are we going to have one of our biweekly, 'I need to figure out what I'm doing with my life' discussions? Because if we are, I'm going to need another cup of coffee."

I kicked him back, making sure to dig a little into his side where I knew he was ticklish.

"No. We're not going to have any kind of discussion at all. No talking allowed," I said.

We amused ourselves for twenty minutes with an activity that had gotten entirely too rare once we'd had kids, then clicked on the television. We spent a vacant hour watching the end of a spy thriller we could just vaguely remember having seen not long before. One of the benefits of the exhaustion that accompanies parenting is the ability to watch a movie or read a book again and again without remembering a single important feature of the plot.

The next morning was Saturday, the one day of the week when Peter wakes up with the kids and I get the morning off. I briefly considered heading back to the gym—I hadn't been there since the morning Bobby's body had been discovered—but I couldn't bring myself to go. It was just too strange and sad to imagine working out there without Bobby. And I was too lazy to work out anywhere else.

I left my family involved in an elaborate game of hide and go seek, which consisted of the kids hiding and then shrieking out their locations while Peter looked for them. "We're in the closet, Daddy! No, the *hall* closet!"

I'd found Dr. Reuben Nadelman in about four minutes on the web. He was an attending physician at Cedars Sinai Medical Center's pediatric oncology unit, and he was in their staff directory. I also found a number of references to him in the *L.A. Times*, including an announcement of his marriage to a Dr. Larissa Greenbaum, a dermatologist. I couldn't find a residential listing for the Nadelmans or for the Greenbaum-Nadelmans (and people wonder why I don't bother to hyphenate) in the phone book. I launched Lexis, a legal search engine, and input the doctors' names in the real estate database. They had purchased a home on Hollyhock Way in Brentwood four years before, the assessed value of which was $1.2 million dollars. I might not have had his phone number, but I'd easily found his address. The World Wide Web—a nosey Parker's best friend.

As I drove through the stone gateway that marked the beginning of the tony Los Angeles neighborhood made infamous by O. J. Simpson's murderous and ultimately unpunished rage, I mused on the coincidence of Bobby being born to one doctor and then adopted by another. Sometimes it seemed like every Jewish mother but my own had gotten her wish.

I wound my way through tree-lined streets past faux French, faux Spanish, and faux English Tudor palaces. Dr. Nadelman lived in a Cape Cod that looked like it had been swallowing the steroid prescription of an

East German swimmer. Bobby had been blessed with a seemingly endless supply of wealthy parents.

I was hoping that on a Saturday morning, at 10:30, the doctors would still be home. They didn't disappoint me.

Bobby's birth stepmother (is there such a term?) led me through the house to a large kitchen papered in yellow roses. Bobby's father was seated at one end of a long Country-French table, reading the paper.

"Reuben, this is a friend of Bobby Katz's," Larissa Greenbaum-Nadelman said, steering me toward a chair and putting a cup of unasked-for coffee in front of me. She pushed a sugar bowl and a coffee creamer in the shape of a cow with an open mouth across the table to me and sat down next to her husband.

Dr. Nadelman nodded his head, folded up his newspaper, and extended his hand. "I wondered if someone would come by. I read about Bobby's death in the *Times*. I was so very sorry to hear about it. He seemed like a nice man."

"He was," I said. "I take it that Bobby came to see you."

"No, but he wrote to me, and we spoke on the telephone." Dr. Nadelman took a sip of his coffee. He was a small man with nothing of Bobby's carefully tended musculature. His dark hair was salted white above the ears. It crossed my mind that he looked Jewish, with his dark eyes and heavy eyebrows, but he could as easily have been Italian or Greek. Then I realized that that kind of thinking was just what I'd found so repellent in Bobby's birth mother.

"Bobby contacted me not long ago. He'd received my name from his birth mother, a woman I knew for a short while many years ago. Both Bobby and his mother were under the impression that I was his genetic father."

"Aren't you?" I asked.

"No, I'm not. When Bobby first wrote to me, I thought that it was possible that I was. After all, I had had a sexual relationship with his birth mother, and we had experienced a failure of birth control. Even then, though, it seemed very unlikely that he was my son."

"Why?" I asked. I was absolutely flummoxed by this turn of events. I had been certain, as Bobby most likely had been, that Reuben Nadelman was his biological father.

His wife interrupted. "You see, Ms. Applebaum, Reuben and I tried for many years to have children. While I had a child from a previous marriage, we never conceived one of our own. Reuben's sperm count was just too low."

Dr. Nadelman nodded. "We finally had our son, Nate, through artificial insemination of donor sperm," he said. "Now, while it's certainly possible for me to have impregnated Susan—after all, all it takes is one sperm—as I said, it's not particularly likely. I told this to Bobby when he called me. I told him about my infertility, and that it was unlikely, though not impossible, that I was his father."

"Do you mind telling me how he reacted?"

Dr. Nadelman shrugged his shoulders. "He was disappointed, I think. Not because he so desperately wanted to be my son, in particular, but because I think he had been so sure he'd found his father."

"Disappointed enough to kill himself?" I asked.

Again the doctor shrugged. "I'm sorry, I really don't know the answer to that. I didn't know him. Certainly not well enough to make a judgment. But he wasn't distraught when we spoke. In fact, he still seemed to hold out a hope that he was my son, despite what I told him about my fertility issues."

"And you don't know for certain that he wasn't your son. As you said, all it takes is one sperm."

"I didn't know for certain, then. I do know now."

"What do you mean?"

"Bobby told me the story of how he came to find out he was adopted in the first place. His diagnosis as a Tay-Sachs carrier led to his determination that he was the biological son of neither of the people whom he had always known to be his parents."

I nodded. I knew that much.

"For that same reason, I could not possibly be his father."

"Excuse me?"

"Tay-Sachs is an inherited condition. It's autosomal recessive. That means that only if both of a child's parents pass on the affected gene will that child have the fatal disease."

I nodded. I knew all this.

"Tay-Sachs *carriers*, on the other hand, receive an affected gene from only one of their parents. That means that either Bobby's birth mother or father was a carrier and passed that gene on to him. Now, as I'm sure you know, Tay-Sachs is a disease found almost exclusively in Jews of Ashkenazic descent. Thus, the gene must have come from his father, because Bobby's birth mother is about as Jewish as the Pope."

I smiled. The doctor had a sense of humor. Not necessarily a good one, but a sense of humor nonetheless.

"Despite the fact that I am Jewish, I am not a carrier of the Tay-Sachs gene," he said. "As you may or may not be aware, Tay-Sachs testing is not a chromosome analysis like, for example, the kind of testing done for Down's syndrome. The Tay-Sachs test involves the detection of an enzyme. Carriers have about half as much of this enzyme called Hex A in their blood as noncarriers. When Bobby told me about his Tay-Sachs, I went and had a blood test to determine my status. It was negative. I'm not a Tay-Sachs carrier and, thus, cannot be Bobby's father."

I felt completely deflated—just as Bobby would have felt.

"Did you tell Bobby that you weren't his father?"

The doctor shook his head. "I would have called him right away, but I didn't have the opportunity. I read about Bobby's death in the papers the same day I received my test results."

I heaved a sigh. "I guess I'm back to the drawing board. I need to find another Jewish man with whom Susan Sullivan had sex at the same time as she had her affair with you."

"Not necessarily," Larissa said.

"What?" the doctor and I spoke in unison.

"French Canadians and certain Louisiana Cajuns also carry the Tay-Sachs gene."

"Really?" I said. "I didn't know that."

"Neither did I," said her husband. "How did you find this out?"

She patted his hand. "After the boy called, I did a little research. I looked at one or two articles on Tay-Sachs."

"Why?" he asked, his brow wrinkled with concern.

She reached up a hand and touched his cheek. "This was before you got the test results back—before we knew you weren't a carrier. I wondered if the Tay-Sachs might have been the cause of your infertility."

"Why didn't you tell me what you'd discovered?"

She smiled gently. "I was afraid it would hurt you. I didn't want you to think that I was still searching for answers. I didn't want you to think I was still tied up in all those horrible knots, that I was still consumed with our fertility issues the way we both were back then, back before Nate was born."

Reuben hugged his wife to him for a moment. In that flash of intimacy, I felt like I could see the relationship these two people shared: the warmth, the love, the respect and caring. I wished so much that Bobby had found out that he was this gentle man's son. The home made by this father would have been the haven the Katzes could never have provided and that Susan Sullivan would not.

"Bobby's father could be either an Ashkenazic Jew or of French-Canadian or Cajun descent," I said, almost to myself.

I sat for a moment, thinking of Susan and her vehemence. And her anti-Semitism. Suddenly, another thought occurred to me. Perhaps Susan Sullivan had protested too much. She had admitted to me that she'd lied to her husband about her education. Maybe she'd lied about much more. Perhaps she'd lied about the results of her genetic testing.

"Is it possible that you *are* Bobby's father, but that his *mother* passed on the Tay-Sachs gene to him? Maybe *she* has Jewish or French-Canadian ancestry."

He looked at me for a moment, surprise in his eyes. "I suppose it's *possible*," he said softly.

13

"WAIT, YOU'RE ASKING *me* for help?" I was astonished. I'd spent so much time, over the past couple of years, begging Al for information and assistance. He'd never once asked me for anything in return, other than to lend a sympathetic ear to his Baroque conspiracy theories.

"Don't make so much of it," he growled on the other end of the phone. "I need a little lesson is all. On mitigation and the death penalty."

I'd unwillingly come straight home from my visit to Dr. Nadelman. What I'd really wanted to do was whip over to the Palisades and shake Susan Sullivan until she told me exactly who Bobby's father was and what was going on. Instead, I'd been treated to a hysterical phone call from my husband. It seemed life on the planet could not continue without a certain lavender tutu that had disappeared off the face of the earth. I described various possible tutu hiding places over the phone, to no avail. Finally, and not a little frustrated, I agreed to come home and search for the offending bit of gauze myself. It took me about three minutes to locate it crumpled in a corner of Ruby's dollhouse, where it had been doing service as the carpet in the master bedroom. I was getting ready to throttle both Peter and Ruby when the phone rang.

"And why do you need my help?" I asked Al.

"Because I took a case, and I want to make sure I'm up on exactly what the hell I should be doing here."

"Details?" I leaned back in the kitchen chair, wrapped the phone cord around my finger, and put my feet up on the table. The kids were in Ruby's room playing Barbie. Peter had retired to his office in a huff and was most likely rearranging his first-series Mego *Star Trek* action figures (still in the original packaging). I could be confident of a few moments of tranquillity.

"It's a death penalty case, and the attorney hired me to replace the mitigation investigator, who went out on maternity leave. Might I say, at this point, that you ladies are never going to get anywhere in your careers if you keep dropping the ball to drop a baby?"

"No, you might not. Okay. So you were hired to help the defense attorney flush out information that will convince the jury to give the guy life without parole and not a lethal injection."

"Exactly. Only I've never done a mitigation case before. The lawyer seems like a decent enough guy, for a lawyer, but he dumped the file in my lap without a heck of a lot of explanation or direction. I want to make sure that I'm investigating the right things. You know, finding things that will actually be useful. No point in coming up with a file full of crap."

"True enough. Okay, here's what I'll do. I'm no expert on the death penalty myself. I'll do a little research, find a couple of articles that describe what specific kinds of things can be used in mitigation of a death sentence, and put it all together for you. When do you need this by?"

"Whenever. Yesterday."

"Seriously."

"Well, you got any time today?"

I cocked an ear to the kids. They'd probably let me do a little legal research. I could always toss them in front of the television if I needed to. With Peter working on a mood, I wasn't going to be able to get away to confront Bobby's birth mother anytime soon, at least not without the kids. And I wasn't about to bring them along to what might end up being a confrontation verging on the ugly.

"Sure, I could put in a couple of hours right now," I told Al.

"Let's do this. Do what you can today, and then meet me tomorrow. There's something I want to show you, anyway." He gave me an address in downtown L.A.

"Where am I meeting you?" I asked him.

"It's a surprise."

THE TRUE SURPRISE was how *nice* all the folks were at the indoor firing range. When I'd pulled up in front of the long, low building painted a pale blue, with an oversized mural of cartoon figures pointing weapons, and saw where it was Al had directed me, I'd had to cool off for a few minutes before going inside. Al knew how I felt about guns. I'd always been a proponent of gun control, but getting shot while eight-and-a-half-months pregnant had pretty well sealed my disgust for side arms and their devotees. In the wake of that nightmare, Al had showed up at the hospital with a bouquet of carnations and a little pearl-handled pistol, complete with its own Roma leather lady's gun purse. I'd sent him and his armory packing. Now, here he was, trying once again to convert me into a gun-toting member of the NRA.

It was, however, hard to stay angry when everyone was so superfriendly. I walked into the building under the banner proudly proclaiming it to be the city's largest indoor firearm range and was greeted by a smiling young man in an Oxford-cloth button-down shirt. He complimented me on my Dodgers cap and invited me to wait for Al in the lounge, a friendly little room with a bank of vinyl chairs and a gurgling coffeemaker. A pleasant, middle-aged woman with gray blue hair molded into perfect curls pressed a flyer about "Ladies' Night" at the range into my hands and complimented me on my new red jeans. Everyone there seemed to like how I dressed.

I willed myself to avoid the plate of doughnuts and homemade cookies sitting invitingly next to the coffee machine and finally compromised by taking just half of a honeyglazed. I was licking my fingers after finishing the second half (it seemed rude to leave a half-eaten doughnut just sitting there on the plate) and leafing through a brochure urging me to practice my shotgun skills with some AA Flyer Clay Targets when Al finally showed up.

"Why are we meeting here?" I asked.

He dumped the black nylon duffel bag he was carrying over his shoulder onto one of the vinyl chairs.

"I needed to get some target practice in. What do you have for me?"

I spent about fifteen minutes describing the various facts about a murderer's history that the California courts consider relevant in determining whether he should be executed for his crimes. I'd printed out a good law review article on the subject. Al was grateful both for the article and for the information.

"You see," he said, "this is why you should go into business with me. You figure out the legal stuff, and I do the legwork. We'd be a good team."

"*You* do the legwork? Please. When I was at the federal defender's office, I didn't just sit behind a desk. You and I went out in the field

together. Or have you gotten too senile to remember our days interviewing methamphetamine addicts and robbery witnesses?"

"Prove it," he said with a smile.

"Prove what?"

"Prove that you're capable of doing something other than prancing
around a courtroom. Come shoot with me."

I gave a disgusted snort. "How would that prove *anything*? I don't have
to shoot a gun to show that I can investigate a crime. I didn't carry a gun
when I tracked down my babysitter after she'd disappeared. I didn't carry
a gun when I confronted Abigail Hathaway's murderer."

"Yeah, well, maybe if you had been the one carrying a weapon, you
wouldn't have been the one bleeding on the floor."

I was about to launch into a speech about how people who own guns
are more likely to be shot with their own weapons than they are to shoot
anyone else but bit back the words. Al and I had had this fight too many
times before.

"Speaking of investigations, have you found out anything new about
your trainer?" Al asked. Clearly he also wanted to preempt our all-too-
familiar debate.

I gave him a quick synopsis of the confusing search for Bobby's birth
parents.

"I'm beginning to wonder if any of this is even related to his death," I
said.

Al shrugged his shoulders and said, "My operating assumption has
always been that there are no coincidences. Here this guy shoots himself—"

"Or someone shoots him," I interrupted. "Don't forget the Palm Pilot."

"You're really stuck on that, aren't you?"

"I just don't think someone would order a Palm Pilot online and then
kill himself before it even has a chance to arrive. And, anyway, Bobby just
wasn't a depressed kind of guy."

"Okay, either he shoots himself, or someone shoots him, and he just
so happens to have recently found out that he's adopted and is looking for
his biological parents. It's got to be linked."

"Because there are no such things as coincidences."

"Exactly."

"It's a good theory. It's certainly the one I've been operating on. There's
just one problem with it."

"What?"

"There *are* such things as coincidences. They happen all the time."

He shrugged again.

"Hey, you wouldn't consider doing me the usual favor and calling one of your LAPD buddies to check on the status of the case, would you?" I asked.

"Sure, if you do one other thing for me."

"Anything!"

"Come shoot with me."

I rolled my eyes. "No."

"Listen to me for a minute. I know you're opposed to the idea of people carrying guns, but don't you think your arguments might carry a little more weight if you actually knew what you were talking about? Try it. Take a couple of practice shots. You might find out that you like it."

"I won't like it."

"How do you know, until you try?"

So I did.

And I did. Like it, that is.

14

ESPITE THE BRIGHT yellow sign informing us that the range was equipped to handle semiautomatic pistols, rifles, and even fully automatic machine guns, and that they would happily rent those weapons out to us if we didn't bring our own, Al gave me a small handgun to shoot with. It was black, and heavy, and the handle warmed up quickly in my sweating palm.

He stood behind me in the little booth and watched as I held out the gun with a shaking arm, took aim at a pink silhouette on a sliding metal rack, and jerked the trigger back. Nothing happened.

"Safety's on," Al said.

"What?" I asked, lifting up my ear guards.

"Safety." He took the gun from me and disengaged the safety with a practiced thumb. "Squeeze the trigger. Don't jerk."

"What?" I had the ear guards back in place.

"Squeeze. Gently," he said once I'd freed up an ear.

"Oh. Okay. Like a camera. Squeeze." I aimed as best I could and squeezed. The gun went off with a muffled bang, and my arm jerked. I squinted at the target. To my utter astonishment, there was a mark on the lower left-hand side of the target. I'd hit it.

"Wow!" I said. "I must be a natural. Check that out."

"Not bad. Try again."

The next time, however, I was anticipating the recoil. I couldn't help but flinch as I pulled the trigger. I looked up at the target. It had suffered no further damage.

I raised my eyebrows at Al and said, "Gee, you're right. It is too bad I didn't have a gun when I was investigating the Hathaway murder. I could have fired at her killer and missed. That would have been both smart and effective, don't you think?"

My sarcasm was lost on Al. He motioned at me, and I lifted up the ear guards. "Why don't you try keeping your eyes open," he said.

That's when I started having fun. The next time, I opened my eyes, lined up the target in my sights, and squeezed the trigger, reminding myself not to flinch in anticipation of the recoil. I blasted a hole at the bottom of the target, just where a man might find it most painful.

After that, I couldn't be stopped. I fired single rounds, taking careful aim. That soon got boring, and I experimented with emptying my gun into the target as quickly as I could. I turned down Al's offer of his shotgun and instead tried out his M-9 semiautomatic pistol. The thing weighed at least two pounds, and it took me a while to figure out how to keep the nose up and my arm steady. Once I had that down, however, it was a little distressing how much fun I had firing off the fifteen rounds.

After a couple of hours, Al and I repaired to an early lunch of doughnuts and coffee.

"I told you I'd make a convert out of you," he said.

I snorted the coffee out of my nose. Wiping at the brown stain on my white T-shirt, I shook my head. "Al, you really don't get it, do you?"

"What?"

"I'm not surprised that I had fun. I mean, there's a reason millions of adolescent boys spend all their free time and money in arcades playing Cop-killer or whatever those games are called. Target shooting is *fun*. I don't have a problem with target shooting. If guns were only available at shooting ranges, I'd be perfectly happy. It's the fact that any certified lunatic can buy an assault rifle and mow down a preschool class that bugs me. Or the fact that every single one of my gang-banger clients has an arsenal the size of a National Guard unit. By the way, their guns are legally purchased as often as not. It's the *availability* of a deadly toy that I find so problematic, not that people have fun playing with them."

He opened his mouth, but I didn't give him time to interrupt. "And don't you dare offer to give me one for my own protection. I have two kids, one of whom is a gun nut. I'm not bringing a gun into my house," I said.

I recognized the look that crossed over his face. His eyes held a very definite "Now's the time to teach them gun safety" kind of gleam. But, to my relief, he snapped his mouth shut in a thin line and even, after a moment or two, managed a smile.

"Well, intelligent minds can disagree, I suppose," he said.

"Yup." I nodded.

TRUE TO HIS word, Al used his cell phone to call a couple of his buddies at the LAPD. His old partner was at his desk and put him on hold while he made a call to the Santa Monica Police Department, where Bobby's case was lodged. He was back within minutes. Al nodded and thanked the guy.

"Well?" I said.

"Closed. Cause of death deemed suicide."

"Are they absolutely sure?"

Al shrugged. "Who knows. But they closed the case."

I stared at him for a moment. "Yeah, well, I haven't closed mine," I said.

15

IN ORDER TO get out to meet Al unencumbered by children, I had dropped Ruby off at a friend's for an all-day playdate and left Isaac sitting in our bed watching a *Zaboomafoo* marathon on PBS, a sports bottle of chocolate milk in one hand and a defrosted bagel in the other. Peter hadn't even woken up when I'd rolled him over to make room for his son, and I'd given Isaac strict instructions that if he needed anything, he should kick his father until he gained consciousness. Despite the fact that I'd left the house almost three hours before, neither of the men in my life had budged.

Isaac's eyes were glazed over from watching three hours of the Kratt brothers engaging in their particular brand of frenzied animal-watching—sort of like Mutual of Omaha's *Wild Kingdom* but on speed and with better jokes.

"Hi, Mama. I'm a lemur," my son told me when I walked in the room. He'd eaten his bagel and used his chocolate milk to paint his face with a couple of lemurish black stripes.

"So you are. Is Daddy still asleep?"

"Yeah."

"Did he wake up at all?"

"Yeah, but he didn't want to watch TV, so he put the pillow over his head."

It was nice to know I wasn't the only neglectful parent in the house. I scooped Isaac out of bed, set him gently on the floor, and whipped the covers off my insentient husband with a shriek that wouldn't have embarrassed a banshee. He leapt about sixteen feet in the air.

"Good morning, darling," I purred.

He growled at me and stomped off to the shower. I followed him into the bathroom and leaned against the cold tile wall.

"I'm going to need you to spend some more of that fabulous quality time with Isaac today," I shouted over the sound of the water.

He grunted.

I DIDN'T CALL Susan before driving over to her house. I figured there was a good chance I'd catch her at home on a Sunday afternoon, and I didn't want to give her the chance to avoid me. The sense of righteous indignation that I'd felt after talking to Reuben Nadelman had abated somewhat, but I was still eager to confront her with what I knew. If I caught her unawares, she was less likely to be able to come up with another in the series of half-truths and outright lies with which she had already tried to confuse me.

I pulled up the long driveway, wondering how once again mine were the only tire tracks in the combed gravel. Did the Sullivan family drive hovercraft? Salud obviously had Sundays off, because a handsome older man with pale, blondish gray hair and a weather-beaten face answered the door. He looked like a man who spent a lot of time outside, even if just on the golf course. He was wiry and thin, but his height gave him the impression of bulk.

"Yes? Can I help you?" he asked.

"Hello, I'm Juliet Applebaum. I'm a . . . a friend of Susan's. Is she in?"

He sized me up for a minute, not having missed the stumble my voice made over the word *friend*. I got the feeling that very little got by this man.

"Please come in." He led me through the now-familiar entranceway and back into a large, sunny kitchen. Half of the room was a fairly unremarkable kitchen with the usual cabinetry and appliances. The other half was graced with an impressive oversized stone fireplace, in front of which stood a large, round oak table. The table was set with pretty blue and white dishes and contained the remains of what had obviously been an elaborate brunch. There was a half-eaten platter of berries carefully arranged by color, and a wicker basket with a bright blue gingham ribbon and a few crumbly muffins and croissants nestled in a matching napkin. Susan sat flanked by two handsome, blond men in their mid-to-late twenties. I recognized one as the young man who had pushed Isaac on the swing. The other was clearly his older brother. The two looked remarkably alike, and they both resembled Bobby to an uncanny degree. He, too, had possessed those same handsome, innocuous features and surferboy blond hair.

A pregnant woman in a pale pink sweater that precisely matched her lipstick, her dark hair held back by a thick velvet band, also sat at the table. Near the fireplace, in a low armchair, sat an elderly woman dressed in a severe navy suit tied at the neck with a floppy white bow. Her long, wrinkled earlobes were weighed down by huge, yellowish diamonds that looked like they could use a cleaning, and she was speaking as I came into the room.

"I wish you'd joined Patrick and me at Mass this morning, Susan. Father Fitzgerald gave a lovely sermon. Truly inspiring. It's been so long since you've heard him speak. When was the last time you went to church, dear?"

Everyone looked up as I walked into the room. When Susan saw me, her face froze, and red splotches began to appear under the freckles on her cheeks and neck. Both young men glanced at her. They wore identical looks of concern.

"Hello, Susan. I was just passing by and hoped we might have a word," I said, the bright tone of my voice ringing falsely in my ears and, I'm sure, in theirs.

"Yes. Yes, of course," she said, rising suddenly. "Let's talk in the garden."

"Susan," the older woman said. "Hadn't you best introduce your friend to us? Or am I the only person who hasn't had the pleasure?"

"Oh, of course. Of course," Susan mumbled awkwardly. "Juliet, this is my mother-in-law, Mary-Margaret Sullivan. Marmie, my . . . friend Juliet." Her voice tripped over the word, as mine had earlier. "Juliet, these are my sons P. J."—she pointed to the older young man who was a bit stockier than his brother—"and you met Matthew the other day. P. J.'s wife, Charlotte. And of course my husband, Patrick."

I smiled politely and shook hands all around. The boys' handshakes were firm, like their father's, but Susan's mother-in-law's palm lay like a bundle of dry sticks in my own.

"We'll be outside," Susan said, motioning me to a set of French doors behind the table.

"Are you all right, Mom?" Matthew asked, his brow wrinkled with concern.

"Your mother's fine," his father said, and the young man blushed and stared down at his plate of half-eaten, congealing quiche.

"It's nothing, honey," Susan said soothingly. "Juliet and I are just trying to work out some problems with the library benefit. Lots of last-minute crises, as usual." The woman sure was a fluid liar. But, then, she'd had a lot of practice. She put a hand on my arm and pushed me out through the door. Her nails dug through my shirtsleeve, and I had to work hard to keep from wincing.

"What are you doing here?" she asked, once the door had closed behind us. "I've told you all about Bobby. Why can't you just leave me alone?" She sat down heavily in one of the Adirondack chairs, and I made myself comfortable in the other.

"Have you?"

"Have I what?"

"Have you told me all about Bobby?"

"What do you mean? I've told you everything I know."

"I went to visit Reuben Nadelman yesterday."

She looked at me sharply, and I could see that she was desperate to know more. She didn't speak for a moment and then, in a small voice, said, "How is he? Is he married? Does he have other children?"

"He's married. And he has one son. At least, he has a son whom he considers his. The boy is not his biological child, however."

"What do you mean?" Susan began twisting the ring around her finger.

"Reuben is infertile. His son was conceived through artificial insemination of donor sperm."

She shook her head. "That's just not possible. If he's infertile now, he wasn't twenty-eight years ago. He was certainly fertile enough to get me pregnant."

"Susan, Reuben Nadelman is not a Tay-Sachs carrier. If he is Bobby's father, then Bobby would have had to inherit the gene from you."

"But, I'm *not* a Tay-Sachs carrier. I told you. I'm not Jewish, and anyway, I took that test, and it came out negative."

I leaned forward in my chair, giving Susan a look that I hoped was piercing. "Well, then you know what this means," I said.

"What? What does it mean?"

"If Bobby didn't inherit the gene from you, then he must have inherited it from his father. And if you don't have it, and neither does Reuben

Nadelman, then Reuben can't be Bobby's father. So who is, Susan? Who is Bobby Katz's father?"

Something flickered across her face, but I couldn't tell what. "There is some mistake. Either Bobby's test was wrong, or Reuben's test was wrong. I know that Reuben got me pregnant."

"Couldn't it have been someone else?" I asked.

"No!" Her voice was sharp and angry. "I don't want to talk to you anymore," she said. "I'm finished talking about this. I have nothing more to say about Bobby or anything else. I want you to leave. You can walk around the house to the front. You know the way." And with that, she rose to her feet and walked unsteadily into the house, closing the French doors firmly behind her.

16

S I DROVE down Sunset Boulevard, I puzzled over what Susan had told me. None of this made any sense. Who was Bobby Katz's real father? Had Susan had another lover, a lover of whom she was so ashamed that she refused to talk about him?

It didn't seem possible that there was someone worse in Susan's mind than Reuben Nadelman. She'd been so worried about not foisting a Jewish child off on an unsuspecting Catholic family that she'd gone to great pains to make sure she gave him to a Jewish family. Yet she'd admitted to me that she'd had an affair with Reuben. What could be that much worse than a Jewish lover in her eyes? *Who* could be worse? I tried to imagine what person would be so unacceptable that Susan Sullivan would pretend to have had a child by a Jew rather than admit to an affair with him. A convicted felon? A relative? Her father? Her father-in-law?

That thought made me slam on the brakes. A silver sports car swerved quickly around me. I inhaled sharply as it bulleted in front of me. Thank God for the other driver's reflexes. I was going to have to figure out a way to cut down on the emotive driving if I wanted to see out my fourth decade. I thought again about the Faye Dunaway-in-*Chinatown* scenario I had shocked myself by imagining. It just didn't make sense, however. Neither Susan's father nor her father-in-law were likely to be Bobby's father. Unless Susan was lying about her genetic test, the man who had contributed his little bundle of chromosomes to Bobby's creation had been a Tay-Sachs carrier. While it was theoretically possible that one of those men carried the gene, it was a ridiculously long shot. And if there's one thing I learned in all my years of investigating and trying cases, it was the logical principle of Occam's razor. The simplest and most obvious explanation is most often the true one.

None of this got me any closer to discovering what had happened to Bobby.

Had he or had he not committed suicide? If he had, was his despondency related to his adoption and what he'd found out about his birth parents, or was there some other motivation for it altogether? I couldn't seem to accept the suicide theory; it didn't make sense, given everything I knew about Bobby. However, if it wasn't suicide, then it was murder. The fact that Bobby had been found with the weapon ruled out a random killing, to my mind. None of the many drive-by shooters and carjackers I'd come across in my public defender days left their weapons behind. Professional criminals, and by that I mean those who engage in illegal behavior for profit, value their weapons. They're attached to them. More importantly, the guns cost money. The last thing these guys want to do is throw money away. If Bobby's death were the result of a random act of violence, the killer wouldn't have left the gun behind.

No, if Bobby was murdered, he was murdered by someone he knew, and that person had done his or her best to make the crime look like suicide. As Al has told me time and time again, look to the family. More often than not, the only people who hate us enough to kill us are those who are supposed to love us the most. The question was, which of Bobby's families? He had so many.

My cell phone rang. The caller ID screen was flashing "Home."

"Hi, Peter," I said. "How are you guys doing?"

"We're good. We just built a model Native American village out of Lego blocks."

"What a good dad you are. And so PC."

"Yeah, whatever. Listen, I'll make you a deal."

"What?"

"I'll give you the whole rest of the afternoon on your own if you do kid duty tonight so I can catch a movie with a couple of the guys."

A few more hours of freedom! "Sure, no problem," I said, doing my best to convey the false impression that I was doing him a favor. "I'll be home before dinner."

"Take your time."

In the background I heard banging and shrieking. "What's that?" I asked.

"Isaac's bringing in the cavalry to attack the village. I'd better go help Ruby rescue the women and children."

I hit the End button and tapped the steering wheel. *Look to the family*, I thought to myself. Bobby and Betsy weren't married, but they were about to be. Maybe I needed to look a little more closely at the person on whose behalf I was supposedly investigating this case. I made a quick right onto Melrose Avenue and headed over to Hollywood.

I FOUND BETSY still sober, to my great relief, and looking much better than when I'd seen her last. She'd finally gotten up the energy to wear something other than sweats. She had on a pair of black flared jeans with neon green roses embroidered down one leg, and a green Lycra top that clung tightly to her body, outlining her breasts and leaving bare the little roll at her midriff. She had a small gold hoop in her bellybutton. Her hair was freshly cut, and she'd put on lipstick. In fact, she looked a heck of a lot better than I did.

"Roy, this is Juliet Applebaum, the client of Bobby's who's been trying to track down what was going on with him before he died. Juliet, this is my friend Roy West."

I shook the hand of the small man who had been sitting with Betsy. He looked about forty, with graying hair cropped close to his head and gold grommets punched into both earlobes. A third bit of gold poked through one of his eyebrows. He looked too old for his metal decorations, and he smelled strongly of cigarette smoke. He took a great swig from the oversized plastic L.A. Dodgers cup he held in his hand and belched softly. There was a bottle of Diet Coke on the coffee table. I was willing to bet the farm that Roy was a friend from AA. The smoking and copious caffeine consumption gave him away.

Betsy hadn't shown much ability to keep on the wagon in the absence of Bobby's positive influence. I was glad to see that she had fallen back in with the AA circle. Hopefully, their support would give her the strength she needed to stay straight.

I told Betsy that I hadn't found out much more about Bobby's birth family, and in fact was even more confused than ever before. I paused, waiting for her response. I didn't know exactly what I was looking for or what I hoped she would tell me. Mostly, I just wanted to get a better sense of her. Could she have had something to do with her fiancé's death?

"Are you sure Bobby's Tay-Sachs test was accurate?" I asked.

She shrugged. "I guess so. I mean, we had it done at UCLA. I can't imagine they would screw it up."

I couldn't either. "Do you think I could take another look through Bobby's things?"

"What are you looking for?"

"I don't really know." I shrugged. "I guess I'm just on a fishing expedition."

"Well, you'll have to fish somewhere else," Roy interrupted.

"Excuse me?" I asked.

"The Katzes came over here and cleaned Betsy out. They took all of Bobby's files, his office furniture, even his books. It was all we could do to keep their hands off the living room furniture."

"Roy said it was mine, and he knew, because he helped me move it in from my old apartment." She smiled at him.

He preened. "I was happy to do it. Lying to those creeps is a good deed."

I looked from one of them to the other. It dawned on me that they might be either sleeping together or inching toward it. A new boyfriend would explain Betsy's transformation from depressed widow to Lycra-clad babe. Or was he new? Was it possible that she'd been seeing him even before Bobby died?

I made small talk for a little while, watching them closely. There definitely seemed to be some kind of chemistry between the two. Betsy brushed against Roy's arm as she picked up his cup to refill it. He put an arm around her shoulder when she mentioned Bobby. It was a comforting gesture, but it seemed more intimate than simply supportive.

"Are you going to keep investigating?" Betsy asked me.

"I don't know what more I can do," I said. "I might ask Bobby's parents if they'll let me see his papers. Maybe they'll let me look through his hard drive again. I can't imagine that I'll find anything, though. It's really a puzzle."

Betsy nodded. "I've been running through this over and over in my mind, and I just can't think of any reason for Bobby to have killed himself. I know I was kind of wrapped up in my own problems, but I still think I would have noticed if Bobby had been depressed. He just wasn't like that. He didn't get blue. If he was bumming, he'd just go work out."

I agreed with this assessment. I certainly didn't know Bobby as well as she did, but in all our time together, he'd never been anything but upbeat. Even when Besty had gotten into trouble, Bobby had retained his positive outlook. He'd been convinced that it was just a matter of working harder to help her with her recovery.

"Bobby didn't kill himself," Betsy said firmly.

"I hate to say this, but maybe it was a drug deal gone bad," Roy said.

"Roy! Bobby would never have done that!" Betsy sounded outraged.

"You can't know that, Betsy. Every one of us is just one step away from using. Maybe Bobby took that step. Maybe he arranged to meet some guy out by the beach and got robbed instead."

The thought had occurred to me right after Bobby's death, but I had dismissed it. Bobby had been the poster child for the recovery movement. It just didn't seem possible for him to have fallen off the wagon. Moreover, Bobby was acutely conscious of the health consequences of using. Methamphetamine had become toxic to his body. It didn't make sense that a man devoted to maximizing his physical performance would risk so much. Perhaps, however, I'd been too hasty in casting this drug-deal scenario aside.

"I know it doesn't seem possible, but maybe Roy has a point," I said. "Think back to Bobby's behavior leading up to the day he died. Was he acting strangely in any way? Did he disappear for periods of time?"

"Juliet, I think I would know if he were using. I mean, for God's sake, the warning signs are, like, tattooed on my forehead. He wasn't."

"But wasn't he being unusually secretive? He kept the adoption thing from you. Isn't it at least possible that he kept his drug use from you as well?"

I knew I was cross-examining her. Peter is forever complaining about this habit of mine. Once you learn courtroom techniques, however, it's difficult to abandon them for the niceties of acceptable conversation. For one thing, they are remarkably effective. There's nothing like an insistent barrage of questions for eliciting a response.

Betsy bit her lip. "He did lie to me for months about the adoption. But I would know if he used. Wouldn't I?" she said plaintively.

I just shrugged my shoulders.

We sat quietly for a little while, and I debated whether or not I should ask Betsy about Candace. That woman was in love with Bobby. Maybe she'd killed him out of frustrated desire. When I brought up her name to Betsy, she shook her head. "No, he didn't say anything. I mean, how could he? He never told me he was adopted, so how could he tell me about meeting some woman on an Internet adoption website?"

I fumbled around for more to ask Betsy but finally gave up. It gave me pause that Betsy had argued against the possibility of Bobby having killed himself. If she had done it, wouldn't she be more inclined to support the suicide hypothesis? I hadn't learned much in my visit, but neither had my concerns been assuaged. For the time being, I wasn't going to dismiss the possibility that Betsy had had something to do with Bobby's death.

17

I SWORE UNDER MY breath as I stood looking at the smashed window of Peter's car. Peter's lovingly tended, vintage 2002. The one I'd insisted on driving. The one I'd parked in front of Betsy's apartment, in a part of Hollywood that verged on the seedy.

The front passenger window was shattered, bits of glass littering the ground and the bucket seat. I glanced in the window and was relieved to see that the radio was still there. For once I'd actually remembered to take my purse with me, so that was safe as well. The fact that it seemed to be an act of vandalism rather than theft gave me little comfort, and I stomped around the car to the driver's side. My breath caught in my throat and my stomach lurched when I saw the words scratched into the side of the car. Someone had written "MIND YOUR OWN BUSINESS" in jagged capital letters.

The words extended along both driver's-side doors and were carved with such force that the orange paint had peeled up around the scratches. I looked quickly up and down the street. At the end of the block, I saw two boys playing around with a broken scooter. They were trying to get up some speed while balancing on the scooter's remaining wheel.

"Hey!" I called out to them.

They looked up at me and then continued with their game.

"Hey!" I said again and walked quickly up the block. They appeared to be brothers; one was about seven years old, and the other looked no more than five. They had dark skin and close-shaved heads, and the older boy wore a gold cross dangling from a hoop in one ear.

"Did you see anyone near that orange car back there?" I asked.

The older boy shrugged his shoulders, and the younger boy giggled.

"Did you?" I asked again.

"Maybe," the older boy said. "How much you pay me to tell you?"

I crouched down next to him and said, in my best mommy voice, "Listen, young man, if you don't tell me who scratched up my car, I'm going to find your mother. I bet she'll make you talk."

He clicked his tongue and said, "I don't know nothin' 'bout your car."

"Fredo, that rich dude was hangin' out by the orange car, remember?" the younger brother said.

"You shut up," the older boy whacked his brother on the top of his head.

"Hey!" I grabbed the older boy's arm. "No hitting."

"Yeah, Fredo! No hitting," the little boy said, his lip trembling.

"Fredo, tell me what happened to my car," I said.

The boy rolled his eyes. "Fine. Whatever. This phat car pulled up next to yours, and this dude got out. That's all we know. Honest. I don't know what he did or nothing. He was just, like, walking around your car."

"Did you see him break the window?"

The little boys shook their heads.

"Do you know what kind of car he was driving?"

"No. It was phat."

"Fat?"

The little boys rolled their eyes at my ignorance. "You know, cool. Awesome. Like a racing car," Fredo said.

"What color was the racing car?"

"Metal," said the younger boy.

PETER'S FACE TURNED a mottled red when I told him what had happened. He rushed out to his beloved car and knelt down next to the driver's-side door. He ran his fingers along the scratches, swearing quietly under his breath.

"I'm so sorry, honey. Really," I said.

"Who did this?" he asked, rising to his feet.

I told him what the two boys had told me. "I'm figuring that by racing car they meant sports car. That's what Isaac calls them, doesn't he?" Among our son's many obsessions was one with the automobile. While Hondas were his inexplicable favorite—he called them Wandas and lovingly stroked each one we passed (it made for slow going on walks)—he

was also enamored of anything he could call a racing car. For some mysterious reason, this included both sports cars and taxicabs.

Peter swore again.

"I'm sorry, Peter. Really I am."

"It's not the car that I'm upset about. I mean, yeah, I'm upset about
the car. I can't even imagine what it's going to cost to fix this. The scratches
go all the way through to the metal. But that's not what I'm worried
about."

"I know," I said.

We went back in the house. I called the police department, and while
I waited on hold to file a report, the two of us ran through the various
people involved in the case, trying to come up with a possible suspect. The
problem was that the only person whom I could even remotely imagine
doing something like that was the only one I could be sure hadn't been
involved. Betsy had been in the room with me the whole time I'd been
parked in front of her house. That left the members of Bobby's birth and
adoptive families, none of whom seemed a particularly likely candidate
for such a brutally juvenile warning. And then there was Candace.

Finally, after I'd waited close to a quarter of an hour on hold, a police
officer picked up the line. I told her what had happened and where I'd been
parked. Then, I said, "I think this might have something to do with the
death of a friend of mine."

The officer, who had seemed up until then utterly bored with the details
of yet another act of destruction of property, perked up. "Excuse me?"
she asked.

"My friend Bobby Katz was found dead in his car a couple of weeks
ago. It appeared to be a suicide, and I understand that the Santa Monica
Police Department has closed the case. However, I think that someone
might have been trying to warn me off any further investigation."

"Are you a private investigator, ma'am?" The cop's voice was frosty.

"No. No, I'm not. I'm a friend of the deceased. I was simply trying to
help his fiancée determine what happened to him. Perhaps you can refer
this to the detectives assigned to the case."

"Ma'am, there won't be any detectives assigned to a suicide if the case
is closed. However, I'm more than happy to pass this information along
to someone in the Santa Monica PD."

I was getting the brush-off. "Officer, listen. If Bobby was murdered, then it's very possible that I just got a warning from his killer. I'm concerned. With reason, I think."

"You said your friend committed suicide."

"No, I said that the case had been *ruled* a suicide. There's a difference." I knew I was coming off high-handed, but I was scared, and she was making me angry.

"As I said, ma'am, I'll pass this along. This is your police report number for insurance purposes." She mumbled a string of numbers and then she hung up the phone.

"Well?" Peter asked. He was sitting at the table, holding Isaac on his lap. Isaac was sucking on a tube of yogurt and had a trail of fluorescent pink down the front of his shirt. I swabbed at the stain with a paper towel.

"Well?" my husband repeated.

"I don't think they're going to do anything."

"Juliet, I'm worried about this."

"I know. I am, too."

"What are you going to do?"

"I don't know. Wait to hear from the police, I guess."

"I won't hold my breath." He kissed the top of Isaac's head. For a split second, I wished I'd taken Al up on his offer. I imagined confronting this fear with a loaded revolver. I couldn't help but wonder if I'd feel safer.

"I'm going to call Bobby's parents," I said.

"Which ones?"

"The Katzes. Maybe they'll let me take another look at Bobby's things. If the cops aren't going to do anything, I'm going to have to track down whoever is responsible myself."

Peter compressed his lips in a thin line but didn't say anything. He picked up Isaac and carried him out to the playroom, where Ruby was busy building a dollhouse out of blocks. I couldn't tell whether he was angry with me for continuing my investigation or whether he understood that it was my only option. I couldn't tell, and I didn't try to find out.

I dug Bobby's parents' phone number out of my purse and picked up the phone. His father answered. Before I could make my request, he said, "Ms. Applebaum, we all appreciate that you are trying to help. However, I must insist that you refrain from continuing in these efforts. It's a violation of Bobby's privacy. And of ours."

I had been expecting something like this. "I understand that you might feel that way, Dr. Katz. But Betsy isn't convinced that Bobby committed suicide. It's possible that I'll be able to uncover enough information to convince the police to reopen the case."

"Betsy is a deluded and manipulative drug addict, who seems to have sucked you into her fantasy or beguiled you into going along with her plans, whatever those may be. What she thinks about Bobby is utterly irrelevant. The police, the coroner, the medical examiner, all agree that Bobby killed himself. Your pursuit of intimate details of his life is not only unhelpful but destructive." The doctor's voice was cold and harsh, but I wasn't giving up. Someone had struck out at me, had threatened me. It was personal now. I was too angry and too scared to back off.

"I'm terribly sorry to have offended you, Dr. Katz. But I have reason to believe not only that Bobby was murdered, but that the murderer is trying to scare me off the investigation." I told him about the warning on my car.

He snorted derisively. "I haven't any idea who did that to your car, Ms. Applebaum. Moreover, it's ludicrous for you to imagine that it had any-thing to do with Bobby's death. You parked in a lousy neighborhood. Be more careful next time." And with that, he hung up on me.

My tenacity in the face of opposition is either my best or worst quality, depending on whom you ask. When I was a child, it was a source of intense frustration to my poor parents, who took a remarkably long time figuring out that the best way to get me to do something was to tell me not to. Peter has proved to be a better manipulator and generally avoids being on the wrong side of my intransigence. In fact, because he's not a particularly obstinate person himself, he has always relished having, as he says, a pit bull in his corner. I myself grew somewhat less comfortable with this particular side of my personality when I began seeing it reflected back at me in Ruby's face. My daughter makes me look positively irresolute; she doesn't have a pliable bone in her body. She came out of me with her little fists balled and raised and has been bashing her way through the world ever since.

I was debating the merits of driving out to Thousand Oaks and blus-tering into the Katzes' home when the phone rang. It took me a moment to figure out that the whispering voice on the other end of the line belonged to Bobby's sister Michelle.

"I'm so sorry about my dad, Juliet. I just want you to know that not all of us think that way."

"What way?" I asked.

"Not all of us think that Bobby killed himself. I mean, I don't. He couldn't have. And I really appreciate what you've been doing. It's *my* fault my dad is all up in arms about this."

"Your fault?"

"Yes," she said apologetically. "I didn't mean to get them upset or to get you in trouble." That was a funny phrase for a grown woman to use. "But when my mother and David told us about your investigation, I tried to convince my parents to let you go forward. I'm convinced that there is more to this than the police think."

"Michelle, why are we whispering?"

"Oh, I'm sorry." I could almost hear her blushing. "I'm at my parents' house, and I'm on my cell phone. In the bathroom. I didn't want my dad to know that I was calling you."

The Drs. Katz were so formidable that they reduced their grown-up daughter, a woman of significant accomplishment in her own right, to a teenager sneaking a telephone call while pretending to use the toilet.

"There are a few things that I'd really like to talk about, and I can't imagine you'll be able to stay in the bathroom for long. Can you meet me?" I said.

"What? Now?"

"Yes. I mean, it doesn't have to be right now, but it might as well be. Did your father tell you that someone threatened me?" I told Michelle about Peter's car.

"Oh no! That's awful. You must be terrified." That was too strong a word. Nervous? Yes. Scared, even. But the feeling of foreboding inspired by the vandalism of the BMW certainly didn't rise to the level of terror. Or so I tried to convince myself.

"I guess I could meet you," Michelle continued. "I could pretend that I have to go into the office."

It took me a while to convince Peter that I wasn't taking any unnecessary risks by talking to Michelle. He finally agreed that I should go but insisted that he come along, too. And, since we were both going, Ruby and Isaac were necessarily invited along for the ride.

"We'll have dinner at the mall," I said brightly, as if the prospect of limp egg rolls and gyro platters was an enticement. Actually, for them it probably was.

By the time we arrived, Michelle was already waiting for me at an orange plastic table in the food court.

I sat down opposite her and waved Peter in the direction of the California Pizza Kitchen. "I'll find you guys in about half an hour," I told him. I was about to ask him to get me a couple of slices of pizza but changed my mind. Michelle was one of those tiny little women who can't find enough size twos to flesh out a decent wardrobe. I amended that to a Caesar salad. With the dressing on the side.

Michelle and I watched Peter and the kids wander off. Ruby was skipping ahead, and Isaac was sitting on his father's shoulders.

"You have a lovely family," she said.

"Thanks. Do you have kids?"

She shook her head. "No, not yet. We're thinking about it, but my hours are really crazy. Larry didn't even bat an eyelash when I told him and my parents that I had to go to work tonight. I probably spend more Sunday nights at work than at home."

"That's hard," I said. I certainly wasn't about to feed her the line about how it was perfectly reasonable to expect to have a demanding career and be an active and involved parent. I'd discovered the folly of that the hard way. But Michelle was at least thirty-five years old, if not older. She didn't have a lot of time to debate the pros and cons of reproduction. No way I was going to tell her that, either.

"Anyway, like I said on the phone, I really do appreciate your trying to help us figure out what happened to Bobby," she said.

If there was anyone who could help me rule out the possibility that Bobby had killed himself, maybe it was this woman, who loved him so much and knew him so well. "I'm sure you've gone over this a thousand times in your mind," I said, "but thinking about everything that happened to Bobby right before his death—Betsy's arrest, his discovery that he was adopted—does it seem possible that he could have been depressed enough to commit suicide?"

She shook her head. Tears welled up in her eyes and threatened to spill over. "I just don't believe Bobby could have done that. He wasn't like that.

I mean, he definitely had a self-destructive side. I guess you know about his methamphetamine problem."

I nodded.

"But he kicked that. Completely. He'd put all that behind him."

"You don't think that what happened with Betsy might have pushed him over the edge?"

"Of course Betsy's relapse made him *sad*, that's only natural. But you should have heard him defend her to my parents. He told them that addiction is a physical and mental disease and lectured them on tolerance and understanding. He was amazing. He stood by her the whole time, and honestly, I don't think he would have abandoned her now, when she's back in treatment and doing so well."

I cringed a bit, remembering Betsy's jag. "What about finding out about the adoption? Could that have depressed him sufficiently?"

Michelle shook her head. "Bobby wasn't depressed or sad about that. I mean, he was furious with our parents for not telling him. But he wasn't upset about being adopted. On the contrary. He seemed really excited about finding his birth mother. You see, our mother is a wonderful woman. She's smart and strong and a real . . . a real . . . " I was tempted to fill her pause with the word *bitch*, but restrained myself. "She's wonderful," Michelle repeated lamely. "But, she's very demanding. And she's not a real affectionate person. Neither is my dad. I think Bobby needed that more than the rest of us did. It's like Lisa, David, and I were kind of hardwired for my parents—we weren't particularly needy children. But Bobby was wired for something else. He always wanted more of a certain kind of attention than my parents could give. And the attention they did give, the way they got involved in our schoolwork, in our grades, well, that didn't usually work out so well for Bobby. He never excelled academically, so the fact that that was the way they showed their interest in him ended up causing him anxiety and stress instead of anything positive."

"It sounds like he didn't really fit your parents' ideal of what a child should be like."

She shook her head. "No, he certainly didn't. After a while, they stopped demanding so much of him; after all, they had the three of us to satisfy them. Don't get me wrong," she said urgently. "They loved Bobby. Really they did. It was just a difficult relationship."

"Why did they adopt him in the first place? I mean, they already had three children. Why did they want another?" I wanted to see if Michelle's answer matched that of her mother's.

"They always planned to have four children—two boys and two girls. They'd even timed everything perfectly so that their residencies wouldn't be disrupted. But then my mom had to have C-sections with all of us. My birth was particularly hard on her, and the doctors were afraid that if she got pregnant again, she might have a uterine rupture. At first I think my parents accepted that. After all, they did wait eight years before they adopted Bobby. But, finally, I guess they decided that they really had to have their picture-perfect family complete with two of each kind of kid. So they adopted a little baby boy."

"Do you think that Bobby was eager to find his birth parents because he imagined that they might give him the kind of acceptance that your parents never could?"

Michelle looked thoughtful. "I suppose that's possible. I only ever really talked about the adoption with him twice. The first time was right after he found out. David told him, and then the next weekend, he asked Lisa and me to meet him at Mom and Dad's. He told us that he had something important to talk about with the whole family. It was pretty intense. He sat us all down in the kitchen and told us that he knew about the adoption. At first my father tried to pretend that he didn't know what Bobby was talking about. I mean, he'd been pretending for so long.

"But Bobby didn't let my dad get away with it. First, he tried to get Lisa and me to admit it, but I guess we were just too freaked out to say anything. I remember Lisa was leafing through a medical journal of Mom's, and she just sat there, pretending to read. I don't even know what I was doing. Probably trying to look invisible."

"What made your father finally admit the truth?"

"Bobby was getting angrier and angrier. I think initially he was trying to protect David so that my parents wouldn't know that he was the one who told, but when they kept insisting that it wasn't true, he told them that David had told him everything. It was horrible. He just looked at Dad and said, 'Stop lying. For once just stop lying.'"

"Your father told him the truth?"

Michelle shook her head. "No, my mother did. She said that it was true, but that it didn't mean anything. That it didn't mean they didn't love him. She even hugged him, which if you knew my mother, you'd know is a huge deal. She's not a hugger."

"How did Bobby respond?"

"He ended up bursting into tears. I did, too, and I swear I even saw a tear in Mom's eye. Bobby told us that he loved us, and that he wasn't upset about being adopted. He asked my parents what they knew about his birth mother, but we all could see right away that the question really upset them. From the very beginning, they were absolutely opposed to his finding out anything about her. I think they finally told him that Jewish Family Services would never tell them anything beyond his birth date and the fact that his mother was healthy. I don't know if they know any specific facts, but I'm pretty confident that even if they do, they wouldn't have told Bobby anything else. Mom especially didn't think anything good could come out of looking for his birth mother. She told Bobby that it was obvious that the woman hadn't wanted him, so he should just concentrate on the people who did. Namely, her and Dad. And us, of course."

"How did it all end?"

"I guess we all just told Bobby how much we loved him again, and he told us that he loved us, too. And then we never really talked about it much as a family again."

"But you talked about it with Bobby?"

"Yeah, one other time. He had given me a free training session for my birthday, so I came down to his gym in Hollywood. He told me that he was looking for his birth mother, and we started imagining what she was like. We figured that she was Jewish, since the adoption had come through Jewish Family Services. Bobby was sure she had been really young, probably a teenager, and that she'd given him up because she wasn't able to care for him. He was confident that she'd be interested in meeting him, particularly since so much time had passed, and he obviously wasn't after anything from her. He said that it was even possible that she was looking for him, too."

"Did he ever tell you that he found her?"

"No, but he did, didn't he?"

I wondered for a moment whether I should tell Michelle what I knew. I decided to; she was Bobby's sister. She loved him. She had a right to know. "Yes, he did," I said.

"And was she a teenager? I mean, when she gave him up?"

"No, she was young, in her midtwenties, but she was married. Her husband was off fighting in Vietnam, and she had an affair."

Michelle nodded." That makes sense, I guess. Was she Jewish?"

"No, Catholic."

"Then why did she go through a Jewish adoption agency? And how did Bobby get Tay-Sachs? Was the father Jewish?"

"He must have been. It's a little confusing." I told her about Reuben Nadelman.

"But if he isn't a Tay-Sachs carrier, and neither is she, then there's something wrong. He can't be the father."

"Right."

"So who is?"

"That's one of the things I've been trying to figure out."

"Did she have an affair with anyone else?"

"Not that she's told me about. But I suppose she must have."

"That person would have to be the Tay-Sachs carrier, then. You know, his father doesn't *have* to be Jewish. The disease is not limited to Jews, it's just more prevalent in the Ashkenazic Jewish population."

"I know. It also appears in French Canadians and Cajuns."

"And in the general population, too," she said, "it's just very, very rare."

We sat quietly for a moment. Then Michelle said, "Was Bobby's birth mother glad when he found her? Was she happy to see him?"

I shook my head. "No. She wasn't. She's still married to the same man and has two kids. I think she was terrified her family would find out about Bobby."

Michelle buried her face in her hands. "Oh, God. Poor Bobby. How awful. How awful to find your mother and have her reject you."

I put my hand on hers to soften what I was about to say. "Is it possible that being rejected by his birth mother, especially given the difficult relationship he had with your parents, might have made him so depressed he would consider taking his own life?"

Her shoulders shook with sobs. "I don't know. Maybe. Oh, poor Bobby. Poor, poor Bobby."

"Michelle," I said, "can you think of anyone who might have wanted to hurt Bobby? Someone who might have a grudge against him?"

She shook her head. "Absolutely not. You know Bobby. He was the most easygoing guy in the world. He would never hurt anybody, and nobody would want to hurt him."

"What about when he was using drugs? Did he make any enemies that you know of?" It's hard to get through life as a drug addict without pissing off a few people.

"No. Honestly. The only person he hurt was himself."

"Was he ever in any trouble with dealers? Was there ever a time when he couldn't pay for his drugs? When he owed money to people?"

She shook her head. "I don't know. I don't really know anything about his life back then. He did a good job of hiding all that from us. Even when he was at his worst, he tried to protect us from knowing the truth. None of us even realized that there was anything wrong until he checked himself into rehab."

I paused for a moment, wondering how she'd respond to my next question. "I have to ask this. Do you think that anyone in your family might have any reason to harm Bobby?"

Her face paled. "No. Absolutely not. We loved Bobby. Maybe we didn't do that good of a job of showing it, but we loved him. None of us would have hurt him. I know that."

I hoped, for her sake, that she was right.

18

OTH KIDS FELL asleep in the backseat on the way home from the mall. Peter carried Ruby out of the car, and I hoisted Isaac onto my shoulder and staggered in behind him. It's amazing how heavy a sleeping toddler is. Shushing each other, we tiptoed through the dark house and gently laid the kids in their beds. I considered wiping the dried ketchup off their faces but wasn't willing to risk waking them. Peter turned the TV on to his favorite B-movie channel, and I went into the kitchen to make myself a cup of chamomile tea. I could already tell I was going to need some help falling asleep.

While I was waiting for the water to boil, I noticed the light flashing on the answering machine. The first message was from my friend Stacy.

"Listen, girl, you just lucked out in a major way. One of my colleagues came back from maternity leave. She told me that her feet grew an entire size while she was pregnant. She used to be a five and a half. Like you. Now she's a six and a half. I bought her entire collection of Manolo Blahniks for you. You are the proud owner of nine pair of stunning shoes. And you owe me nine hundred dollars."

I was about to pick up the phone and describe to Stacy exactly what my life was like and how drastically it would have to change to accommodate nine pairs of secondhand stiletto heels, when the answering machine began its next message. An electronically distorted voice warned me, "If you care about what happens to your kid, mind your own business."

In my years dealing with criminals of all sorts, I'd never once been threatened. I'd represented drug dealers who had never been anything but polite. I'd had young men from the Crips and the Bloods treat me with respect and affection. My heroin addict bank robbers never intimidated me. Even the violent offenders had been decent to me, if not to their victims.

I'd made prosecutors mad enough to call me all kinds of terrible names, but no one had ever threatened my physical safety. Now, while investigating a supposed suicide, someone was menacing my children.

"What the hell was that?" Peter stood in the doorway, looking grim. Wordlessly, I hit the Replay button and together we listened to the ominous voice.

While the message played, I dialed *69 but was informed by a polite automaton that the call return feature couldn't be used to return our last incoming call.

"Caller ID?" Peter said.

I pressed the button on the back of the receiver. It flashed "Private Caller." I shook my head.

"No luck," I said.

"I'm calling the cops."

"Good idea."

The Los Angeles Police Department proved itself courteous and prompt, if not particularly reassuring, although I'm not sure what Peter and I expected them to do. Two patrol officers came out to the house and walked around the yard. They didn't find anyone, but then we hadn't expected them to. Peter had taped the threatening message off of our digital answering machine with the microcassette recorder he used to take notes for his scripts, and he gave the tape to the officers.

When they left, he turned to me. "What are we going to do?"

I shook my head. "I don't know. Tomorrow morning, I'll call the Santa Monica Police and talk to whoever was assigned to Bobby's case. Maybe they'll reopen it, given all this."

Peter began pacing back and forth. "Should we leave the house? Go to a hotel or something?"

I shook my head. "I don't think so. I mean, the warning was to stop. I'm obviously not going to do anything tonight, so I think we're probably safe."

"Probably? Juliet, do you honestly think that's good enough? The guy threatened our kid. Are you willing to take a chance? I'm sure as hell not."

Something occurred to me. "Why just one?"

"What?"

"Why did he, or she for that matter, threaten just one of the kids? Why not both?"

Peter stared at me like I'd gone mad. "I don't know, and frankly I couldn't care less. Threatening one of them is good enough for me. I'm having a hard time understanding why you aren't more upset about this."

"I *am* upset. I'm scared and I'm angry, but I'm also going to do my damnedest to find out what's going on. Why did the person say 'kid' and not 'kids'?"

Peter sat down in a chair and ran his fingers through his hair. It stood up in agitated spikes all over his head.

Suddenly, I had a brilliant idea. "I'm going to call Al," I said.

"What?"

"Al. I told you he's gone into the independent investigation business. I'm going to hire him to protect us. It probably won't cost any more than going to a hotel, and I know I'd feel safer with him around. Who knows how long it'll be before the police take me seriously, let alone find out who's been doing this? At this point, I'm not even confident I'll be able to convince them to reopen Bobby's case."

AL SHOWED UP an hour later, accompanied by a lanky young woman with dark curls held off her face in a ponytail tied with a purple beaded elastic band. She was wearing tight lavender jeans and an LAPD sweatshirt and carried the long duffel Al had brought to the shooting range.

"Never leave weapons in an unattended vehicle," she said by way of greeting and extended her hand to me. I shook it, marveling as I did so at the tiny gemstones imbedded in her purple nails.

"You must be Robyn," I said.

"Yup. Nice to meet you. My dad talks about you all the time. He says he'd like you a lot if you weren't such a bleeding-heart liberal."

Al groaned, and I managed a smile.

I turned to my husband. "Peter, this is Al's daughter. The Olympic biathelete."

"Just an alternate," she said, shaking his hand firmly.

"Peter," Al said. "How would you and the kids like to spend a couple of days with my daughter at our cabin in Big Bear? There's no snow on the ground, and it's too cold to swim, but you guys could do some hiking. We've even got a hot tub."

Peter frowned at me. "Is this really necessary?"

I liked the idea. With Peter and the kids out of town, I could concentrate on tracking down the source of the threatening messages without having to worry about them. This situation had stopped being one I could investigate while lugging Isaac and his stroller around with me. Moreover, Robyn, with her rippling muscles, talonlike fingernails, and bag full of guns, looked to be the ideal bodyguard.

"I think it's a terrific idea," I said. "You were just telling me that we should take these threats seriously. I think you're right. I think we should make sure the kids are safe. And I'm sure they'll be safe with Robyn."

Peter looked over at Robyn, and she nodded resolutely.

"Okay. Fine. Let's all go, then," he said.

"Peter," Al interrupted. "If I were you, I'd feel the same way. I'd want to get my little lady out of harm's way." I bristled at this, but he ignored me. Robyn rolled her eyes and we shared a rueful smile at her prehistoric father's blatant sexism. "But Juliet's the only person who can figure out who's responsible for the threats. She's got to retrace all her steps over the past couple of weeks and try to come up with a list of suspects to take to the police officers investigating the case. But don't you worry. I'll take good care of her for you."

That really was too much. "Thanks, Al, but I can take care of myself. I could definitely use another person to help me investigate, though. If you're volunteering," I said.

Al opened his mouth to retort, but Peter spoke first. "Robyn can take the kids up to Big Bear. I'm staying here with you. What if this guy is serious? No way I'm letting you be here by yourself."

I kissed him on the cheek. "That's so sweet, honey, and I really do appreciate it. But Ruby and Isaac don't know Robyn. We can't just send them off with someone they've never met. Plus, I don't think Robyn signed on for babysitting duties."

The young woman shook her head. "There's not a lot I can't handle, but I think a couple of little kids might be beyond me."

I said, "One of us has to go with them, and like Al said, if we're going to figure out who is responsible, I've got to stay here."

We could all see Peter struggling with himself. It has always amazed me how even men who've grown up believing that women are their equals and are competent and strong enough to protect themselves, even men who would call themselves feminists, have a ribbon of machismo running through their personalities. Peter and I certainly have a marriage of equals. Not even the fact that he was currently the sole wage earner had changed that. Nonetheless, when faced with the possibility of peril for his woman, I could see my white knight aching to pick up his lance and head off to battle. Except he knew as well as I did that somebody had to take care of the kids.

The look of resignation in my husband's face inspired me to give him another kiss on the cheek. His pride wounded by the indignity of having to run out of town, he shook me off. I turned to Robyn.

"It's late. Do you want to wait until morning before heading up to Big Bear? You can take the guest room, and I can make up the couch for you, Al," I said.

"You know, I think I'd rather go now. I don't want to try to drive through morning rush hour. The freeways will be empty now, and we'll make really good time. That is, if you don't mind," Robyn said, turning to Peter.

"That's fine," Peter said, surrendering. "I'll just go pack a few things. Juliet, you get the kids' stuff together. How long do you think we'll be gone?"

"A couple of days, no more," Al said. "Don't worry about food and things. Jeanelle's been up at the cabin for the last few days doing some work in the garden. I'm sure she's got the kitchen fully stocked."

"Does she mind my family invading like this?" I asked. "I hate to impose on her time away from the city."

"Not at all. Not at all. She's looking forward to the company. Jeanelle loves kids, and since she's not likely to get a grandchild any time soon, she's delighted to have yours to play with." Robyn rolled her eyes once again and settled herself into a chair to wait for us to pack and get ready.

While Peter put together an overnight case for himself, I packed two or three tons of supplies for the kids. Every time I travel with the children, I remember my days of adventure travel when I saw the sights of Asia and South America weighed down by nothing more than a lightweight backpack and a camera. Nowadays, it takes a semitrailer, two forklifts, and a U-Haul just to get us out for a morning in the park. By narrowing down their wardrobes to just the bare minimum, I managed to fit the kids' clothes, bath supplies, baby bottles, hats, extra shoes, toys, and pills, drops, and bandages for any and all emergencies, into two oversized suitcases. Another bag held a supply of juice boxes, rice cakes, Cheerios, and raisins, with a package of chocolate chip cookies tossed in to guarantee good behavior. They were ready to go.

Miraculously, neither Ruby nor Isaac woke up when we carried them out to the car and loaded them into their car seats. I kissed them on the cheeks, softly enough not to wake them, and watched as they pulled away. I felt a pang in my chest and realized that I'd never been away from Isaac before. This was our first overnight separation. I wondered what my sweet little boy would do when he woke up and found me gone. Have a blast playing cops and robbers with Robyn, probably.

"She won't let the kids near the guns, will she?" I said to Al.

He flashed me the fish eye by way of reply.

19

B Y THE TIME I got up the next morning, Al had already made the guest room bed with military precision. I resisted the urge to bounce a quarter off the bedspread and went into the kitchen, where I found him eating a bowl of bran flakes.

"Important for regularity," he said.

"Too much information, Al," I replied and poured myself a cup of coffee. "Are you on the clock?" I asked him.

"Huh?"

"The time clock. Am I paying you your hourly rate as we speak?"

"I don't bill while I'm sleeping or eating. Otherwise, yes, ma'am."

I settled myself on the stool opposite him. "I'd love to have the help, and I'm happy to have the kids and Peter out of harm's way, but I don't think we can afford both you and Robyn."

He swallowed the last mouthful of his cereal and took a noisy gulp of coffee. "How 'bout we work out a swap for services?" he said.

"What do you mean?"

"I provide some muscle on this little project of yours, and the next time I need some advice from a legal eagle, you help me out."

I considered his offer. It had been relatively painless to do Al's legal research. Surely I could offer him those services without impinging too much on car pool and playdates. "Deal," I said, and we shook on it.

We began to draw up a list of all the people with whom I'd had contact over the course of my investigation into Bobby's death. Once we had the names all down on paper, I studied the list.

"Candace," I said.

"Candace?"

"She's the creepiest. She's the one who makes me the most uncomfortable. She's weird, she's unpleasant, and she seems to have built up her relationship with Bobby into a great, unrequited love affair. And she saw Isaac but not Ruby when I tracked her down at her job. It makes sense for her to have threatened my *kid* instead of *kids* because she has no way of knowing I've got two."

"Okay, let's go find Candace."

20

AL AND I decided that the benefit of surprise was worth risking the chance that Candace wouldn't be at work. We lucked out. When we walked into the Starbucks across from the Westside Pavilion where she worked, we immediately saw her sitting at one of the little round tables, gripping the hand of a young woman who was weeping into a crumpled tissue. We paused in the doorway and listened.

"Brittany, I know you are doing the right thing. Because I know *you*. You and I have a special bond, a deeper connection than normal people. Our shared abandonment has given us a unique nexus—a union of souls."

The younger woman smiled tearfully at Candace. "You've helped me so much." She hiccuped.

"And you've helped me. We're lost birds, you and I. Two lost birds, clinging to one another in a tumultuous ocean."

"Like a couple of albatrosses," I whispered to Al. He grinned.

We walked over to Candace's table, and I cleared my throat. She looked up at me, clearly irritated at the intrusion, and frowned.

"Yes?" she said.

"It's me, Candace. Juliet Applebaum. Can we talk?"

"I'm very busy right now."

The young woman shook her head. "No, no. That's okay. I've got to go." She stood up and hugged Candace. "I'll E-mail you, okay?"

"I'll be expecting it."

The woman left the café, and Candace turned to me. "I really have to get back to work."

"Take a minute, Candace," Al said, pulling up a chair and sitting down at the table.

"Who's he?" she said to me without looking at Al.

"A colleague. Listen, Candace, we'd like to talk to you a little more about Bobby's death."

The words were barely out of my mouth when she started shaking her head. "I really don't have anything to say. I've moved beyond that whole thing. I'm concentrating on Brittany right now."

"Excuse me?"

"Bobby's gone, and I'm sad, but there are things I need to do. Brittany needs my help. I've got to get back to work." She got up and walked away, ducking under the counter and busying herself at the coffee machine.

Al and I looked at each other, and he raised his eyebrows. We left the store and stood outside for moment.

"What the hell was that about?" he asked.

"I don't know. It's hard to imagine that she could have just threatened to harm my kids. She didn't seem the slightest bit scared or worried when she saw us."

He shook his head. "More like just not interested."

"She could be faking it."

"She could be."

"So, now what?"

Al rolled his eyes at me. I blushed. "Well, what would you do if you were still a cop?" I asked him.

He shrugged his shoulders and replied, "Interrogate."

"Okay. Let's interrogate her. It's, like, the tiniest problem that we can't arrest her or assert any kind of authority whatsoever, but hey, let's go for it."

"Watch and learn, honey. Watch and learn." He turned and headed back in the door of the café.

I muttered something under my breath about not liking to be called honey, and followed him inside. He ambled up to the counter and leaned on it.

"Candace, we'd like to have just a moment of your time. Can you spare that? For Bobby's sake?" His voice was almost a purr.

She shook her head angrily.

"Let me buy you a coffee," Al insisted. "What kind do you like? A mocha? A latte? How about one of those wonderful frozen things?"

"I hate coffee," she said.

I raised my eyebrows and looked around the café, a veritable shrine to the brew.

"A juice, then," Al said. "And a cookie. For Bobby's sake. Because we all cared about him and want to find out what happened to him."

"Okay, okay," Candace said. She poured herself a glass of milk and took a cookie from the case. "That'll be three dollars and seventeen cents," she said.

Al handed her a five-dollar bill. She ostentatiously dumped the change in the tip cup and ducked under the counter. Then she motioned to us to move to the back of the café. We followed her and sat down at the little table she indicated.

"So, what do you want from me?" she said.

"Just your help. That's all," Al replied in the same honeyed tone with which he'd convinced her to come out from behind her counter.

"How 'bout we start with the most obvious thing. Just a formality really," he said.

"What?"

"Where were you when Bobby was killed?" His voice had suddenly turned stern. Candace flushed, and I held my breath.

"I dunno. Home. I'm always home at night."

"But you don't remember that night specifically?" Al asked.

"No. I mean, why would I? I didn't know he was going to die."

Al turned to me. "Juliet, what was the official time of death?"

I blanched. Had I ever found that out? Al's jaw clenched almost imperceptibly.

"I can prove where I was, no matter what time he died," Candace said.

"Excuse me?" I asked.

"I mean, I can show you where I was."

"At home?" Al asked.

"Yeah, but I mean, I can show you where I was online. I'm always online."

"All night long?" I asked.

She blushed again. "Yeah. Mostly. Until three or four, at least. That's where I am every night. All you have to do is check the websites. My posts will all be there. Dated and timed."

"How would we be sure that you didn't just change the date and time on your computer?" Al said.

"Because we can check the posts of the people who replied to her," I said with a sigh. She had seemed such a likely suspect.

"Do you want to look?" Candace said. "I have my laptop." Candace went back behind the counter and pulled out a battered computer carrying case. She plugged the computer into the phone jack and began typing. I spent the next ten minutes bent over the counter at an uncomfortable angle, charting the course of Candace's depressing online existence. The woman had begun posting messages on various boards at 7 P.M. Her last post was at 5:12 A.M.

"If there's nothing else you want, I'm going to get back to work," she said finally, a victorious note in her voice.

Al and I made our way back to the car. "We'll check the time of death. Maybe it's after 5:12."

"Maybe," Al said, sounding doubtful.

We got in my car and slammed our doors almost in unison. Jiggling the keys in my hand, I said, "Okay, let's start from scratch. What's the first rule of investigating a murder? Look to the family." And then my cell phone rang. It was Michelle.

"I couldn't get the whole Tay-Sachs thing out of my mind," she told me. "It was driving me crazy all night. I mean, of course it's possible that Bobby got the gene from someone with no connection to an at-risk group, but that's just so unlikely."

I agreed with her. "I can't help but feel that if we figure out the source of Bobby's genetic condition, we'll have more of a clue about why he died."

"That's what I was thinking. So, when I got to work this morning, I started searching the medical and genetic databases I work with. You're not going to believe what I found out."

"What?" I said, not doing a very good job of keeping the impatience out of my voice.

"You already know that approximately one in every thirty to thirty-five Ashkenazic Jews, French Canadians, and Louisiana Cajuns is a Tay-Sachs carrier."

"Right."

"Well, it turns out that there is another group with an almost equally high incidence, although for some reason it isn't generally known."

By now I was ready to reach into the phone receiver and yank the words out of her throat by force. "Who?"

"One in every fifty Irish people, or people of exclusively Irish descent, is a Tay-Sachs carrier."

I leaned back in my seat. Major Patrick Sullivan, scion of one of Los Angeles's most prominent Irish Catholic families. Bobby's mother's own husband. He was Bobby's father. But how could he be? I'd considered that possibility more than once but had dismissed it each time. Susan Sullivan herself had told me that there was no way Bobby could have been her husband's child. She said that the only time she'd had sex with her husband in the months before her pregnancy was the time she'd flown out to Japan to meet him on his leave. According to Susan, that had been at least a month before her birth control had failed her with Reuben Nadelman. But, I remembered, she'd also said that Bobby had been born a little early. What if he was, in fact, the product of the Japan leave but had been born a few weeks late, rather than a couple of weeks early?

I thanked Michelle for her research and said a hurried good-bye. Waving off Al's questions, I dialed Susan Sullivan's number. I heaved a sigh of relief when she herself answered the phone.

"It's Juliet Applebaum. Please don't hang up," I said.

"What? What do you want from me? Can't you please leave me alone?" She whined.

"I just have one question for you. Do you remember how much Bobby weighed when he was born?"

"What? Why are you asking me that?"

"Please. It's important. Do you remember?"

"Yes," she whispered, after a pause. "I didn't hold him. I couldn't bear to. But I asked them whether it was a girl. I'd always wanted a girl. The nurse told me that it was a boy and that he weighed seven pounds seven ounces. I've always remembered because of the drink. You know, seven and seven."

Seven pounds seven ounces. Heavy for a baby born early. Maybe a little small for one born two or three weeks late.

"Susan," I asked. "Did your husband participate in the cystic fibrosis study?"

"No, of course not. He's not a blood relative of my niece."

"Then he never did the genetic screening that you and your sons did?"

"No."

"Susan, is it possible that Bobby was your husband's baby after all?

That he wasn't born early but rather a little late, maybe ten months or so after your trip to Japan?"

There was silence on the other end of the line, and then, unexpectedly, the phone went dead.

I turned to Al. "I'll tell you all about it on the way," I said.

"Where are we going?"

"Pacific Palisades."

He shrugged his jacket off and tossed it in the backseat. That was when I noticed the brown leather holster clipped to his belt. I almost told him not to bring the gun, that we wouldn't need it. I don't know why I didn't. Maybe I should have. It's hard to say.

21

$\mathcal{S}$ALUD ANSWERED MY ring. She recognized me but didn't seem any more eager to let me in than she had been the last time.

"I go see if Mrs. Susan in," the maid said.

"*Podriamos esperar al dentro?*" I wheedled. "*Por favor?*" Once again my attempt at conversing in her own language seemed to charm her. She flashed me a silver-capped smile and looked at Al.

"*El es un amigo mío,*" I said, and Al smiled pleasantly.

Salud opened the door and ushered us in, burbling in a Spanish so rapid and thickly accented that I could make out only every couple of words. I nodded and said, "*Sí, claro,*" a few times although I had no idea what I was agreeing with.

She looked at Al and then, in a loud, slow voice, as though speaking to the infirm, said, "You stay here. I get Mrs. Susan."

Al and I watched silently as she hurried up the stairs. Al whistled softly as he looked around the marble entryway.

"Classy," he said.

"Old money. Or, as old as it gets around here. Patrick's family made it big in the gold rush and then even bigger in Southern California real estate."

A few moments later, Salud came down the stairs. This time her tread was heavy and slow.

"I am sorry, you go now," she said, motioning us toward the door.

"*Que pasa con la señora?*" I asked.

"You go now," she said again, refusing to reply in Spanish.

"Tell Mrs. Sullivan that we need to talk to her. It's very important," I insisted.

"She no want to talk to you. She say you go now. So you go."

I looked at Al, and he shrugged his shoulders. Then I started to get angry. I wasn't entirely without sympathy for Susan Sullivan. I could only imagine what the woman was feeling, faced with the possibility that thirty years ago she'd made a horrible mistake. But Bobby Katz was dead, and I wanted answers. I wasn't about to let his birth mother hide out from me. I was getting ready to tell Salud that she should inform Mrs. Susan that she could either talk to me or to the police when the door opened and Matthew Sullivan walked in.

The blond young man was jangling a set of keys in his hand. He wore a buttery-soft, brown leather jacket and those nubbly soled driving shoes that you see in catalogues but nobody ever buys. Nobody outside of a Connecticut country club, that is. His face stiffened when he saw me, and then he smiled politely.

"Can I help you? Juliet, is it? My mother's friend from the library benefit."

"Er, right. The library benefit. I'm just here to talk to your mother for a moment."

"Mr. Matthew, Mrs. Susan say she no want to see the lady. She say the lady should go home," Salud insisted.

The blond man shrugged his shoulders. "I'm afraid my mother is busy, Mrs. Applebaum. You'll have to come back some other time."

"Matthew, I don't know your mother from the library. I need to speak to her about something personal and urgent. Why don't you go upstairs and tell your mother that if she won't talk to me, I'm going to have no choice but to go to the police with what I know."

His face blanched. "What are you talking about?" he said.

"It's personal. Just tell her."

He looked over at Al. "Who's that? Are you a cop?" His voice was hoarse and worried.

"I'm a colleague of Mrs. Applebaum's," Al said. "Go tell your mother that we'd like a few words. If you don't mind. " Al had perfected his calm but firm cop's voice. Matthew looked for a moment like he was about to follow the gently given instruction. At that moment, the door opened again, and Patrick Sullivan walked into the house.

"Hello?" he said in a questioning voice. "What's going on here?"

His son turned beet red and began to mumble something unintelligible.

"Mr. Patrick, Mrs. Susan say she no want to talk to these people, but they no leaving," Salud said.

"Can I help you?" His voice was cold and foreboding.

For a brief second, I considered spilling the story to him, Susan's feelings be damned, but I couldn't bring myself to completely destroy the life she was so intent on keeping intact and undisturbed.

"We were just leaving," I said and mentioned to Al to follow.

Susan's husband waved to his son. "Please see them out," he said.

Matthew jerked the door open, and Al and I filed through. As I walked by the young man, I reached into my pocket, pulled out a business card, and pressed it into his trembling hand. In a low, hurried voice meant for his ears only, I said, "This has my cell phone number on it. Tell your mom that she might be able to catch us on our way to the police station."

We'd parked the car on the circular driveway right in front of the house. As we pulled around to leave, Al said, "Well, so much for that."

"Do you think she's just having some kind of hysterical breakdown at the thought of having given up her husband's baby, or do you think she knows something about Bobby's death?"

He shrugged his shoulders.

"Maybe she killed him, and she's having a hysterical breakdown because she just realized that she killed not just her own son, but her husband's, too," I said.

"Maybe who Bobby's father is has nothing at all to do with his death."

I hit the brakes and turned to Al. "You were the one who was so big on the no-coincidences theory!"

He shrugged his shoulders, and I shook my head at him. Before I stepped on the gas, I looked back up the long driveway through my rearview mirror. A silver Audi TT and a gold Lexus coupe were parked around the side of the house in front of the three-car garage. Neither had been there when we'd arrived. I pulled into the street and headed toward Sunset Boulevard. Suddenly, I remembered the little sports car that had zipped by me on the PCH the last time I'd visited Susan Sullivan. I remembered the racing car that the boys said they'd seen when Peter's BMW had been vandalized. I pulled over to the side of the road with a screech and turned to Al.

"That's the car," I said.

Al raised his eyebrows questiongly, and I reminded him about the boys and described the car that had almost rear-ended me.

"The Audi. It's got to be the Audi."

Al wasn't convinced. "It's possible. But if we call the detectives with nothing more than the possibility that the racing car the kids described could have been maybe the same Audi that blew by you on the highway and that might maybe be the same Audi that's in this driveway, even though thousands of those cars are floating around the city right now, they're going to laugh in our faces."

I knew he was right. "Well then, let's get them something more than that."

He looked at me for a moment as if trying to figure out whether I was determined or foolhardy or both. Then he patted the gun strapped to his waist. "All right. Let's."

22

T FIRST, NO one answered our ring. Then I leaned on the bell. After a couple of cacophonous moments, Patrick Sullivan wrenched the door open and glared at us.

"Look here, I've had about as much as I'm willing to take of you. My wife doesn't want to see you. Get away from my front door and off of my property before I call the police." He hunched over into my face and spoke through gritted teeth. I felt a thin spray of spittle and didn't wipe my cheek, although I desperately wanted to.

"Mr. Sullivan, my friend Bobby Katz is dead. He was shot in the head, and I think your wife knows something about how and why he was killed. And, frankly, I'm betting you or your son Matthew knows, too."

His eyes narrowed. "What are you talking about?" I couldn't tell if his ignorance was real or feigned.

"Mr. Sullivan, if you want to call the police, by all means go ahead and do so. I'm sure they'd be interested in exploring your family's involvement in Bobby's death. Alternatively, you could let us in and help us figure out what may well be an innocent explanation for all this."

Patrick Sullivan stared at me, his face inscrutable. Then, suddenly, he stretched out his arm and opened the door wide. "Come in," he said.

He led us through the circular entry hall and into the living room. We stood on the crimson Chinese carpet in the middle of the room. He didn't invite us to sit down.

"Wait here. I'll get my wife," he said and left us, clicking the door shut behind him.

Al rocked back and forth on his heels. I paced nervously.

"Do you have *any* idea what you're going to say when he drags the woman down here to talk to you?" Al asked.

I scowled at him. "More or less. Have some faith."

We both turned to the door when it opened, expecting to see Susan Sullivan. Her son Matthew stood there instead. He was pale and sweaty, and his breath came in shallow gasps, audible across the room. He looked like he'd been running or crying.

"Get out! Get out of here!" He tried to shout, but his voice cracked and came out an awkward squeal.

"We're here to talk to your mother, Matthew," I said.

"Get out!" This time he managed the yell.

I could see Al firming up his stance out of the corner of my eye. His feet were planted shoulder-width apart, and he'd assumed a barely detectable crouch. He was ready to spring at the young man if he needed to.

"Hey, Matthew," I said in a conversational tone. "Is that your Audi or your dad's?"

His face turned beet red, and he lunged at me. Al, moving more quickly than a man of his age has any right to, stepped between us. He grabbed Matthew around the shoulders with one arm and swung him away from me. Matthew wiggled frantically in his grip. Before I could make it across the room to the grappling men, Matthew had somehow managed to yank one arm free of Al's, and he was punching wildly. The two men slipped on the edge of the carpet and fell to the ground with a thud. I saw Al's hand fumbling with his holster as I ran to help him subdue Matthew. I had just reached the two when I heard a pop like a piece of wood snapping in two. Suddenly, Matthew was pointing the gun at Al, who knelt, hunched over, holding his right hand against his chest. His index finger was bent at an unnatural angle, and he groaned.

"Get over there with him," Matthew said, swinging the gun in my direction. It wobbled in his trembling hand, and I was terrified that he would accidentally pull the trigger. I walked quickly over to Al and helped him to his feet. We backed away from Matthew. Al and I both stared at the gun. Matthew followed our gaze and suddenly pulled back the safety.

"I can shoot it now," he said, and he made a sound halfway between a giggle and a groan. Sweat was pouring freely down his forehead, and he hitched up his shoulder to wipe it away. At that moment, his parents walked into the room. Susan gave a strangled cry and began to run to her son, but Patrick yanked her back.

"Matthew! What the hell do you think you're doing? Put that gun down!" Patrick bellowed.

Matthew's back was to the door, and he turned slowly, keeping the gun aimed at Al and me.

"You go stand with them, too," he said, the words hissing from his throat.

"What the devil—" his father began.

"Do it!" he shrieked, and the Sullivans joined us where we stood, backed against the long sofa.

"Sit," he said, his voice almost gleeful, as though he was relishing the opportunity to force us to comply. Patrick did not seem a man who took orders willingly, certainly not from his son. It was obviously an unusual pleasure for Matthew to feel power over his father.

Al, Susan, and I sat, but Patrick remained standing. "Sit down, Dad."

"Look here, Matthew. This is ridiculous. Hand me the gun."

"No."

Patrick took a step forward. "Come on, son. Give me that gun."

"I'll shoot. I will. Stop!" The young man's teeth were gritted shut as he tried to keep his voice from quavering. Patrick kept moving forward, and Matthew suddenly swung the gun in the direction of his mother.

"I'll shoot her!" he screamed. And his father stopped stock-still. Susan whimpered.

"Shut up!" her son screamed at her. "This is your fault. All of it. You're a . . . a slut! That's what you are. You're a whore!"

The woman's chest rose and fell with her sobs. Matthew kept talking. "I knew you'd done it. I knew it as soon as the genetic counselor told me I had that Jew disease."

"Son, son, what are you saying?" Patrick's voice had lost its authoritative swagger. He sounded afraid.

"It's not what you think, Matthew," I said calmly and slowly. Everyone looked at me except Al, who kept his eyes fixed on the gun in Matthew's hand.

"What do *you* know?" Matthew snarled.

"You tested positive for Tay-Sachs, right? You're a carrier?"

"No! You're not. You can't be," Susan cried. "You said you weren't. And you can't be."

"I lied! Of course I lied. You and P. J. each said you didn't have any of the three diseases. And then Dad said of course you didn't because Sullivans are a strong breed. How the hell was I supposed to tell you that I had it? How? Particularly since I know what it means!"

"You *don't* know, Matthew. You're making a mistake," I said.

"What are you talking about?" Patrick said. "Matthew, Susan, what the hell is she talking about?"

I didn't reply to Patrick. I kept talking to Matthew quietly but firmly. "Bobby got in touch with you, didn't he?"

The young man nodded. "He said he was my brother. He asked me to meet him, and I did. He told me that she didn't want to have anything to do with him but that he hoped I might. He told me about the Tay-Sachs, and that's when I knew I had to do it."

My chest tightened, and I could feel my eyes begin to burn as tears collected in them. "Matthew, did you hurt Bobby?" I asked in a soft, gentle voice.

"I had to," he whined.

I could hear Susan's harsh, ragged sobs and willed her silently to keep her mouth shut. Patrick seemed stunned and unable to speak.

"I had to," he repeated. "He wasn't going to leave it alone. He wasn't going to go away. He was going to make her tell Dad, and then Dad would find out about me. I couldn't let that happen. I couldn't let that happen." He turned to his father. "I know you hate me. I know you're just looking for a good reason to cut me off. You want to throw me out, but you don't think you can, right? Right?"

This time it was Patrick who sobbed. I turned to look at him, expecting to see him reduced to tears. His eyes were absolutely dry.

"You were afraid that if Bobby forced your mother to tell your father about him, then Patrick would find out about you, too?" I asked, again keeping my voice low and calm.

He nodded.

I continued. "You're afraid that you're not your father's son, aren't you?"

"I'm *not* his son. She had an affair. She had an affair, and she got pregnant, and she had Bobby and gave him away. And then she kept on seeing the guy, and she had me. I don't know why she didn't give me up, too." He stared at Susan and cried, "Why did you keep me? Why didn't you give me away like you gave away my brother?"

Susan didn't answer. She had her hands clasped over her mouth, and she rocked back and forth, moaning. Patrick stared at his wife, rage and disgust warring on his face.

"You're wrong, Matthew. You *are* your father's son. And so was Bobby. Your mother did have an affair while your father was in Vietnam, and she did give Bobby up for adoption, but you're wrong about the rest, Matthew."

Matthew shook his head furiously, but his eyes narrowed as he looked at me.

"Bobby didn't come from the affair your mother had. Bobby is Patrick's son, too. Just like you are. Tay-Sachs doesn't just affect Jews, Matthew. Anyone can have it. Anyone, especially the Irish. It's almost as common in the Irish population as in the Jewish. You inherited the Tay-Sachs from your father."

"What?" the young man whispered. "What?"

"Patrick *is* your father, Matthew. And he was Bobby's."

"No. No he's not. Is he? Is he?" The young man shrieked, first at me and then at his mother.

"I don't know, I don't know," Susan whispered.

At that moment we all heard the faint sounds of sirens. We stiffened as they grew closer and closer. Matthew's arm began to sink to his side so slowly that it was at first almost imperceptible. Al and I both rose to our feet, also slowly. Matthew said nothing, he just continued to lower his arm. I stepped to one side of him and Al to the other. Al reached out his hand and carefully and deliberately removed the gun from Matthew's now limp palm. He slipped it back into the holster attached to his belt. The police found us thus, Al with the gun securely clipped in its place, Matthew trembling, just barely managing to keep to his feet, and Susan and Patrick sitting next to each other on their lovely and expensive sofa, frozen in despair.

23

THE POLICE KEPT us there for quite a while. I'm sure it was Al's status as a retired member of the LAPD that finally convinced them that it was safe to take our names and telephone numbers and let us go on our way. We drove in silence down Sunset Boulevard. I wasn't thinking about what had happened so much as I was trying to figure out the best way to break the news to Bobby's fiancée and his family. I knew the police would inform them, but that could take some time, and I certainly owed it to Betsy and Michelle to tell them myself. I didn't realize how distraught Al was until he cleared his throat. I looked over at him sitting in the passenger seat. His face was blotchy under a sheen of sweat.

"Are you okay?" I said. "What's wrong? Are you feeling all right? Should I pull over?"

He shook his head and cleared his throat once again. "I'm . . . I'm very sorry. Truly. And I'll understand if you don't want to partner with me anymore."

I took a quick right into the parking lot of a big box store and pulled the car into a spot. I turned off the engine and turned to face him. Looking him full in the eye I said, "What the hell are you talking about?" Although I knew. Of course I knew.

"My gun. I let that kid get hold of my gun. You could have been killed. I let him overpower me, and I endangered both our lives."

To a man who had always been as physically powerful as Al, the vulnerability that comes with age must be devastating. How impossibly painful it is to acknowledge that you are no longer able to protect yourself and others, when that has always been your primary occupation, the source of your identity. If your physical strength is one of your paramount skills, what must it feel like when that begins to go?

I'd often wondered how it was that Al made the transition from law enforcement to defense investigation so easily. It had never seemed to bother him that his job was no longer to protect and defend but rather to work toward the release of those who he'd once been so committed to incarcerating. Sitting next to him in the car, I understood that it had only seemed to come naturally to him. Perhaps the job of defense investigator had enough of the trappings of the police—he investigated, he searched, sometimes at least, for truth—that he could feel like he was still in the business of protecting people. At the moment when Matthew wrenched the gun from his hand, Al must suddenly have confronted the fact that not only was his job no longer to protect the public, but he was no longer even able to protect himself and those he cared about in the way he once had.

"You didn't *let* him get your gun," I said. "You didn't let him do anything."

Al shook his head and knotted his old man's hands, gnarled like tree branches, in his lap. His index finger was swollen and red. There was something very wrong with it.

I reached out my own hand and rested it ever so gently on his. He flinched slightly. "Al, listen to me. I know this is hard. I know twenty years ago, hell, even ten years ago, Matthew would never have gotten your gun away from you—"

Al grunted. "He should never have been able to lay a hand on my gun. Not then, and not now. Never."

"Al, the guy's in his early twenties. He's strong and young and out of his mind. Crazy people are capable of amazing feats of strength; you know that. He was desperate, and he got lucky. I mean, look at your hand! He snapped your finger! There's no way you could have held on to the gun."

Al stared at his swollen finger and gave it an angry shake. He immediately winced in pain.

"I've got to get you to a doctor to have that taken care of. It looks excruciating."

He looked for a moment like he was going to object, then he shrugged. "Don't worry. I'll get it looked at. Some bodyguard, huh?"

"You're not my bodyguard. You're my *partner*."

He raised his eyebrows at me. I waved him off. "Look, I want to break this news to Michelle and Betsy in person. You coming?" I asked. He nodded. "Should we stop at an emergency room?"

"Let's do it later," Al said. "If we go now, we'll be there all day waiting for them to deal first with the coke-head gang-bangers bleeding to death."

That's my buddy Al, always able to toss a slur even in the midst of exquisite agony.

Before I pulled out of the parking lot, I handed him my cell phone and asked him to call Big Bear and let everyone know that the police had Matthew in custody and that the kids were no longer in danger. Al spoke quickly to Jeannelle—Peter and Robyn had taken the kids out for a hike— and then I called Michelle. I tracked her down at her lab. I didn't want to tell her on the phone, so I asked her if we could come see her.

As soon as Michelle met Al and me in the lobby of her building, she ushered us back through the double doors marked "Authorized Personnel Only" to a small office kitchenette. She pulled a first aid kit out of a cupboard and held out her hand for Al's. With a quick snap, she'd straightened out his finger. He'd winced briefly, but by the time she'd taped it to a tongue depressor, he was smiling.

"Thank you, dear. You just saved me about three hours and three hundred bucks at the ER."

She said, "It was just dislocated, but I'm happy to oblige. Actually, I like being reminded that I'm also a real doctor now and again."

Al and I took Michelle up on her offer of coffee, and we sat at the Formica table in the sterile little kitchenette and told her how her brother had died. She cried, but it seemed as much with relief as sorrow. Knowing that Bobby hadn't killed himself, and knowing why Matthew had murdered him, gave her some sense of peace. More, certainly, than she'd had before.

"It just seems so pointless," she sighed, wiping tears from her eyes.

"It almost always is, in my experience," I said. "People never kill each other for very good reasons. It's usually about love, or jealousy, or some horrible misunderstanding. And it never feels justified to those left behind."

Michelle asked me to leave it to her to tell her family, and I was only too happy to agree. After my recent conversation with her father, I'd been dreading seeing him again. And we still had to break the news to Betsy.

I called Betsy from the car but got a busy signal, so we just headed over to Hollywood.

Betsy's door was opened by the same man who had been there when last I'd seen her. He had a cigarette clenched in his teeth, and he squinted his eyes against the smoke curling from the end. He was holding a roll of packing tape in one hand and a thick magic marker in the other.

"Yes?" he said. "Oh, right. The detective girl."

Al nudged me in the side with his elbow, but I ignored him. "I'm a lawyer, actually. Is Betsy around?"

Roy took the cigarette out of his mouth and ground it out in a little while saucer that looked like it had been serving as his ashtray for quite a while. "Nobody told you?" he said.

"Nobody told me what?"

"About Betsy?"

My stomach knotted in dread. "What happened?" I asked.

"Betsy had a positive urine test. Her probation officer had her arrested."

I wasn't surprised. I looked around the shambles of the living room. Cardboard boxes rested on every available surface.

"You're packing?" I asked.

"She asked me to. Her lawyer told her she's looking at a few months in county, at the minimum. Since she's getting evicted at the end of the month, she asked me to take care of her stuff for her. I'm putting it all into storage."

"She's going to jail?" I asked. "Not into a drug treatment facility?"

He nodded. "Sick, isn't it? I mean, the woman has a disease, but instead of giving her the medicine and therapy she needs, they throw her in jail. Where, incidentally, she'll be able to get as much crank as her little heart desires."

I shook my head. "Ridiculous."

I could feel Al aching to put his two cents into the conversation, surely to comment on how using drugs is against the law and people who break the law deserve to go to jail, but I silenced him with a glare. The last thing I was interested in at the moment was one of our trademark political debates.

"Are you planning on visiting her?" I asked.

"Once they let me, yeah, I will."

I told him what had happened and asked him if he would be willing to pass word on to Betsy. I also promised that I'd go to county jail to visit her.

I guess I wasn't surprised that Betsy hadn't managed to stay sober. Most addicts don't. Drug addiction is a complicated thing. It seems to take some remarkable combination of support, security, and will to kick the habit. And even with all that to help them, many people still end up locked into a cycle of using that destroys them and those around them. I hoped Betsy would survive her months in county and come out with the strength and desire to try again. I wasn't about to lay any money on it, though.

24

AL AND I drove down La Brea toward my house in silence. Finally, as I pulled in the driveway, I said, "Okay, I'll do it."

He looked at me, puzzled. "Do what?"

"Go into business with you. But in a really limited way."

"Go on."

"First of all, I need completely flexible hours. I mean, I've got to be able to pick Ruby up at school, take care of Isaac, take the kids to play-dates. All that."

He shrugged. "That's fine by me. Work when you want to work."

"And I don't want to commit to a firm number of hours or anything like that. If you need some legal research done, and I'm free, then I'll do it. But I can't promise anything."

"What an attractive offer," he said.

"Those are my terms. I don't really want to go back to work, anyway. I'm a stay-at-home mom. I'm happy that way."

"Sure you are."

I decided to ignore that. "How are you going to pay me?"

"I'm not."

"What?"

"I'm not going to pay you. The clients will pay you. If I've got work for you, and you can fit me into your busy schedule, then you'll do the work and we'll bill the client. Whatever they pay me for your time, I'll give to you."

"Okay. That sounds fair. Oh, and one more thing."

"What?"

"I'm not carrying a gun. Ever."

"We'll see about that."

"I'm serious, Al."

"Okay, okay."

"Do we have a deal?"

"Yes, I believe we do."

We shook on it.

After Al went home, it occurred to me that it might be a good idea to have some welcome-home presents waiting for the kids. Actually, the most important person to reward was probably Peter. I headed out to the Toys "R" Us on La Cienega, across from the Beverly Center, and meandered up and down the aisles for a while. I found a truly disgusting doll for Ruby that would pee after drinking a bottle and poop after being fed a special powdered pap (sold separately). She would love it. I picked out a Johnny Lightning Speed Racer Mach 5 for Peter. As for Isaac, it didn't take me long to find the perfect gift. When I got home, I wrapped everything in some Chanukah paper I found under my bed and sat down at the kitchen table to wait.

It took them quite a while to make it down from Big Bear—it had snowed that morning—and, finally, I was bored enough to whip up a batch of chocolate chip cookies. I had eaten my way through half the cookie dough and most of the cookies, too, when I heard the car pull into the driveway. I ran down the back stairs and greeted them as they tumbled out. The kids were squealing and ruddy-cheeked from their adventures in the snow. Peter looked exhausted and very happy to be home. We hugged, kissed, and staggered up the stairs with all their bags and boxes.

Sitting on the floor in the living room, my husband and I cuddled as Ruby and Isaac tore the wrapping paper off their presents.

"You okay?" Peter asked.

"Now I am," I said, kissing him on the cheek.

Suddenly, Isaac screamed in delight. "A gun! A real gun! A gun! A gun! A gun!"

"A gun?" Peter was obviously shocked.

"A purple water pistol," I said.

"Don't we have a rule against guns?"

"Relax," I said. I picked my son up onto my lap and kissed him on his round, soft cheek. "Isaac and I know it's just pretend. Right, Isaac?" He took aim at me with the purple pistol, right between the eyes, and squeezed off a round, point-blank.

"Pow," Isaac said. "You're dead."